Can't Say No

"The only man who could take advantage of me is you, Mr. Prescott. And you are not interested!" Vanessa hissed in sheer frustration.

Ralph stared at her, doubting his hearing. "What?"

"I will not be climbing in bed with Ron. I don't find him attractive. I don't want him."

"But you find me attractive?" he quizzed.

"Absolutely." Vanessa would have liked to smile and gaze longingly into his dark eyes, but she was shaking so badly, her teeth were chattering. She forced herself to say, "I want you, not Ron. But you're wrong if you think I'm looking for a husband. I'm not."

Leaning back in his seat, Ralph asked candidly, "Tell me, Miss Vanessa, exactly what do you have in mind?"

Recognizing this was the opportunity she'd waited for, Vanessa spoke before she lost her nerve. "A single night with you, Ralph."

By Bette Ford

CAN'T SAY NO
AN EVERLASTING LOVE
UNFORGETTABLE

BETTE FORD

CAN'T SAY NO

AVON

An Imprint of HarperCollinsPublishers

This is a work of fiction. Names, characters, places, and incidents are products of the author's imagination or are used fictitiously and are not to be construed as real. Any resemblance to actual events, locales, organizations, or persons, living or dead, is entirely coincidental.

AVON BOOKS
An Imprint of HarperCollins*Publishers*
10 East 53rd Street
New York, New York 10022-5299

Copyright © 2008 by Bette Ford
ISBN 978-0-06-114350-2
www.avonbooks.com

First Avon Books paperback printing: September 2008

Avon Trademark Reg. U.S. Pat. Off. and in Other Countries, Marca Registrada, Hecho en U.S.A.
HarperCollins® is a registered trademark of HarperCollins Publishers.

Printed in the U.S.A.

10 9 8 7 6 5 4 3 2

This book is a special thank you for my close friends and loving family members who have prayed for me, and unfailingly helped in countless ways during the good and not so good days in the past year. Love you all.

Remember the wonders He has done, His miracles and the judgements He pronounced.

Psalm 105:5

One

It was a late-spring day, not a cloud in the sky, despite the chill in the air. Vanessa Grant had been rushing around since she'd overslept that morning. Even though she was late, she fought the urge to pound on the steering wheel of her dated SUV. As usual, the Metropolitan Detroit traffic was hopelessly snarled due to freeway construction.

She didn't bother to glance at her reflection in the rear-view mirror. She knew her small African-American features, her toffee brown skin and dark brown eyes, showed just how tired she was. She'd not intentionally neglected herself, but there was always someone or something that needed attention. And there was never enough time to kick back and relax. Not that she was complaining, for she dearly loved her family and never regretted becoming her younger brother and sisters' legal guardian when they'd lost their mother, six years ago.

This morning was no less hectic than most. By the time Vanessa had her family dressed, packed, fed, and in the car, she was indeed ready for the minivacation she would be sharing with her girlfriends. After dropping the kids off, she headed for the home of her best friend, Brynne Armstrong.

Brynne had invited all six of her bridal attendants to fly down to spend four days and three nights, in Atlanta's

Buckhead district. They were all thrilled, looking forward to being pampered in the day spa at the luxurious hotel. The all-expenses-paid trip was Brynne's way of thanking them for all they'd done to make her upcoming wedding perfect.

Brynne would be marrying Devin Prescott, her longtime sweetheart and father of her three-year-old daughter, Shanna next weekend. Although Devin was the quarterback for the St. Louis Rams, he was from Detroit and part of a large, close-knit family.

Vanessa, along with their good friends and fellow book club members, Laura Murdock, Trenna McAdams, and Maureen Hale Sheppard, were in the bridal party, as well as Brynne's soon-to-be sisters-in-law, Anna Prescott Mathis and Kelli Warner-Prescott.

"Finally." Vanessa sighed as she stopped her SUV at the security gates outside Brynne's gated community. After giving her name to the security guard on duty, she was waved through.

"Oh, no," she wailed as she pulled into the crowded driveway and parked behind Maureen's car. Evidently, she was the last one to arrive. Slamming her car door, she hurried to the back to retrieve her garment bag and makeup case.

Vanessa and Brynne had formed the book club in the hopes of sharing a beloved hobby by participating in lively book discussions and developing new friendships. The five single ladies decided early on they didn't need to have a man in their lives to be happy or fulfilled. Maureen, Laura, and Brynne worked together at the Sheppard Women's Crisis Center. Trenna owned the nursery school where Brynne's daughter, Shanna, attended. Of the five, Vanessa knew that at six feet she was the painfully shy one. The others teased her good-naturedly because she couldn't remember the last time she'd been out on a date.

But Vanessa wasn't like the other "Elegant Five" book

club members, who were into fashion, shopping, and, for those still single, men. Although single, what little free time she had away from the children was spent designing glamorous evening gowns and wedding dresses, dresses she couldn't imagine herself wearing. She kept to herself the fact that the closest she had come to being intimate with a man was the fantasy lover who filled her dreams.

"It's about time you got here!" Brynne complained as she hurried out to help Vanessa with her luggage. "I was worried, afraid one of the kids was sick."

Vanessa smiled as she hugged her petite, beautiful friend. "Nothing like that. Just took forever to get us all out of the house. The twins were so excited because they will be staying several nights with friends, I couldn't get them to settle down last night. And Lana couldn't decide what to take with her." The twins were six and would be in first grade in the fall, while Lana, seventeen, would be starting her senior year in high school. "Where is your sweet baby girl?"

Brynne smiled. "Shanna's with Devin's parents. She loves spending time with them. She won't even miss me."

The foyer was crowded with luggage and people. Vanessa received hugs from her friends.

Laura Murdock was the first to scold, "What took you so long?" as she kissed Vanessa's cheek.

"Leave her alone. She's here now, and we're going to Hot 'Lanta," Maureen Hale Sheppard, said with a welcoming smile. She owned and ran the Sheppard Women's Crisis Center.

"Kelli and I would have been happy to pick you up, Vanessa," Anna Prescott Mathis volunteered. She had recently married Vanessa's boss, Gavin, and was Wesley and Devin's baby sister.

"I was fine. Just running a little late," Vanessa said with a smile. She was surprised that the married ladies didn't mind leaving their gorgeous husbands behind. "Kelli, I love that outfit."

"This old thing?" Kelli teased, referring to the designer pantsuit. "Got it last week on sale." Before she married the Detroit Lions' star quarterback, Wesley Prescott, the tall beauty had been a full-figured model. Now she spent her days caring for their toddler.

"You missed the show, girlfriend." Trenna McAdams laughed, clapping her hands excitedly. "We got an eyeful."

"Really?" Vanessa asked, looking from one to the other. "What happened?"

"Laura has a new man," Brynne teased.

"New man? What about Ralph?" Vanessa blurted out, then immediately wanted to take back the name, afraid she had given herself away.

Laura scoffed, "Ple-e-ase! Old news. Ralph has never been more than a friend."

Vanessa frowned. The last she'd heard, Laura had been interested in Ralph Prescott. She couldn't help wondering what had gone wrong between Laura and Ralph.

How had Laura overlooked the fact that the six-foot-seven-inch confirmed bachelor was not only gorgeous but very wealthy? Ralph, like his cousins, had been a professional athlete. He didn't bother to hide what he was, a player. There was no shortage of adoring women in his life.

There also was no doubt that Vanessa's life would have been simpler if Ralph, her private fantasy lover, was someone like Denzel Washington. Then the odds of her ever meeting him would have been remote . . . no one could guess her secret. More often than not, she'd awakened trembling from the heat of Ralph's beautifully shaped lips ravishing hers.

To make matters worse, Vanessa had gotten to know the "real man" during the planning of Brynne and Devin's combined wedding shower and engagement party. She had seen why so many women couldn't turn the brother down. The combination of a ready sense of humor, smooth masculine charm, and dark African good looks proved to be irresistible. Ralph had it all. To make matters worse, they were frequently paired together because he was Devin's best man and she was Brynne's maid of honor.

Since the engagement party, where she'd danced in his strong arms, Vanessa's fantasies about him had intensified. At odd moments during the day, her thoughts would fill with daydreams of him. She often felt the need to reassure herself that everything would be fine as long as she didn't act on her fantasies and kept them locked in her dreams, where they belonged.

"Well?" Vanessa couldn't stop herself from asking, "If not Ralph, then which one?"

Weddings were generally hectic and exciting affairs, and this one would be no exception. Vanessa still hadn't gotten over the fact that Devin's groomsmen were all attractive pro athletes. Plus four of the seven men in the bridal party were eligible bachelors.

Although Brynne continued to deny it, the ladies believed it was her doing. Not that the single women were about to complain. Vanessa had been the only one made uncomfortable by the news although she wisely kept that to herself.

"None of the groomsmen," Brynne said, laughing. "And just think how hard I would have had to work to get Devin to pick gorgeous, unattached men for you single ladies. Lucky for you, he made his own decision."

Maureen asked, "You call kissing your good-looking fiancé work?"

"She did more than kiss him," Laura teased.

They all broke into giggles.

"Good thing, I'm going to marry him . . . make an honest man out of him." Brynne's pale brown cheeks were flushed with color. "I assure you, I would have given it my all, *if* I had talked him into it, but I didn't."

"You did, and are we ever glad." Trenna laughed until tears streamed down her pretty brown cheeks.

"You all are so wrong! We were talking about Laura. What did I miss?" Vanessa persisted.

"How many times do I have to tell you, ladies, that Jeff isn't my man," Laura insisted. "My car wasn't working, and he simply gave me a ride over here. We're friends."

"Yeah, sure," Trenna said, rolling her eyes. "I don't kiss my male friends on the mouth. We shake hands!"

That sent them off into more peals of laughter.

"Grab your bags, ladies. The limo just drove up," Brynne said excitedly.

"Limo?" Trenna gasped. "Brynne, I could easily get used to this kinda luxury. You better hang on to that man."

She came back with, "I plan to."

Brynne was the last to leave the house, making sure the burglar alarm was set and the doors locked. The chauffeur had his hands full, trying to get all their luggage into the trunk, while the ladies climbed into the sleek gray car.

"Champagne anyone?" Brynne offered, lifting the open bottle that had been chilling in an ice bucket.

"Don't mind if I do." Laura flashed a grin, accepting one of the fluted crystal glasses being passed around.

Vanessa was the only one who shook her head. "None for me."

"Oh, come on," Trenna complained.

"You know I don't like the taste of alcohol."

"Loosen up, girlfriend. One sip to toast our trip won't kill you," Maureen urged.

"Yeah, girl. Loosen up," Laura joined in.

Vanessa shrugged, reluctantly accepting a glass.

"To a safe trip and a good time!" Brynne raised her glass.

"Hear, hear," the others echoed, clinking glasses.

They laughed and teased each other all the way to the airport, where a private Learjet was waiting for them on the tarmac.

The small jet was one of a fleet co-owned by business partners Devin and Ralph Prescott. The jet's lavish interior was designed to appeal to their wealthy and celebrity clientele. Nothing had been overlooked. There were fresh bottles of chilled champagne and soft drinks, along with an array of tempting hors d'oeuvres and finger sandwiches waiting for them. Soon they were strapped into plush leather armchairs, ready for takeoff.

Laura teased Brynne in a whisper loud enough for the others to hear, "Aren't you worried about your man always being around such attractive women?" She referred to the pretty flight attendant.

"Yes. But after more than four years apart, why should I be concerned?" Brynne shook her head. "Now that we're finally going to be together, I'm not worried about a single thing."

"That's right! She knows her man loves her," Vanessa said from where she sat next to Brynne.

"Vanessa is right," Maureen said, seated next to Trenna. "Brynne has nothing to worry about. She's survived worse and deserves happiness." She lifted her glass. "To Brynne."

"Hear! Hear!" the friends cheered.

"Thank you one and all." Brynne smiled. "I'm so looking forward to a mud wrap."

"Honey, yes." Trenna nodded. "Can I have a massage every day we're there?"

"Absolutely." Brynne laughed.

Then Trenna asked, "Devin's not upset because you're leaving him on his own, the weekend before your wedding?"

"Nope. He's been in St. Louis for business meetings. I

just hope he finds his way back to Detroit before the wedding next Saturday."

"He'll make it," Vanessa assured her, sipping from a glass of sparking apple cider. "It was nice of him to let us use one of his planes."

"What a way to celebrate the holiday! I hope Hot 'Lanta is crawling with gorgeous men," Laura added, "Poor Devin."

Brynne quipped, "You make it sound as if I'm going to give him a reason to worry."

"Not at all." Laura explained, "But you two haven't seen each other in two whole weeks."

"I miss my honey," Brynne said around a long sigh.

"Get used to it. Once the football season starts in earnest, you're going to spend a lot of time apart." Anna sighed. "Look what poor Kelli and I have to put up with."

"There is nothing poor about either one of you lucky ladies, married to two pro-football players. Forget the time apart. Think of all the money. That should keep you warm," Laura joked.

"Shut up, Laura," Vanessa, Maureen, and Trenna said at the same time.

Brynne added smoothly, "To each his own. But I'd much rather have my man's muscular arms around me."

"Me too," Kelli and Anna said at the same time, then laughed.

Vanessa silently agreed. Unfortunately, a special man and romance were nowhere on her horizon. Even if she were lucky enough to meet a man, the odds were, he wouldn't be interested in a woman with a ready-made family.

Vanessa had been twenty and her sister Lana only eleven when the twins, Curtis and Courtney were born, and they'd lost their mother from childbirth complications. Since then family had come first with Vanessa. She shouldered the responsibility as best she could. Her dreams of finishing college, designing elegant evening gowns, and owning her own bridal boutique had to wait. If she were lucky, she might be able to squeeze in a class once Lana was in college.

Her friends believed she had let her personal life go when there was no need. That there were men who wouldn't object to a ready-made family. Vanessa strongly disagreed. Besides, she didn't have the inclination or free time to find out if she was wrong.

So what if she had another fifteen years or so before she learned what every woman on this planet seemed to know already. There were worse things than not knowing what it was like to be with a man. Until then, her fantasies would have to do.

Vanessa bit her bottom lip. Fifteen years? It felt like a lifetime. Maybe she should be thinking in smaller terms? Maybe she couldn't have *forever,* but a single night of lovemaking with the right man? It would be akin to bottling a taste of heaven. After one night she would have something that could never be taken away. A sweet memory that could be examined whenever she felt lonely. She held in the sudden scream of delight bubbling inside of her.

"I wouldn't be surprised if Devin flew in for the weekend," Maureen announced with a smile.

Brynne shook her head. "Not a chance. Devin knows this is a ladies-only spa weekend. No men allowed."

Trenna teased, "But what if he showed up? Are you saying you'd send him packing?"

"Of course."

Six pairs of eyes twinkled with laughter when they all yelled, "No way!"

Two

"What's your problem, cuz?" Wesley Prescott asked as he stretched his long legs out in front of him.

Gavin Mathis said, "Yeah, you've been scowling since we boarded the plane. Are you and Devin about to go under?"

"Not likely," Ralph Prescott muttered. His sour disposition had nothing to do with the financial report on his laptop, showing another sizable increase in their quarterly profits. They'd made more than enough to add comfortably to their fleet of private planes.

Ralph had been fortunate. He was born into a loving family with both parents. Unfortunately, his folks had been killed when he was only twelve. He'd gone to live with his father's younger brother, Lester and his wife Donna, and their children. The adjustment hadn't been easy, but Ralph had eventually landed on his feet when he realized he was home . . . genuinely loved and accepted as one of Donna and Lester's own.

When Devin and Ralph started their business, they had more money than either one of them knew what to do with. The private airline had been a sizable risk considering they knew next to nothing about planes or running an airline. The small commuter airline business had nearly been bankrupt when they took it over. Since professional help was needed, the first thing they'd done was hire an old friend of Lester's, Carl Snyder. He'd been a crack pilot in the military for a number of years. He was interested in starting his own business but lacked the necessary capital. It had been Devin's idea to turn it into a private air service for the wealthy. With Carl's knowledge, combined with Ralph's and Devin's business skills and celebrity connections, they soon had the business up and running. Together, the three men had turned the small operation completely around.

One of the first things they'd done was make sure that even a man of Ralph's size, six feet, seven inches, 190 pounds of solid muscle, was comfortable in the compact space of a Learjet. Whatever creature comforts their wealthy clientele, many of whom were professional athletes, required were available. The jet's main cabin contained a small granite-tiled galley kitchen, a fully stocked bar, a built-in mahogany desk, complete with telephone, computer, and fax machine, plush leather armchairs and sofa. The rear of the cabin housed a luxuriously appointed bedroom-and-bath suite.

"Well?" Gavin prompted.

Ralph acknowledged, "Our little business has been growing so fast that Devin and I are going to have to sit down and take a hard look at what we want to do next. Carl manages the aeronautical aspects of the business, and since I'm no longer playing basketball, the day-to-day responsibility of running the business has fallen on my shoulders."

The business was also cutting into Ralph's assistant coaching career at the University of Detroit, as well as the work he enjoyed doing for low-income boys at the community center. And then there was his active social life.

Wesley teased, "Lighten up, cuz. You should be on top of the world with a weekend of fun and golf, as well as real Southern food. Plus you've got your pick between the four beautiful single ladies in the wedding party. Chill out, you won't see Gavin and me working this weekend."

Ralph was determined to ignore both men, who were relaxing in matching leather armchairs across the aisle, with soft drinks in hand. Wesley and Gavin not only played football for the Detroit Lions but had been best friends since their college days. The two also co-owned a successful string of sporting goods stores across the country.

"You two started this mess," Ralph snapped. "You're nothing more than a couple of 'sell-outs.' Giving up your freedom and bachelorhood. If that wasn't bad enough, my main man will be joining your sorry ranks in a little over a week. It's a disgrace that I'm the only bachelor left in this family, other than fourteen-year-old Wayne."

Wesley and Gavin roared with laughter.

It was Gavin who sobered enough to say, "You don't know what you're missing, my man."

"Yeah, sure," Ralph grumbled.

"May I get something for you, Mr. Prescott?" the pretty flight attendant asked Ralph with a hopeful smile.

"No thanks," he mumbled, aware of the other two looking on with knowing grins.

It wasn't business, his coaching job, lack of time, or his traveling buddies that had put the scowl on Ralph's face. He had been fine until Devin called last night to invite him, along with the other groomsmen, to fly down to surprise the ladies.

The fact that Alex, Marvin, and Ron were tagging along with Devin and were known "players," shouldn't have bothered Ralph, especially considering his own slightly tarnished reputation. The single guys were understandably looking to have a good time with Brynne's lovely bridesmaids.

Clearly Devin was missing Brynne. And Wesley and Gavin were not going to let their wives leave them behind.

No, what was really bugging Ralph was Ron's interest in Brynne's maid of honor, Vanessa Grant.

It had been obvious to anyone with eyes in their head that since the engagement party, Ron had gone out of his way to monopolize Vanessa. That meant it was up to Ralph to see that Ron didn't take advantage of her.

Vanessa was what his uncle would call a "good girl." A decent man didn't mess with her unless he was ready to walk down the aisle. Ralph swore beneath his breath, infuriated by the mere thought of it.

Evidently Wesley heard the comment. "Come on, Ralph. You can't be upset that Devin is finally getting his family? He has been crazy in love with Brynne for more than four years."

"No! I'm glad for him. He won't be able to breathe easy until after the ceremony, and she's signed on the dotted line," Ralph grudgingly admitted.

Gavin asked, "Then what's got your nose out of joint?"

"Has to be a woman," Wesley surmised. "Who is she, Ralph?"

"I don't have a female problem. I leave that to you married guys. All I'm trying to do is get some work done."

"Working on a holiday weekend? That's not like you. Wes, you could be right." Gavin laughed. "Tell us more. Who is she? This is one lady I've got to meet."

"Absolutely," Wesley put in.

"Very funny," Ralph snapped.

Wesley surmised, "You'd think with four beautiful single women on the trip, he'd be in hog heaven."

Ralph wasn't about to admit that his traveling companions had hit the mark. He was on edge because of a special lady, only she wasn't his. Somehow, Vanessa had managed to do what no woman, outside of his family, had done . . . brought out his protective instincts.

He'd be the first to acknowledge that when it came to women he was just as susceptible as the next guy. He'd adored females from the time he was old enough to understand there was a difference. It was no secret that he liked everything about them, from the smell of their skin, their soft curves, and their sexy voices, to their small feet. Short, tall, slim, plump, none of that mattered to him, as long as they were female. He even found the puzzling way women viewed the world fascinating.

Unlike the women he and Ron enjoyed, Vanessa wasn't out there using her beauty and sexuality to trap a man. Both men considered the male-female maneuvers as nothing more than a game, and in the end if said male and female ended up in bed together, then both sides could claim victory.

Ron had to see that Vanessa wasn't like the party girls who followed the teams or hung around the trendy clubs "on the ready." There was no doubt in Ralph's mind that Vanessa didn't have the experience required to stand against a smooth brother like Ron. If he put on a full-court press, she would end up right where Ron wanted her . . . in his bed.

Why hadn't Devin asked Ralph's old friend, Scott Hendricks, to be his groomsman? The NBA player was from Detroit, and he was single. More important, he respected the rules. Unlike Ron, who considered all women fair game.

Ralph bit back an expletive. He didn't have a clue why the matter weighed on his conscience. Vanessa, although beautiful, didn't draw men to her in droves. And it wasn't as if he thought she was sporting a halo. Odds were she'd been involved with at least one guy, someone who apparently had taken advantage of her innocence. Ralph would be willing to bet that after getting what he wanted, the lowlife had moved on. It would explain why she had been off men for so long.

Obviously, Vanessa was so caught up in raising her family and her job that she wouldn't know what hit her until it was too late. Like some lame black knight, Ralph was chasing after her to make sure he'd be on hand, just in case she needed his help.

Ralph couldn't help wondering if he was going soft in his old age, not that thirty-one was old. What he should have been doing was trying to figure out why he felt the need to play hero.

It didn't bother him that the women he dated were out for what they could get. It was part of the game. His lady friends thoroughly enjoyed the expensive restaurants or the gifts of fine jewelry or elaborate trips in private planes and limousine rides. He could afford to indulge them because he was assured of getting what he wanted, a beautiful woman in his bed for a time.

"Mr. Prescott, is something wrong? Is there anything I can get for you?" The flight attendant was once again at Ralph's side. They'd hired her as much for her good looks as her skills. All of the employees at Prescott Air were top-notch.

Annoyed when he caught Wesley and Gavin exchanging knowing grins, Ralph hastily said, "Nothing, thank you. When do we land?"

"In twenty minutes, sir." Smiling seductively, she was practically purring when she whispered, "Are you sure, I can't get you . . . something?"

Ralph stared at her for a long moment. She was certainly gorgeous, with short black curls, creamy pale brown skin, dark eyes, and full, painted lips. Oh, the girl definitely had it going on, yet his body didn't stir. Frustrated because he genuinely wasn't interested, he shook his head, no. Although he made a practice of not messing around with the hired help . . . decidedly bad for business . . . that didn't account for the change in him.

Ralph hadn't had sex in weeks, not since that blasted engagement party. Although he wasn't about to share that information with anyone, certainly not his traveling companions. Not that they would believe it. He could hardly believe it himself!

Trying to relax, Ralph leaned back in the large leather armchair and stretched his long legs out in front of him. The former Los Angeles Lakers' star forward had been at the top of his game when he'd gotten hurt. He'd gone up for a rebound and ended up on the bottom of the heap, with a broken shoulder and collarbone. The injury had ended his career, and he'd left the bright lights of LA and the game he loved.

Ralph had gone back to the University of Detroit, where he did graduate work to complete a master's degree in finance and business. Before he knew it, he was working with his former college basketball coach as his assistant and found he enjoyed helping aspiring college athletes. Most of them dreamed of playing pro ball but had no idea how to handle what came with it . . . the money, the fame . . . and the women that inevitably were part of the multimillion-dollar contract. For Ralph, the NBA had not been about any of those things, only the sheer love of the sport. The money was a sweet added bonus.

A large number of the kids he worked with came from single-parent households and didn't have positive males in their lives. In an effort to make a difference, he often spoke at both middle schools and high schools around the city, as well as volunteering his time at the city's community centers.

Unfortunately, Ron wasn't the only problem Ralph was having with Vanessa. If only he could get her out of his mind! It started so unexpectedly. His body hardened each and every time he recalled her incredible softness while they'd slow-danced at that blasted engagement party. The scent of her dark, silky skin, the texture of her thick black hair, and the sound of her voice had him aching with need whenever he so much as thought of her. And he thought of her too doggone often for his peace of mind.

"It can't be me!" Vanessa whispered aloud.

She gazed into the bathroom mirror, turning her head from side to side, not quite believing what she saw. Her dark, creamy skin looked beautiful, and she had never, even once, thought of herself as beautiful.

Their minivacation had been a wonderful idea, and she was having the time of her life. Vanessa couldn't get over the exquisitely appointed suite they were sharing. There were four bedrooms and baths, a spacious living/dining room, as well as a fully equipped kitchen.

After breakfast, they'd spent the day enjoying the spa facilities. Nothing had been overlooked. Lunch had been brought to them as they'd been pampered from head to toe. When they returned to their suite, Brynne had arranged both a makeup artist and hairstylist to help them prepare for an evening out on the town.

Vanessa's long and thick black hair had been curled to frame her face, while the back had been left to flow down her back.

"What's all that noise?" Vanessa asked as she entered the bedroom she was sharing with Laura.

"You will never believe it!" Laura said excitedly as she tossed her robe on the end of one of the queen-size beds. In a cream satin teddy, Laura picked up the cream dress waiting for her. "Devin just arrived. He came to surprise Brynne. You should have seen the girl's face!"

"Really?" Vanessa laughed.

"Yes! And he didn't come alone. All of his groomsmen

are with him. They're all dressed in custom-made suits, ready to take us out on the town. Girl, can you believe it!"

"Ralph is here!" Vanessa nearly screamed as she sank down into the nearest armchair.

"Ralph, Alex, and . . ." Laura stopped, to stare at her friend.

"I wish I could have seen Brynne's face when Devin walked in," Vanessa said, trying to calm her racing heart.

"Well, well, well." Laura grinned.

"What?" Vanessa hedged as she stepped into the black knit dress that she knew would cling to her generous hips and show too much thigh with its uneven hem. Frowning, she wished she had bought another dress . . . something that would cover her from neck to toes. Unfortunately, it was the only dress she'd packed. She recalled the red, off-the-shoulder evening gown, she had sketched. She imagined wearing it while on Ralph's arm. Too bad it was only just a pretty fantasy . . . not real.

"No wonder you were questioning me about Ralph. You've got a crush on him!" Laura laughed. "I can't believe it! And to think, whenever you've heard his name in the past, you acted as if he was the number one dog in the pound. Why all the secrecy?"

Staring down at her French manicure nails, Vanessa said miserably, "Because I knew you would do just what you did. Laugh!"

"Aw, honey lamb." Laura came over and gave her a hug. "I was just playing with you. There isn't one single thing wrong with the man. Are you kidding? Half the women in Detroit are chasing after Ralph Prescott."

"My point exactly! And he's probably slept with all of them at least once!" Vanessa exclaimed, while anxiously smoothing the fabric covering her hips.

"Oh, come on. The man is gorgeous and rich. Of course

women are chasing him down. We'd both think something was wrong if they weren't after his gorgeous behind."

"I'm not looking for a man. And if I were, it wouldn't be a low-down, womanizer like Ralph Prescott," Vanessa said bitterly.

What she didn't say was that he was too much like Gregory Cummingham, the twins' heartless father, for her peace of mind. She wasn't about to repeat her mother's mistakes. No way was she going down that dead-end road.

"And what are you going to do if he approaches you?" Laura asked as she zipped Vanessa's dress.

"Run!" Vanessa quipped. "Besides, it doesn't matter. The kids come first with me. Even multimillionaires wouldn't want to be saddled with a ready-made family."

"Girl, you are too much. I'm talking about a date, not a lifetime commitment. Loosen up, will you? Have some fun for a change. You are twenty-six, not a hundred and six. Enjoy yourself!" Laura gripped Vanessa's shoulders. "If he asks you to dance, say yes. Okay?"

Vanessa smiled sheepishly. "Okay. I know, I'm overreacting. Thanks."

She gave Laura a hug before moving to stand in front of the mirrored dresser. She turned, checking out the front and back views. Frowning at the way the vee neckline dipped low enough to bare her ample cleavage.

Why had she gone shopping with Brynne and Laura? Those two had convinced her she could not only wear something sexy but look good in it. Why had she listened? Now she was stuck. The dress cost too much to throw out. If it hadn't been on the clearance rack, she could have returned it. Who was she kidding?

If it hadn't been on sale, she never could have been able to afford it, not on her tight budget. As much as she loved to design and sew, the clothes she made were for the children.

For herself, she daydreamed and sketched, but that's as far as it went in the family. The majority of the evening gowns she sketched were for small, elegant women, like Laura and Brynne. She'd sketched a few gowns with Kelli in mind, but had never shown them to her.

Not that she didn't think full-figured women deserve lovely things. Yet when it came to herself, it would be a waste. She wasn't going to need the red evening gown or a wedding dress. She certainly couldn't wear either to the grocery store or work.

"Vanessa?"

"Laura, tell me the truth. Do you think I should change? I brought an off-the-shoulder white blouse and jeans for to-morrow night."

"Stop it! You look great! We all do. How could we not look good, with all the work we've had today?" Laura giggled as she presented her back to Vanessa. "We have to hurry. Now zip me up, please."

Vanessa was still undecided as she helped Laura with her dress.

Picking up her small evening bag, Laura smiled. "Now, stop stalling. Our escorts for the evening are waiting."

Vanessa's heart was pounding as she took her own small, plain black purse and followed the other woman into the living room.

There was laughter and chatter. Everyone was there and seemed to be having a great time. Laura hadn't exaggerated. The men looked fabulous and were dressed for an evening out. Vanessa's smile was forced as she did her level best not to so much as glance at Ralph Prescott.

"Look who's here." Brynne beamed. One look at her twinkling eyes told the whole story. Devin stood behind her with his arms wrapped around her tiny waist.

They all laughed.

"You ladies look beautiful." Ralph grinned. His dark eyes moved from Kelli and Anna to Trenna and Maureen, then Laura and Brynne, before they eventually rested on Vanessa.

Blushing, Vanessa wondered if it were her imagination or if Ralph's gaze had truly lingered on her. She was uncomfortably aware of him as she fought for composure. Even though Ralph was among over six-foot-tall, broad-shouldered, and attractive men, he alone held her gaze. He was incredibly male, with his rich brown skin, bold African features, and, close-cut black hair. Unlike the other women, who were all laughing and talking, Vanessa shyly dropped her lids, unable to meet Ralph's dark eyes.

Laura asked, "So what gives? We weren't expecting you very handsome men."

"Yeah," Trenna and Maureen put in, while Vanessa was busy studying the toes of her black pumps.

Alex Goodman, a smooth-talking linebacker for the St. Louis Rams, grinned. "We wouldn't dream of disappointing you beautiful ladies. We can't have you here without proper escorts to show you the town. How does a scrumptious dinner, followed by dancing all night long, sound to you ladies?"

Boisterous feminine cheers went up then, and everyone seemed to be talking at once.

"You look hot," Ron Daniels, smiling widely, said close to Vanessa's ear.

The Rams' wide receiver was one fine man. Yet there was something about him that Vanessa didn't like. He was too good-looking. She had no illusions as to what he wanted from her . . . sex. On more than one occasion, she had nearly set him straight and told him the answer was no. But then she would realize she could be wrong, and it was best to simply let it go.

"Thank you. How have you been, Ron?"

"Can't complain," he said. His beautiful light brown eyes gleamed. "Save me a slow dance?"

She smiled, nodding, annoyed that her fantasies were about one man . . . the one who hadn't so much as approached her.

"Let's go, everybody," Devin called out. "We have two limousines waiting for us." He led the way with Brynne's small hand clasped in his.

As they walked to the elevator, Laura asked Vanessa in a whisper, "You okay?"

Vanessa whispered back, "I'm fine. Just had a bad case of nerves for a few minutes there."

"Ron's right. You do look hot, but watch your step with that one. He's slick. Knows all the right moves," Laura cautioned.

Vanessa laughed. "You got that right."

She had no comeback when Laura revealed, "You-know-who has had his eyes on you the entire time."

Three

Brynne and Devin shared the first car with Kelli and Wesley and Anna and Gavin, while the single ladies rode in the stretch limo with the unattached men.

Vanessa told herself she had no business feeling disappointed. She should take Laura's advice and concentrate on having a good time. Didn't matter who sat where or who danced with whom. All the guys were fun.

Yet later, when Ralph tapped Ron on the shoulder and insisted it was his dance, she laughed and went willingly into the other man's arms.

It didn't matter that her heart rate had suddenly accelerated and her breath had quickened. Even though all the men were tall, Ralph was the one who made her feel small. He towered over her, even in her heels. As his clean male scent enveloped her, and his warm chest pressed against her breasts, Vanessa found herself tongue-tied. It was as if her brain stopped working the minute he got too close.

"You are awfully quiet," Ralph said in his deep, husky voice.

"What do you mean?"

"Whenever I am near, you seem to clam up, but when you're with the other guys, including my cousins, you're all sweet smiles. Do I need a breath mint? Or could it be my looks offend you?" he asked with a straight face.

"You are joking, aren't you?" Vanessa blinked in dismay.

"Absolutely." He smiled. "Do I make you nervous?"

Vanessa blushed. "A bit. You're smooth. I can understand why women seem to throw themselves at you."

"But not you."

"What is this? I thought we were here to have fun? You make me feel as if I'm on the witness stand."

Ralph smiled. "You're right. So how do you like Atlanta?"

"I haven't seen a lot of it, but so far it has been exciting. So much to do."

"Enjoying the spa treatment?"

"Loved it. When we planned the trip, we didn't expect you fellows to follow us," she teased.

"It was a last-minute kind of thing. Good chance to relax, play some golf, and burn the candle at both ends."

Vanessa nodded, keenly aware of his lean, long length against her as they moved easily in time to the music. The song ended, but rather than release her, Ralph kept her at his side.

"You're a good dancer," Ralph said quietly.

Before she could think of a response, Ron appeared at their side, just as the music started again.

"May I?" Ron asked.

Vanessa was looking at Ron, therefore missed the look of disappointment in Ralph's dark eyes.

"Thank you," Ralph said to her, dropping his hands as he stepped back.

Ralph swore as he mumbled to himself. The guy didn't know when to stop. He suspected Vanessa wouldn't understand if he cracked Ron's jaw just to make a point. One wrong move, and Ron would be picking himself up off the floor. Rather than join the soon-to-be-newlyweds, who sat snuggled up in the corner of a banquet booth, Ralph headed for the bar.

"What can I get you?"

"A beer," he grumbled, keeping his back to the dance floor. He would be fine as soon as he figured out what exactly was going on with him. He should have stayed in Detroit spending the weekend with any one of his female friends, taking care of business. But, no, he had to come chasing after Vanessa. Telling himself the woman needed someone to look out for her. She was like a goldfish in a pondful of sharks. Ron definitely had his eye on the statuesque beauty—a beauty who didn't have a clue about her own sexual appeal. Talk about built for days–she had it all and then some.

And what was he doing? Counting the number of dances she had with other men? He was losing his mind. Why should he care? Vanessa was a grown woman who had taken care of herself, as well as her three siblings, for a number of years. If she wanted to dance with Ron or anyone else, who was he to object?

"Thanks." He didn't pick up the glass or move away, instead he stared broodingly into the frothy brew.

It had all started going a little crazy for him the night of the engagement party. It wasn't like he'd just met the woman. He'd known Vanessa for several years, since she started working for Gavin well before Gavin and Anna got married. They had even talked on the telephone and planned that stupid party.

On that particular night he'd taken a long, hard look at Vanessa, as if really seeing her for the first time. There was no denying that she was gorgeous in a long, dark green dress, with a slit on one side, giving him a view of incredibly beautiful, long, sexy legs that seemed to go on forever.

Whenever he recalled that night, all he could think of was having those gorgeous legs wrapped around him and his shaft deep inside her sweet heat. He didn't have a clue as to what she'd done to herself other than applied a little makeup and left her hair down to curl around her shoulders and pretty face.

Her dress had thin straps and a low-cut bodice that drew his eyes, like a starving man to a feast. Her breasts were high and ripe, her skin was as creamy as whipped, dark brown chocolate. When she smiled at him, his shaft suddenly lifted, hardening as if he hadn't had sex in years. He was immediately hot and ready for whatever she was offering.

And he hadn't been the only man in that blasted ballroom looking at her. Ron couldn't take his eyes off her all night. Hell, Ron still hadn't stopped chasing after her. Ralph's jaw had clenched when Ron asked Vanessa to dance, then pulled her against his chest.

Like the other members of the bridal party, Ralph hadn't brought a date. By now, they were all friends and always had a good time whenever they got together.

Stunned by his sudden interest in Vanessa, Ralph had even gone as far as to discreetly question his cousin, Anna. He had been determined to find out if Vanessa was involved with anyone. And on that he'd been lucky. Anna hadn't caught on, which was a bonus. He would never have heard the end of it if Anna had realized.

Ralph had a reputation for never going after inexperienced women. Lucky for him the beautiful, Miss "V" practically had "inexperience" stamped all over her forehead.

Ignoring her that night had proven impossible once he had discovered from just a single slow dance that Vanessa's six-foot, curvy frame fit his body perfectly . . . as if they were meant to be lovers. From that moment on, the wanting never seemed to stop.

Nevertheless, Ralph knew he was wrong for her. Vanessa was looking for a "forever" kind of guy. And he had no choice but to respect that and keep his distance. There wasn't one woman on God's green earth worth sacrificing his freedom. No way was he going down, not like his cousins and Gavin.

There were any number of women he could call to ease the ache in his jeans. When he got home he planned to pick up the telephone and take care of that problem.

"Something wrong, bro?" Devin asked as he joined Ralph at the bar.

"Not a thing."

"Then why are you scowling?"

Ralph shrugged. Deciding a change in topic was called for, he asked, "Where is your fiancée? I haven't seen you two apart in hours."

"Ladies' room. And you won't." Devin grinned. "See us apart, I mean."

Ralph shook his head. "You got it bad. Why are you doing this man? There is still time to stop this insanity."

"Insanity? Hardly. Love happens to most of us. Who knows, it could happen to you!" Devin grinned, sipping from his glass. "As wild as it might seem, you, too, are susceptible."

"Hell no! Just because Wesley, you, and Gavin have gone under doesn't mean I'm next."

Devin roared with laughter. "It's not a disease."

"Devastating to life as I know it," Ralph quipped with a frown, taking a long swallow of his beer. "Dev, you're so far gone, you don't even realize you are throwing your life away. One week to go. And that is it! No more fun and games."

"I'm looking forward to it, not back. My lady has it all. Come on. Trenna and Brynne are at the table. So what do you think of her?"

Ralph lifted a brow, "Trenna? She gorgeous, just like all the ladies. So what?"

Devin shook his head. "Come on."

Vanessa had no idea why she was uncomfortably aware of Ralph's dark, brooding gaze when she and Ron rejoined the others.

"Enjoying yourself?" Laura asked as she sank into a chair.

Vanessa smiled. "Yes, how about you?"

Before she could answer, Devin said, "I don't know about you guys, but Brynne and I are heading back. It's after midnight, and the fellows and I have a 7:00 A.M. tee time. Can we do this again tomorrow night?"

"Absolutely," everyone agreed.

"Why don't we stay until closing, then walk back to the hotel?" Ralph suggested. "Drinks on me!"

The singles cheered while the married couples were ready to call it a night.

"Count us in," Trenna said, referring to the ladies. After waving good night to the others, they were soon up on the dance floor doing the Electric Slide.

Later, the moon seemed to be hiding behind a ribbon of clouds, but the air was warm, with only a light breeze. After leaving the noise and excitement of the nightclub behind, Vanessa realized Ralph was only a few steps behind her.

"Nice night," he said casually.

"I can't believe how crowded the streets are. Does anyone ever sleep in this city?"

"This is Friday night of a holiday weekend. Sleep when you get back home," he said, chuckling.

"How far?"

She had to look up to meet his eyes, unusual for her, a woman six feet in flats. Despite her three-inch heels, he topped her by a good four inches.

It was rare that she could look up at any man and feel utterly feminine. How could she not? He was such a macho male, all broad shoulders, trim waist, and long legs.

"A few blocks. Don't tell me you're tired?"

"Not at all. You've been here before?"

He smiled. "A few times."

Vanessa almost asked for the name of the woman he'd traveled with, but decided against it. With Ralph, there were always women. A dozen questions entered her head, but she didn't ask any of them. What was the point? His love life had nothing to do with her.

"Watch it." Ralph caught her arm, keeping her from walking out into the busy intersection.

"Thanks. It would help if I watched where I was going." Vanessa shivered with awareness as his large hand touched her bare skin. Goodness, there ought to be a law against that much sex appeal. The man was downright dangerous to her peace of mind.

"We'd like to keep you around," he teased.

When he slowed his steps, she found herself doing the same. She watched as the distance between them and others increased.

"We should hurry," she said, glancing anxiously at the others.

"You're safe. I know where we are. Besides, I'd like to talk to you without being overheard."

She glanced at him. "Sounds serious. Is something wrong between Devin and Brynne?"

He shook his head. "Nothing like that. Are you seeing anyone?"

"What?"

"As if you don't know. Dating anyone special?" he clarified.

"Why do you ask?"

"I'm curious. Well?"

"No, I'm not. How about you? Can't say the same?" she teased.

"No one seriously. I don't do serious. Besides, this isn't about me."

Feeling as if her stomach had dropped to her feet, Vanessa had to work to conceal her disappointment. She scolded herself. She knew what Ralph was . . . a player. No surprises there.

Not bothering to hide her annoyance, she said, "I don't get it. You aren't interested, so why the questions?"

"Ron is interested . . . more than interested in you. Have a care. He's a womanizer."

"Like you," Vanessa reminded him.

"Yeah, but unlike me, I don't go after innocents."

Vanessa laughed, hoping to hide her dismay. "You know nothing about me."

"I know you are looking for love, commitment, and happy-ever-after. Ron has been checking you out. He's intrigued, and he likes a challenge. Watch yourself, he . . ."

She stiffened. "I'm no novice, nor am I a teenager. I didn't ask for your help. I don't need it." She stomped off, not caring that she didn't know where she was going.

Ralph caught her hand before she could move away. "I'm sorry. It came out all wrong. I just want you to watch yourself around Ron. That's all."

She quipped, "Is this where I'm supposed to say thank you?"

"Hell no," he snapped. "Excuse me. I'm not looking for thanks. I just don't want you hurt."

Vanessa tilted her chin up a notch. "Ron can't hurt me, Ralph. I'm not attracted to him." She didn't add that he was the only one who could.

He smiled as they turned onto the block of their hotel. "Good."

"But let me ease your mind. I make my own decisions and my own mistakes. I don't need help."

It wasn't until she tried to move away that she realized Ralph was still holding her hand. She pulled free, scowling at him.

"You're a beautiful woman, Vanessa. I am not the only man in our group who noticed. You got it going on, with those long, sexy legs."

"What is this? I told you, I don't need your protection." She was determined not to let his compliment go to her head. Why would she? It meant nothing to him.

He stood staring down at her, his lips tilted at the corners as he teased, "Don't be angry. I thought we were friends. Friends look out for one another. Or at least that was my understanding."

Vanessa sighed. "You're right. We are friends. I certainly couldn't have put that huge engagement party together without your help. Or combined the male-female formal wedding shower. With all your teasing, you made it fun. Let's leave it at that. Good night." She kissed his cheek before she hurried away.

Vanessa was conscious of his dark eyes on her back as she crossed the lobby to the bank of the elevators. Laura would have put an extra sway in her hips. Vanessa didn't dare. She fought the urge to run back and tell him that as far as she was concerned none of the other men held the least bit of appeal for her.

Yet he was everything her mother had warned her to steer clear of in a man. Ralph had good looks, smooth talk, and plenty of charm. There was no doubt he knew his way around the bedroom. Was it any wonder that he filled her dreams?

When she let herself into the suite, Vanessa was not surprised to find her friends in the sitting room.

"Where is Brynne?" she asked as she dropped down on the sofa beside Maureen and kicked off her heels.

"I give you three guesses. And they all begin with the letter 'D.'" Trenna laughed.

"What took you so long? Checking out the moonlight?" Laura teased.

"Very funny," Vanessa said. "Did you ladies have a good time?"

"Remind me in the morning to kiss Brynne's feet for insisting that Devin's groomsmen be single." Trenna giggled.

"Amen to that," Laura echoed.

"It has been fun," Maureen said before she teased, "Ron seems to be taken with you, Ms. Vanessa."

"I don't understand it. I haven't encouraged him," Vanessa confessed. "It's embarrassing."

"What difference does it make? The guy is a jock . . . and a millionaire," Trenna insisted. "That's what matters. He can take care of you like a queen."

"They are all millionaires. So what?" Maureen observed. "They're good-looking and fun. It's not like we're looking for husbands."

"Speak for yourself!" Laura worked her neck for emphasis and sent them all into a peal of laughter.

"I don't know about you, ladies, but I'm exhausted." Maureen yawned. "See you all at breakfast."

"Sounds like a plan. 'Night," Trenna said, giving out hugs before following Maureen.

Laura waited until she heard bedroom doors close, then asked, "Anything happen, you want to talk about?"

"Not really. Ralph seems to think Ron wants more than a few dances."

"Really? That is interesting."

"No, Laura. He thinks I needed to be warned. I'm 'innocent,' his word not mine." Her exasperation was all over her face.

"So. Use it to your advantage."

"How? I don't need another brother."

"If you want the man, go after him." Laura smiled. "Good night."

"That's all you have to say?"

"Mmm-hmm." Laura laughed before she went into the room they were sharing.

After releasing a frustrated sigh, Vanessa wandered around the beautifully appointed living/dining room. She didn't so much as consider going to bed. Her thoughts were too jumbled to allow her to sleep. First she examined the jade figurine, then ran a finger over an etched crystal vase. Eventually, she stood in front of the window gazing out at the ink-dark sky. Could she do it? Did she have the nerve to go after Ralph? More important, what would she do with him if she caught him?

First she had to get over being shy, uncomfortably so, especially around him. She wasn't like her friends. She'd never gone after a man. Ralph was right. She was an innocent. She might as well have it tattooed on her chest. And she wasn't attracted to any of the other men . . . only Ralph. He was the one who filled her dreams and made her wake trembling with desire.

If she did nothing, the dreams would eventually be all she had. She would never know his kisses . . . his lovemaking. She nearly screamed "no."

Frowning, Vanessa admitted to herself that she wanted to be like other women. She was tired of not knowing, tired of feeling less than other women. She wanted to flirt and tease the man she desired most. She wanted Ralph to be her lover.

She wasn't looking for an engagement ring or any type of commitment for that matter. One special night would be enough. Surely, she could persuade him to give her one long, wonderful night? But how? What would she say?

She'd been shy her entire life. Now suddenly she was supposed to boldly ask him to sleep with her because she was curious. She wanted to know what the love songs were talking about, what the rest of the world was getting, and she wasn't.

Four

"I can't believe it," Vanessa whispered to Ralph, then blushed. She had no idea how many times she'd said it since she'd won $1,000 in the nickel slot machine in the casino. "Things like this don't happen to me."

"Sure they do." He laughed as he spun her out, then back on the dance floor. The rhythm and blues poured out of the loudspeakers as they moved in time to the music.

"It's all right to be happy, darlin'. Just don't spend it all in one place," he teased as he tightened his arms around her.

"I don't intend to spend any of it, at least not on me," she quickly explained. "With three growing kids, they always need something. My guess is most of it will go toward school clothes and supplies. It would be great if I could put it aside for Lana's education. She starts her senior year in the fall." Beaming, Vanessa said, "I'm so proud of her. She's an excellent student. It hasn't been easy for her with just me in her corner."

Ralph tucked a loose curl behind her ear. "I imagine it hasn't been easy for you, either. The congratulations go to you, Vanessa. You're the one who has done a remarkable job."

Vanessa blushed, warmed by the sincerity of his compliment. "Thank you." She laughed, then surprised herself when she teased, "I'd better watch my step. You are a charmer. Does it come naturally, or did it take years to perfect?"

Ralph threw back his head and laughed, apparently surprised by her candor. "I was born this way. I've always enjoyed females. I grew up knowing they're special."

"Oh, yeah? You're smooth," she replied, laughing.

Ralph chuckled. "I was fortunate to grow up around a remarkably talented woman. Donna Prescott is a special lady. She treated me like her own."

Vanessa nearly stopped dancing to stare up at him, pleased by his openness. "No wonder, I've always liked Mrs. Prescott. She is not only nice but a genius, to turn you three rough-and-tumble boys into accomplished men."

"She had help. My uncle was no slouch." He laughed. "Hmm, I'd better watch myself. I can't put anything over on you, can I? You know my entire family."

Smiling, Vanessa nodded. "One of the perks of my job."

"You like working with Gavin and Anna?"

"Oh yes. Never a dull moment. I admire what Gavin does for the black community. So many kids are getting the education they could never afford on their own because of his scholarship program."

"Gavin is one of the good guys."

"So are you. Anna has talked about your work with teen boys at your college. And I heard about the new community center you and your cousins are building in your Uncle Lester's name to honor him. I'm impressed."

"Thanks." Ralph's voice seemed gruff with emotions. "Lester Prescott is a great coach and has done a lot over the years for the community. He's done so much for me personally. He's shown us boys what it is to be a man." His voice was filled with emotion when he admitted, "Sorry, didn't mean to get so sentimental."

Vanessa nodded, touched by his trust in her. She was disappointed when the music ended. Their time alone passed too quickly.

It was Vanessa's turn to blush, embarrassed by her fascination with him, while he treated her as if he were her big brother. She'd been trying to be assertive, but evidently he still didn't realize she was interested.

Dropping her arms, she said, "You had good reason to be proud of your aunt and uncle. They're a remarkable couple, who aren't afraid to give and receive love."

"Thanks for the dance," he said as he guided her through the crowd with a hand on the back at her waist.

Vanessa forced a smile, wondering if she'd blown another opportunity. How was she ever going to get him in bed if she didn't have the nerve to come out and ask him? Ralph wasn't going to come on to her, especially when he was acting as if she needed his protection from Ron Daniels. She'd done everything but come right out and tell him that she wanted him, not Ron. It was harder than she imagined. She'd even dreamed last night that he'd made hot sizzling love to her. She had wakened that morning thinking about Ralph . . . not Ron.

"My turn," Ron said, a few steps from the long table the bridal party shared.

Vanessa urged, "Give me a few minutes to get something to drink." She hurried away, annoyed with the way Ron ogled her. She was dressed in the white off-the-shoulder knit top that she'd embellished with sequins to show off her ample bustline and small waist. It was a big mistake, for she felt as if her white jeans were clinging to her hips like nobody's business. Trying to look sexy, she'd left her hair down, and her only jewelry was bold, gold hoops. Laura had assured her that she looked hot. For once in her life, she wanted to sizzle. She'd been hopeful that Ralph's eyes would linger on her.

If only Ron hadn't jumped between them. The last thing she needed was Ralph to keep thinking she was interested in what Ron was offering. She didn't want Ralph's defenses in place. She didn't need his protection. What she wanted was for him to pay attention to her.

She'd come to a decision. She wasn't looking for a relationship with Ralph, only a single night. For years, she'd let her natural shyness and her jealousy of his women keep her away. No one had guessed that she was drawn to the man, not even her close friends. Vanessa let out a frustrated sigh as she joined Trenna and Maureen at the table. The two other ladies were also taking a breather from the dance floor.

"Everything okay?" Maureen whispered, glancing between Ralph and Ron.

"Just great," Vanessa hissed, wishing she could be candid but afraid the men might overhear. This was a "Laura" kind of problem. Things like this never ever happened to her!

Ron joined them at the table, taking the chair across from the ladies, while Ralph made his way to the bar.

"This music is slamming tonight," Ron said with a grin.

Maureen and Trenna nodded, then asked him question after question about the upcoming football season.

Vanessa was grateful for the reprieve. Maybe she should come right out and tell him she wasn't interested. The weekend was supposed to be fun. Why was he on her heels every time she turned around?

"Here you go," Ralph set a tall glass of sparkling water with a lime in front of Vanessa. Before she could even thank him, he was asking if the other two women needed fresh drinks.

She watched the way Trenna and Maureen both smiled at him, as if the sun and moon revolved around him alone. Neither lady required a drink, but both appreciated his easy smile and thoughtfulness.

Vanessa dropped her gaze, hating the sudden twinge of jealousy eating at her. For a moment, she'd forgotten the game she was playing. Ralph was not hers. He was fun and available to the woman who happened to catch his eyes at that moment.

Just for one night she wanted to be the one who captured his interest. A single night of love was all she was after, then they would both go back to their individual lives. What should she do or say? Or was it too late? Had she blown it?

In the morning they were all going to service at a quaint little church near Decatur. Afterwards, they had planned to have brunch at the hotel before heading back. On this trip, the ladies would be flying back to Detroit with Wesley, Gavin, and Ralph while Devin and his teammates returned to St. Louis.

Only one week to go before Devin and Brynne would exchange vows and become husband and wife. Time was running out. Vanessa's chance of convincing her fantasy man to be her man for one special night would disappear. Next Sunday, the reality of taking care of her family would once again be prominent.

Vanessa suddenly decided the perfect time for them to get together would be after the wedding. Now all she had to do was to find a few private minutes alone with him before they returned to Detroit to convince Ralph. As long as Ralph realized that she wasn't trying to trap him, everything should be fine. It could work. It really could. All she needed was to . . .

"Wow, that was great." Laura said, breaking into Vanessa's thoughts. "These folks know how to party."

"You have not seen anything until you see the blow-out we've planned for our reception." Devin grinned as he pulled Brynne down into his lap.

Vanessa wasn't really listening. Her mind whirled with ideas.

As Ralph slowly sipped his beer, his temper gradually eased. He kept his gaze on his cousin Anna as she talked about the food planned for the wedding reception that her catering company would be handling.

Rising to his feet, he reached for Anna's hand. "Dance with your cousin. Can't have this jerk monopolizing your time," he joked, punching Gavin in the arm as he passed by. Once they were on the crowded floor, Ralph concentrated on having a good time.

Anna laughed up at him as they moved in time to the fast beat of the music. "This trip has been so much fun, but next Saturday it will be all over but the shouting. Brynne will be a Prescott!"

Ralph shook his head, bewildered. "If you told me a year ago that Devin was going down like this, I'd never believed it."

"Going down? Not hardly. The man will finally have his family together. He's waited four years to make Brynne his wife and complete his family."

"It's a colossal mistake. The man can't see what he's losing."

"What? Lonely nights? Meaningless encounters?"

"He is losing his freedom. None of that other stuff matters," Ralph joked.

Anna laughed, moving with the music. "You are so wrong. But that's all right. One day you are going to meet that one special lady, and you won't know what hit you. All I ask is for you to call me. I plan to be there to see you fall on your face. Promise to call me!"

"Very funny, only I'm not laughing. You're wrong. Not me. I like my life the way it is."

"Yeah, that's the point. Your precious freedom won't be enough. You remember that old Natalie Cole song, 'Can't say no'? That will be your middle name, lover boy." Anna playfully patted his cheek, then threw her head back and laughed.

"I remember the song, but it ain't gonna happen. Now shut up and dance." Ralph couldn't help chuckling. It was official. His baby cousin was so in love with her husband, Gavin, she could no longer see straight.

Anna was wrong. There was not a woman alive who could turn his life inside out to please her. Evidently he was the only one in the family who was safe from that "love" kind of craziness.

It wasn't like he had anything against marriage. It worked for his family members, but that didn't mean it was right for him. He grinned. There were just too many beautiful women out there to settle for only one. Marriage was like inviting a man to a feast, then serving only mashed potatoes. What a waste.

When the music switched to a slow tune, he felt a tap on his shoulder.

"My turn," Gavin said, taking his wife into his arms.

Chuckling, Ralph started back to their table. Halfway there, he noted Ron leading Vanessa back out on the dance floor. Instead of continuing on to ask one of the other ladies to dance with him, he veered toward the bar for a fresh drink.

While he waited, he promised himself that he'd find time before the weekend was over to sit Vanessa down and lay it out for her. She was so caught up in enjoying the time away that she simply was not taking his warning seriously. After their talk, his conscience would be clear, and they could both get back to having a good time.

When they returned to the hotel, Ralph caught Vanessa's hand. He said close to her ear before she could join the others at the bank of elevators, "If you're not sleepy, have a drink with me on the hotel patio?"

Vanessa blinked at him, trying not to show her surprise. She smiled. "I'd like that."

"Good. This way." He waved to the others as he led her along the corridor to the rear of the property.

Softly lit, small round tables and chairs had been set up along the patio railings, surrounding a beautiful marble fountain. The patio opened into the lush garden lit by tiny clear lights in the trees. Despite the late hour, nearly every table was occupied.

Ralph found an empty table near the fountain. Holding her chair, he asked, "What would you like?"

"Sparkling water with lemon, please." Suddenly nervous, she clasped her hands in her lap. She couldn't stop wondering why they were here. Had he picked up on her attraction to him? Her heart began to race at the possibility. Vanessa was determined not to let her inherent shyness hold her back from this bold and charismatic man.

Forcing a smile, she asked, "So what's on your mind?"

Ralph arched a black brow. "No beating around the bush, huh?"

"Why bother? What's on your mind, Ralph?"

He looked into her eyes when he said, "You are on my mind, Vanessa. We've all been having a great time these past few weeks, with the parties and the combined shower. Now with this weekend away from home, it's become more than fun and innocent games."

Vanessa's heart was pounding so hard in her chest she could hardly fill her lungs. That was all she needed was to pass out cold at the man's feet. She took a deep breath, hoping for calm. She needed her wits about her if she were to get the words past the lump in her throat.

"And?" she prompted.

"And I wanted to sit down with you to explain why Ron's intentions aren't honorable."

"What!" Vanessa snapped. "You invited me here to talk about Ron?"

"Of course. You would not take my warning seriously the other night. I thought, if we sat down and brought it . . ."

Disappointed, she interrupted, "You thought wrong. As far as I can tell, Ron has no designs on me. And even if he did, so what. It takes two . . . and I'm not dancing." Vanessa was so angry, she nearly grabbed her purse and stormed out. Only the realization that there was only one more weekend left. If she wanted to turn her fantasy lover into her reality, she'd better act now. Her back was not only against the wall, it was rubbing her skin raw.

"You're angry. Why?" he said with a frown. "Vanessa, you're beautiful, both inside and out. I don't want to see you hurt or taken advantage of by anyone. Especially not a man who doesn't appreciate you."

"The only man who could take advantage of me is you, Mr. Prescott. And you are not interested!" she hissed in sheer frustration.

Ralph stared at her, as if he doubted his hearing. "What?"

"I will not be climbing in bed with Ron. Not because you say so, but because I don't find him attractive. I don't want him."

"But you find me attractive?" he quizzed.

"Absolutely." Vanessa would have liked to smile and gaze longingly into his dark eyes, but she was shaking so badly, her teeth were chattering. She forced herself to say, "I want you, not Ron. But you're wrong if you think because I am taking care of my family, it means I'm looking for a husband. I'm not."

She nearly laughed at the relief she saw on his handsome face. What did he think? That she was proposing? She couldn't have him thinking she was trying to trap him into marriage. She needed his cooperation, not have him running for the closest exit.

Leaning back in his seat, he asked candidly, "Tell me, Miss Vanessa, exactly what do you have in mind?"

Recognizing this was the opportunity she'd waited for, Vanessa ignored the fear cramping her stomach, and blurted out before she lost her nerve, "A single night with you, Ralph."

Shock was stamped on his bold African features. "Wait, I must have misunderstood . . ."

"There is no mistake. I'm asking to spend one night . . . all night in your bed," she rushed ahead to say before she lost her courage, "When we part in the morning, both of us will go back to our normal lives. Next Saturday evening will be good for me. How about you?"

Ralph caught the waiter's sleeve before he rushed by and gave their order. Then he turned his intense dark eyes back to Vanessa. "Don't play with me. You aren't like the women I hang out with. We both know you haven't been around the block. So talk to me. What is this about?"

Forcing her facial muscles to relax, Vanessa sighed softly. "My history with other men is not the issue here. I am serious, Ralph. I'm not asking Ron to sleep with me. I'm asking you for . . ."

"Wait one minute. Are you threatening to go to Ron if I don't agree to sleep with you?" he demanded to know.

"I didn't say that! Ron has nothing to do with this discussion. Why are you so shocked? What's the matter, honey? Did I jump down from that pedestal you placed me on?" Despite her teasing tone, she was exasperated. "I'm twenty-six. Old enough to know what I am asking for . . . what I want. Don't you dare tell me that I'm the first woman to proposition you, because we both know that would be a bold-faced lie." She took a calming breath, before she went on to say, "Please, don't underestimate my intelligence. You change women every other day. There is always a new lady on your arm."

A muscle jumped in his jaw, as if he were grinding his teeth. He stared at her while sipping his drink. He stopped the waiter. "Bring me another one."

Vanessa lifted a beautifully arched brow, pouting her red-tinted full lips. "What's wrong, big guy? Are you saying you're not attracted to me? If that's the case, then say so. I don't plan on begging." After draining her own glass, she said, "Just say no, Ralph, and I will be out of your face like that." She snapped her fingers for emphasis.

His voice was gruff, deeper than normal, when he replied, "I can't say no." His eyes lingered on her soft lips. "I want you."

Vanessa's velvet brown eyes went wide. She reached across the table, deciding she needed something stronger, and took the fresh drink from his loose grip. She took a sip of his scotch, then made a face. "Nasty."

Ralph threw back his head and released a deep throaty laugh that seemed to ease some of the tension between them. "Not to your liking, I take it."

Vanessa shook her head wondering how much more her poor nerves could take. She meant every word. After all, she wanted him, but she wasn't about to beg for his lovemaking. After all, she had some pride.

He ordered her favorite soft drink before he gave her his full attention. He lifted her small hand and covered it with his much larger one, unknowingly causing tingles to race along her spine.

She forced herself to say, "You haven't said no, but you also haven't said yes either."

"Tell me why."

Vanessa wasn't about to answer that loaded question, especially when the response was so inherently personal. Instead she hedged. "But I've told you. I want to experience your lovemaking. We've gotten to know each other these past few weeks. Quite frankly, I think you're one sexy man."

Ralph smoothed his thumb over her red-painted nails, his gaze on her full lips. "Come walk in the garden." He slid his chair back and reached for hers. She shook her head, not rising to her feet.

"Not until I have your answer. Do we have a date next Saturday night?"

He smiled. "We do."

Vanessa allowed him to help her rise and took the arm he offered realizing she was suddenly hot. It had nothing to do with the temperature. Although it was close to two in the morning, and the night air had cooled considerably, Vanessa felt as if she'd swallowed a hot chili pepper.

It had finally sunk in. Ralph said yes. Now what? The nerves that had cramped her stomach felt as if they were jumping all over the place.

They walked along the curved walkway that meandered through the lush grounds. The trees twinkled, as if filled with sparkling lights. There was beauty everywhere she looked, honeysuckle and azaleas in full bloom.

"Nothing to say," he asked. He turned her to face him and gently cupped her shoulders.

Vanessa swallowed with difficulty. Unable to get any sound out of her suddenly dry mouth, she licked her lips.

Ralph's eyes were on her mouth.

He surprised her when he asked, "What if I want more than one night? We can have the whole weekend. Let me escort you to the rehearsal dinner Friday night?"

Vanessa insisted, "Ralph, this is a private matter. Between the two of us. I don't want the others to play guessing games, trying to figure out what we might be sharing."

Ralph lifted her chin until he could see her eyes. "Are you absolutely sure this is what you want?"

"Yes," she managed to get out.

Before she could collect herself, Ralph was sliding his arms around her small waist and pulling her against his wide chest. "One kiss. Then we'll know if we're sexually compatible."

He waited for her nod. Once it came, he covered her mouth with his. There was nothing simple about that kiss. First his mouth soothed, then caressed her soft lips; when they parted for him, Ralph tenderly thrust inside, ready to explore and fully taste her mouth.

He groaned, "Sweet," as he deepened the kiss even more. He didn't stop until he was suckling her tongue, intent on learning all her tantalizing secrets.

Vanessa quivered with incomparable desire. She moaned, sliding her arms around his trim waist, needing to be closer, eager to feel her breasts against his broad, hard-muscled chest. He felt good, so right, while his clean male scent enfolded her. She wanted, how she wanted. She tightened her inner muscles, feeling empty deep inside where she'd never felt empty before. Suddenly, she was hungry for him, and what she instinctively knew only he could give her. Shyness kept her from rubbing herself against his hard thigh.

Ralph was the first to move back. Slowly, he lifted his head and stared into the depths of her eyes but said nothing. His breath seemed as uneven as hers.

"You are a mystery, Vanessa Grant. Your lips are incredibly soft and so sweet. I'm looking forward to holding your beautiful body close all night long." His voice deepened even more when he said, "I promise. You will not be disappointed."

Vanessa trembled, whispering, "I have no doubts. Good

night." She turned and hurried back the way they'd come. She didn't slow until she was in an elevator. She gave silent thanks that she didn't have to wait.

It was only after the elevator door closed that she let out the breath she'd been holding. Wrapping her arms around herself, she smiled triumphantly. Proud that she'd done what she'd set out to do. For one special night, he was hers. Next weekend! It could not get here fast enough to suit her.

Five

Church service, brunch, the plane ride, and even coming home to an empty house had all passed in an unbelievable whirl. Vanessa just knew she would fall asleep the instant her head touched the pillow. She'd been wrong. The weekend's excitement hadn't worn off; a glance at the bedside clock confirmed, two o'clock in the morning. And she could not shut off her brain. She'd had so much fun!

"If you're so happy, why can't you sleep?" she grumbled as she punched her pillows.

There was no need to search for an answer. Her reason was tall, dark, incredibly gorgeous, and kissed like a dream. She hadn't said more than a few words to Ralph the entire day. It was understandable, considering they were never alone.

Vanessa had held it all in. Even Laura couldn't get anything out of her. She wasn't ready to share. As much as she loved Laura, Brynne, Trenna, and Maureen, Vanessa didn't plan on sharing the details of her agreement with Ralph. She still hadn't completely processed it all. And she'd spent hours going over every word.

Who would believe it? It seemed like something out of a movie. She'd gone and made a date to spend the night with a man she wasn't sure she even liked. It was crazy! Totally unlike the shy, safe woman she'd always been. She was not one to take risks. Yet here she was, planning the most gigantic gamble imaginable . . . sleeping with Ralph Prescott.

She did like him! Over the past weeks, Vanessa could honestly say there were lots of things she liked about Ralph Prescott. He was more than a rogue and womanizer. Even a lowlife player had a few good points. Take Greg Cummingham. He, too, was all those things, yet he had fathered the twins. Ralph was not nearly as bad as Cummingham. And he was part of a wonderful family.

Despite Ralph's tremendous financial success and good looks, he was a regular guy who was down-to-earth. He'd been considerate and protective of her and revealed a genuine interest.

Even though she hated his reputation with women, that hadn't stopped her from fantasizing about him day after day or dreaming about him night after night. Disagreeing with the way he ran his sex life certainly hadn't kept her from asking for a night in his bed. Ralph was man enough to make even a large woman feel ultrafeminine. When he'd looked at her, kissed her, and complimented her beauty, for a moment Vanessa had actually believed him.

To say the man was shocked when she propositioned him would be putting it mildly. Vanessa giggled as she recalled his shock, yet he hadn't ignored or dismissed the question. He took her seriously. She grinned suddenly, intrigued by the possibility he found her as attractive as she found him. Her heat raced at the thought. But why was she taking this so seriously? They would share what some people might consider no more than a one-night stand.

This night wouldn't be what either one of them would call normal. Yet it was something Vanessa longed to share with Ralph. For one magical night, she could be like her girlfriends. She would experience her special man's lovemaking. And then she would go back to her regular routine of taking care of kids and working while trying to balance it all on her own. What mattered was that she would walk away with a beautiful memory that no one could take away from her.

Vanessa was not the only one having trouble sleeping that night. As Ralph prowled the dark confines of his large, luxurious den he couldn't stop thinking about Vanessa. Why hadn't he refused? He had certainly felt the need to walk away from what his instincts warned was a trap, which was ridiculous. It was Vanessa he was dealing with, a woman he knew he could trust.

Yet he couldn't say no, especially after seeing the longing in her eyes. He suspected a refusal would be a crushing blow. For such a quiet, unassuming lady, she had thrown him off-balance. He still couldn't believe it.

If someone had told him how the evening would end, he would have argued them down and sworn they weren't talking about the lady he'd known for years. Vanessa Grant? No way! And he would have been wrong.

Ralph swore beneath his breath. The lady had shocked him. He still hadn't wrapped his mind around the fact that Vanessa had propositioned him. For a few moments he'd been busy trying to figure out who the woman was, and what she had done with Vanessa. Vanessa was a good girl. She didn't sleep around. Any man with half an ounce of self-respect would assume she'd temporarily lost her mind.

Ralph called himself every kind of fool he could think of. Of course when he finished, nothing had changed. He still faced the same reality. Next Saturday, he had a date with Vanessa. And he would not be kissing her good night at the end of the evening. When it was all said and done, they would be sharing a bed.

He had a single goal. To see to it the beautiful lady got what she wanted. He planned to pleasure her until she couldn't so much as recall Ron's name. All he had to do was figure out how he could manage that without her winding up hating him and him hating himself.

What she asked went against his grain, yet he could not, in good conscience let her go to another man. Despite what she said, he believed she could be tempted by Ron. That possibility left him coldly furious. She had asked him to become her lover. He accepted and was going to honor that promise.

He also hadn't gotten over the fact that he would have preferred to make it a weekend date, while she insisted on limiting their arrangement to a single night. She had also decided to keep their agreement between the two of them. He didn't like it, not that he planned to broadcast their arrangement. After one lousy night they both would walk away, as if it had never happened.

Sprawling back in an oversize armchair, he laughed without amusement. It wasn't as if he hadn't been there and done that. He'd never been big on relationships. His way, when it was over, no one was left holding a bag of disappointments or hurt feelings. It was no big deal. So why didn't it feel right?

He'd be a bold-faced liar if he didn't at least admit to himself that the taste of Vanessa's sweet mouth had not been nearly enough. She had left him painfully aroused. To make matters worse, whenever she'd got within touching distance today, he ached. One taste of her lips had left him eager for more. He wanted her . . . badly. Right or wrong, good or bad, he couldn't walk away from what she was offering, not in this lifetime. He could think of a hundred and one reasons, why he shouldn't give in to her tempting beauty. None of those reasons mattered. He was a man of his word. He was going to keep his promise. And he would deal with the unavoidable consequences later.

* * *

"Courtney Ann, if you don't sit still, I will never get finished. I thought you wanted your hair up like mine?" Vanessa scolded her six-year-old sister. She'd brushed her hair into a high ponytail, secured it before pinning the curls in place. She left loose hair to frame the little girl's brown face.

"I'm tired, Nessa, why did Curtis get to play, and I can't." She pointed to her twin brother, who was parked in front of the television with his collection of small cars on the living-room sofa and had been ordered not to move. He was dressed in a pale gray tuxedo.

Vanessa smiled. "Curtis is not going to be a flower girl, like you and Shanna. He has to carry a ring, while you get to drop the flower petals. Right?"

Courtney nodded eagerly. "Right!"

"You look so pretty. Now, be still for a few minutes and let me finish." Vanessa went to work with the curling iron. Before she could finish, Curtis was in the door of her bedroom.

"Can I go sit on the sunporch? I won't get dirty on the swing. Honest."

Vanessa saw the mischievous gleam in his dark brown eyes, the swing he had in mind was not on the sunporch but in the backyard. He looked so handsome in his suit and white shirt, with the rose vest and bow tie matching the bridesmaids' dresses. She smiled, "We don't have time to play, sweetheart." After finishing the curls, Vanessa pinned a cluster of tiny pink roses into her sister's hair. "All done, Courtney."

She had barely gotten the words out of her mouth before Courtney, in a white ruffled slip and tights and white patent-leather shoes dashed past Lana on her way into the living room to join her twin. "Courtney!"

Lana laughed. "I'll get her dress and help her into it. You

finish getting ready. We can't have the maid of honor in her robe."

"You look beautiful. Turn around let me see the back," Vanessa gushed.

Lana was dressed in a dark green vee-neck ankle-length chiffon-layered dress. Her hair was curled around her shoulders, and her soft brown skin was lightly made up.

Vanessa smiled, proud of her sister and the way the dress she had made turned out. She had designed and embroidered all the bridesmaids' dresses, but had only made her own as well as Brynne's wedding gown.

"Thanks. I'd better hurry. The limousine will be here soon." Vanessa sighed, gazing at her sister. "Are you sure you don't mind driving the kids and yourself to the church? I can call Brynne and explain."

"Stop worrying. We will be fine. Now you hurry and finish up. Brynne is expecting you and the other ladies to help her dress. She is going to look lovely in that bridal gown you designed especially for her."

Vanessa smiled. She'd always loved sketching clothes and sewing. She was especially honored that Brynne had decided to wear one of her creations for her wedding. She'd learned to sew at her mother's knee. It wasn't until she was in her teens that she began to design bridal and evening gowns. She'd been working on a degree in business and hoped to open her own bridal boutique one day. After her mother passed, she was forced to postpone those plans. Once the children were in college, she hoped to go back and finish her own degree. In the meantime, she had her collection of sketches to build on.

"Oh, Nessa, I can't wait to see all the dresses. The wedding is going to be so beautiful . . . all your designs. Mama would have been so proud." Lana kissed her cheek. "Hurry."

She gave Vanessa a tiny shove before she closed her bedroom door.

Smiling, Vanessa turned to gaze at the dress spread out
on her bed. The dark rose silk was strikingly beautiful but
plain, with its square neckline and long, flowing skirt cut on
the bias, except for the ivory embroidered midriff accentuat-
ing her trim waist. All the bridesmaids had picked Vanessa's
designs that best flattered their figure types. Thank heaven
Brynne had insisted on hiring two seamstresses to do the
actual sewing. Vanessa concentrated on the bride's gown.

It was a true labor of love. The beautiful strapless, ivory
silk gown's midriff and train were embroidered with white
silk ribbon flowers and pearls. It was no secret that Brynne
could afford a Vera Wang gown, if she chose because, like
Maureen, she came from a well-to-do family.

As, Vanessa stepped into her dress, she smiled. She hadn't
expected Ralph to ask her to be his date for both evenings.
Although flattered, she decided to exercise caution, prefer-
ring to maintain their privacy. Last night at the rehearsal
dinner, she'd stayed as far away from him as she could. He
called several times earlier in the week to try and change her
mind, but in the end, he respected her decision.

The first time he'd called, she had been at the sink and
nearly dropped the phone into the soapy dishwater. She was
shaking by the time she'd dried her hands. With the phone
to her ear, she ignored the curious look Lana had sent her as
she hurried into her room and closed the door behind her.
She had been thankful that the twins were playing a board
game out on the sunporch.

When he asked if he could see her some night that week, she
had been shocked but quickly insisted it wasn't necessary.

Ralph seemed disappointed. When he reminded her that
he really wanted to take her to the rehearsal dinner, she was

relieved that he couldn't see her because she could not stop smiling.

There was a lengthy silence, then he asked about Saturday night. But Vanessa insisted she had to make sure the kids were settled. It would be simpler if later she met him at his place.

He sighed softly, said he was looking forward to Saturday night, then hung up. This had seemed like the longest week, and now that it was only hours before the wedding, she was a nervous wreck. Vanessa stared at her image in the mirror. Her eyes filled with fear. Her face was made up, her thick hair pinned into a knot, and loose curls framed her face. She wore her mother's choker-length pearls and matching stud earrings. She couldn't help pondering what Ralph would think. Would he like what he saw? Would he still find her desirable?

"The limo is here, Nessa!" Curtis yelled, pounding on her closed door.

When she opened the door, he nearly fell in. "I heard you, Curtis." She leaned down and kissed his cheek. "I've got to go. You be good and listen to Lana."

He nodded his understanding.

"Courtney, come give me kiss. You heard what I said to your brother. It goes for you, too." After kissing her, Vanessa smoothed her hair. She paused to hug Lana before asking anxiously, "How do I look?"

"Good," all three of them said at once.

Vanessa laughed. "Right answer. See you at the church. And please don't be late. And drive carefully."

"We'll be there early," Lana promised, urging her to the door. "Bye."

Vanessa joined her friends inside the limousine. Like her, Trenna, Laura, and Maureen were in dark rose silk dresses, embroidered with ivory. Vanessa's heart raced with joy. "You all look wonderful. Where are Kelli and Anna?"

"They are meeting us at Brynne's," Maureen exclaimed. "You're right. We do look fabulous."

They all laughed.

Trenna confessed. "I'm so nervous. You'd think I was the one getting married."

"I know what you mean," Vanessa echoed, knowing her jittery nerves had more to do with what would happen after the wedding. The unanswered question that swirled through her mind was did she have the nerve to go through with their plan. What if she chickened out at the last minute? Ralph would have every right to be furious.

"We are going to party tonight," Laura cheered.

"Absolutely," Trenna added.

Maureen reached over to squeeze Vanessa's hand. "I have never looked so good. And it's all your doing. This dress turned out beautifully."

"Thank you." Vanessa beamed.

"I'd love for you to design a gown for both me and my grandmother, for the women's center annual fund-raiser. This year it's going to be a black-and-white ball."

Vanessa's eyes went wide with excitement. "I don't know what to say." She smiled, afraid to believe. Maureen wore beautiful clothes, most of which were bought in New York during fashion week. Maureen's grandmother often appeared in the society pages of the newspaper. She was a patron of the arts and had founded the Women's Crisis Center.

"Your designs are wonderful, Vanessa," Maureen insisted.

Vanessa's smile was filled with sincerity. "Thank you. Let's hope Brynne's happy with her wedding gown."

Kelli and Anna were already there. Brynne was a nervous wreck, and the ladies went to work getting her and little Shanna ready. When they were done, they stood back to admire their handiwork.

"You are so beautiful," Vanessa whispered with tears in her eyes.

"It's not me. It's this dress." Brynne was an exquisite bride. The dress fit perfectly. She also wore a diamond tiara and layers of a long ivory veil that flowed to the floor. At her throat was a diamond-and-pearl necklace. She had teamed it with matching earrings and bracelet.

"Mommy, you look like a princess!" Shanna beamed up at her.

"So do you, sweetheart. Turn for me." Shanna happily whirled. Her pale pink lace dress had an empire waist like Courtney's.

"Are we ready, ladies?" Anna asked eagerly.

They were in Brynne's bedroom.

"Not yet. I have something for you." Brynne opened the dresser drawer and began to hand each of them a slender box, a well-known, jewelers' name printed on the lid. She thanked and hugged each one of them in turn. "Okay. Open it!"

The ladies squealed with pleasure when they found diamond bracelets with their initials in eighteen-karat gold forming the clasp.

There were hugs and kisses all around. Brynne scolded that no one could cry, or they would have to start all over. And she didn't plan on being late for this wedding.

"Let's get moving, ladies. We've got men to impress," Kelli insisted.

Every one laughed and started moving to the waiting limousines.

Vanessa stood smiling in front of Ralph, Brynne, and Devin on her left as the photographer took picture after picture of the wedding party. They were all lined up in front of the church. Shifting from one tired foot to the other, she struggled with her frazzled nerves.

"Tired?" Ralph whispered, close to her.

"Of smiling . . . yes," she whispered back. Curtis and Courtney stood in front of her. "My feet are what's aching."

"Hmm, I'll see what I can do about that later," Ralph said into her ear. His voice was low and sexy, so much so, if she hadn't been listening closely, she would have missed the comment. She stood stunned as shivers of desire caused her heart to pound in her chest. Before she could collect her thoughts, her little brother tugged on her hand.

"Nessa, I'm tired," Curtis complained.

"I'm hungry" Courtney added.

"It shouldn't be much longer. Smile," she coaxed.

Just then Shanna, who was being held by her dad, said in a loud whisper. "Daddy, I've got to go . . ."

"Me too," Curtis and Courtney chimed in.

Vanessa smothered a laugh, "Come on." She motioned for Shanna to join them.

"If you like, I can take Curtis," Ralph offered, drawing her eyes to the smoldering heat in his dark hungry gaze.

Vanessa, used to doing nearly everything on her own, nearly refused until she saw her little brother's smile. Evidently Curtis found a short time in a man's company appealing, reminding her that growing up in an all-female household wasn't easy for him. He missed not having a father in his life. Unfortunately, there were some things she couldn't do for him, no matter how hard she tried.

"Yes. Thank you." She smiled up at him.

The responsive warmth of Ralph's smile momentarily caused her to forget what she was supposed to be doing. Shanna swiftly reminded her of the need to hurry by tugging at her hand. By the time the two little girls were finished, Vanessa had regained her composure. She didn't want anyone to guess how uneasy she'd been all day. Or how eager she was to be wrapped in Ralph's strong arms.

One thing was clear. Vanessa would chicken out if she let herself dwell on what could happen later that night and didn't just relax and let go. She'd been waiting a long time to feel like a woman. She had no doubts that Ralph was the only man to handle this special job.

Six

"You look surprised," Vanessa blurted out nervously. "As if you weren't expecting me." She stopped suddenly. "I shouldn't have said that."

Ralph smiled as he backed away from the door, allowing her entrance into the spacious foyer of his home. It was after eleven before they were able to get away.

"Why not? It's true." He eased the colorful silk-fringed shawl from her shoulders. "Pretty."

Vanessa blushed, not knowing if he was referring to her or the shawl, a gift from Brynne. She resisted the urge to tug down the black, clingy dress she'd worn last weekend. When she selected it, she recalled how he had looked at her and complimented her.

"Thank you." She lifted her chin and pulled back her shoulders. She wasn't going to start the evening hiding what God had given her.

Ralph's smile widened as he dropped her shawl over the back of the chair flanking a tall, high-polished, ebony table. "Would you like a tour?"

Smiling, her hands clasped tightly in front of her, she nodded.

Ralph offered his arm, and she took it. He had changed also. He was wearing a navy T-shirt and jeans that followed the lean lines of his tall muscular frame. His feet were bare on the gold-and-beige marble floor.

"Living room." Directly across the hallway was a large and beautifully furnished beige-and-wine room. They walked through the spacious formal dining room, decorated with oriental-style table, sideboard, and high-backed, cushioned chairs.

"Beautiful," she said, as they entered the spacious kitchen, with granite countertops and stainless-steel, state-of-the-art appliances. From there, they walked through the fully equipped game room, home theater, and downstairs to the indoor basketball court and pool area. They ended the tour in the luxuriously furnished den at the back of the large house.

She moved to stand in front of the French double doors, glad her nerves had eased somewhat. "What can we see from here?" Vanessa asked as she peered into the dark.

"The outdoor pool, tennis and basketball courts," he said, leaning against the mantel, where candles flickered in the fireplace.

"Goodness. All this for one man," she exclaimed, then covered her mouth. "I didn't mean to . . ."

Ralph laughed. "Relax. You didn't offend me. My aunt said the same thing when she first saw the size of the house and grounds. It's large, but then I am a big man. Besides, it was a great investment. How many cars can one man drive? Two's my limit."

"According to Jay Leno, several garages full," she joked.

Ralph chuckled. "I'm not that flashy. I was raised in modest homes, first with my folks, then my aunt and uncle and cousins. Believe me, I have enough stuff."

Large leather sofas faced each other in front of the fireplace. A lush leather recliner was positioned opposite. A large flatscreen television was mounted above the marble fireplace.

The desk was near the floor-to-ceiling bank of windows. The drapes were wine silk and the thick area rug in lush burgundy, red, blue, and cream covered the hardwood floor.

Vanessa nodded. "I like this room. It's not only beautiful but comfortable." Then she let out a small gasp as she felt his lips brush her nape. She'd been longing for his touch, to be held by him. Finally, she was here.

She stared at the tray filled with assorted cheese, crackers, finger sandwiches on the wide ottoman in front of the sofas.

He took her hand, urging her over. Once she was seated, Ralph didn't sit beside her but went over to the built-in shelving that housed the bar. He leaned down to open a small refrigerator and lifted out a pitcher of an iced drink.

"Tea," he explained as he filled two long-stemmed crystal glasses. He handed her a glass before he sat down beside her and stretched his long legs out to the side of the ottoman. "Hungry?"

"You've thought of everything." She took a sip, hoping she wouldn't choke; her nerves were back the instant he sat down, her senses suddenly on high alert.

"I do my best," he replied, his dark eyes caressing her creamy dark skin.

"In a second, you are going to tell me you cook, clean, and decorate," she teased, surprising herself. Finally, she was able to relax a bit more.

"Cook, yes. Clean and decorate, no. I have a housekeeper. My aunt and cousin Anna decorated my home, Gavin's homes, and Devin's home here and in St. Louis. They also did my house in Los Angeles before I moved back here."

"You guys are so spoiled." Vanessa laughed, determined to overcome her fears. She was here because he wanted her. She had waited forever to be alone with him, his attention solely on her.

"With love, absolutely." Ralph grinned. "That's family. And it goes both ways."

Vanessa nibbled on a sandwich. "Mmm, good."

"Anna's recipe for homemade sandwich spread. Deviled egg?"

Impressed, she asked, "When did you have time to do this?"

"This morning. It wasn't hard. I really do know my way around the kitchen. My aunt made sure all her children knew how to take care of themselves. We all had a night to cook at home. Anna is not the only chef in the family. She just has the degree to back her up." He shrugged. "Normally, I don't take time to put together more than breakfast. I've gotten lazy. I'm on the list of bachelors who have their weekly evening meals prepared by Anna's catering company. I always have a freezer full of something good. It's a great service for me and profitable for them."

Vanessa nodded. Anna and her business partner, Janet Matthews, had started their catering business working out of Anna's home kitchen. They made and delivered homemade meals mainly for the Detroit Lions' football team's single players. Gavin had been one of Anna's clients before they fell in love and married. Although both women were married, their business was still going strong. Plus, there was no shortage of weddings, banquets, graduations, and baby showers in the metro area in need of a good caterer.

Ralph was studying her as he took a healthy swallow of ice tea. He surprised her when he asked, "Why so quiet? You aren't nervous, are you?"

Vanessa stiffened, then took a deep breath. "I suppose I'm still in shock. I don't know what I expected. Your house is fabulous, but you don't need me to tell you that. It's all a bit overwhelming."

Judging by his expression, he liked her response. "It's a

house, Vanessa. Nothing more than a boatload of stuff. I thought you could see past the obvious."

"Obvious?"

"To what's important."

"Oh," Vanessa said, wondering if he was ever going to kiss her.

He took another sip of tea, watching her. After returning his glass to the tray, he asked, "What are you thinking?"

"Why?"

"Your eyes are soft, kind of dreamy."

Vanessa blushed.

He insisted, "Tell me."

"I was wondering if you were ever going to kiss me."

"Absolutely." He looked deep into her eyes before he placed a finger under her chin, tilting her face toward his. He pressed his firm lips against hers. His kiss was soft and almost tender, causing Vanessa to relax against his broad chest.

She sighed softly, allowing him access to the interior of her mouth. As his tongue stroked hers, Vanessa stopped thinking and began feeling. He aroused a wealth of emotions. She kissed him back, turning until her full breasts were pillowed against him. Lost in a maze of sensuality, only the need to breathe forced her to pull away.

Her breathing, quick and uneven, her eyes met his. His dark gaze seemed to glow as he studied her full red lips.

"So sweet," Ralph whispered, his voice rough with need, an instant before he pressed open-mouthed kisses against her throat.

Vanessa shivered, having no idea her neck was so sensitive, especially behind her ear, until Ralph warmed the area with first his breath, then his tongue. She trembled as desire traveled along the surface of her skin, spreading to her nerve endings. Embarrassed when her nipples quickly turned into beads of need and her feminine core moistened, Vanessa didn't want him to guess how much she longed for him. She quickly moved away.

"What's wrong?"

Vanessa blinked as she forced herself to think, to find an answer that did not reveal her vulnerability to him. "Nothing," she lied, reaching for her now-watery glass of tea. She drank it anyway.

"Vanessa, if you're uncomfortable with anything I did, tell me."

"Why would you think that?"

He shrugged. "I'm not trying to take advantage of you."

Needing to know, she asked, "You no longer want me?"

Although he chuckled, it held no humor. His voice was deeper than normal, almost gruff when he admitted, "One thing a man's body does not do is lie. If you care to look, you can see how much I want you. But I also don't want you to have any regrets."

"I don't." Although curious, she was too embarrassed to look down.

"Then why are you hugging one end of the sofa rather than being in my lap?"

"I doubt your lap could hold me." She giggled, trying to joke at her own expense.

Ralph grinned. "You have nothing to worry about. I can't wait to fill my arms and hands with your sexy curves. So-o-o, explain to me again why you're so far away when I want you here." He patted his muscled thighs.

I can do this, she repeated to herself as she scooted over to his side.

"Better?"

"It will do." He placed kisses across her throat, then tongued the hollow at the base of her throat. "You like?" he whispered.

"Mmm," she moaned.

He moved his hand to her waist. "Or do you like this better?" he asked before pressing his mouth to hers. One kiss moved into another, and yet another. He squeezed her waist before moving his hand to her breast.

"You're so soft, Vanessa. So much woman," he whispered as he kissed her again, stroking her tongue with his while worrying the hard crest of her breast. "Mmm," he sighed, as she moaned. He continued to squeeze her nipple until it pebbled even harder.

Vanessa trembled in his arms.

"You're so beautiful . . . let me touch you, baby. Let me see you and taste you."

She nodded, her eyes closed, her breath rapid. He needed no further encouragement. He unzipped her dress, pulling the straps down, easing the clingy fabric from her arms and down past her waist.

Vanessa, caught up in the seductive magic of his hot, hungry kisses, didn't consider protesting as he unhooked the front clasp of her strapless bra and peeled the cups away from her full breasts. She whimpered in protest when his mouth left hers, then gasped aloud as he tongued the erect dark brown nipple into aching need.

"Sweet," he whispered as he played with the other nipple. He took her peak into his mouth, then began to suck hard, causing Vanessa to call out his name, moaning aloud as hot sparks of desire shot through her system. She unwittingly crossed her legs, pressing her thighs tightly together.

"Good?" Ralph lifted his head to gaze hungrily into her velvet-dark eyes.

She caressed his face, unwittingly urging him back down to her arching breasts. Ralph seemed to understand what she needed; he moved to the other globe and treated it to the same sizzling-hot attention.

She was whimpering so by the time he lifted his head that he studied her face, before he asked "Do you want me as much as I want you, beautiful?" Ralph licked her plump bottom lip.

Vanessa nodded, unable to find the words to express her needs.

"Then show me." Ralph paused, his mouth close to hers but not close enough.

"How?" she murmured, mesmerized by the sight of his firm lips, longing to lick his lips as he'd licked hers.

As his hot eyes moved down her throat over her ripe breasts and back to her lips, he couldn't fail to see her blush.

"I want you on my lap, beautiful."

"I'm Vanessa," she said hotly.

"Oh, I know who you are. Tonight, you are my Vanessa . . . mine. And I think you're beautiful. Come on, stand up and take that dress off." He patted his thighs. "I want you here."

Flustered, and unsure of herself, nonetheless she was where she wanted to be . . . with him. She stood on unsteady legs and pulled her dress down her shapely hips, past her thighs, to the floor.

"Vanessa," Ralph crooned, as she stood in front of his spread thighs in nothing more than black bikini panties and thigh-high black hose.

"You are so incredibly beautiful and sexy," he murmured throatily, clasping her waist as he guided her down until she sat facing him straddling his powerful thighs. When he reached for the hem of his T-shirt, she pushed his hands away and took charge.

"Let me." She was shaking but managed to get the shirt over his head. She'd been waiting for what seemed like forever to see him, to touch him.

He leaned back, smoothing his palms on her long legs. He caressed up her silky bare thighs.

"See anything you want, help yourself, sugar," he teased.

Vanessa trembled, wanting, but afraid to caress him.

His copper brown chest gleamed, firm with hard muscles. Both his pecs and biceps were well developed while his abdomen was trim and his stomach taut. In short, in her estimation, he was the beautiful one.

Vanessa's lids dropped as she felt him lift her breasts, using the heat of his tongue to lick one globe. She was sobbing by the time he had taken both nipples in turn and suckled. When he pulled back, he only went back far enough to study her face.

He said, quietly, "You okay?"

Caught in a frenzy of emotion, sensation, and sexual desire, Vanessa could only nod.

He released a sigh before he kissed her, long and deep, as he wrapped his arms around her. He said into her ear, "Let me hold you." He must have heard her murmur of agreement because he tightened his arms even more. As his hard muscle meshed with her cushiony softness, they both sighed at the pleasure.

Vanessa had thought she knew what to expect, had thought she was prepared for this. The instant her bare flesh met his, she realized she didn't have a clue. Never had she given so much of herself physically and received so much from another, yet she wanted so much more. She felt empty deep inside and knew that only he could give the fulfillment she craved.

Even now he was holding her as if she were delicate, made of spun glass. And she hated it. She wanted it to stop, but she didn't know how . . . didn't know how to tell him what she needed.

Giving in to her need, she began to slowly move her

hands over his wide shoulders and down his back from nape to spine while kissing the side of his throat. His husky groan made her smile her satisfaction and unwittingly rub her aching nipples against him.

Ralph eased back, putting space between them. Her closed eyes fluttered opened, a question in their brown depths.

She gasped as she felt him cup and squeeze her sex. "What are you doing?"

"Making you hot for me." He lowered his head again to her aching nipples and took one into his mouth to suckle while he found and repeatedly worried her clitoris through her silky panties. He didn't stop until she cried out as she reached a climax.

Panting, Vanessa rested against Ralph, her hand over his heart as she tried to make sense of what had just happened.

Ralph held her tight until her breathing gradually returned to normal. Then he slid her along his hard, long, muscular thighs until her moist folds moved against the length of his erection, teasing them both. They both groaned at the contact, despite annoying layers of clothing separating them.

"How long has it been for you?" he asked, kissing the sensitive spot on her neck.

Vanessa shivered but not from desire. "Why?" she asked, startled by his interest. He hadn't asked before. Why was he asking now?

"It's not something I normally ask, but because it's you, I want to know all your sweet secrets."

Vanessa lifted a brow, then attempted to tease seductively, "Judging by what I'm not wearing, I'd say you know just about all there is to know about me, sweet man."

Ralph laughed throatily, kissing the warm scented place where her neck and shouldered joined. "Mmm, I'd say there is one very special place I haven't discovered."

Weak with relief, she stroked a hand down his chest. "Don't let me stop you," she whispered.

His kiss was hard, urgent, then his lips softened, and he began to tease her mouth open. When she parted her lips, the kiss deepened as he stroked her tongue with his own. He didn't stop until she was moaning his name. His large hands moved down the line of her smooth back to curve on her lush behind.

"You've got me hot and rock hard, I can't think straight. All I know is that I need you. I want to be inside you, my beautiful Vanessa."

"Yes . . . yes," she practically sobbed, her need matching his.

He revealed huskily, "I've been fantasizing about having you in my arms, in my bed. This past week felt like a year."

She looked at him, not knowing what to think or say. Yet she was afraid to believe he was sincere. She needed no reminder that she was with Ralph Prescott, a man who had his pick of women in the "D." For this special night she was all his . . . all night long.

She let out a startled screech when he stood up, his strong arms supporting her plump bottom. She quickly wrapped her arms and legs around him.

"Put me down before you hurt yourself."

"Not likely. I routinely bench-press much more than you weigh, beautiful."

"But where are we going?"

"To bed." He laughed. His long legs moved easily through the house to the staircase. Eyes closed, she held on as he mounted the stairs. He wasn't out of breath when he reached the top landing. He turned right, moving down the carpeted hallway. He passed several closed doors on both sides of the hall. He slowed as they approached a set of double doors that was partially opened. He used a shoulder to push them wide and entered a huge bedroom. He walked between a set of sofas facing each other and flanking a stone fireplace. He moved on to an oversize bed.

She let out a gasp when he placed her in the center of his bed. A dark red velvet comforter covered the biggest and longest bed she had ever seen. Her head rested on crisp white silk-covered pillows. A single lamp was lit on one of the nightstands. Both the carved headboard and nightstands were made of dark, rich cherrywood.

As he reached on either side of her and eased down the comforter and top sheet, she lifted her hips.

"Comfortable," he teased, a hand braced on his hip.

Vanessa merely nodded, as if she were in a daze. Ralph's eyes never left her as he pulled off her panties and rolled her hose down her long legs.

"Don't move," he whispered huskily. "Let me look at you."

Vanessa doubted she *could* move, as she struggled to accept the moment had finally arrived. She was in Ralph's bed.

He was the first to break the silence when he said "Do you have any idea how unbelievably sexy you are?" He didn't wait for her response, but said, "Your skin is like dark, creamy chocolate. To think you've been hiding those dangerous curves beneath your clothes all this time. So beautiful. From now on, that's what I'm going to call you . . . beautiful."

"Stop," she begged. "You're embarrassing me."

"But why?"

In an effort to distract him, Vanessa slowly ran a hand up one long, muscular, denim-covered thigh. She stopped before she reached the prominent ridge declaring him male.

His lids drooped, then he urged, "Please don't stop."

She turned to swallow down an attack of nerves and slowly moved her fingers over the large bulge, from the thick base to the broad crest. When he released a husky moan, Vanessa jerked her hand back, afraid she had done something wrong.

"Please . . . don't stop."

When she hesitated, Ralph took her hand and curved her fingers over his shaft, moving it along his hard length. She stroked over him twice before he took her hand in his. At her questioning look, he unsnapped his jeans and carefully eased down the strained zipper.

Vanessa knew she should look away but didn't. Her natural curiosity had taken over. She wanted to see Ralph, every inch of his muscular frame, bare, for her eyes only. Her gaze never left him as he pushed the jeans down his hips and legs. She watched as he pushed down a pair of navy knit boxers, then stepped free of both.

She knew her eyes were wide as she took in his full length. There was nothing small about him anywhere. He opened the top drawer in the nightstand and placed a box of condoms on top.

"I didn't forget," he said as he sat down beside her and placed kisses down the middle of her rib cage to her stomach.

He whispered, "Open those long, pretty legs for me, beautiful."

Seven

She had a single thought that consisted of a solitary word . . . hurry. Burning with an unrelenting hunger that only he could ease, Vanessa obeyed, and in doing so, she offered her all, without fear or hesitation. For this one magical night, he was hers alone.

Ralph released a heavy sigh as he settled between the expanse of her long, shapely legs and eased her toward him. He caressed his way up the outside curve of both legs, then leaned forward, pressing his lips to hers before he sank back and kissed his way back up her inner thighs. At her startled gasp when he pressed a kiss against her feminine curls, Ralph hesitated. When she made no further protest, he parted her plump folds and found her slick with feminine moisture. He moaned her name as he slid a finger deep inside her sheath.

At the sound of her whimper, he husked into her ear, "You are so incredibly tight. Relax, beautiful." He moved until he could take her nipple into his mouth while he played in her heat, increasing the friction while pressing his palm against her exposed clitoris.

"Oh . . . ah," Vanessa cried out, turning her head from side to side as her enjoyment grew. She arched her back, losing touch with everything but how he made her feel. Added to that, the increased suction on Vanessa's taut nipple caused her senses to go wild, sending her into yet another release.

Before she could gather herself, Ralph's hard body covered hers. His eyes burned hot with desire as he stared down into her velvet-dark eyes. Her hands caressed down his broad back as he pushed a firm thigh between hers, spreading her legs even more. Her eyes went wide when she felt the unmistakable pressure of his rigid sex. Using the broad crest of his thick shaft, he parted her soft folds, moving against her damp opening. Ralph's breathing was as uneven as hers as he teased her softness, giving her time to adjust to his size.

"Ralph . . ." she moaned.

He said her name as he slowly pushed forward.

He growled into her ear, "Relax, sweetheart. I won't hurt you." He kissed her.

Vanessa tried to relax but whimpered in pain when he reached the natural barrier deep inside.

He stopped moving. His entire body stiffening.

As the burning eased, the pleasure returned. Vanessa moaned, needing to feel more . . . all of him. "Hurry," she urged.

He growled, "Why didn't you tell me?" through gritted teeth.

Even though she sensed his anger, that didn't stop her from wanting him . . . now.

Instead of answering, Vanessa arched her back, lifting her legs to encircle his waist. His response was a groan and deep shudder.

Licking his neck, she whispered "Please . . . Ralph. I need you, all of you." She was beyond pride as she pleaded with him to finish. When he didn't move, she followed feminine instinct. She tightened her inner muscles around his hard shaft, stroking him, milking him.

He covered her mouth in a hard, punishing kiss, then

he thrust forward past the barrier until he filled her completely. Vanessa cried out at the pain. Taking a deep breath, she rested with her lips at the base of his throat. She kissed him there again and again. Growing frustrated when he remained still, she wiggled her hips beneath him.

Ralph moaned huskily, then began to ease out slowly before plunging into her sheath, repeating the movement again and again. Each stroke was deeper, harder than the last, as he gripped her hips, showing her how to move with him. All too soon Vanessa climaxed, her entire body quivered, and he quickly followed as his large frame convulsed into an earth-shattering release.

Ralph had used his arms to support his upper body. Then he dropped down beside her, his breath quick and uneven. He said nothing for such a long time that Vanessa began to worry. She was certain she'd pleased him. Despite her lack of experience, her instincts told her she couldn't be wrong about that.

Determined to push the negative thoughts away, she concentrated on that one positive . . . she hadn't failed. She'd done what she set out to do . . . turned her fantasy into reality. Making love with him had been better than she imagined.

"Why didn't you tell me?" he said tightly.

"You sound angry." Suddenly uncomfortable with their nudity, she reached down and pulled the sheet up to cover them.

Ralph turned his head toward her, a muscle jumped in his jaw as if he were grinding his teeth. "Why didn't you tell me that you had never been with a man?"

Nervously smoothing the sheet covering her breasts, Vanessa took a few minutes to collect her thoughts. Of all the things she imagined might happen between them, this conversation wasn't one of them. She'd foolishly assumed he wouldn't notice. Why was he making such an issue of it?

"I asked why didn't . . ."

"I heard what you said. I just don't understand why you are so angry about it. It was my decision to make, not yours."

"I don't believe this!"

He swung his feet down to the floor, his back to her. He walked through a set of double doors into what she saw was a hallway. Both sides of the hall were lined with closet doors. At the other end of the hallway was another set of doors. He disappeared inside what must be the bathroom.

Vanessa sat up in disbelief. This was nothing like she imagined it would be afterwards. Where was the romance? He hadn't held her close. Instead he was truly angry with her. If anyone should be angry, it should be her. Why did her lack of experience matter? Why was he letting it ruin what they had shared?

Frowning, she dropped her hands over her face. He hadn't taken anything that she hadn't wanted to give. Oh, she wanted him all right. For weeks she'd been desperate to know how it would feel to have him deep inside her body. Evidently it hadn't been as good for him as it had been for her. For her, it had been sheer magic. Why wasn't he pleased? He'd climaxed! That had to mean something, didn't it?

Feeling absolutely stupid, she listened to the sound of the shower being turned on. No, no, no! It was not supposed to end this way! She sniffed unhappily. Well, sitting and crying about it wasn't going to fix things. She had to do something, that is, unless she wanted their special night to end now, right this minute.

Brushing her tears away, Vanessa yanked the sheet off the bed and wrapped herself in it. Walking over to his dresser, she used his brush to bring order to her thick curls. Taking a deep breath, she knocked firmly on the bathroom doors.

There was no answer. Calling his name, she pulled them open and looked inside. The room was done in taupe granite and bronze features; a row of thick white towels were heating on the towel warmer.

It was not the opulence of her surroundings that held her attention. Ralph stood in the center of an oversize, clear glass shower stall, water rushing from multiple showerheads.

He was all smooth hard muscle on one powerful bare frame. His broad, rich brown back narrowed into a trim waist, and taut yet nicely rounded buttocks, with long, muscular legs, and narrow feet. His head was down, his hands braced against the wall as water cascaded over him. He must have sensed her presence, for he turned to glance over a broad shoulder.

Vanessa could read his expression through the sheet of water. He stared at her before turning his back on her.

Suddenly furious, Vanessa marched over, yanked opened the shower door, and stepped inside. She yelled over the sound of the spray, "What is your problem, Ralph Prescott? You are the one who invited me here. Do you want me to leave? Is that why you are treating me this way? If that's the case, just say the word, and I'm gone!"

Before she could say more, he yanked her inside and against him.

Burning with need, Ralph took her sweet mouth again and again. The more he tasted her, the more he wanted. When she whimpered in protest, he softened the kiss, soothing her with gentle strokes of his tongue. How had she managed it? She was turning him inside out, crazy with desire. Once was not nearly enough. When she melted against him, he pressed kisses down her throat. He tugged the sheet tucked over her magnificent breasts until it dropped onto the marble floor. He didn't want anything between them . . . nothing from preventing him from feeling every one of her voluptuous curves.

For tonight she was his dark, chocolate beauty. He never dreamed that this shy, quiet woman was so hot or that she could make him forget everything, but her. He felt as if his head had blown off when he came inside of her. He'd never even come close to feeling that way before.

"Vanessa . . ." he groaned, pressing her cushioned soft breasts into his chest. The magic between them was starting again. One minute he was furious . . . the next he was wild with need. How had she gotten past his anger? How had she made him forget that she'd kept her virginity a secret?

He still couldn't believe that he hadn't made himself pull out . . . and he had tried. This untried virgin had done something no woman had ever done. Vanessa had caused him to lose control completely.

"You feel so good."

"Oh Ralph." Trembling, she wrapped her arms around him, holding on tight.

He took another taste of her lips, then he reached for the bar of milk soap he preferred. When his hands were covered in lather, he slowly moved them over her body, from her soft throat to her sleek shoulders. Satisfied when her lids closed and she trembled with need as his soapy hands slid over sensitive breasts, Ralph paused to tug her nipples into peaks. Once they were swollen and taut with desire, he moved sudsy hands over her soft skin down to her stomach. Vanessa moaned in earnest. He was holding her up by the time his soapy fingers played first in her nest of ebony curls, then focused on caressing her ultrasensitive folds. He took his time before he found and worried her feminine core until the bud was swollen from need, and she begged him to take her.

Ralph was so hungry to have her yet again that only a kernel of common sense kept him from taking Vanessa against the wet marble without protection. He switched off the water, then, with more haste than grace, carried her into the bedroom wrapped in a bath sheet, another fresh towel over his shoulder. After he placed her on her feet beside the bed, Ralph dried her hair.

"Sorry, it got wet," he said, between kisses.

"I'm not sorry about anything." She stared up into his eyes.

He stared at her for a long moment before taking her kiss-swollen bottom lip into his mouth to suck. "Sweet . . . so sweet," he groaned. At her responsive shiver, he deepened the kiss until they were both breathless.

Ralph picked up a new packet from the nightstand, but before he could do more than open it, Vanessa took it from him.

Her beautiful dark eyes pleaded with him when she asked, "Please let me."

He didn't even consider objecting, when there was nothing he wanted more than to have her softness on him. He nearly lost it when she gently caressed him from the thick base of his shaft to the sensitive crown.

Suppressing a moan, he released a pent-up breath when she finished unrolling the condom down his hard length. He relaxed, showing her how he like being stroked.

"Thank you." He kissed the side of her neck, then slowly unwrapped her towel as if she were a gift especially meant for him. She was glorious, and he told her so.

He kissed her again and again, caressing and squeezed her lush hips. Quickly drying off, he stretched out on the bed. He chuckled at her look of surprise as he took her hand, urged her to sit astride him, his hands on her hips as he guided her down onto him.

His gaze heated as he watched her eyes widen as he carefully filled her. He enjoyed the way her eyes softened and her breath quickened even more as she moaned her pleasure.

"You are open and wet for me. Can you feel how much I want you, Vanessa?"

She nodded, as if speech was beyond her at that moment. He studied the way her lids closed, her beautiful eyes hidden as he lifted her. She sank onto his throbbing shaft, but this time she slowly took all of him. He growled his pleasure from deep in his throat.

"I don't know what I'm supposed to do now," she confessed.

"Just relax and enjoy," he whispered back as he wrapped her in his arms until her sweet breasts pressed against his chest. He waited, giving her time to adjust. He indulged himself, kissing her again and again. Once she seemed comfortable, he guided her hips, whispering. "You're in control. Move as slow or fast as you want, beautiful."

Vanessa's eyes searched his as she carefully moved along his pulsating length. He closed his eyes and groaned huskily at her tight, wet heat. It took all his control to wait until she was ready. The wait was sweet agony. He growled his pleasure.

"Good, Vanessa?"

She nodded as she began to quicken their pace. Judging by her facial expression and the way her inner muscles tightened around him, he suspected she was close to completion. He reached between their bodies and caressed her slippery feminine pearl. Her entire body stiffened as she shuddered in his arms. Her strong release triggered his own and he climaxed mere seconds after she did.

Exhausted, he held her close as their breathing returned to normal. Their bodies were still joined as he kissed her hungrily, not wanting to let her go. She'd done it again, given indescribable pleasure. Everything about her pleased him. His body began to harden, again.

"Didn't you . . ." she questioned.

He chuckled, saying huskily, "If you are asking if I came, the answer is yes." He rubbed her soft cheek with his. "What can I say?" he asked, moving a caressing hand down her back. "I can't get enough of you. Relax, I'm not going to take you again. I don't want you sore." Easing out of her, he rested on his back. He was tempted to leave the light on, so he could look at her, but it was late, and they were both tired. After turning off the lamp, he held her close, relishing her soft curves.

He whispered in her ear, "You okay?"

Vanessa nodded. "It has been a long day. I wonder where Devin is taking Brynne."

"Private island near Hawaii."

"Sounds wonderful. I'm surprised he kept quiet."

He yawned. "Sorry."

"Tired?" she asked, moving a hand over his chest.

"Mmm." He sighed deeply. "We should talk."

"About what?"

"I need to understand why now and why you chose me. But it will keep until morning." He brushed his lips against her temple while moving his palm soothingly up and down her arm. Her skin was so soft all over.

Smiling, he closed heavy lids.

Vanessa lay on her side, her head on Ralph's chest, her fingers spread low on his concave abdomen. Judging by his deep breathing, he was asleep.

Carefully, she slid her leg from beneath his. He stirred, his brow creased in a frown, and he tightened his arm around her waist.

"Come back here," he grumbled in a deep, gravelly voice.

"I'm going to the bathroom."

"Mmm," he mumbled, never opening his eyes, but dropping his arm to his side.

Quietly picking up her things, Vanessa hurried into the bath. After using the facilities, she took a quick shower. As she stared at herself in the mirror, she realized how tired she felt and that she looked a mess. Last thing she wanted was to talk about what happened.

How could she make him understand why when she couldn't sort it out herself? He made her feel things she didn't want to feel. How could she admit she had a school-girl crush on him? Or that he filled not only her dreams, but her daydreams?

She re-dressed in panties and hose and tiptoed out of the bedroom. Finding the rest of her clothes in the den, she finished getting dressed and let herself out.

She had originally planned to stay the entire night and part of the following day. But that had all changed the instant he decided they needed to talk. Her car was parked in the spacious circular drive. She didn't congratulate herself until she was out of his subdivision and on Twelve Mile Road. It didn't matter if it was close to three o'clock in the morning. She could sleep as late as she liked.

Eight

Ralph was livid! He couldn't remember ever being so upset. Naturally he'd been disappointed when he awoke and found Vanessa's clothes gone. He assumed she was downstairs, perhaps preparing his breakfast. He'd showered quickly, not bothering to pull on more than a well-worn pair of jeans. When all the downstairs rooms had been searched, including the kitchen, his disappointment ballooned into a full dose of anger.

First she led him to believe she had some experience with men. Then she had gone on to break her promise to spend the entire night and part of the next day with him. Not one to openly display his feelings, he was shocked at his inability to put his hurt aside and move on.

Rather than join his folks at the ten-forty-five church service, Ralph had subjected his body to a punishing workout, ending with laps in the pool.

Fortunately, his temper cooled enough for him to at least act civil, so he'd gone over to have Sunday dinner with his family. It was a Prescott ritual that they honored; regardless of how busy everyone was during the week, they came together on Sunday. He rarely missed Sunday dinner, mainly because he hated to disappoint his aunt.

Only this week he had planned to spend the day in bed

with Vanessa. As he drove over, he wondered if he'd run into her. It was possible, as her little brother and sister were spending the weekend with his folks. He recalled his aunt's mentioning that the twins were going to help entertain Shanna while her parents were on their honeymoon.

Yeah, it would be interesting to run into her. He had a few choice words to say. If nothing else, he would demand an explanation. He deserved that much! It would help if he had an idea why she'd run. Sure he had been upset when he discovered she was a virgin. Any man would be. But they had made up, or so he thought, until he woke up alone.

He swore when he pulled into the drive and didn't see her van. Anna and Gavin's Navigator, as well as Kelli and Wesley's Cadillac, was parked in the drive.

"This has never happened to me," he muttered aloud. If anyone was sneaking out, it was generally he. He didn't like waking up in an unfamiliar bedroom. He'd had enough of that when he was in the pros, traveling with the Lakers for so many years. When he retired from the game, he promised himself the days of not knowing where he was were over.

A few of his lady friends had not been pleased when he didn't stay. But that didn't stop him from leaving when the lovemaking was over. Expensive gifts or flowers always soothed those ruffled feathers and eased his way back, if he chose. Until last night, he hadn't dealt with a woman who didn't know the rules.

He wasn't interested in a long-term relationship. He didn't want any form of a relationship. He was no fool. Relationships were how his cousins ended up married.

The man-woman thing was nothing but a game. And he was a master player. Everything had been fine until last night.

What was she up to? Despite the trick she had played on him, he seriously doubted she knew what she was doing. It was not a game to her. He'd bet his last dollar that she wasn't playing at anything.

His first mistake had been not following his gut instinct. When she propositioned him, he had been wrong to agree . . . his answer should have been a flat-out no.

It wasn't as if he hadn't been approached before by attractive women. They were generally after money, or out to trap him in any way they could . . . mainly marriage. It had been going on since he turned pro. Thanks to his uncle, he and his cousins had never had trouble recognizing their ulterior motives. What was different this time was Vanessa. Her interest in him had come as a shock, especially since he'd always considered her to be a good girl. Now he was forced to deal with the fallout from a guilty conscience.

Because Wayne and Kyle, Gavin's younger brother, spotted him and called his name, there was no turning back. The men were outside manning the barbecue grill, while the ladies were inside, Ralph had no choice but to stick it out. Before he reached the lawn, Shanna came running to him with her little arms out wide. She was followed by the Grant twins.

Ralph grinned as he swung Shanna up for a hug and kiss on the cheek. He also scooped up Vanessa's baby sister, Courtney, causing her to squeal with laughter. With the girls back on their feet, he bent down to tickle Vanessa's baby brother, Curtis, on his tummy, sending him into giggles. When Vanessa came to pick up the twins, he intended to be there. If she couldn't make the trip, he planned to volunteer to drop them off. Vanessa wasn't going to be able to hide from him. Just imagining her surprise widened his smile.

After dinner, Ralph was the one forced to conceal his disappointment when he learned from his aunt that the twins were staying another night. Donna would be dropping the twins at kindergarten in the morning since the public schools' summer vacation didn't start until the following Thursday.

Ralph wanted to howl his frustration. He'd given his word that he would not seek her out afterwards. His word was not something he gave lightly. But they needed to talk. He needed to understand why.

Lana knocked on the open bedroom door before she walked across a hardwood floor to the queen-size bed. "Nessa? Are you sick?" she asked as she sat down beside her sleeping sister.

Vanessa mumbled into the pillow. "What time is it? And how did you get home so early?"

"Early? It's after three. Marisa's mom dropped me off. Why are you in bed in the middle of the afternoon?"

Vanessa rolled on to her back and covered a yawn. "Just catching up on some sleep."

"The twins aren't home yet." Lana curled up at the end of the bed, resting her back against the footboard.

"Mrs. Prescott asked if they could stay another night." Vanessa propped herself up against the pillows. The beautifully carved mahogany bedroom set with a large sleigh bed, along with matching armoire and dressing table had originally belonged to their grandparents, and had been lovingly created by her grandfather. It had been passed down from her mother to her. It gave the room an old-fashioned charm.

The heavy desk near the window was often used to hold Vanessa's aged Singer sewing machine or the embroidery machine. The embroidery machine was the last gift her mother, Leah, had given her for Christmas. A large corkboard on the wall above the desk was covered with drawings of her most recent designs.

"Sis, look at your hair. It looks like you had a good time last night," Lana teased.

Vanessa covered her face, laughing. "Forget my hair. Tell me about you. Did you and Marisa have fun?"

Lana grinned, kicking her shoes off so she could tuck her legs beneath her. "We always have so much fun. We stayed up most of the night talking." Her beautiful brown face was relaxed and carefree.

Pleased, Vanessa vowed to do as much as she could to ensure it stayed that way. Lana took life much too seriously. She'd been so young when forced to deal with the loss, first of their father, and then their mother. Vanessa did her best for all her siblings. Unfortunately, during the summer months, Vanessa would have to rely on the seventeen-year-old to watch the twins while she was at work. Even though, she paid Lana, Vanessa wished things were different. She wanted her sister not to be so serious all the time, to spend time with her friends and just concentrate on enjoying herself, before she had to settle down for her last year in high school.

"So what about you? Did you stay and dance the night away?" Lana asked eagerly.

Vanessa dropped her lids. She didn't enjoy lying, especially to her sister, but she couldn't exactly reveal the truth either. She hedged. "I had a great time at the reception. Wasn't the wedding fabulous! The dresses came out better than I imagined, and Brynne was so beautiful."

"Absolutely! I was so proud of you, getting all those bridesmaids' dresses designed and embroidered, not only on time but beautifully. You did a great job on Brynne's dress!" Lana enthused. "How did you feel when you saw how good they looked . . . all together?"

"Overwhelmed." Vanessa laughed, getting up to hug her sister. Over dinner and during the evening, the sisters discussed the wedding in detail. Vanessa revealed that she'd been approached about designing a one-of-a-kind evening gown for one of the Metro area's wealthy ladies, Judge Quinn Montgomery's wife, Heather. Brynne had told everyone, who bothered to listen that Vanessa had designed her bridal gown.

At times Vanessa felt daunted by the challenge ahead. There was never enough money to take care of all the things that children needed. She rarely had extra money or time to spend in the fabric store or even to look in the high-end boutiques. Vanessa adored clothes, especially the beautiful gowns found in New York, Paris, and Milan. But her reality was a full-time job and children to care for. For now she could only dream about going back to college to finish her degree in business so that she could someday have a boutique with her name on the door.

It was strange that she loved designing beautiful evening gowns, especially bridal gowns, because Vanessa never expected to be a bride. Fortunately, she knew the difference between dreams and reality. Her feet were firmly planted on the ground. One romantic night, with the exciting man who filled her fantasies, didn't mean a lifetime of love and commitment. Ralph was a fantastic lover, but he would make a lousy husband.

The fantasy ended when she drove away. Tomorrow was a workday, and she would go back to doing her thing. She had plenty to keep herself occupied, work, kids, and saving what little extra money she had. It was up to her to make sure the kids had what they needed.

Later, the two sisters were curled on opposite ends of the sofa, watching an old Halle Berry movie on television, when Lana asked, "Nessa? You aren't going back to sleep on me, are you?"

Vanessa blushed, embarrassed that she'd been caught daydreaming about Ralph. She didn't have to pinch herself to remember last night. Her feminine core was tender, proof

enough that she'd slept in Ralph's bed. He'd actually made
her feel beautiful. She'd blushed even more, accepting that
her fantasies about him were tame compared to his raw sexual need. She knew from experience that his reputation as a
gifted lover hadn't been exaggerated. It was a fact that . . .

"Nessa?" Lana prompted.

Vanessa said, "It's late. I think I'll turn in. What about
you? You have school in the morning. Three more days
until vacation." Uncurling her long legs, Vanessa stood and
stretched before reaching for the empty popcorn bowl and
empty lemonade glasses on the coffee table.

"Can I see the end of the movie? It's only thirty minutes,"
Lana begged.

Vanessa smiled. "Okay, but you've seen this movie 101
times."

"I know. I can clean up those few dishes."

"No. You can finish the movie, then go on up to bed."
Vanessa bent down to kiss Lana's forehead. "I like just the
two of us spending time together."

Lana grinned. "Me too. Although I miss the twins."

"Me too. They'll be back tomorrow with plenty to talk
about. I'm sure they did a great job last night and today of
keeping Shanna entertained."

"I bet. Those two never stopped talking."

Vanessa went past the dining room and into the kitchen.
It didn't take long to wash the leftover dishes. The old house
was roomy and well loved. Vanessa and Lana had grown up
here. Back then, her parents shared the big downstairs bedroom and bath while the two sisters occupied the upstairs
bedrooms. The small back bedroom had been her mother's
sewing room. Vanessa fondly recalled spending time at her
mother's side, learning how to sew.

When the back porch had been screened in and converted
into the sunroom, which ran the length of the house, the

family had often spent many happy hours there, especially during the hot summer months. Under the old oak tree in the backyard was where the swing set had been placed. Their father had built the brick barbecue pit. Vanessa, Lana, and their mother often shared a picnic lunch under that old tree on warm summer days. There were so many happy memories of their time together.

Vanessa was drying her hands when she heard her sister calling good night. Switching off the kitchen light, Vanessa called her good nights. She took her customary walk through the house, checking that the doors and windows were all locked and the alarm set, before she entered her own room and got ready for bed.

The alarm system was something she had installed after her mother passed, more for her own peace of mind. The old neighborhood didn't feel as safe as it used to. Perhaps it was the weight of being solely responsible for the babies and her little sister that caused the unease.

After washing, conditioning, and blow-drying her permed hair, Vanessa creamed her skin before sliding into her big empty bed. Hugging her pillow, she had only to close her eyes to recall the sweet magic of being cradled against Ralph's wide chest. He was not soft and cushiony like the pillow she squeezed against her. She recalled his clean, male scent and the deep timbre of his voice as he made love to her.

By the time he had finished making love to her, her entire body shivered from incomparable pleasure. She had relished the caress of his large, yet surprisingly gentle, hands and the amazing heat of his firm lips and tongue. This once she indulged herself, allowing her senses to take flight as she relived the utmost joy they reached together. Her hips unconsciously moved against the firm mattress as she remembered his seductive allure as he licked, then tongued her breasts. He didn't stop until she reached her very first climax. She hadn't even known she was capable of reaching such heights of pleasure.

"Goodness," she whispered aloud as she remembered the excitement and pleasure she found from his steel-hard shaft deep inside. Initially the pain had surprised her, but once she was relaxed, she was able to let go, and that was when the sheer enjoyment began. The only word she could think of to describe the sensation was incredible . . . that was until Ralph had started quizzing her.

He had nearly ruined their night by demanding answers. And when he hadn't received them, he'd gone off alone, which had upset her. In fact, she was proud of the way she hadn't caved in and let her inherent shyness stop her from following him into the shower. She had surprised herself, yet it felt right at the time. She couldn't let their one night slip away without at least trying to hold on to the romance.

Vanessa couldn't stop blushing when she recalled the hungry look on his dark, strikingly handsome face when he pulled her into the shower stall with him . . . sheet and all. It was embarrassing that she hadn't recalled they didn't have a condom! It had been Ralph's quick thinking, not hers, that had prevented a major disaster.

What she wasn't proud of was the fact that she'd been too much of a coward to stay and face him and at least try to answer his questions. She had run away. She could only imagine his reaction when he woke and discovered she'd broken her promise to him and fled. Of the two of them, he had kept his part of their agreement, while she had broken hers.

Had he been angry? Or had he only been disappointed? Perhaps he was so accustomed to the fickle ways of women that he hadn't reacted at all? With a disappointed sigh, she accepted that it didn't matter. Theirs had been only a single, admittedly incredible, night of pleasure. It had been more than she expected.

Covering a yawn, Vanessa acknowledged that tomorrow was a workday. Time for her to get back to the world of raising kids, work, cleaning, washing, and cooking, and when she could find the time, sketching and designing beautiful evening and bridal gowns.

Maybe when the twins were out of high school, she'd actually consider looking for Mr. Right? It was a possibility. In the meantime she wasn't foolish enough to fall for a man whose life revolved around the next female challenge. While some men collected baseball cards or model airplanes, Ralph collected women. And that was okay with Vanessa, as she wasn't really involved with him.

She should be jubilant. She'd done the impossible. She'd become sexually involved with him without being emotionally involved with him. Few women could say that! Also, she had discovered the mystery of human sexuality. When it was all said and done, the night they had been together was a slam dunk as far as she was concerned. She didn't have a single regret.

Ten days since Devin and Brynne's wedding, and Ralph still hadn't gotten past his anger, or disappointment. He'd really tried to push away his encounter with Vanessa and move on. It hadn't worked. Nothing worked. He felt as if he was left with only one option, and that was to seek the lady out. She had all the answers. And he intended to find out why she broke her word . . . why she forced him to break his promise.

After identifying himself, the security gates swung open, and Ralph followed the drive around to the side entrance of the Mathises' home. He frowned as he parked behind Vanessa's aged SUV.

He was downright furious that she had left him no alternative. It would be easy for her not to take his calls or slam the door in his face. If he came to her workplace, she had to hear him out.

Pasting a smile on his face, he knocked at the door before letting himself in. "Hey! Where's everyone?" he called as he followed the hallway past the laundry room, bathroom, and into the large, bright kitchen.

"Will you look who's here! In the middle of the day, no less," Anna smiled as she came over to give him a kiss on the cheek.

Ralph gave her a hug. "You saying I'm not welcome? What you got smelling so good in here, Little Bit?" He called her by the childhood name she hated, just to bug her. "I'm hungry."

Laughing, she asked, "You came for food?"

"Why not? You're the chef in the family." He casually leaned back against the counter rather than going straight to Vanessa's office. In hopes of avoiding suspicion, he had no choice but to bide his time. "Where is everyone?"

"Gavin has a meeting at the Lions' headquarters. Kyle is over at Mama and Daddy's hanging out with Wayne. That leaves Vanessa, me, and the housekeeper." She teased, "You couldn't find any food between here and the campus?"

"None that you made. Well, what do I smell? Fresh-baked cookies?"

Anna pointed to the cookies cooling on a rack. "Oatmeal with walnuts." After taking out homemade sourdough buns, Anna reached into the refrigerator for sliced turkey, roast beef, ham, and cheeses, then began putting together a hero sandwich topped with lettuce and her special chopped-olive spread.

Ralph washed his hands in the sink before he walked around to take a seat at the raised central island. "How's the cookbook coming?"

Anna had been collecting and writing family recipes,

some dating back to slavery. She grinned. "Fabulous! I have a publisher interested. I should know something soon."

With a huge smile, Ralph gave her a big hug. "That's great! I'm proud of you, cuz; I knew you would do it."

"That is high praise, indeed, coming from an overachiever like you. How are the plans for the community center going? Wesley said Daddy has no idea what you fellows are up to."

Lester Prescott had worked at the old neighborhood high school for years as a coach. He had helped many young boys, who would otherwise have gone to the gangs, finish high school and go on to higher education. Anna's brothers and Ralph had decided to honor him for all his years of dedication by using their old home as an integral part of community center in his name. It was due to open next summer.

Ralph laughed. "That's been the hardest part, keeping Uncle Lester in the dark. But everything is right on schedule. We're going to break ground soon for the indoor pool, indoor basketball courts, tennis courts and track and field." The Prescott men had bought the surrounding lots and now owned the entire city block.

"There is no way you fellows can do all that without Daddy catching on." Anna warned as she put together the sandwich. "I don't know how you have kept it out of the papers. This is big news. What do you think about the architect? You talked to him, right?"

"He's good. I had a meeting with him yesterday. I wish I had remembered to bring the most recent plans, so you and Gavin could look them over. I think you guys will approve."

"Sounds great. We have to get together with Wesley and Kelli soon to get this done. How does next Friday night sound? I'll do dinner, then we can all get together and make a decision. When Brynne and Devin get back, we'll have everything all set to go. Oh, Ralph, you've done so much of the legwork already. I can't wait for the dedication ceremony. Daddy and Mama are going to be so happy." Anna wiped away tears.

"He deserves it. They both do. We've got less than a year to get it done." Ralph grinned. "Watch your mouth. Aunt Donna is too sharp for words. Nothing much gets past her."

"Me! I know how to keep my mouth closed. But that means making sure Kyle and Wayne don't find out."

"I think the boys can keep a secret," Ralph boasted.

"Hardly." Anna placed a plate filled with the sandwich and a mound of coleslaw on the place mat in front of him, then handed him a cloth napkin. "Please, Wayne tells everything he knows."

"When are the newlyweds flying back?"

"I'm not sure, but soon. Devin's got to get back for camp."

"I hate that they are going to be in St. Louis. Mama and Daddy will be sorry to see Shanna leave." Anna smiled.

"I know. They wanted to keep her for the summer, but Brynne and Devin would never agree to that. They will only stay long enough to close up Brynne's house and his condo," Ralph said.

"Shanna is such a doll baby." Anna asked, "What do you want to drink? Lemonade? Beer?"

"Bottled water." Ralph said between bites.

Anna teased, "So what's her name?"

He nearly choked. It was a few moments before he recovered enough to ask, "Who?"

"Whoever? You always have a new lady. Tell me about the latest one."

Nine

Ralph took a swallow of water before he forced a grin. "No one you know."

"Aw, come on. There is always someone new. Tell me," Anna teased.

"Nothin' to tell."

She frowned. "That's not like you to keep secrets. And you haven't brought anyone to Sunday dinner with you in ages. What is going on? Spill it!"

There was no way he could be frank, not without breaking his promise. No way could he reveal that he hadn't been near another woman, not since he'd made love to Vanessa. He wished he knew what was going on. That was the main reason he was here . . . to get some answers.

Instead of answering, he took a huge bite of his sandwich.

Exasperated, his cousin rolled her eyes at him. "Keep your secrets! Both Kelli and I agree that the way you're going, you will never find anyone willing to put up with your womanizing ways."

Ralph chuckled, finishing his lunch. "Do I look worried? There are plenty of gorgeous women in Detroit. I wouldn't want to disappoint a single one of them," he teased. Wiping his mouth on his napkin, he asked, "Will you wrap some cookies for me, Little Bit? I want to say hello to Vanessa before I take off."

"Okay. She's in her office. You know the way."

"Thanks." Ralph pinched her cheek playfully. "Did I ever tell you that you're my favorite female cousin?"

"Ha-ha! I'm your only female cousin."

Ralph grinned at the sound of Anna's laughter. His smile slipped as he walked down the carpeted hallway. He stopped at the closed door, took a fortifying breath before he knocked once, then walked in. Vanessa was on the telephone. She looked up with a smile on her lovely face until she saw him, then her forehead creased in a decided frown.

"I'll call you back, Lana," she said into the headset she was wearing. She dropped the telephone on top of the stack of papers on her desk. "Ralph, why are you here? I thought we agreed . . ."

He closed the door then crossed his arms over his chest. Quirking an ebony brow, he said, "Hello, Vanessa. Surprised to see me?"

"Naturally, I'm surprised. We agreed to keep our distance after . . ."

"After you ran out on me?" he quizzed.

A muscle jumped in his cheek as his dark eyes moved from her flawless, dark brown face, long hair pulled up into a thick ponytail. The only jewelry she wore was a pair of small, gold hoop earrings. She looked so doggone wholesome, with little makeup, other than the dark red covering her lush, full lips. A huge departure from the sexy vamp who had shared his bed.

Ralph's body wasn't fooled. He wanted them both . . . he wanted her. Her magnificent breasts might be covered by a crisp white blouse, and her lush hips and unbelievably long legs concealed by jeans. That didn't change the fact he knew what was hidden beneath those plain clothes. His shaft began to harden in readiness, and his nostrils flared as he inhaled her oh-so-enjoyable feminine scent. He swallowed with difficulty, aching to have her beneath him again, with her thick, black curls spread across his pillow.

Her beautiful eyes went wide before she quickly dropped her lids, hiding her thoughts behind ebony lashes. "What do you want?"

"I'll give you one guess." When she remained silent, he said with a charming grin, "Now that we're on the same page, let's move on to this weekend. Darlin', would you prefer to spend it in the Caribbean? Which island? Martinique or St. Thomas?"

"Neither. We had an agreement. One night. It's over," she said firmly. The only evidence of impatience was the betraying pout of her plump bottom lip.

His heart pounded as he considered taking that lip into his mouth to suckle. Instead he rested a hand on the edge of her desk. "We also agreed to spend that entire night and part of the next day together. What time did you leave? Five? Six? When I woke at six-thirty, you were gone."

"So what if I left a little early? We did the deed. We both enjoyed it. It's over!" she snapped.

Ralph scowled; he didn't like being dismissed. She was acting as if what they shared meant nothing to her. He wasn't used to being rejected. He was used to being the one who walked, not the other way around.

His voice was deceptively soft, when he said, "I didn't come here to pick a fight. I came for some answers. There was a lot left unsaid. Why didn't you tell me?"

"I don't know what you mean." She turned away.

He swallowed a cussword. "You know exactly what I mean. Answer my question."

When she remained silent, he snapped, "You tricked me. If I'd known I would be the first, I would never have gone through with it. You distracted me in the shower. Not again. I want an answer."

"And I can't believe you are even here! I expected you to have moved on to the next lady on your long list. What happened to the man who always keeps his word?"

Feeling the need to defend himself, he thumped his chest. "The way it looks from where I'm standing, neither one of us kept our stupid promise. You walked. And I came for answers."

"Please! We both got what we wanted that night. It was sex, Mr. Prescott. No more . . . no less. Now go away and leave me alone!"

He shot her a furious glare. "With pleasure." He yanked the door open and walked out. His long legs swiftly eliminated the distance to the kitchen. He paused to kiss Anna's cheek and grab the wrapped cookies. "Thanks for lunch, cuz. Got to run. See you, Friday, for dinner."

Ralph didn't slow down until he was in his car. He couldn't remember being angrier or more aroused. He had to get away from Vanessa before he did something crazy, like reminding her no matter what she said, he had been the man she'd wanted inside her.

"Just sex," Vanessa mumbled aloud as she fought back tears. It sounded right. Too bad it wasn't how she really felt. But that was cool. If she kept saying it, sooner or later, she might actually believe it.

She sat with her head in her hands, not believing the words that had come out of her mouth. She only said them to protect herself. She'd been terrified that he would touch her and realize she'd been harboring a schoolgirl crush for him. Her only hope had been to make him angry. She'd done it, but she was the one left feeling miserable.

Why had he come? It didn't make sense. Didn't Ralph

Prescott have enough women running after him as it was? They both knew she was not his type. It was so outlandish, it was laughable, only she wasn't amused. The painful truth was, Vanessa had too much pride ever to admit to being infatuated with the man.

Their memorable night together hadn't ended the way she would have liked, but it was over. As far as she was concerned, it was a sweet memory she would keep in a secret part of her heart, to be examined and enjoyed at her leisure.

What she couldn't understand was why he was upset. He was acting as if this was something that had never happened to him, which was ridiculous. The man was a well-known ladies' man, for heaven's sake! They both knew it was only a matter of time before he moved on to his next female conquest. Why was he so put out?

The only reason she could come up with was that he didn't appreciate her being the one to walk away. Was that it? She'd wounded his pride? Was he on an ego trip?

Vanessa suddenly smiled, relieved that she'd finally understood. Now she wouldn't waste time trying to put a foolish romantic spin on something as basic as injured male pride. Nor would she mistake a case of lust for something complicated . . . such as love.

With a lighter heart, she dialed her home telephone number. When Lana answered, she said, playfully, "How do you and the twins feel about going out for dinner for burgers and hot fudge sundaes? To celebrate summer vacation and day camp on Monday?"

Vanessa laughed at the twins' squeal of approval in the background. She heard a click signaling another call. "That's the other line. Have to get back to work. See you around five thirty. Bye. Hello, Mathis Enterprises. How may I help you?"

* * *

As Vanessa printed out congratulatory letters to notify students that they would be receiving scholarships for the fall semester, she also praised herself on remaining levelheaded.

She hadn't heard from Ralph in two blissful weeks. Nor had she been tempted to contact him. Her days were full, and she rarely had time to spare him much thought. Only at night, when she was in her bed, did her defenses fall, and the bittersweet memories returned.

"Vanessa, have you talked to Brynne today? Have you heard the news?" Anna said with a wide smile as she dropped down into the empty visitor's chair in front of the desk.

Pausing to pull the neat stack of letters out of the printer tray, Vanessa shook her head. "Haven't talked to her since they were here in Detroit. What's up?"

"They are flying in for the family barbecue on the Fourth! I can't wait to hug my little niece. I just got off the telephone with my mother. She's excited that the entire family will be together for the holiday."

"That's great, Anna." Vanessa smiled. "I miss not being able to see them whenever I like. Have you started on the menu, yet?"

"The menu is almost set." Anna began rattling off dishes from porterhouse steaks to lobster tails.

"Wow. Sounds delicious," Vanessa said, returning to her desk and beginning to fill envelopes.

"You are coming with your family, aren't you?" Anna urged eagerly.

Vanessa swallowed down an immediate refusal. The last place she wanted to be was anywhere near Ralph Prescott. "I thought it was a family gathering? I couldn't possibly impose."

"You're family! Since Gavin and I are hosting, naturally, all our employees are invited. Wayne and Kyle will be here, so Lana will have someone close to her age. And she's welcome to bring a girlfriend, if she'd like." Anna laughed, "I'm sure Shanna is looking forward to seeing you and her favorite playmates, Curtis and Courtney."

Vanessa's heart sank, seeing no way out. Ralph was bound to be there, with his current lady. Vanessa didn't have a single doubt he had a new lady friend. She would just have to deal with it. When she'd asked him to be her lover, she hadn't realized it would mean the end of their friendship.

"Vanessa?"

Vanessa forced a smile. "Sorry. Thanks for inviting us."

"Does that mean you're coming?"

"We'd love to come. It will be good to sit down and have a long talk with Brynne." Vanessa hoped her reluctance didn't show. This was Ralph's fault. She'd like nothing more than to smack him upside his head. "Is there anything I can bring?"

"Nope. Just you and the kids and your bathing suits."

Dawn Johnson clung to Ralph's arm as if she were a drowning victim going down for the final time. They'd met the week before at a popular night spot. She didn't even so much as try to hide how thrilled she was that he was 'ex-NBA' and had invited her to a family picnic. As soon as she heard his last name and zeroed in on his championship ring, she was in love.

Ralph was used to women assuming he was serious because he brought them around his family. He didn't bother explaining that her only purpose was entertainment, in a nutshell to keep his mind off Vanessa Grant.

Nor was he concerned that his folks would read more into the situation. They knew he enjoyed female companionship and dated frequently. His family had been giving him a hard time because he hadn't brought a date to Sunday dinner in weeks.

Dawn would suit his purpose by smiling and hopefully stopping the pointed questions on his nonexistent love life. His male cousins would be shocked if they knew that he hadn't slept with Dawn and wasn't interested. As far as Ralph was concerned, the twenty-two-year-old five-foot-two-inch beauty was nothing but eye candy.

"Hey, Ralph," Wayne, bouncing a basketball, called. "We've been waiting for you to get here, so we can play some ball." He indicated his best friend, Kyle.

"Hey, Ralph." The other boy grinned.

"Hey yourself." Ralph smiled, glad that Gavin's younger brother's troubled days of sullen moods and a huge chip on his slender shoulders were long gone. Kyle knew he was loved and wanted by both Gavin and Anna.

Cushioned lawn chairs were placed around the veranda, which ran the length of the house. Wesley and Devin were lounging while Gavin manned the grill and Lester supervised. The pool was located on the other side of the guesthouse and tennis courts.

Ralph promised, "We'll play ball after we eat. Okay?"

"Cool." Wayne grinned, then said to Kyle, "Let's go talk to Lana and Marisa at the pool."

"Hey!" Ralph said, greeting the men. After introducing his date, he playfully punched Devin on the arm. "When did you get in, old man?"

Devin grinned. "This morning. Shanna and Brynne are inside with the ladies."

"Looks like marriage agrees with you."

The other man laughed. "You won't get any complaints out of me."

"We're going on inside. I want Dawn to meet Aunt Donna." Ralph ushered her in through the side door. He called out, "Anyone here?"

"Uncle Ralph," Shanna squealed as she rushed to welcome him.

"Hi, sweetie pie." Ralph swung her up so she could put a wet kiss on his lean cheek. "Where you been?"

"In Louis!" she exclaimed. "Did you miss me?"

"Oh, yeah!" After a hug, he placed her on her feet.

"Mama's here, too!" She took his big hand and tried to drag him into the kitchen as she chattered nonstop.

Following along, he caught Dawn's hand so she would not be left behind. He immediately dropped it the second he saw Vanessa seated at the center island beside Brynne. His gaze momentarily locked with hers before she looked away.

His heart raced as he studied her. Vanessa looked good in a perfectly ordinary navy swimsuit with a deep vee neckline that caused his hungry gaze to linger on her lush breasts. Unfortunately for him, her gorgeous, long, sexy legs were hidden in knee-length denim shorts. Her thick curls had been pulled back into a ponytail. Had it only been two weeks since he'd seen her? It seemed much longer. By the looks of things, she was still ticked at him. Why? If anyone had a right to be ticked, it was he.

He fought the urge to swear beneath his breath, pasting a broad smile on his face. "Hey, ladies." He made the rounds, kissing his petite, pretty Aunt Donna's cheek, then Anna, Kelli, and Brynne. He told himself he had no reason to feel guilty as he introduced Dawn to everyone. Vanessa was the one who had made the rules, he was only going along with her game plan.

For the first time in memory, he was uncomfortable with the way his date clung to him. Dawn was grinning as if she'd won the lottery, and he was the jackpot. If this was a sample of the way things were to be, he was ready to pack up his marbles and go home.

Just then Vanessa's twins raced into the kitchen. They yelled, "We're ready, Nessa!" They were dressed in swimsuits and flip-flops, like Shanna.

"Hurry, Mommy! Let's go slide!" Shanna said excitedly.

Donna explained, "Gavin and Anna set up a waterslide for the little ones."

"Yeah!" the kids cheered, jumping up and down.

Even little Kaleea, at fifteen months, giggled, clapping her tiny hands and pumping her plump legs as if she was also ready to go.

"Don't tell me you want to go, too." Ralph chuckled as he took the baby from her mother, Kelli, and placed playful kisses on her plump cheeks. She gurgled and put wet baby kisses on his face.

Ralph laughed, giving her a playful whirl before handing her back to Kelli.

"Nessa!" the twins complained.

"Let's go." With her back to him, Vanessa, a child in each hand, urged them outside, not offering him more than an ice-cold hello.

Shanna and Brynne followed.

"What's wrong, baby?" Dawn asked, clinging to his arm.

"Not a thing." Ralph forced a smile, working to hide his frustration. Why hadn't Anna warned him? He was many things, but stupid wasn't one of them. He would have never brought a woman if he'd known Vanessa was going to be there. What was she thinking? But then, Anna didn't know anything about the unforgettable night he'd shared with Vanessa.

He was tempted to release a pointed swearword. Rather than trying to change Vanessa's mind, he would be stuck with Dawn. He'd thought he'd done a decent job of putting that night behind him and moving on. But one disdainful glance from Vanessa's beautiful eyes had proven he was dead wrong.

All it had taken was one look at Vanessa, and he was hard, ready for more of her sweet loving. The hunger hadn't gone away. One sexual encounter with her had left him eager for more. His mind might be saying he didn't want a relationship, while his body was screaming for more. What now? All he was certain of was that, given some time alone with Vanessa, he might be able to work her out of his system.

Curtis's and Courtney's loud complaints caused Vanessa to realize she was practically running to get away from Ralph. "Upset" was too mild a word to describe how shaken she was from seeing Ralph with his new lady. Darn it! She was everything Vanessa could never be . . . small and beautiful. Vanessa knew she had no business caring at all. One night was all she asked for and wanted. So why were her feelings genuinely hurt that it hadn't taken him long to move on? It made no sense.

Stop it! she silently warned herself. She was overreacting . . . nothing more. She had done what was best for her. She'd gotten out before she became emotionally involved. Thank goodness it wasn't possible to fall in love in one night. She had been careful to protect herself from emotional devastation. She had nothing to worry about. She was merely tired and hadn't been sleeping well lately. Once she'd gotten a full night's sleep, she'd be fine.

"Gavin and Anna sure know how to throw a party," Brynne said as she settled in one of the cushioned chaises several yards from the pool where the teenagers were hanging out.

Wayne asked from near the deep end of the Olympic-size pool, "Can we go in?"

Vanessa nodded, taking the chair beside Brynne. She reminded the little ones, "No running or pushing. Play nice!"

As soon as the kids moved out of earshot, Brynne demanded, "Give it up, girl. What's going on with you and Ralph?"

Rather than tell an outright lie, Vanessa hedged, "Why do you ask?"

"Maybe because I've known you longer than five minutes? Get real. You seem upset back in the house. Did he say something to upset you?" Brynne's concern was genuine.

Vanessa didn't know where to begin. He had done nothing but upset her since the night they spent together. She wasn't ready to share what she'd been up to on Brynne's wedding night. Besides, she didn't want her friend worrying about her. Brynne had been through so much worse. This was her time for joy. And Vanessa was not about to load her mess onto her dear friend's shoulders. These days Brynne glowed with happiness. No, Vanessa couldn't do or say anything that would change that.

"Ralph is being his natural womanizing self. No woman in her right mind would take him seriously. I just hope his new 'friend' doesn't get her feelings hurt expecting too much from him. He reminds me of Greg Cummingham, the twins' dad, and I see red! No biggie," Vanessa ended with a forced laugh.

"I know. But someday he is going to settle down. And when he does, the woman he has fallen in love with will be one lucky lady."

"What makes you say that?" Vanessa demanded.

"I can't explain it. I just have this feeling that once he gives his heart . . . Ralph's going to be just as devoted and loving a husband and father as his cousins and uncle. Maybe more so. He's a Prescott, after all."

"Maybe." Vanessa didn't even try to hide her doubts. "How many hearts is he going to break in the meantime? My advice to any woman interested in that one is, if she knows what's good for her, she'll keep her distance." Glancing at her sister and her sister's girlfriend, Marisa, who were laughing at the boys' antics in the pool, she confessed, "I'm worried about Lana. I wish she didn't have to stay home all summer babysitting for me. She has too many responsibilities as it is. I wish she wasn't so serious all the time."

"Lana is a great kid. And she's having fun today. Stop worrying."

Vanessa leaned back in her chair when she saw the twins and Shanna squealing with laughter, taking turns going down the waterslide. "I know you're right."

Brynne laughed. "I am right. Lana is hardworking and a good student. You couldn't ask for anyone more reliable to stay with the twins. Besides, knowing you, I bet you have every minute of their day scheduled."

Vanessa released a guilty laugh. "I do. But as you know, Lana is an excellent swimmer, and she has worked hard to earn her certificate to be a lifeguard. It's a great way for a teenager to earn extra money."

Brynne shook her head. "Forget the guilt trip. You can't find anyone better to take care of the twins or love them more. You're being too hard on yourself."

Vanessa sighed, knowing everything Brynne said was true. "Lana will be starting her senior year in the fall. And I don't want her to feel as if she's missed out." Vanessa didn't add that she was doing everything she could to make sure Lana would be able to go to college the following year. She'd never touched the money their father had put aside for Lana's education. Even though Vanessa's college money had gone to caring for them while the twins were babies, Vanessa had no regrets on that score. But what their father had put away no longer stretched very far. College expenses were rising every year. Vanessa had to make up the difference.

Brynne reached out and squeezed Vanessa's hand. "You

know I understand how difficult it can be raising kids on your own. All the hard decisions come back onto your shoulders. You're doing an amazing job with all of them." Until Devin came back into Brynne's life, she had been a single mom, raising her daughter alone.

Vanessa nodded. "Thanks, Brynne. That means a lot to me. Do you have any idea how much I've missed you? And it's only been a few weeks?"

Brynne smiled. "I miss you also. But remember, I am only a phone call away. St. Louis isn't that far. Anytime you need to talk, call me."

"I'm glad that raising Shanna alone is no longer your responsibility. So how do you really feel about being back in St. Louis? That can't be easy."

Brynne shook her head. "St. Louis may not have changed, but I have. I'm not the same frightened young woman who ran home to Detroit to hide from my problems. Now, I couldn't be happier. But don't get me wrong, I have my moments when it all comes back, but Devin is there to hold me." Then Brynne laughed. "And I especially miss my friends in the book club."

"But you're truly happy?" Vanessa persisted.

"Oh yes. Devin is so good to me. But then we would never have gotten back together if he hadn't been so giving and understanding. I still feel guilty about keeping him and Shanna apart for so long."

Vanessa shook her finger at her friend. "Get over it. Devin has. And Shanna is crazy about her daddy."

Brynne laughed. "That she is. Look!"

The twins and Shanna came down the waterslide with their arms wrapped around each other's waists, giggling the entire time.

"She misses you and the twins."

"We miss her." Vanessa had babysat for Brynne when Brynne had to work late.

"What do you think of Ralph's new lady?"

Vanessa candidly revealed, "Doesn't matter, she won't last. They never do with him."

Brynne shook her head. "My goodness, you are getting cynical, girlfriend." She was somber when she admitted, "Don't laugh, but for a while, I wondered if you two might be interested in each other."

"Do I look stupid?"

Brynne giggled. "Ralph adores kids. Shanna and Kaleea both adore him. And from what Devin tells me, Ralph's heading the Lester Prescott Community Center."

"And what does that have to do with me and Mr. Commitment Phobic?" Vanessa asked, almost sharply.

"I keep telling you, he's no worse than his cousins. Wesley and Devin were out there womanizing with the best of them until they fell in love. I had serious doubts about my man when we first met. The women were chasing him like crazy, and he wasn't running."

"Now wait one minute! What are you up to Brynne Armstrong Prescott? Tell me you're not seriously trying to hook me up with Ralph?"

Bursting into a fit of giggles, Brynne nodded. "I don't see why not."

"I've already given you 101 reasons, but you're not listening. I'm going to say this once, then we're going to both drop it forever. Leave it alone."

"Okay . . . okay." Brynne laughed, throwing her hands up in defeat.

"Thank you. Now tell me about Devin's place. Are you happy with it? Or are you secretly house hunting as we speak?"

Brynne shook her head, then began telling Vanessa her plans to redecorate their home. She went on to tell her about the office space she'd found that might be suitable for the new women's center she planned to open in St. Louis.

Ten

By the time the food was served, Ralph wanted out. He'd had enough of Dawn's hints about their future. Also, he was sick of the cold glares he'd been getting from Vanessa whenever she caught him looking her way. She had been acting as if he were in the wrong when she wasn't busy ignoring him.

"What's wrong, son?" Donna Prescott said, drying her hand on a dish towel. He'd just brought a load of trash into the kitchen. "And don't tell me nothing. You're as grumpy as an old bear."

After dumping the load into the trash compactor, he came over and kissed her temple. "I'm fine. There is nothing to worry about."

She frowned. "I don't like it when any of my chicks are unhappy. You know you can always come to us with anything. Your uncle and I love you."

"I know. I've always known that." Dredging up a playful grin, he asked, "What do you think of Dawn?"

"No more than you do. Why'd you bring that poor girl? She's clearly infatuated with you, son."

"She barely knows me. We've known each other less than a week. In fact, this is our first date."

Impatient with him, Donna insisted, "Ralph, it's as clear

as the nose on your face that she thinks because you brought her here to meet your family, there is something special between the two of you."

"That's ridiculous," he dismissed.

"You need to be frank with her. There is no point in hurting her needlessly. It's not like you to pretend you want more than friendship."

Resigned, he said, "I'll talk to her. Thanks, Aunt Donna."

"Now are you ready to tell me what's really bothering you?"

Before he could plead ignorance, Anna and Gavin came in with empty serving bowls.

"Mama, you are not supposed to be in here working," Anna scolded, hurrying over to take a dish from her.

Just then Kyle and Wayne came racing in, then Kelli with the baby. Ralph was grateful for the reprieve. Since the closest bathroom was in use, he headed toward the one in the central hallway. As he reached for the knob, the door swung inward.

Ralph and Vanessa collided. Quick reflexes kept her from bouncing off his wide chest. He clasped his hands at her trim waist to steady her.

He grinned. "Are you okay?"

"I'm fine." She took a hasty step back.

"Sorry, didn't mean to bump into you, but I'm glad we have a few minutes to talk."

"No." When she turned to move around him, he sidestepped, directly into her path.

"Ralph!" Placing her hands on her shapely hips, she inadvertently captured his hungry gaze.

"Well, at least you looked at me. Shall we go in? Or would you like to have this discussion in the hallway?"

"Don't you have to use . . ." She gestured toward the facilities.

He grinned. "I can wait."

Sighing heavily, she finally backed inside, crossing her arms beneath her full breasts. "Say what you have to say!"

Ralph closed and locked the door behind them. Leaning a broad shoulder against it, he said, "I can explain about Dawn."

"Don't bother. What you do, and whom you see, is none of my business."

"If I'd known you were going to be here, believe it, I would have come alone."

"What difference does it make?" She glared at him.

He snapped, "A lot. I don't generally bring a date while trying to get next to another woman."

Vanessa reached up to pat his cheek before she said sarcastically, "Don't worry. You'll get over it."

"I doubt it. Dawn is a nice woman, but I'm not involved with her. We only met last week. We're not lovers."

Vanessa patted a sandal-encased foot impatiently. "I didn't ask."

"Nevertheless, I'd like you to know." Uncomfortable from his unusual need to be candid about his love life, he said, "If you don't . . ."

"Ralph, you don't owe me anything, least of all an explanation. Now, please say what you have to say so I can leave."

"Vanessa . . ."

Evidently, she'd heard enough. "You have less than one minute to say what you have to and let me out of here, or I'm going to start screaming for help."

"That won't change what we shared or what we both . . . still want. You can't tell me that you didn't enjoy our lovemaking. It was magical. And that doesn't happen every day." He eliminated the space between them, backing her up until she stood against the granite countertop, his chest practically touching her breasts. "You know it's true."

"It doesn't matter now. Why can't you get it through your head that one night was enough for me."

"It wasn't nearly enough for me," he snapped, cupping her shoulders.

"Don't touch me," she hissed.

Frustrated, Ralph dropped his hands, shoving them into his pockets. "I don't believe this! As my uncle used to say, you are making a mountain out of a molehill."

"And you're confusing me with Dawn. She's the one who can't keep her hands off you. I'm the one who is not interested."

He ran an unsteady hand over his close-cut natural. "Why are you making this so difficult?"

"You're wrong. I'm simplifying things. No woman in her right mind would want to be involved with a man incapable of committing to any type of a relationship, certainly not this one."

He longed to yell that that was no longer the case, but held back. He stared at her while wondering if it could be true. Did he want a relationship with Vanessa? Or was he merely aggravated because she had decided not to see him again? He felt powerless to make things right between them.

"One night has spoiled a perfect friendship," she complained.

"It wasn't my idea," he put in, unhappy with the way things stood between them.

"Thanks for reminding me," she hissed. "I was trying to make a point. Our friendship is gone, a huge mistake that can't be corrected."

Ralph swore beneath his breath. He honestly didn't have an answer. All he was sure of was that she was right. They couldn't go back. It had also proven to him that she was the only woman able to get and keep him hard. That night didn't have to be a mistake. Nor did it mean they couldn't try to find a workable solution.

"I know it looks bad, but beautiful . . ."

"It is bad! Instead of trying to talk trash to me, you should be out there respecting the lady you're with today. Ralph, women aren't Barbie dolls. You can't trade one for the other."

Ralph dropped his lids, hoping guilt wasn't written all over his face. "Vanessa, you made up the rules to this game we're playing. Why does it have to be so complicated? I wanted to make love to you, then. I still want you. One night was not enough. You're an incredibly beautiful woman."

"Stop!" Her eyes flashed with dark fury. "I've listened to every single word. Now let me pass."

"Why? It's the truth." Frustration, anger, along with relentless determination were pulling him in different directions at once.

"Not another word. Let me pass."

He resisted the urge to yank the door off its hinges. Opening the door, he couldn't stop himself from warning as she passed, "I'm not one to give up, Vanessa. You might want to work on figuring out what you're afraid of. You can't tell me it wasn't good between us."

She gasped, pausing for only a second before tossing back, "We both got what we wanted but lost what was important. Our friendship."

Later that same night, Ralph sat outside on the cushioned lawn chair on the balcony off his bedroom. Despite the late hour, the only cool air stirring came from the ceiling fan overhead. Wearing only a pair of worn cutoffs with his bare feet propped on the waist-high wrought-iron railing, he stared out toward his distant property line.

Swallowing the last of a bottle of imported beer, he

scowled. The day had gone from bad to worse by the time he'd walked Dawn to her front door. To say the lady was ticked when he turned down her offer to come inside would be putting it mildly. Things went downhill swiftly when he'd attempted to explain why he didn't think it was a good idea for them to continue seeing each other. She wasn't having it. She slammed the door in his face.

He didn't blame Dawn for being upset. Aunt Donna was right. He hadn't given the young lady an ounce worth of attention all day. He'd used her as a distraction. Partly to take his mind off Vanessa, but mostly to divert his family's interest in his love life. It had turned out to be a total failure.

To make things worse, no matter how hard he tried, he couldn't seem to take his hungry gaze off Vanessa. One glance at her smooth, creamy skin and lush, full curves and he was hard, throbbing for more of her wet heat.

Ralph didn't need to be told he'd messed up. Vanessa had been right. He had no business chasing her down while he had another woman on his arm. He couldn't even blame her for being angry. He was just plain wrong.

Swearing aloud, he hadn't kept his promise to let it go. She had been clear when she said she wasn't interested. He was the one who couldn't move on. One taste of her sweetness had left him clamoring for her. He'd made a colossal mistake when he thought he could sleep with her, then go back to doing his own thing, as if nothing had happened.

It was crazy. He might be able to make sense of this mess if he didn't find her so irresistible. Although shy, Vanessa was also beautiful and sexy as all get-out. And those unbelievably long, shapely legs left him with a relentless hard-on. What he wouldn't give to see her in a very short red dress and a pair of red high heels. He released a deep groan, frustrated by his body's constantly yearning.

For the first time in memory, Ralph couldn't get a woman

out of his head. And he'd genuinely tried. Since that night he had slept alone, yet wakened each morning craving Vanessa.

Recalling how he had cornered her in the bathroom of all places, he muttered aloud, "I may have lost this time, but there will be a next time, sweetheart."

The house was quiet when Vanessa walked out to the screened-in sunporch. Today had turned out to be a Fourth of July, she wasn't likely to forget. Sitting down on the swing, she tucked her legs beneath her. She wore a thin summer gown and robe. The twins had still been talking about all the fun they'd had at the Mathises' party when she tucked them in. The highlight for Curtis and Courtney had been seeing Shanna and playing on the waterslide. Lana had also had a great time.

For Vanessa, the highlight had been leaving. She sighed heavily. That wasn't fair or true. She adored Ralph's family. Anna had worked so hard to make sure that everyone, from the Mathises' employees, their families, and her own enjoyed themselves. Ms. Tillman, the housekeeper, didn't have family, but she, too, had a great time. Gretchen and her family also enjoyed themselves. Everyone had fun . . . everyone but Vanessa. The Prescotts really were a wonderful family . . . too bad Ralph was one of them.

If only Ralph hadn't come. He had spoiled her day. And why was the man so stubborn? He was known to be a love-them-and-leave-them kind of guy. So why hadn't it worked this time? She still couldn't believe that Ralph had actually backed her into the bathroom, then closed and the locked the door.

The man had more than his fair share of nerve! He used his long, powerful body to block the door and keep her there. Why did he even bother? Just what had he hoped to gain?

Another go-round in bed? Why? She wasn't even his type. His beautiful date was everything she wasn't.

Maybe it had been an ego thing? Maybe he had to be the one to end it? They had agreed to one night of mutually satisfying sex. And they'd gotten what they wanted. Yet he was the one to change his mind. Why? He evidently couldn't stand the thought that she had left a few hours early? If that was the case, then it had to be about ego.

"Now what?" She wanted to throw her hands up in frustration. It shouldn't matter to her what Ralph Prescott did. She had done what was best for her.

Dropping her head until her chin rested on upraised knees, she knew that wasn't exactly correct. When had she started lying to herself? Yes, she had walked out, but she couldn't forget not one minute of what they had shared.

Every night since their night together, she had only to close her eyes to see him as he had been that night. His long, strong body covering hers . . . filling her to the point of bursting. She had no idea that a woman could want a man so desperately. She trembled from the memory of his hard, intense lovemaking, which seemed endless. She hadn't wanted him to stop . . . not ever. The pleasure went on and on, until it overwhelmed and consumed her. And he'd made love to her again and again. More important, she hadn't wanted to leave him.

For the first time in her adult life, Vanessa felt like a woman . . . complete in every way . . . able to open herself and pleasure her man. Vanessa couldn't hold back a smile. She had no doubts that she pleased him. He held her close while she'd convulsed in his arms, his body also shaking from the force of his own release. He had held her so tight she could barely catch her breath . . . and she had loved every minute of it. It felt so good . . . so satisfying. At that moment she was all woman . . . his woman.

As his breath slowly eased that night, he had caressed her, his hand gentle . . . tender. He'd stroked her back, her face and neck, her breasts, cradled her against his wide chest.

Vanessa shivered from the sweetness of the memory just as she replayed it in her mind every night. She had tried to put it out of her mind, but for some unknown reason hadn't been able to do so.

Staying away from the memory was easier said than done. Again and again, she forced herself to push him away. Even when she managed not to think of it or him for a few hours, it always came back. She saw him every night in her dreams. Ralph made love to her while she slept, and she woke recalling the feel, the taste and the pleasure of being one with him.

Filled with frustration, she began pacing the length of the porch. While she was wasting time trying to forget that one night, there was no doubt in her mind that, right this minute, he was in bed with his new lady friend.

Sure, he claimed he wanted her back, but that didn't mean anything when it came to his selfish masculine needs. How many women had he slept with since the night they shared? Two? Three? Ten? Regardless of his claims, Ralph was a known womanizer.

She would be much better off if she reminded herself of that fact every time the memories rushed into her thoughts. The fact that she hadn't wanted to leave him had frightened her. It reminded her of her mother and how the love for a womanizing man had ruined her life.

Ralph was capable of being just as heartless as the twins' selfish father. While her mother had given Greg Cummingham all her love and devotion, he, in turn, had walked away the minute he learned she was pregnant. Her mother had never recovered from the heartache and shame of having to face being unmarried and pregnant alone. Even though the doctors claimed she had died from complications due to childbirth, Vanessa believed that her heart had been broken beyond repair, and she had simply given up on life.

Wiping at the tears seeping beneath her lashes, Vanessa vowed she wouldn't make the same mistake. No, it would be a huge mistake to let Ralph get close enough for her to fall in love with him. Once was more than enough to answer all her questions about making love. It had also been enough to leave her longing for more. She'd been left with enough . . . incredible memories that at times they nearly drove her to distraction.

Today had proven what she'd always known. Only a genuine womanizer would be bold enough to try and talk one woman into his bed while he was escorting another. Being close to him, smelling his clean male scent, seeing his firm lips and dark penetrating eyes were enough to convince her that she was darn lucky to have left him that fate-filled night with her heart whole.

Ralph's looks alone were enough to explain the steady flow of females willing to risk it all for just the opportunity to get close to him. Add in a generous dose of the Prescott charm, blend with keen intellect, quick wit, then combine with an enviable bank balance and mix in excellent health and sexual attraction, was it any wonder that Ralph would never lack for female companionship?

Vanessa's time would be better spent concentrating on what was most important, taking care of her family and working toward her goals to finish her college education and design beautiful bridal and evening gowns.

"I've wasted enough time on that man," she muttered aloud, then got up and went into the small utility room behind the kitchen, where an overflowing basket of clean clothes waited on top of the drier to be folded or ironed and put away.

* * *

"I didn't hear you this morning," Lana said into the telephone.

Vanessa was at her desk, sipping a steaming mug of coffee. "You were sleeping so peacefully, I decided not to wake you."

"The twins weren't so considerate." Lana laughed.

Joining in, Vanessa asked, "Did you see the bowl of tuna salad left for sandwiches in the refrigerator? And I also left a list of books you and the twins might want to check out while you're at the library. If you have time, would you pick out something on business accounting for me?"

"No problem. But Nessa, it's summer vacation. We're supposed to have fun every once in a while. You have us scheduled to go somewhere almost every day." They were fortunate that the public library was only a block from their home. The neighborhood community center, three blocks away, had art classes and recreational programs for kids that included use of their pool during the summer months.

Vanessa laughed. "Okay. But call me if you need anything. I'll be in the office most of the day."

"All right. Talk to you later."

Gretchen and Vanessa spent the morning working on the proposed budget for a dinner dance to generate funds for the following year's scholarship fund.

Gretchen had left for a meeting downtown with several high-school counselors. Vanessa was preparing a list for Gavin of proposed tuition hikes across the country when Anna came into the sunny home office Gretchen and Vanessa shared.

"Try this," Anna said, as she placed a small tray on Vanessa's desk.

Vanessa smiled. "Smells good," she said, accepting a bowl of savory stew and a homemade buttered yeast roll. Anna was close to finishing her cookbook. Trying out new recipes was a perk of Vanessa's job. "Mmm. It's wonderful."

"It's lamb stew. I changed it a little. What does it need?"

"Nothing as far as I can tell." She relished the taste, closing her eyes. "It's delicious. When is the cookbook coming out?"

"Next summer if I can get all the kinks worked out. Do you think it needs more curry?"

Vanessa took another taste. "Not for me; I'd say it was fine."

"Thanks, Vanessa. I'll pack it up and take some over for Mama and Daddy to try out. There's more if you get hungry later. I also baked a fresh batch of sweet potato bread with walnuts this morning. There is a loaf with your name on it ready for you to take home on the counter. See you later."

"Thanks." Vanessa laughed. "I'll never lose weight around here."

"Why bother? You always look great," Anna called over her shoulder. "If Gavin calls, tell him to call me on my cell."

"All right." Vanessa went back to the list. She enjoyed her job. If it weren't for her goals, she would be content to work for the Mathises. She thought it was wonderful that Gavin and Anna had decided not to limit the scholarship fund to only low-income graduates with the highest grades but to average students as well.

Vanessa had finished her lunch when the telephone rang. She said automatically into the receiver, "Mathis Enterprises."

"Hello, Vanessa. It's Ralph. How are you?"

Her heart rate accelerated at the sound of his deep male voice. She wasn't about to tell him that he didn't need to identify himself. She knew his voice . . . knew too much about him, including the feel of his warm caresses as he stroked her nude body. Memories of his long body pleasuring her filled her thoughts.

"Vanessa . . ."

"I'm well, thank you." She waited, refusing to say his name. Finally, she asked, "May I take a message for Anna or Gavin?"

"I called to speak to you, beautiful. Would you like to go out to dinner with me? I have a plane ready to fly us to the Keys. I know of a restaurant that has the best lobster and Key lime pie in the state of Florida. We'll have time to walk on the beach in the moonlight, that is, if you insist on coming back tonight."

Eleven

Ralph frowned when he heard Vanessa's laughter. "What's funny about a dinner invitation?"

"Will you get real? The answer is no. First of all, it's a weekday. Second, even if I were crazy enough to even go across town with you, I still have three hungry kids at home expecting me to prepare them dinner tonight. Last and most important, we have an agreement. I suggest you call one of your money-hungry little friends for entertainment. Tell me, is stubborn your middle name?"

Ralph couldn't help laughing. The lady meant business, but so did he. He intended to see her, and soon. He wasn't about to take no for an answer. Not when he knew he was capable of making her purr, again. He was looking forward to hearing that sexy sound she made when she came . . . purring only for him.

Around a wide grin, he said, "Who told you my middle name? Here I was thinking it was a family secret. Tell you what, don't worry about cooking tonight. Leave dinner up to me. Does your family like Chinese?"

"Yes, but that doesn't mean . . ."

"It means we have to eat. See you," he said, ending the call.

He shook his head. Talk about stubborn. The girl could

give lessons. She was right about one thing. The ladies he normally hung out with would never turn down his offer . . . any offer. In a sense, Vanessa had done him a favor. She'd reminded him that his lady friends weren't only interested in his winning personality. They were after him for all the advantages his hefty wallet could provide.

There was no doubt that Vanessa had her feet firmly planted on the ground. The man who won her heart would have more going for him than moonlight and roses. She was nobody's fool.

A few hours later, Ralph was leaving a meeting in Coach Gardner's office when he ran into an old friend he hadn't seen in some time. "Well, well. I don't believe it. When did you get back?" Ralph playfully slapped his longtime friend on the back. The two had been teammates and friends at U of D and the NBA.

Scott Hendricks grabbed Ralph for a bear hug. "Man, it's good to see you. How have you been? Missing the NBA?"

"Somewhat. It's been an adjustment," Ralph admitted. "Man, it's good to see you. Are you just passing through the 'D'?"

Scott shook his head, surprising Ralph. "No, I'm back for good. I bought a place in Bloomfield Hills."

"So, the rumors are true. You've given it up?"

"That's right. I gave it ten years. Now, it's time to hang up the uniform and pick up the textbooks."

Ralph was shocked. The other man had been an A student working toward a degree in chemistry when he quit U of D after his sophomore year and been drafted in the NBA. "Wow! Giving up the big bucks for a test tube. Well, if anyone can do it, you can, Scott." Ralph glanced at his watch. "Look I've got to run. I plan to put in a few hours at the Malcolm X Community Center. Maybe I'll run into you there. You know Dexter Washington and Charles Randol."

Scott laughed. "Of course. Both of them are old friends. Back in the day, that center helped keep my nose clean. I hope, once I get settled, to put in some volunteer time. But, I'm here to drop in on Coach. Is he in?"

"Yeah." Ralph punched him playfully in the arm. "Stop in to see me on campus. Better yet, give me a call. We can hit a few balls."

"Sounds good. Later."

Ralph had a smile on his face as he headed for the parking lot. It had been great to see Scott. But Ralph knew his good mood was mainly because he was going to get some of what he needed . . . a chance to see, and, with some luck, spend time with, his lady.

Vanessa might not be ready to admit it, but they definitely had something going on between them. But it was going to take a great deal of work on his part to persuade her to give him another shot. He planned to prove her wrong. Friends can be lovers! Why not, if it was what they both wanted? They could make up their own doggone rules.

Vanessa was still angry with Ralph even later that afternoon when she parked in her driveway. He was full of himself, but even an egotistical jock like him wasn't bold enough to show up at her door with dinner. No way! She tried to laugh at herself for imagining the worst.

Ralph Prescott, smooth-talking charmer with millions, was used to women falling at his feet. Once he realized his romantic offer had been turned down, he wasn't about to waste the evening of seduction by having dinner with Vanessa and her three kids. He was most likely flying to the Keys by now, sipping champagne aboard his private jet with one of his gorgeous lady friends. Goodness knows, he had enough women to choose from.

She called out a hello, as she unlocked the screened, side door.

Judging by the squeal of laughter coming through the back sunporch everyone was playing in the fenced-in backyard. Ignoring the neat stack of bills that had evidently come in that morning's mail and dropping her purse on the hall table as she went back out the side door, she walked past the detached garage.

"Hi!" she called, as she opened the gate and walked across the thick carpet of grass.

"Nessa!" the twins yelled, and ran to give her a hug. As usual, they were talking over each other, telling her the day's events.

When Vanessa sat in one of the swings on the old but sturdy wooden swing set that her father had put up for her when she was a girl, Courtney climbed on her lap facing her, so they could swing together. She pushed off. Curtis pouted for a moment, then climbed up the ladder to the overhead platform and slid down the curved slide. Lana took the other swing and began talking about the trouble the girls next door had gotten into with their parents.

"Are you listening, Nessa?" Lana quizzed.

"We have any ice tea?" Vanessa asked, pumping her legs to go higher as she kissed her giggling baby sister's cheek.

"Yes, we do. I'll get it." Lana got up and headed toward the house.

"No name calling," Vanessa warned Curtis, who had taken the empty swing.

"Okay, but I'm next!" he insisted.

"Look who's here," Lana said, stopping to greet the man walking through the gate and into the backyard.

"Hey." Ralph smiled.

Vanessa rose, placing Courtney on her sandal-covered

feet. Curtis ran over to greet Ralph. She was forced to smile, aware of the twins' curious gazes moving between the two of them.

"He brought dinner." Lana peeked inside the huge bag of Chinese takeout he carried. Excited, Lana said, "Enough for everyone, by the looks of it."

"Just happened to be in the neighborhood, right?" Vanessa crooned, careful to keep the anger and frustration out of her voice.

Ralph laughed. He dropped down until he was at eye level with the twins and held out his hand. "Hi, Courtney. Hi, Curtis."

Courtney blushed, but smiled, too shy to put her tiny hand in his for a handshake.

Curtis stuck out his chest and offered his hand. "Hi, Mr. Prescott. How tall are you? Are you bigger than Shaq?"

Ralph shook Curtis's hand. "Shaq has a few inches on me. "I'm six-seven, but I can jump higher than he can," he boasted, his twinkling dark eyes rested on Vanessa. "Since I wasn't sure what everyone liked, I brought a little of everything, including plenty of egg rolls."

"Yeah!" Curtis spoke for them both, and the twins giggled.

"How nice, Mr. Prescott. You shouldn't have gone to so much trouble." Vanessa, folding her arms beneath her breasts, suddenly remembered what she looked like. She was in a pair of comfortable jeans and a pink knit sleeveless blouse. She hadn't put on more than a little powder and lip gloss, both of which were long gone. Her hair was pulled back in a ponytail. She told herself it didn't matter. He wasn't staying for dinner.

"Mr. Prescott, you can stay for dinner, can't you?" Lana asked.

"Yes!" the twins said excitedly.

Ralph's dark eyes danced as he looked expectantly at Vanessa. "I'd love to, if it is all right with you, Nessa," he teased.

Forcing a smile, Vanessa knew she had no choice, and said, "Oh please, you must join us."

"I'd love to, but everyone has to call me Ralph. Not Mr. Prescott."

Both the twins clapped their hands, jumping up and down excitedly.

"Nessa," Lana called back over her shoulder, "you coming?"

Vanessa, suddenly in a hurry to get away, nearly bumped into her sister, who had stopped to open the gate. Lana gave her sister an odd look, causing Vanessa to ask, "What?"

"You tell me. Are you upset because I let Mr. Prescott, I mean Ralph, in the gate without asking you first?" Lana rushed on to say, "I'm sorry. I let him in because I thought he was your friend. I didn't think you'd mind."

Vanessa kissed her cheek. "Nothing's wrong. And you're right. Ralph is a friend of mine."

"But you're upset."

Vanessa forced a smile. "I'm just surprised. Now get going. We've got people waiting to be fed."

Evidently relieved, Lana laughed, motioning to the large bag she held. "No worries. He brought enough to feed a small army."

Vanessa was forced to swallow a scream of frustration. She didn't want her sister to see how very upset she was. If she were a swearing woman, she could have turned the air blue. He knew exactly what he was doing. He'd backed her into a corner, and there was nothing she could do about it in front of her family.

"Goodness!" Vanessa exclaimed, once they were inside the roomy kitchen and she saw how much food Ralph had provided. Rather than his generosity endearing him to her, she wanted to give him an earful, but she would have to wait until she could talk to him alone. Instead of grinding her teeth together in mute frustration, she put Lana to work setting the table while she began heating the food in the microwave and filling serving bowls.

"Should I use Grandmother's tablecloth?" Lana asked

"No. We are eating in the kitchen."

Lana had been on her way to the china cabinet to get out their mother's good dishes. "Why?"

Vanessa pointed at the cabinet where the everyday dishes were stored. "Ralph is a friend, not company."

Even though Vanessa had seen how comfortable Ralph was with his teen cousin, Gavin's brother Kyle, and even his two little nieces, she nonetheless was shocked how quickly Curtis and Courtney warmed to him. Even Lana, despite her shyness, was laughing at his corny jokes. By the time the meal had ended, all three kids were hanging on his every word, especially Curtis. When Ralph volunteered to put up a basketball hoop and show Curtis how to play, Curtis was beside himself with excitement. It was painfully obvious that the little boy lacked male attention.

Afraid that Ralph was going to disappoint the child, yet at the same time determined to keep Ralph as far away from her family as humanly possible, Vanessa didn't know if she should tell him to stay away or demand he keep his promise. Her need to protect her family won out.

With a forced smile, she volunteered to walk him to his car. Before she could start yelling at him, he kissed her temple.

"You don't have to thank me. I enjoyed dinner."

"Thank you!" she huffed indignantly.

He chuckled, and teased, "Yes, thank me. After all, I did bring the meal, saving you the effort. Seriously, you have a great family, Nessa." He used the nickname the kids preferred. "I'm sure it can't be as easy as you make it look. The twins are well adjusted and happy. And Lana is a sweet girl. I applaud you. You've done a remarkable job. And you've done it on your own."

Surprised by the compliment, Vanessa was unsure if he was sincere or putting her on . . . trying to get next to her. His approval warmed her heart, the last thing she needed or wanted. She blinked rapidly, struggling to push the tender emotion away. She wasn't going to take it or him seriously. In the end, the good manners her mother had drilled into her prevailed.

"Thank you," she whispered.

"You are welcome." He smiled. "I'll see you tomorrow." Then he climbed into his dark red Navigator and started the motor.

When she knocked on his passenger-side window, she repeated, "Tomorrow?"

"Yes, I promised Curtis I'd put up the hoop and teach him my game."

She shook her head firmly. "That's not necessary. I'll come up with some kind of excuse so . . ."

"It's necessary, Nessa. Once I give my word, I keep it. I thought you knew that. Bye."

Before she could say more, he pulled away from the curb and drove off. Resisting the urge to fling a few choice words at him, she settled for kicking a few loose rocks and muttering to herself.

How did he do it? How did he get the better of her? She had told him more than once what she thought of him. Why didn't he just give up? By the time she walked inside the house, she was relatively calm. The twins were plopped down on the area rug, watching television, and Lana was curled up on one end of the sofa, talking on the telephone to one of her friends. Silently, Vanessa promised herself that she would tell him tomorrow to get a life and leave her alone.

The next afternoon, when Vanessa pulled into her drive, she couldn't decide if she was relieved or upset to see Ralph's Navigator parked in front of the house. While she didn't want her little brother disappointed, neither did she want to deal with Ralph. For her there were no easy answers.

She was annoyed when she put the car into park and discovered that her hands were shaking. She took several deep, calming breaths before she got out. It was then she noticed the shoulder-high, basketball hoop mounted on the garage door. At the end of the drive, both her sisters and brother were running after a bouncing basketball. Ralph seemed to grab it out of the air, handling it with ease. Then he passed the ball to Curtis, who caught it and went in for the basket. Everyone cheered when he made it.

Ralph spotted her first, and, before she knew it, she was playing on Lana and Courtney's side, against Ralph and Curtis. The fellows beat the girls, twenty-five to eighteen.

To Vanessa's relief, he turned down her obligatory dinner invitation, stating a previous engagement. While she was busy wondering if his refusal was because of Dawn, the woman he had taken to his family's picnic on the Fourth, Ralph invited her family over to swim in his pool and stay for dinner on Friday evening. All three children quickly accepted before she could get out a refusal. With a satisfied smile on his face, he waved good-bye and was halfway down the drive before she said a word.

"Ralph!" Vanessa called after sending her family in to wash up for dinner.

Laughter danced in Ralph's dark eyes. "What? Did you

come up with an excuse for not coming on Friday?"

"As a matter of fact, I have." With a hand resting on one hip, she said, "Sorry. We're busy."

"Doing what? Avoiding me?"

"Exactly. I'd appreciate it if you don't come around the children. I don't think it's a good idea."

Ralph frowned. "Don't you think you're taking the problem between us a bit far?"

She shook her head. "No, I don't. You're the one who showed up here, food in hand last night. Today, I come home, you're playing ball with my family. Enough of this! I'm not going to get tricked into being obligated to go to your place, then having to return the favor."

He lifted a brow. "What are you afraid of, Vanessa? Having a good time? That the kids like me, or I like them? Tell me, what's got you on the run."

"I'm not running. I hate to crush your ego, but not wanting to be involved with you isn't illegal. Including my family in your little game is plain wrong."

"Come over here and say that." He pointed to the sidewalk space in front of him.

Vanessa lifted her chin, refusing to back down. She walked up to the spot and repeated, "I'm not . . ."

The next thing she knew she was in his arms.

"Yes?" he said softly. His warm breath fanned her neck.

Vanessa shivered, closing her eyes as awareness traveled up and down her back. "We can't . . ."

"We aren't," he whispered, brushing his lips over her temple. "Why can't we continue to be friends?"

When she realized she was touching his chest, she took a quick step back. She needed to think, and she couldn't do that with him so close. "It won't work."

"It will if that's what we want. On the Fourth, you told me

that you mourn the loss of our friendship. I don't want our friendship to end, either. And there is nothing wrong with friends spending time together. Is there?"

"No," she said carefully, trying to decide if she had stepped into a trap.

"Good, then we agree. Besides, I enjoy spending time with you and your family. I've got a pool, and all three kids like to swim. Why should they be disappointed because you and I messed up?" When she remained silent, Ralph prompted, "If I didn't know better, I'd think you were afraid even to try. Are you afraid?"

"Of course not. Stop trying to put words in my mouth. The problem is, I'm not sure I can trust you to keep your hands to yourself."

"Can't trust me?" He grinned, lifting a dark brow. "Or yourself?"

Vanessa crossed her arms protectively over her chest. "Believe me, I can keep my hands to myself."

He grinned. "Good. Then we don't have a problem. See you Friday around five. Need directions?"

Realizing she had just backed herself into a corner, Vanessa sighed heavily. "No. We'll be there."

"Good."

Watching as he waved, got into his vehicle, and drove away, she could not help feeling as if she'd just jumped into the deep end of the pool.

Twelve

Vanessa woke with a start. Her entire body tingled from a dream so vivid it felt real. She moaned, hugging her pillow. She was exhausted. For the last few days, she'd been unable to sleep, busy trying to figure out if Ralph had been right.

Over and over, she asked herself one question. Was she afraid of him? Her immediate answer was of course not! Yet the question nagged at her. Maybe she was afraid, but not of him. If anything she feared how he made her feel.

She'd been a quivering mass of nerves when he challenged her to approach him, close enough to touch. Yes, she'd boldly placed herself right in front of him. While he'd kept his hands to himself, she had been the one doing the touching. His closeness had sent her nervous system into high alert.

There was no question that she'd been . . . trembling with awareness. It was a struggle not to lift her mouth to his, to feel that firm, warm pressure of his lips against her. Who was she fooling? She'd wanted more than his mouth, she'd wanted him . . . every muscle-packed inch.

The worst was when he had brushed his lips against her forehead. At that moment, she'd nearly lost it. She'd practically given in to the desire to press her breasts against the muscles of his chest. It had taken all of her willpower not to rub herself against him. Talk about brain freeze. She'd been so needy, so hard-pressed for his body, that her nipples were aching, throbbing with longing for the heat of his mouth. She had no idea how she found the strength to resist.

Thank goodness, he hadn't known about her struggle. It was clear to her now that she never should have slept with him. She should have gone through life not knowing what she'd missed. It would have been so much easier.

Now, instead of getting on with her life, she was struggling to get over him. She was being tormented by dreams of their lovemaking, vivid dreams that left her filled with yearning for more of his unforgettable brand of lovemaking. And she had brought this on herself. The blame was hers alone.

How could she have been so naive? She had honestly thought a single night in Ralph's bed would answer all her questions. Well, it had done that, but it had left her longing for what she couldn't have . . . more of Ralph Prescott. She felt like an addict. Yet he was worse than any drug known to man. AA couldn't cure what ailed her. And she was not about to have her name added to the long list of women who had put their lives on hold in the hope that someday he'd remember their names.

She groaned wearily, knowing she wouldn't be able to get back to sleep. Five o'clock in the morning. Friday . . . the day they were scheduled to go swimming and have dinner at his place. She was learning that regret was a terrible thing. And her regrets seemed to be mounting. Knowing she should have refused to go didn't matter now. She could not disappoint the kids. They were so excited, talking about little else.

How had he found out her family's likes and dislikes so quickly? After two visits, he knew that the entire family's favorite sport was swimming. Lana was so good at it she'd trained to be a lifeguard, and the twins had taken their first swimming lessons when they were babies. It was an indulgence that Vanessa had been unable to deny, despite the cost of the lessons. Their family took advantage of the community center's year-round indoor pool.

Vanessa scowled. Ralph knew the children would find his invitation irresistible. She pounded her pillow, wishing it was his face. They were going, but only this one time—she planned to make sure it would never happen again.

"Hurry, Nessa!" the twins called from outside the dressing room.

"I'm coming!" Vanessa was dressed in her old, faded, navy blue swimsuit. It didn't matter that she didn't have a trendy new suit, designed to attract a man. It wasn't about that. With the twins, she didn't have a choice. If they were in the water, she had to be ready to go in, just to make sure they were safe.

"I've got them!" Lana said from the hallway.

"Coming!"

Tucking a towel around her waist, Vanessa turned her back on her reflection. She'd had enough to worry about without focusing on how big her behind was or that her thighs touched when she walked. Instead she hurried out before she changed her mind and ran for the car.

"Ready." Vanessa gave her family a warm smile, automatically taking Curtis's hand so he wouldn't go dashing out. Ignoring the nerves in her stomach, she said, "Remember, no running around the pool area." It was less stressful and simpler to keep her thoughts on the children.

She'd been a ball of nerves since Ralph opened his front door and let them into his large, beautifully decorated mansion. He'd been dressed casually in faded jeans that hugged powerful thighs. A plain white T-shirt covered his wide chest, broad shoulders, and taut midsection. His feet were bare.

He'd showed them around as if Vanessa had never been there. The children enjoyed seeing the game and home the-ater rooms. When Lana asked why so many bedrooms, he laughed, explaining with so much family, and out-of-town friends, he wanted plenty of room. Vanessa was glad he didn't show them the den . . . it held so many memories. Ralph had left them in the hall outside the dressings rooms.

Vanessa and the kids entered the huge, beautifully tiled, green-and-blue room, two of whose walls were floor-to-ceiling glass framing the Olympic-size pool. A set of French doors opened into the lush grounds.

"Find everything?" Ralph was already there waiting for them. He frowned at the towel around her waist.

Vanessa, busy looking around, jumped at the sound of his voice. Curtis and Courtney went off in peals of giggles.

She felt the heat of his dark gaze caressing along her throat, down to her arms, and lingering on her ample breasts. "Yes, thanks." She forced a smile.

"Look!" Lana said.

Vanessa heard the loud squeal of excitement from the twins. They were practically jumping up and down as they stared with wide eyes at the huge waterslide at the shallow end of the pool.

"You shouldn't have," Vanessa exclaimed in disbelief.

"Why not?" Ralph asked from directly behind her. She shivered as his warm breath caressed her nape.

"The expense. And don't tell me you did this for yourself. I know better."

Vanessa, aware that the twins where right there, their lit-tle ears taking in every word, let the twins go over to take a closer look with a warning not to run. She waited until Lana followed the twins, intrigued by the rushing water.

Annoyed, Vanessa said, "Why would you do something

like this? Wasting your money. Now I'll never get them to leave."

Evidently realizing she was really upset, Ralph said, "Vanessa, I can afford it. It really isn't a big deal. I have a teenage cousin, Wayne, then there is Kyle, plus my two little nieces. I also have friends with kids. I like having my family and friends over."

Vanessa nodded, aware that she was overreacting. Just the upkeep of this house probably cost more than she made in a year. How had she forgotten he was wealthy? She was surrounded by opulence. Dropping her lids, she found herself unwittingly studying the bold masculine bulge beneath his tight black trunks.

"Don't . . ." he whispered huskily.

"What?" she managed to get out before she realized she'd been staring at his crotch. Her cheeks were hot with embarrassment that he'd caught her in the act.

"Don't look at me as if you'd like another look at what's beneath the trunks. If we were alone, it wouldn't matter because there's no doubt that I want you . . . badly."

She blushed, forcing her eyes away. Before she could blink, he'd dived into the deep end of the pool and swum to where the kids were playing in the water. She was thankful the twins and Lana hadn't waited for them.

"Come on in, Nessa!" Courtney called, waving frantically.

"It's your turn to slide!" Curtis laughed.

The afternoon passed quickly. Everyone was having a great time. Vanessa found she was able to relax and enjoy herself. Like Lana, Ralph was an excellent swimmer. And all three children laughed at his horseplay.

Although the twins were hungry, they didn't want to get out of the pool. Eventually, Vanessa was able to coax them out. Sitting in lounge chairs and wrapped in towels, Vanessa and the twins yelled at the top of their lungs as Lana and Ralph raced. They had dived into the deep end and were swimming laps side by side. While Curtis pulled for Ralph, Vanessa and Courtney cheered Lana on. Lana won, but Vanessa suspected Ralph had let her pass him.

Only because of their growling stomachs was Vanessa able to urge the kids into the showers and get them changed in the dressing rooms. Everything they might need—soap, lotions, stacks of thick towels—was waiting for them.

Ralph had gone up to his room to shower and change while Lana and the twins rushed to get ready and a thoughtful Vanessa took her time. She had not changed her mind. Unfortunately, she hadn't had an opportunity to let him know this outing would be their last.

"You could get lost in this place. It's so big," Lana whispered, as they followed the taupe-carpeted hallway back toward the front of the house.

Vanessa nodded, keeping an eye on the twins. "Where is the kitchen?" She fought the urge to tell the children not to touch a thing as they passed cream walls displaying spectacular paintings and sculptured pieces done by prominent and talented African-American artists.

Lana laughed. "Down the central hallway, past the game and theater rooms . . . I think."

Vanessa warned softly, "Curtis, slow down. There's no need to run." She was embarrassed because she should have been busy watching where they were going and not thinking of Ralph.

Turning to the right, Lana said confidently, "This way."

They went under a wide archway into the spacious state-of-the-art kitchen, decorated in shades of beige and taupe. There were gold-and-brown granite countertops and a long center island. A large round, butcher-block dining table sat in front of a set of French doors that led out onto a patio.

"Anna and Mrs. Prescott did a great job decorating," Vanessa marveled.

"Thanks." Ralph grinned as he came in through the patio doors. "I bought this house as an investment, while I was still playing basketball for the Lakers. It didn't feel like home until I moved back to Detroit."

"It's really lovely. Is there anything you need me to help with?" Vanessa asked, glancing at the large table, empty except for a crystal bowl of fruit in the center.

"It's such a nice night, I thought we would eat outside on the patio." When she smiled and nodded, he said, "This way." He urged them through the double doors to a spacious redwood-planked veranda that curved along the side of the house.

Outdoor lights revealed redwood furniture cushioned in a maroon-and-green leaf pattern. There was an outdoor kitchen including built-in stainless-steel refrigerator, sink, and countertops as well as a stainless-steel grill.

"How about some volleyball?" Ralph asked, the kids agreeing before he'd finished speaking. He'd strung a net, low between two steel-anchored poles. A large basket of balls sat nearby. Soon Curtis, Courtney, and Lana were engrossed in the game.

"Come on. You can keep me company." Ralph gave Vanessa's hand a quick squeeze. While he worked, she relaxed in a lounge chair near the grill, her feet up as she sipped a glass of lemonade.

Not used to being idle, Vanessa asked, "Are you sure there is nothing I can do to help?"

"Nope. The potato salad and coleslaw are waiting in the fridge," he said as he worked at the grill. Corn on the cob steamed in their jackets on an upper rack away from the flame, while thick T-bone steaks and steak burgers were sizzling away.

"I'm impressed," Vanessa admitted. "I didn't quite believe

it when you said you knew your way around the kitchen. I haven't tasted anything yet, but I'm impressed."

He laughed. "I suppose it's only fair to withhold judgment until after dinner."

"When you do praise my expert culinary skills, and I assure you that you will," he boasted, "my aunt is the one who deserves the credit. She is an exceptional cook. Why do you think Anna is a chef? Aunt Donna. She made sure all of her kids knew how to take care of themselves. We all had chores."

"I've always thought Donna Prescott was a smart and talented lady," Vanessa said sincerely. His aunt had a generous and down-to-earth way about her that had always made Vanessa and the kids feel welcome. Donna and her husband were genuinely warm, caring people. And their home was like a haven. Even though their children were wildly successful, it wasn't about the money but the love.

When she looked up, Vanessa found herself returning Ralph's smile as he flipped the burgers. For a few moments, she'd been so engrossed in watching him that she had forgotten all else. She was relieved when he asked if she would fill the glasses while he loaded the serving platters. She told herself she was more than ready when her family joined them at the table.

She didn't need any reminding that Ralph's devastating smiles and lethal charm were the reasons so many women were thrilled to end an evening in his bed. They were willing to take whatever they could get in exchange for an opportunity to reel him in. In return, he'd wine and dine them, then sleep with them. The sex was his ultimate goal. When he'd had his fill, he was ready to move on to the next pretty face. And there was never a shortage of women eager to play the game with him.

And in their case, Vanessa had gone after Ralph. She

wanted to unravel the mystery of what goes on behind closed doors between the male and female. And she knew Ralph had all the answers . . . he was the expert.

She hadn't been prepared for her once-tried body to take such a liking to his that she continued to crave his male attention. Only her pride had saved her from making a complete fool of herself. All it took was a look from his dark, hot gaze, and she was wet, ready for his hard length. It was shameful, the way she was constantly fighting her need for him.

For the life of her, she couldn't figure out why he'd come back for more. She wasn't egotistical enough to believe her lovemaking had gone beyond the ordinary. She hadn't had a clue as to what she was supposed to have been doing. She hadn't even known how to move . . . let alone give him pleasure. No, it could not have been that good for Ralph.

So why, then, was he chasing her? Apparently, he really resented the fact that she'd walked away before he made that same move. The male ego was evidently more powerful than she'd realized. The man was dangerous to any weak-willed, empty-headed female. Talk about trouble. So what was. . .

"More corn?" Ralph held out the platter, that blasted masculine charm in his dark eyes, and blatant sexual appeal all over his handsome face. Even his teeth were too even . . . too white . . . perfect!

Determined to be ruled by her head and not her hormones, she kept her voice cool when she said, "No . . . I can't eat another bite." Glancing at her family, she forced a smile, "Dinner was wonderful."

"Great." Lana smiled, wiping her sticky fingers on a napkin.

Ralph grinned but refrained from saying, "I-told-you-so."

"Tired, baby girl?" Vanessa asked as she caressed her little sister's cheek.

Courtney merely nodded, hardly able to hold her head up

as she rested against Vanessa's side. Curtis was no better. The chair was the only thing holding him upright. His dinner was only half-finished.

"Ralph, we're going to have . . ."

His laugh was deep and throaty. "I can't believe that Curtis, human dynamo, has run out of steam." Ralph rose slowly to his feet. "You and Lana get your things. I'll carry these two."

"There's no need. Lana and I . . ."

"Thanks, Mr. Prescott," Lana interrupted, then remembered he'd asked her to call him by his first name. Blushing, she said, "I mean, Ralph." Lana began gathering the plates.

"It's my pleasure. Don't bother with that, Lana. It was my turn to entertain and clean up," he said with a wide smile.

Lana returned the smile. "Thank you for everything. We had so much fun."

Vanessa was feeling guilty. Just because she resented the way he blasted his masculine charm her way didn't excuse a lack of good manners. "Lana is right. Dinner was delicious. And we enjoyed the use of your pool. Thank you for inviting us. The twins really enjoyed themselves. Please, let Lana and me help, at least clear the table." She reached for the platter of corn.

"Nope. No need," he insisted as he carefully lifted Curtis. When he easily picked up Courtney, she rested against his chest, an arm around his neck. He started moving toward the open French doors. Lana followed them into the house. When Vanessa reached the foyer, Lana had their purses and duffel bags.

Ralph paused, surprising Vanessa when he said to her sister, "Lana, you're a strong swimmer. You and the twins are welcome to use the pool and waterslide anytime you'd like. You have my cell, just give me a quick call to make sure I'm home."

Beaming, Lana nodded eagerly. "Thanks, Ralph." Excited, Lana squeezed Vanessa's hand.

Resisting the urge to smack him, Vanessa said, "That's kind of you, but . . ."

"I'm not being kind. When I'm in town, most mornings I work out of my home office. If I'm home, you and the kids are welcome."

Steaming, Vanessa thrust her purse on her shoulder and followed the others to the front door. She didn't say a word, even as Lana helped Ralph place the children in their car seats and fastened their seat belts like an expert. Once Lana was buckled into the passenger seat, Vanessa hesitated.

She had no trouble recognizing the satisfied smile on his handsome face, thanks to the light from the sconces mounted on either side of the wide door and the small torches lining both sides of the walk and the circular drive.

Vanessa said to her sister, "Be right back," before she hurried toward him. She was careful to keep her back to her sister and her voice low. With her arms crossed tightly beneath her plump breasts, she hissed, "You haven't won this stupid game you're playing, Prescott."

"It's not about winning, beautiful. You have it all wrong. I'm not playing a game with you," he said quietly.

"Really? You can't fool me." It took every ounce of her control, not to scream. "You are playing . . . a sex game. And you're trying to use *my* family to manipulate me."

He stepped forward until they were eye to eye. "No games . . . sex or otherwise. And I would never use your family in any way. You don't know me well, yet. If you did, you would realize you just insulted me. And I'm tired of your insults." He let out a deep breath as his eyes moved over her small features. Then he said, very softly, "Every time we're together, I learn something new about you. Tonight, I learned that I scare you, and when you're scared, you strike back."

Dropping her arms, Vanessa glared up at him, her hands now balled into two small fists. "You know nothing, Ralph Prescott! Did you hear me?"

"Oh, yeah. Any louder, and Lana and the twins will also hear you, beautiful."

She hissed, "Enough! Stay away from me and mine."

He said, "Take a moment before you crawl into your empty bed tonight. Ask yourself one question . . . why are you so frightened. I guarantee the answer won't have a thing to do with me. I haven't so much as touched your hand tonight, beautiful. So why are you shaking?"

"I'm not afraid of you! And if I'm shaking, it's because you make me so angry I can't stand it!"

"Then why were you trying to hide under that stupid towel, wrapped around your waist? Surely, you don't think I've forgotten the shape and feel of the delectable curves of your hips and thighs? Sorry, beautiful." He tapped his temple. "It's all up here, every sweet detail."

By the time she whirled around and practically ran to her SUV, she was furious. Lucky for her, Lana was talking excitedly on her cell, and the twins were dozing. No one noticed that Vanessa wasn't smiling as she drove away, refusing to so much as glance in Ralph's direction.

Later that night, her temper had gradually eased enough for her to stop pacing her bedroom and get into bed. She was fed up with Ralph yanking her chain . . . manipulating her into seeing things his way. What she needed was a plan of her own. Ralph, evidently, had one. He was too confident, too sure of himself, while she was sick and tired of simply reacting to his moves. And she'd wasted enough time wracking her brain trying to figure him out and getting nothing but a headache for her trouble.

Turning off the bedside lamp, she couldn't say she was pleased with her decision to come up with a plan, but she was determined. It was quite simple. Once she had her own plan in place, he wouldn't be able to rattle her. So what was this wonderful plan? What could she do?

"That's it!" Vanessa suddenly sat up in bed. That was what she would do while he ran around driving his fool self crazy. "Let him!" Let him waste his time and come by every single day of the week . . . it wouldn't matter to her. All she had to do was wait him out. Eventually, he would get fed up with the situation and bow out. In the meantime, her kids would have a ball, using his stupid old pool and waterslide. Vanessa clapped her hands with glee, smiling from ear to ear.

So, as Ralph's impromptu visits moved from one week to the next, Vanessa found her tension around him disappearing. The kids certainly enjoyed Ralph's attention. And she had to give him credit. He never came empty-handed. He either brought along a take-out meal, board game, video game, or newly released DVD that was always age appropriate.

Vanessa was proud of herself. While he thought she was caving in, she was merely waiting him out. Eventually, he'd get tired of pretending to like her and her family and not getting what he really wanted . . . sex. He was in for one long dry spell. And it would serve him right.

The past few times, while the kids and Lana had enjoyed his pool, Vanessa walked around in her new dark red bathing suit without trying to see if he was busy checking her out. Although she felt his gaze, she was relieved that she hadn't caught him staring. Perhaps, it proved her plan was working . . . familiarity breeding indifference on his part.

So what if in the late evenings, after the twins were in bed, and Lana was upstairs in her room either happily chatting on the telephone or reading and watching television, Vanessa and Ralph actually talked about nothing important. He told her stories about his family, told her about his business. And she talked about her family, her growing-up years.

Her dreams of becoming a designer and owning her own store. They didn't talk about anything serious.

It was true that she'd often ended up laughing, as he recounted an episode of his growing-up years as part of the lively Prescott household. His family was exactly what they appeared to be, a warm, caring, and close-knit family, involved in each other's lives.

Vanessa hadn't expected Ralph to tell her about the volunteer work he did at the Malcolm X Community Center. Or his work, coaching at University of Detroit. There was no doubt, he genuinely liked kids. He revealed that he and his cousins were planning a big surprise for his uncle's retirement next spring.

He'd laughed when he explained the latest effort to keep his Uncle Lester from finding out that on their old family property they were building a community center complex for the neighborhood kids his uncle had worked so hard, over the years, to help, and that it would be named after his uncle.

Vanessa was amazed at how full Ralph's life was. He, in essence, worked two full-time jobs yet made time to do volunteer work. He believed in giving back. She was touched that, despite his full schedule, he found time to play with the twins and he listened to Lana and took her concerns seriously. Also she was shaken that she often found herself staying awake, thinking about him.

Vanessa had been surprised when Ralph started to end their evenings with a hug and the brush of his lips against hers. Then he'd walk off to his car, whistling like he'd won the lottery. He never asked for more. Yet while he held her, she felt the hard, unmistakable proof of his desire. He felt so good that she was beginning to worry that she might be the one to weaken and do the asking.

Thirteen

Things were going well, yet Vanessa couldn't help wondering if in her efforts to beat Ralph at his own game she was, in essence, allowing him to get too close to the children. It was clear that all three of the children admired and respected him, especially Curtis.

Her little brother clearly missed not having a father. Evidently he longed for what Vanessa couldn't provide, a man with whom to talk with and do things.

The girls were a lot like Vanessa. Neither was outgoing, and they didn't make friends easily. Yet once the new person had gained their trust, they had a friend for life.

She vowed, as she pulled into the driveway, to do a better job of spending less time with Ralph. After all, she knew first hand that Ralph's charm could be lethal.

Determined, she ignored the way her heart raced as she glanced at his SUV parked at the front curb. "I need help," she called, balancing several bags of groceries and her purse. Awkwardly, she managed to put her key in the locked screen door.

"Hi," Ralph said with a wide smile. He scooped up the bags. "Where do you want these?"

"Hi. The kitchen table. Thanks." After greeting the twins

and Lana, she gave Lana her keys. "There's more in the van."

She went into her bedroom, dropped her purse in the armchair, and took a moment to freshen the makeup she had applied that morning. When she went into the kitchen, Lana and Ralph were busy, with the twins helping them put away the food. In the past few weeks, Vanessa hadn't realized how accustomed they'd all grown to Ralph being in what she'd always considered her private domain.

She said, "Ralph, I didn't expect you today. Didn't you say you had a conference call with a new airplane manufacturer?"

He smiled at her, then went back to washing, then cutting an apple in half for the twins to share. "I did. The call went well. We're ordering two new planes."

"Congratulations! That's wonderful." She knew how important the new planes were to his expansion plans. Vanessa resisted the urge to walk up to him and give him a hug.

Ralph grinned, his dark eyes sparkling. "Thanks. I didn't realize how much I wanted to go forward with growing the airline until I talked it over with you the other night. The private jet service is a fast-growing industry. As time goes on, I'm finding it means more to me than merely an investment."

Vanessa blinked, warmed that he trusted her enough to discuss business matters with her.

When he reached for another apple, she shook her head. "Ralph, don't give them another one. It will spoil their dinner. Now, all of you get out of here so I can get dinner started."

"Come on, Ralph." Curtis tugged on his arm. "Let's finish shooting hoops."

"Not until we see if your sister needs help."

"Aw, that's girl's work," Curtis sneered.

"Some of the best cooks are men." Ralph moved toward

the hall bathroom. "I'm going to wash up. Courtney, come on, you can help."

Curtis pouted for a second, before he said, "I want to help, too."

"Then come on," Ralph said from over his shoulder.

Vanessa laughed as Curtis raced to keep up. As she began rinsing off the ingredients for coleslaw, she listened to Lana reprise her day. When the three of them returned, she announced, "We're having sloppy joes, homemade fries, and coleslaw." She pointed to a large bag of potatoes in the pantry. "They need scrubbing."

Lana and Vanessa exchanged an amused smile as Ralph and Curtis got busy.

Courtney looked up at Vanessa. "What can I do?"

"You can help me make the Kool-Aid." Lana smiled.

Vanessa was pleased not to hear sexist remarks coming out of her little brother's mouth. She also was surprised by how quickly the meal came together with all of them working. She nearly laughed out loud as she imagined what Laura would say about Ralph's antics. There evidently was no limit to the lengths a man would go in order to seduce a woman.

She was serving dessert, the brownies she'd bought at the supermarket, when Ralph mentioned, "Vanessa, would you and the children like to go to Disney World? I'm flying down to Orlando Thursday morning, on business. I'm sure I can talk Gavin into giving you a few days off. How does a long weekend of fun at Universal sound?"

Before she could respond, the twins were on their feet, jumping up and down in their excitement while Lana squealed in delight.

"You can't be serious," Vanessa had to shout, to be heard over her family's enthusiasm.

"What did you say?" Ralph asked, laughing at the children's antics.

Vanessa shocked them all when she jumped up and pounded her fist on the dining-room table. Furious and upset, she had to stop this before it went any further. She shouted, "I said NO!"

Instantly, the room was quiet, with all eyes on her.

To the children, she said in a calm voice, "I'm sorry, but we can't afford a vacation at this time. It's too close to the end of the summer. You will be starting school in a few weeks. All our extra money has to go toward school clothes and supplies."

"But Nessa," Courtney begged, "please!"

"I've never been on an airplane!" Curtis pouted, his thumb going into his mouth, something he never did unless he was very upset.

Lana didn't say a word, but Vanessa could tell by her face that she was as disappointed as the twins.

Vanessa sat down, so she was eye level with the twins. She held out her arms, and they both came over to stand on either side of her chair.

Frowning, Ralph had to clear his throat, before he said; "I'd be happy to pay for . . ." He stopped when he saw the glare she sent his way.

With a protective arm around each child, Vanessa said to him. "Thank you, but we can't." To the children, she soothed, "I'm very sorry. I know how much you would like to go. Unfortunately, we can't have things we can't afford to pay for. Maybe, next year, we can save up and plan for the family to take a Disney vacation. Courtney, Curtis, do you understand?" Both twins nodded, as tears rolled down their smooth brown cheeks. She said softly, "Please tell Ralph thank you for inviting us."

They managed to mumble a thank-you, then with lips poked out, hand and hand the two stumped their way upstairs. Without a word to anyone, Lana began stacking the dishes, then took them into the kitchen. The room was heavy with silence when she returned for another load.

Shaking from suppressed emotion, Vanessa said, "Lana. I'll finish up. Would you, please, go up to the twins? I need to speak to Ralph privately."

Lana nodded her head, then hurried upstairs.

Ralph rose to his feet. "I apologize. I didn't mean to upset everyone."

"What did you think would happen? Ralph! Why did you ask me something like that . . . to go to Disney of all places, in front of my family!" She threw her hands up in the air in a helpless gesture when she'd much rather punch something . . . namely him.

"Look, I know I messed up. But, Nessa, it was an honest mistake." When he reached for her hand, she snatched it away before he could make contact.

"Honest mistake? Hardly! You were trying to trick me into going away with you." She let out a frustrated sound of sheer rage. "For a little while, I thought I might be wrong about you," she said, holding up her hand to stop him. "But tonight proved, as nothing else could, not only can't I trust you, but we live in two different worlds." On trembling legs, she picked up a dish and carried it into the kitchen.

Ralph was right behind her. "What is that supposed to mean? I told you it was an honest mistake! And I apologized." He swore beneath his breath, before he said, "I don't get it. Why did you refuse my offer? The hotel bill won't be a problem. I would be happy to take care of the entire trip."

"No!" she nearly screamed.

"Why not?" he snapped. One large hand rested on his lean hip. "You're acting as if I'm trying to do a terrible thing here. I'm not trying to buy you."

"No, what you're trying to do is get me to sleep with you, by any means possible. What I don't understand, is why you can't take no for an answer? And why are you using my family to get what you want? Ralph, that's lower than low."

"You think I deliberately pulled the kids into our problem!"

"Of course. If you give it half a second's worth of thought, you'll see that's exactly what you did!" She glared up at him, her arms crossed beneath her full breasts, unknowingly drawing his eyes to them. "You listen up, Prescott. I won't stand for it!" Unable to look at him another minute, she busied herself with squirting dish liquid into the sink and turned the hot water on full blast.

Ralph swore beneath his breath as he paced the length of the kitchen. When he stopped, he was directly behind where she stood at the sink. She felt the heat of his breath on her nape. She managed to switch off the water, but she refused to turn and meet his gaze.

He taunted, "Afraid to look me in the eyes?"

Vanessa turned so fast she had to use the edge of the counter to steady herself as she glared up at him. Why did he have to have the best set of shoulders in Detroit? Why was he so tall and so darn good-looking? And why did he have to have every woman in the state running after him?

"Vanessa, you can't honestly think that I used the kids to get close to you." His voice was low and angry.

"I meant every word. You have been nothing, if not determined to get what you want. Tonight, you went too far. What kind of lowlife takes advantage of children to get what he wants? Never mind! Just leave!"

A muscle jumped in his jaw. He snarled, "It looks as if we were both wrong. I thought we were working on rebuilding our friendship. You said it was what you wanted. I also thought you knew me well enough to realize that I care about you and those kids. I'd never hurt you, intentionally, or your family, for that matter." He stopped abruptly, waiting for her response.

"There is no excuse for what you did. I have two little ones, hurt for no good reason, and a disappointed teen. It's your fault!" she ended tightly.

"Did you hear anything I said?" When she didn't respond, he snapped. "I didn't . . ." He sighed wearily. "I'd better go before I say something I'll regret. Don't worry. I won't be back."

Vanessa listened for the front screen door to close. Only then did she walk through the living room, and slam and lock both sets of doors. In an effort to keep busy, she plunged her hands into the soapy water. After washing dishes, she cleaned the kitchen. She'd just poured herself a glass of ice tea and sat at the kitchen table to sulk, when she heard Lana on the stairs.

"How are the twins?"

Filling a glass with tea, she said, "Don't worry. They will be fine by morning once they get over the disappointment."

"I don't think it's going away that fast."

Sipping her drink, Lana surprised her when she asked, "Why did you say no? Ralph can easily afford the trip even if we can't. He was going anyway. I don't get it, sis. He's your boyfriend."

Vanessa's eyes went wide. "Ralph isn't my boyfriend. He's a friend."

Her sister sent her a disbelieving look, before she said, "Come on, Nessa. I've seen the way he looks at you. He likes you! And you like him. What's the big deal?"

Vanessa couldn't believe she was having this conversation with her little sister. Lana was growing up fast, and Vanessa wasn't sure she liked the change. It was obvious that Lana assumed she and Ralph were lovers.

She paused, taking a few minutes to think before she spoke. Screaming at her sister was clearly not the answer. She'd made a point of always being frank and not keeping secrets, but some things were not appropriate because of Lana's age.

"Ralph and I are friends, but even if there was more to it, I would never allow him, or any man, for that matter, to take care of me or my family. That's my job, not Ralph's. The only way it would be acceptable would be if we were married." She hesitated before she said, "My beliefs don't have anything to do with how much money he has. It's how our parents raised me. We come from a long line of strong people who worked to take care of themselves and their families. After Daddy died, Mama went back to work to take care of us. She never lived off a man. I won't either."

"But—"

Vanessa interrupted, "Let me finish. Times have changed for some women. There are women out there looking for a man willing to pay for whatever they can get. Doesn't matter if it's their nails, hair, clothes, or their rent. It's not the way to be on equal footing with a man. When a man takes care of you, I believe that both of you are being cheated. He feels used, as if all you want is what he can give you. And you have nothing to feel proud of . . . you lose your pride and sense of accomplishment. Lana, I have to be able to hold my head up, and I do that by being my own woman. I'm willing to wait until I can afford to do better on my own. Do you understand?"

"Yes, I think so." Lana nodded, swallowing the last of her drink.

"Good, because someday you may have to decide for yourself what is right for you."

Lana giggled. "I don't have time for boys. I get all A's. And I plan to keep on getting A's all the way through college. Someday, I'm going to not only be a lawyer, but argue in front of the Supreme Court," Lana ended proudly.

Vanessa smiled. "That's my girl."

Lana grabbed a small bag of chips and a banana. She stopped by her sister's chair and hugged her. Before she headed for the stairs, she paused, "You know, sis, I don't think Ralph meant to make you mad. He cares about you, even I know that. And he was only trying to do something special for our family. There is nothing wrong with that." She called from over her shoulder, "'Night!"

Stunned, Vanessa hadn't expected that last comment. She had hoped her sister would agree with her, not take up for Ralph. But then, Lana had no way of knowing what had gone on between the two of them. Nor did Lana need to know what some men were willing to do to get what they wanted from women.

For weeks now Ralph had been pressuring her to pick up where they left off, after Devin and Brynne's wedding. She was not in the wrong. This was about s-e-x. One night wasn't enough for him. And he wasn't going to let a little thing like her family stand in his way.

Letting out a growl of frustration, Vanessa decided she might as well take advantage of the quiet and get some work done. She flipped through her sketchbook to the wedding gown she started earlier. After several tries to get the sleeves right, she threw down her pencil. Her concentration was practically nonexistent. The sleeves still didn't look right. And the skirt was all wrong. Giving up, she flipped her sketch pad closed. What next?

She picked up the novel she was reading for her book club's upcoming meeting. After reading the same page three times, she gave that up. It was pointless. Her thoughts kept returning to her disagreement with Ralph.

After a hot bath, Vanessa got ready for bed, then went

up to check on the children. All three of them were asleep in Lana's double bed. Although each of them had their own rooms, Vanessa wasn't surprised to find Courtney, not in her own bed. Courtney didn't like to sleep alone. Most nights, she slept beside her brother. Although Courtney adored her own pink feminine room, she'd also crawl in with Lana. Occasionally, both twins slipped into bed with Vanessa.

When she came back downstairs, Vanessa double-checked all the locks in the house and set the alarm. Too restless to sleep, she curled up on the sofa in front of the television. Unfortunately, the old Diana Ross and Billy Dee Williams movie didn't hold her interest. She'd seen it several times, but that wasn't the problem. Normally, she enjoyed seeing an old favorite again and again . . . but not tonight.

She still couldn't believe how the dinner had ended. For a time she'd relaxed enough with him to let her guard slip. She'd also discovered some unexpected things about him. He was more than a sexy smile. She was getting to know the man behind the charming roguish façade he showed the world.

He was a man who many might say had the world wrapped around his little finger. Women fought to get close to that sophisticated, confident smooth talker. Vanessa sensed there was so much more to him.

She'd seen him with his younger relatives and knew he was warm and caring with them. She had not expected him to reveal that side of his personality to her family, yet he had. He was a busy man, on a tight schedule; nonetheless, he made time to listen to their concerns and offered more than a quick pat on the head.

He had been wrong to ask in front of the kids. But, unfortunately, she couldn't dismiss the pain she'd seen in his dark eyes when she had accused him of using her family to get close to her. He had allowed her a glimpse of the inner man.

The hurt had been real. He'd gone as far as to admit he cared for her. Even Lana thought she'd been too hard on him.

Was she wrong? Had she overreacted and let her fears get the best of her? Since the night they'd shared together, she had been struggling to keep her distance. Because of her fear of repeating her mother's mistakes, had she let one thoughtless invitation ruin the friendship that her entire family had enjoyed? A friendship she valued more that she wanted to admit. Her accusation had indeed been harsh. Maybe too much so? Covering her face with her hands, she moaned unhappily. Suddenly, she realized she'd made a mistake.

She owed him an apology. Ralph might be many things, but he wasn't a cruel or selfish man. His offer to pay their way had been genuine. Clearly, he had been devastated about upsetting the children. His mistake had been asking in front of the children.

What now? If she'd been woman enough to get in his face to tell him what she thought of him, then she should be woman enough to apologize the same way . . . to his face. With a weary groan, she clicked off the set and went into her bedroom to get dressed. She had to do this, and she'd better do it tonight, before she lost her nerve. As long as she kept her dress down and her mind on their friendship, she was safe.

She went up to tell Lana she was going over to Ralph's. She wouldn't be out long. Her sister laughed and told her not to hurry back on her account. Vanessa didn't like to leave Lana alone at night with the kids, but tonight she felt a sense of urgency. She kissed her sister good night, locked up, and turned on the alarm before she left.

That same night, Greg Cummingham was working in his plush home office. He should be concentrating on crafting the criminal case for Jackson Jacob. Jacob was one of the most powerful men in the state and deserved his complete focus. Greg had made it to the top by devoting his considerable legal skills to getting his clients off no matter how guilty they were.

Greg was a senior partner in one of the most prestigious and lucrative law firms. in the Midwest. He was the only black partner, and because he was a fierce competitor with unrelenting determination, his name was constantly in the press and his face in the media. He was the go-to man with a reputation for delivering, no matter what.

Women had always been drawn to him. And he certainly enjoyed them. Quite honestly, he could count on one hand the number of females who said no, and that had been years ago, while he was on his way up. He saw no reason why it would change. He had enough money to keep them or get rid of them and their little problems. He'd been accused of being unbelievably selfish, but he considered that to be an asset.

Greg hadn't expected to fall in love. But he'd fallen hard for, not only beautiful, but smart and popular television journalist, Sheila Adams. She cohosted, *AM-Detroit*. Greg wasn't about to let this one get away. He surprised everyone when he married her.

Sheila was special, and, more important, she made him happy, both in and out of bed. For the first time in his life, Greg found himself putting someone else's needs ahead of his own.

Unfortunately, they'd only been married a few months when she'd gotten it in her pretty little head that they needed a baby to make their lives complete. When Sheila had been unable to conceive the old-fashioned way, she'd talked him into going to a fertility specialist, which eventually led to in vitro fertilization treatments at more than ten thousand dollars a pop. After six failed attempts, Sheila was inconsolably disappointed. He couldn't bear putting her through that again, yet he knew it was only a matter of time before she rebounded and wanted to try again.

Greg knew he had to intervene, especially since he had the means to end this wild merry-go-round! He had to tell her . . . he had to tell her about the twins and soon. But how much to tell? The truth was not an option. She would never understand the circumstances of their birth.

They were perfect, considering they had no mother to complicate matters. Afraid of losing her, he held back. Sheila was so tenderhearted, especially when it came to children. There was no need for her to know he'd never loved the twins' mother nor have an interest in them, until now.

He had to tell her. He simply couldn't handle seeing her keen disappointment and tears each month when she had her period. She was depressed for weeks, and only the hope of trying, yet again, would lift her spirits.

There was a soft knock on the open door, then his beautiful Sheila hurried over to his desk and climbed into his lap. She could have been a model, with her tall, slim body, soft honey brown skin and long curls.

"Darling, I know you're busy, but we need to talk." She caressed his jaw as she pressed her lips over his. Greg sighed, because he knew by the look in her dark eyes what she meant. She wanted to try another trip to the fertility doctor.

"No," he said firmly.

She blinked in surprise. "What do you mean, no?"

"I don't want you hurt. You think I don't know what's going on in that gorgeous head of yours? No more trips, Sheila, to that quack of a doctor." At the shimmer of tears in her eyes and the tremor of her bottom lip, he kissed her soft cheek tenderly.

"But why? You know how much I want to have your baby. Please, my heart, I thought you wanted it, too?"

"Hush, sweetheart . . . don't cry."

"But if we don't try . . ."

"There is another way—"

She interrupted, "But the doctor said we—"

"I don't care what that doctor has to say. We can have my child without you going through this torment every month," he snapped from sheer frustration.

Startled, she said, "I don't understand." Her forehead creased in a frown.

"Let me get it out, without interruption. Okay . . . my precious love." As he kissed her soft cheek, he realized he was shaking.

She nodded, then looked at him expectantly.

Greg took a deep breath, hoping for the best, despite the fear and doubt at the pit of his stomach. In the confident voice that he used in the courtroom, he continued, "I ran into an old friend I hadn't seen in years. At one time, I dated his cousin. Anyway, when her name came up in conversation, he looked at me in shock, then told me she'd died in childbirth. I got this odd, funny feeling in my gut. I didn't even know she was expecting. Suddenly, I had to know when the baby was born. I don't know why, but it was weird. Anyway, she had twins, and they're six now. When he told me they were born during the summer, I knew they were mine."

Sheila merely stared at him in stunned dismay, while his heart nearly stopped, choked with fear. He'd done it. Now it was out of his hands . . . beyond his control. Somehow, he'd managed not to jump in and rush to defend himself. It took everything in him to keep quiet. He'd dealt with enough criminals to know that his guilty conscience could only work against him, causing him to give in to a natural tendency to loosen the tongue and let the lies pour out one after another.

He was many things, but not a fool. So he waited, knowing their future depended on how convincing he had been.

"Are you sure?" she finally whispered.

"Well, as much as I can be, under the circumstances. We were not married, but Leah was not the type of woman to sleep with more than one man at a time. She was a widow and had not been involved with anyone since her husband died. No, those twins are mine. To make sure, I had one of the firm's private investigators look into it for me. I learned that the twins were born in June. I'm certain they are mine. Of course, we will have blood tests done. My name is already on their birth certificates."

She screamed with sheer joy. She began raining kisses all over his face, from his forehead, cheeks, nose, and to his mouth. "Oh my darling! It's wonderful news! I don't mean about the poor woman dying, but it's fabulous for us. It's the answer to our prayers. You are happy, aren't you, my love? Please tell me you are. You aren't mad at me, are you?"

"Mad at you?" He laughed. "Never!" He released a deep throaty chuckle.

"Good. Why didn't you tell me right away? As soon as you heard?"

"Oh, no. I didn't want you disappointed if the twins weren't mine. It killed me, not being able to tell you. Do you think you can accept them?"

"Accept them!" she exclaimed, lifting her face to kiss him. "I love them already. Now tell me every single detail. Are they identical? Boys or girls? I've been hoping for girl, but you probably want a little boy. Where are they? Are they in foster care? Please, don't say they've been adopted."

"Wait . . . wait!" He grinned, thrilled by her enthusiasm. He silently congratulated himself on a job well-done. He couldn't have hoped for a better response. "They aren't identical. A boy and a girl. I don't have pictures. What I've learned from the report is that they live with two older sisters. The oldest one is in her late twenties, the youngest one is seventeen."

At the tears trickling down her cheek, he paused, "What's wrong, my angel? Why are you crying? I thought you were pleased. If you'd rather not do this, then we can leave them where they are."

"No!" She quickly wiped the tears away. "I'm just so happy. I'm overwhelmed with joy that I can't contain it all. My love, I want them. Please say you want them, too."

Greg cupped her face, lovingly. "Of course, I want them. I'm sure the older sister will be relieved that she no longer has to care for them. You, my angel, will make a wonderful mother. I think from now on I'll call you 'angel.' Only an angel would consider taking over the care of two children from a past relationship. You are perfect. And I love you because you don't feel threatened."

"Of course I don't feel threatened. I have no reason. I know you've had relationships before we met, and I also know you're a good man. You aren't some lowlife who would neglect or ignore your child. I'm so proud to be your wife. You are so wonderful. Once you learned about the twins, you were instantly prepared to deal with the consequences of a past mistake." She jumped up, asking, "So how soon can we get the twins? I have so much to do. I have rooms to decorate . . . toys to buy. And clothes! They are going to need clothes. How soon, my darling?"

Greg leaned back in his chair. "I'm not sure, but I promise you it shouldn't take very long. I will hire the best child custody lawyer we can find and get the ball rolling. No more visits to the fertility doctor?"

"None," she promised.

"Good."

Sheila hugged him. "I'll leave all the legal matters to you, my love, and you leave the shopping and decorating to me. Honey, please, let the lawyer know that I want to adopt the twins. I want to be their mother."

"You will be, my angel. I promise you."

Fourteen

On the drive home, Ralph swore aloud. "Why did she make things so damn complicated?" He'd done everything he could think of to convince Vanessa that he was no threat to her and certainly not her family. Why would he want to hurt her little brother and sisters? Deliberately or otherwise? She had to see that it was a ridiculous idea.

How had something so simple as his desire for her gotten so out of hand? He swore in frustration. Vanessa was hardly the first female he had desired, and he assured himself she wouldn't be the last. So why was his desire for her eating away at his control?

It was bad enough that he wanted her to the point that he couldn't walk away from her. It had gotten so that many a night he hadn't wanted to go home to an empty house. But instead of dropping by his folks' for a home-cooked meal and a little chatter, or even Wesley's or Anna's place, he'd been parking himself at Vanessa's table like a lost puppy. She had become a habit that, if truth be told, he didn't want to break. He had to at least speak with her every single day if he couldn't see her.

He didn't mind having to share her with the children. He was fine as long as he knew at the end of the evening, he would be rewarded. His reward, alone time . . . having her to himself. That time with her was more than worth the wait. Some nights, they merely talked, but as he watched her eyes light up, or she told some anecdote about work or the children, he could feel the pleasure. And he lived for the moments when her defenses would crumble, sometimes it would be for only a few minutes, and her entire body would lose the protective stiffness she imposed on herself. She'd let herself go, and her sweet body would sway toward his. It was all he could do not to take advantage when her defenses were down. He lived for those precious moments.

Furious, he swore long and hard as he put his body through a punishing workout. He wasn't sure how his fool-proof plan had backfired. All he knew was he wasn't ready to let it go, not over a stupid mistake. He wasn't going to give her an easy way out. She claimed she wanted his friendship. Well, friends don't just walk away when things are rough.

Vanessa could tell by the look on his face that she was the last person he expected to find at his door. He blinked twice, as if to clear his vision.

She spoke quickly, hopefully before he slammed the door in her face. "I suppose I should have called first. May I come in?"

Ralph's famous charm was notably absent when he stepped back. "Come on in."

She waited until he'd closed the door, before she said, "I know it's late, but this can't wait until tomorrow."

He said tightly, "What? Did you find something else to accuse me of? Robbery? Child abuse?"

Vanessa looked everywhere, but at him. "I came to talk. This won't take long, but may I please sit down?" She was beginning to worry that her unsteady legs might not hold her. Even though, the air-conditioning kept the hot night pleasantly cool, she shivered.

His voice was tight with anger. "Excuse me for forgetting the manners my aunt drummed into my head." He gestured toward the formality of the large living room rather than his den. He was right behind her, switching on a Tiffany-style floor lamp. He motioned to the two large, deep-cushioned, burgundy sofas, facing each other in front of a large marble fireplace. As she crossed the room, the sound of her heels on the hardwood maple floor was muted by a luxurious, patterned area rug.

Gratefully, she sank down on the end of the sofa, clasping her trembling hands in her lap. She nervously smoothed the layers of her orange-and-gold floral sundress. It was two years old, a gift from the kids. She hoped it would bring her good luck. Struggling to find the words to convey her feelings, she worried her bottom lip, then remembered she was wearing makeup and stopped. Impatient with herself, she waited for him to speak.

"Well?" Ralph prompted. Not bothering to sit down, he leaned a broad shoulder against the impressive marble mantel. The large mirror above the picture-lined shelf reflected the beauty of the room.

She forced her eyes to meet his dark gaze. "I came to apologize. I was upset, I overreacted, and I said things I shouldn't have said. Once I had time to cool down and think, I knew your offer wasn't meant to hurt anyone. You have been thoughtful and generous to my family. In fact, you've gone out of your way to include the children whenever possible. I'm sorry, Ralph. Can you forgive me?"

The stiffness left his big frame, but he continued to study her. "You surprised me. I didn't expect you to say that, but I'm glad you did. I'm also sorry. I didn't mean to upset the kids." He paused before he revealed, "I don't know if I've ever told you how much I admire the way you care for your family. You've done a remarkable job."

"Thank you." Deeply touched, she felt some of the tension she'd been holding inside slip away. "I probably should have waited until tomorrow instead of coming by so late."

"No problem. It's barely eleven. Would you like something to drink? There is ice tea, soft drinks, juice?"

"Diet Pepsi, if you have it." She blushed, aware of his gaze moving over her.

Ralph chuckled. "I may have Pepsi, but I doubt I have diet anything, other than water."

She laughed. "Ice tea, please."

By the time he returned, her jitters had settled a bit more. He placed the small tray with two tall glasses of tea on the coffee table.

Cupping her drink in both hands, she attempted to tease, "Don't worry. I won't stay long."

Instantly, he turned serious. "Don't rush on my account. You're always welcome in my home."

"Thank you," she said, while wondering if he was merely being polite. The man had an active social life. For all she knew he could have a late date or plans to go out.

He took the seat across from her. Rather than reach for his drink, he studied her.

She surmised, "You're still angry."

Ralph shook his head. "No, what I am is confused. I don't know where I stand with you. Until tonight, I thought we were getting to know each other. Getting closer. If not lovers, then at least I thought we were repairing our friendship. Now, I don't know what to think. You're here, yet you said you don't want anything to do with me. You were quite clear when you said you don't want me near your family. Nothing has been resolved."

"That's not . . ."

He interrupted, "Please, let me finish." Rising, Ralph began to pace between the fireplace and the set of bay windows, but he made no effort to fill the prolonged silence.

Unable to look away, Vanessa's heart raced with a combination of fear and excitement. What was he really saying? Did he want her to go or stay? Or was that it? He wanted her to make the decision. What did she really want from him? Did she even know?

She came tonight because she'd hurt him and knew it was up to her to make things right. Okay . . . the unvarnished truth. Despite what she'd said and done to protect herself, Vanessa knew she wanted the man. She wasn't thinking about forever. She wasn't even thinking about tomorrow. All she could focus on was the here and now.

She wasn't even sure how it happened. She didn't even remember rising, but suddenly she was in Ralph's arms, with her breasts pressed against his chest and her arms wrapped around his neck. She hung on to him, needing his solid strength. Although she couldn't seem to find the words, she stood on tiptoes and lifted her face until she could reach his hair-roughened chin. It wasn't enough. What she wanted was his mouth.

He released a deep groan, dropping his head until she caressed his fleshy bottom lip with her soft tongue. She licked first the right, then the left corner of his mouth before slipping her tongue deep inside. There was no hesitation on his part as his hands spanned her waist, then he followed the slope of her back, over her plump bottom, cupping her softness.

He brought her into the heat of his long length until his heavy erection pressed against her stomach. She shivered, trembling with desire, thrilled to discover he wanted her. His long, steel-hard shaft brought back poignant memories of how he felt inside her. Goodness yes, Vanessa needed Ralph . . . wanted him now.

Why had she fought so hard against it? And why had it

taken her so long to get back to this place and this man? They felt so good together . . . so right. This was so much better than any fantasy or dream she'd conjured up.

As he fed her kiss after hungry kiss, the pulsating need throbbed deep inside, moistening her feminine core. Had she ever been more needy . . . felt so incredibly empty?

This was how she awoke during the night, aching for him. It was not make-believe. Ralph was real. Allowing her feminine instincts to guide her, Vanessa pressed the ultrasensitive crests of her breasts into his chest. She rubbed her sex against the firm contour of his muscular thigh. Even though she was nearly faint from lack of oxygen, she moaned a protest when his mouth left hers. Why? Why had she gone so long without him? Oh, she needed this. She needed him.

When she raised her hand to trace the line of his jaw, he pressed a kiss into the center of her palm. But he surprised her when he shook his head.

"Why did you stop?" she forced herself to say, while her stomach filled with nerves.

His voice was gruff when he said, "No more misunderstandings. I want to make sure we are on the same page. If we take this further, it will be what we both want."

Dropping her lids, she whispered, "Ralph, this is crazy . . ." Her voice was so husky with desire that she couldn't even try to hide it.

He made a frustrated sound in his throat, his voice harsh with need when he grated, "Not to me. Now tell me what I need to hear. Or this ends now."

She stared at him in disbelief, but evidently, he meant what he said. He didn't break down but waited for her response. When she still didn't say anything, he let go, dropping his hands to his side and stepped away.

Vanessa grabbed his hands, whispering, "Are the words so important?"

"Absolutely."

Vanessa stared at the base of his throat for a few moments before she said in an urgent whisper, "I'm here because I want to be with you. Make love to me, Ralph."

His nostrils flared as if he were filling his lungs with her scent. And his heated eyes never left hers as he gripped the hem of his crewneck T-shirt and ripped it away from his body. Dropping the ragged edges, he unsnapped his jeans and began easing the zipper down.

Her breath hitched in her throat when he reached for her with both hands, pulling her back to him. "I need you now," he growled an instant before he captured her mouth with his.

There was no finesse in that kiss. There was nothing soft or coaxing about it. It was wild, exactly what she needed to reassure her that he indeed wanted her as much as she wanted him . . . hot, raw, and insistent.

"Yes . . . oh yes," she managed to get out when he freed her lips.

Her lips were tender, swollen from his kisses, but she didn't make a single complaint as she rained kisses down his dark throat and chest. His skin was hot against her lips, her tongue. He filled her senses.

"You're wearing too many clothes," he complained.

He quickly pulled the zipper down the back of her dress, pushing it off her shoulders and down past her hips until she could step free of the garment. He pressed a kiss to the base of her throat as he reached behind her to unhook her lacy beige bra. Only when it fell to the floor did he release a ragged sigh. His hands clasped her waist, then slipped beneath the lace band to push the beige bikini panties off her hips, down her long, shapely legs.

"You're so beautiful," he said huskily as he held her close until her body hugged his long length. "Feel how badly I want you . . . Nessa. How desperately I need you." His open mouth slid down the side of her throat before lingering to lave the feminine-scented hollow.

Frustrated when Ralph pulled back, she released an impatient sound deep in her throat, watched as he shoved his jeans down his lean hips and long, muscular legs. His body was still tight, the well-toned body of an athlete. He had not let himself go. Even though he'd been out of the game for a few years, he was the beautiful one.

He surprised her when he dropped to his knees, wrapping his arms around her soft hips. He buried his face between her creamy brown breasts and filled his hands, cupping her round bottom, squeezing her lush softness. He carefully placed a series of kisses down her rib cage to her stomach. He placed hot, wet kisses on her soft, flesh, pausing to tongue her belly button. Vanessa trembled as desire raced along ultrasensitive nerve endings.

"Ralph . . ." she begged, bracing her hands on his broad shoulders, uncertain if her legs would continue to hold her upright.

His response was to slide his mouth lower still . . . he placed tender kisses in the ebony curls that covered her sex. She let out a surprised squeal when his tongue warmed the place he'd just kissed.

"Nessa, you are so wet, so ready," he groaned as he followed the sweet curve of her feminine mound. He stunned her when he tongued the outer fleshy folds, then bathed her fragrant softness with the hot wash of his tongue.

"Ralph . . ." she begged, while shaking her head. Shoving her hair away from her face, she realized she was still wearing heels and trembling so badly she could hardly stand.

"Please don't tell me to stop. Let me really taste you . . . the way I've wanted to do for so long," he said urgently. His large hands cupped her ripe buttocks. He rhythmically squeezed her softness, at the same time inhaling her woman's scent as he waited for her response.

Aching with need, she nearly screamed his name. Wild with frustration and eager for the full strokes of his tongue, she begged, "Oh . . . please. Don't stop!" Suddenly feeling herself falling as her legs gave out, she clung to his shoulders. He tightened his arms around her and held on to her.

"Let go . . . I've got you," he said as he eased her down onto her back. "You okay?" he asked, his face buried in her full breasts.

Vanessa surprised them both when she giggled. "I have never been better." Her humor quickly turned to moans as he suckled a dark peak, taking it deep into his mouth to enjoy. Not wanting the other to feel cheated, he moved to tongue the other nipple, drawing it into his mouth as he gave her the hard suction that caused her to quiver with longing.

She remembered saying his name, then the next thing she knew, his mouth was between the plump lips of her mound. He kissed her there, then used his fingers to hold her slick folds open to the hot strokes of his tongue. He tasted her as if she were a rich, creamy dessert.

She whimpered as sensation after sensation battered her. He didn't ease up but continued to pleasure her. He relished her sweetness as if he were starving for what only she could give him. When he moved to lave her ultrasensitive swollen nub, she gasped, quivering uncontrollably. When he took the aching bud into his mouth and suckled, she lost touch with her surroundings.

Vanessa was lost in a mad whirl of wild sensations. She screamed her enjoyment, convulsing in a white-hot, earth-shattering orgasm. It was a while before her awareness returned, and she even realized where she was.

She wanted to ask him why, but couldn't find the words, let alone have the nerve. Who was she kidding? She could barely form a coherent thought. He cradled her in his arms. Tears of sheer bliss ran unchecked down her cheeks. When she opened her eyes, she quickly blinked in order to see him clearly.

Ralph's intense gaze captured hers as he stroked down her back, calming, soothing her. "You okay?"

Vanessa, certain her voice would fail her, nodded, then flushed with embarrassment as she recalled how he had pleasured her and that she had relished every second. "I still can't believe . . ."

Ralph dropped his head, following the slope of her throat to the valley between her breasts. "No need to blush, beautiful. We did nothing wrong, certainly, nothing to be ashamed of. I've wanted to know everything about you, including the way you taste on my tongue, since the night we first made love. I wanted it badly but held back because it was our first time. I didn't want to shock you."

"Did you . . ." she stumbled over the words.

"Did I enjoy pleasuring you with my mouth? Do I want to do it again?" he asked, as he kissed the upper swells of her breasts.

Although embarrassed, she nodded, wanting to know the answer to both questions.

"Absolutely. You taste honey sweet . . . wonderful." He chuckled, deep in his throat, as he watched her blush.

Before Vanessa could collect her thoughts, he licked the sensitive peak of her right breast. When she gasped, he laved her until her ebony nipple stood at attention, as if eager for more of the same.

"You are so beautiful," he said, into her ear. Then he dropped his head to kiss the other tip. She was both amazed and touched by his generosity. His focus had been on her pleasure, not his own. She called out his name, and his response was to increase her enjoyment by sucking the aching peak.

Once more she was lost in a maze of exquisite pleasure. Vanessa could only moan when he returned to her other breast. He gave it the same keen attention and didn't stop until she called out his name. She shook her head even though desire pulsed persistently, and she instinctively tightened her empty passage. She pushed at his shoulders until he lay back.

"It's my turn to pleasure you," she insisted. Her hands moved over his chest and flat stomach. Unsure of herself, she hesitated at touching his shaft.

Ralph said close to her ear, "It's okay, you don't have to do anything you don't want."

Her eyes met his. "I want . . . to do it right."

"There is no wrong way for you to touch me," he replied, his voice heavy with need.

"Show me, please."

He took her hands, showing her how to stroke him, from the thick base to the broad crest of his hard sex.

"Mmm." He surprised her when he caught her hands. "It feels so good, but I want to be inside you."

She nodded, "Yes, please . . . now."

Vanessa didn't have to ask twice. He grabbed a pillow from the sofa, dropped it on the rug, and positioned it under her head. He reached into his jeans, pulled out a condom from a pocket, and quickly sheathed his pulsating shaft.

Her breathing was uneven as she waited expectantly with her eyes closed. When she felt him caressing her inner thighs as he covered her mouth with his, Vanessa whimpered, opening her body for him. He pressed forward, caressed her moist opening, then thrust inside.

"Oh . . . yes . . ." Vanessa cried out, as Ralph filled the emptiness.

He stopped, giving her time to adjust. Pressing his mouth against the place where her shoulder and neck joined, he inhaled her scent, kissing her tender flesh. When he gently scraped her soft skin with his teeth, she trembled, turning her head until she could kiss his forehead, his lean cheek. He groaned when she worried the corner of his mouth with her tongue. He growled, giving her full access to his mouth.

As she tightened around his aching shaft, it was even sweeter. He groaned his pleasure, deepening the kiss. Suddenly, he quickened his thrust, giving her the deep, hard strokes she longed for. Vanessa lifted her legs, wrapping them around his hips and rubbing her breasts against his chest as she clung to him.

As the pleasure spiraled, she lost her grip on reality. She called his name as she climaxed. Her orgasm caused him to quicken his pace even more, and soon he shook from the force of his own. He cried out. Her face rested against the base of his neck, her arms tight around his waist.

As her breathing gradually slowed, she closed her eyes, her entire body relaxed and sated. Ralph smoothed her hair away from her face, caressing her cheek. His kisses were slow and intoxicatingly sweet. Vanessa sighed at the tenderness of the moment. She wondered if she'd ever felt so cared about or cherished. She stiffened as the worries she'd pushed aside began to fill her thoughts, reminding her that nothing had really changed.

Ralph asked, "Are you okay, beautiful?"

"I'm fine. How about you?"

His laugh was deep and raspy. "I couldn't be better." When she shifted, he moved to her side, rubbing her soft hip. "I'm sorry. I should have carried you up to my bedroom. I couldn't wait that long," he confessed.

Suddenly embarrassed as she mentally pictured him struggling to lift her, she quickly changed the subject. "I'm sorry, but I can't stay long." When his brow creased into a frown, she hastily added, "Please don't be angry. I don't feel right leaving the kids alone at night. Lana is only seventeen."

Since their argument, she realized, she'd changed. His feelings mattered to her. What alarmed her was how much they mattered.

He smiled sheepishly. "I understand." He tightened his arms around her in a fierce hug, whispering, "You're right, beautiful. You have to go although I won't lie. I can't help feeling a bit selfish and wishing I could fall asleep with you in my arms . . ."

Fifteen

Vanessa smiled, secretly wishing the same thing, but decided to keep her thoughts to herself. She wasn't ready for these new, tender feelings. They frightened her, caused her to feel vulnerable to him, something she didn't welcome. She certainly wasn't prepared to share her emotions with Ralph. Nor was she ready to examine them closely herself.

After placing a playful kiss on the tip of his nose, she began hunting for her clothes. Ralph lay with his hands behind his head, a huge smile on his face. She turned and caught him watching her.

Hands on her hips, she said, "What are you doing?"

"Enjoying the view," he teased.

"A little too much." She couldn't help noting the way his sex was hardening, then blushed.

"Little?" He lifted a brow.

"I didn't mean!" she hastily said, then covered her face with her hands. It was difficult enough dressing with him watching her, but to discuss his impressive proportions!

Laughing, Ralph rose to his full height.

"It's not that funny!" she said from over her shoulder as she fumbled with her bra clasp.

He pushed her hand away and did it for her. When he finished, he swept her hair away from her nape and kissed it. Rather than turning toward him, she picked up her dress. She stepped into it, smoothing it down her hips and thighs. With her panties wadded in her hand and her purse under her arm, she turned toward him. She was surprised to see he was also dressing.

"Be right back." Before she could rush off, he cupped her shoulders. "There are fresh towels and soap in the vanity. Toss the towels in the hamper when you are done." At her look of shock, he shrugged. "My aunt. She explained that even a bachelor should have certain things in his powder room for his female guests."

"Powder room?" she teased, and smiled at his embarrassment.

Vanessa decided she would choose to be grateful to his aunt rather than jealous of the other females he'd entertained. In his wine-colored half bath, she found everything she needed, a stack of cream hand towels, minisoaps, and some things she didn't need, small tubes of toothpaste, toothbrushes, tampons, condoms, and a small first-aid kit. She recalled how well stocked his dressing rooms in the pool area had been. But this was different. Or maybe she was different because she cared.

When she returned, he was completely dressed, including sandals, and was standing in the foyer, where he picked up a set of keys. Her curiosity got the better of her.

"Going out?"

"Yeah." He smiled. "I'm going to follow you home. Want to make sure my lady gets home safely. You did make sure your alarm was on when you left the house?"

"Of course." She lifted her chin.

"Ready?"

She nodded. He ushered her outside. After locking the door behind him, he walked her to her car and held the door for her.

Before he could close it, she said, "You really don't have to go through so much trouble. I'm fine . . . really."

He leaned in and pressed a soft kiss on her lips. "I plan to make sure that you stay fine, beautiful." He closed the door, and then jogged to his Jaguar, parked a few yards away.

As she waited for him, she couldn't help grinning. She understood as never before why women found him so downright irresistible. The brother was not only smooth, but an incredible and unselfish lover. His priority had been to pleasure her to the utmost degree. Evidently, he could write a how-to book on making a woman feel cherished since he had done that and then some.

Was it any wonder women chased him down? Despite her inexperience, there wasn't a doubt in her mind that he knew his way around a woman's body. He'd actually made her toes curl.

She was humming as she drove home, aware of the way her body still purred from the sweet loving he'd given her.

Vanessa wasn't surprised when Ralph got out of his car and linked hands to walk her up to the front door, where she had left the porch light on.

Holding her close, Ralph asked, "What are we, Nessa? Friends or lovers?"

Smiling, she said, "Both."

Ralph grinned. His kiss wasn't long but was indeed sweet.

Close to her ear, he reminded her that he was flying out of town on business and wouldn't be back until Monday. Then he said, "I'm going to miss you. Would you and the kids have dinner with me Monday evening?"

She smiled at him and nodded. Then she playfully bit his bottom lip before she licked the hurt tenderly and kissed him again. At his husky groan, she smiled and whispered bye. Hurrying inside, she locked the door behind her.

As she leaned back against it, she let out a weary sigh. It was very late, and she was tired. But that wasn't what caused her to sigh. She was new to this game they were playing, but that didn't mean she wasn't going in blindfolded. They agreed to be both friends and lovers. She assured herself that as long as she was careful and didn't yearn for more, she would be fine. The danger came from being greedy . . . wanting it all. Love had no place in their agreement. Nope! It was the sure way of getting a huge dose of heartache.

She hadn't realized until now, but Ralph had been the perfect choice for her. He was no more interested in that four-letter word than she was. Vanessa fell asleep with a smile.

Saturday mornings were often lazy, with no need to rush anywhere. The twins liked to curl up on the living-room rug in front of the television and watch cartoons. Lana liked to sleep late, and no one bothered her until eleven. Vanessa also liked to stay in bed only with her sketch pad, working on new ideas.

Although she'd slept well, Vanessa had dreamed . . . dreamed of a fabulous wedding . . . her wedding. Her entire family had been there. Rather than focus on the fact that Ralph was her groom, she concentrated on creating the spectacular wedding gown.

It was beautiful in its simplicity. The gown had to be made in raw silk that would ripple when she moved. It had clean, straight lines with an off-the-shoulder design. An inch-wide trim of seed pearls and tiny cream silk-ribbon-embroidered rose buds saved the bodice from looking too plain. The long, tight sleeves were sheer, but the cuffs were also covered in seed pearls. Her hair had been pinned up in an elaborate French twist, and the sheer veil was anchored by a row of cream roses.

As Vanessa stared at the drawing, she decided she'd never seen anything more beautiful. This gown, to do it justice, had to be embroidered by hand. It was a shame she'd never have a reason to make it.

For years, Vanessa had dreamed of wedding gowns but never one for herself. Rather than examine her emotions, she flipped the page and began designing a deep green silk, one she envisioned her sister would wear to her prom.

Knocking briefly on the open door, "Hi," Lana said, around a yawn. "Busy?"

"Nope, did you sleep well?" She smiled.

"Mmm-hmm," Lana stretched as she crossed the room to sit on the end of the bed. Leaning her back against the footboard, Lana said, "What happened? Did you and Ralph make up?"

Vanessa didn't look up from the pad. "Yes, not that it's any of your business, Miss Nosy."

Lana laughed. "Good. Are we going over there to swim later? Because if it's okay with Ralph, I'd like to invite Marisa to join us."

"Not today. Ralph has gone away on business. He won't be back until Monday. We're on our own this weekend." She tapped her chin as if in thought. "I bet I can come up with lots of things that need to be done. You and the twins can clean your rooms. There's laundry to do, the kitchen and bathrooms are in need of cleaning. Take your pick."

Just then, the twins ran in and jumped into bed on either side of her.

"Nessa!" Lana complained. "I'd hoped to visit with Marisa this weekend."

"That's fine. If everyone pitches in, we should be done with the house by four. Why don't you call and invite her to dinner? If her folks say it's okay, she can stay over and go to church with us."

Lana jumped up and hugged her. "Thanks, sis. I'll go call. Can we make our own pizzas?"

Vanessa smiled. "Sure."

Lana called, "Thanks," while racing for the stairs.

"Can I have pineapple-and-ham pizza?" Curtis asked. Evidently the only part of conversation that interested him was the food.

"Anyone with toys and clothes on the floor or unmade beds can't want pizza. That also goes for anyone still in their pajamas," she said with a straight face.

"That's not fair!" Courtney insisted.

"Sure, it is. I want pizza for dinner, so I'd better get moving." Vanessa pushed back the cotton blanket.

"Me too!" Curtis yelled, jumping up and running for the stairs. Courtney looked at her sister for a moment, then took off after her twin.

As she showered and dressed, Vanessa was proud of the fact she hadn't wasted time reviewing the previous night or worrying about what was said afterwards. What was the point? They decided what was best for them. No one else's opinion mattered. Vanessa was not fooling herself. More than likely, Ralph would be the first to look elsewhere. And it had nothing to do with her. It was simply his way, which would be fine with her.

This way there would be no surprises. She knew what she was up against. She knew her man. That was how her mother made her first mistake. She'd underestimated Greg Cummingham. Her second mistake, Leah had fallen deeply in love with him. Those two blunders had cost her everything. She gave him her power and left her heart open to hurt and devastation. Unfortunately, her mother never recovered from Cummingham's callousness.

Vanessa was confident that wouldn't happen to her. She had her eyes wide open. Ralph was not her weakness. For now, he brought her pleasure. And that was enough. She wasn't deceiving herself by trying to make "for now" last. She wasn't looking for "forever."

That didn't mean she wasn't looking forward to seeing him on Monday evening. In fact, she was sorry that she had not suggested they go out alone. So what if she was feeling selfish and wanted to keep him to herself. It was ridiculous, considering her family always came first with her. Oh, well, she shrugged.

However long Ralph's infatuation lasted, it would be enough. When it ended, she wasn't going to self-destruct. They'd go back to being just friends, with no regrets for either of them.

Although her workday had been no more hectic than usual, Vanessa rushed in the door somewhat breathlessly. She had less than an hour to get ready for the evening ahead.

"Where is everyone?" Vanessa called.

"In the kitchen," Lana called back. "We've had our showers, so the coast is clear."

Vanessa smiled. She hoped that meant there would still be some hot water. "No more than a snack. I don't want you all to spoil your dinner," she said as she walked into the kitchen.

The twins rushed to give her a welcoming hug. To save time, she'd laid out their things before she had left for work. She wanted things to run smoothly.

"There's a letter for you from an attorney's office." Lana sent her a questioning glance when she entered the kitchen. "I left it in your room."

Not having a clue to what it might be about, Vanessa nodded. "Okay thanks." She hurried into her room, undressed, and put her hair in hot rollers. In her robe, she rushed into the bathroom.

She showered, did her makeup, styled her hair, then dressed in white jeans and the off-the-shoulder top she'd worn while they were in Atlanta. She'd picked it because of the wonderful memories associated with the trip.

It wasn't until she lotioned her hands that she remembered the letter. Vanessa recognized the prominent law firm. A glance at the bedside clock assured her, she had ten minutes before Ralph was due. She could spare a few moments before she had to check on the kids.

Opening the envelope, she was more curious than alarmed when she began reading the legal papers. Her hands were shaking and her eyes filled with tears by the time she reached the bottom of the document.

"Nessa! Ralph is here!" Curtis yelled.

"Coming." She dried the tears, did a last-minute touch-up, then put the letter into the envelope and hid it in the bottom of her lingerie drawer.

"Sorry to keep you waiting," she said with a forced smile.

Ralph's eyes momentarily locked with hers. "No problem." He met her in the center of the living room and after kissing her cheek, he unknowingly gave her what she needed most, a hug. If he was surprised that she clung for a moment too long, he didn't show it. "You look nice."

"Thanks. Everyone ready?" Vanessa give each child a once-over, then finger combed Courtney's bangs, straightened Curtis's collar, and smoothed the back of Lana's blouse.

"Where are we going?" Curtis and Courtney asked eagerly.

Ralph smiled, "That's up to your beautiful sisters."

"Why?" Curtis demanded.

Ralph chuckled, "When they are happy, we're happy. Vanessa? Lana? Courtney?"

The ladies looked at each other, then said at once, "The Olive Garden."

Ralph whispered to Curtis. He nodded and hurried over to the screen door and held it open for the ladies. The last to leave, Vanessa handed Ralph her door key as she passed. After locking up, Ralph ushered them down the walk.

When Vanessa went to get Curtis and Courtney's booster seats, he stopped her. "No, need. There is nothing for you to worry about. I took care of everything." He squeezed her waist as he urged her toward his gleaming Navigator. He helped her into the front seat, then went to check that the twins were buckled into a brand-new set of booster seats and Lana was strapped into the middle seat.

"We all set?" Ralph asked as he slid into his seat.

"Yes." Vanessa, touched by his forethought in regard to her family, blinked back tears. Aw, oh, tears signal emotional distress. Not good. She knew she had to be cautious. She was feeling too much, which made her vulnerable.

Ralph could be all charm. Not that she thought he would take advantage, but she was used to being in control. Tonight, she was a very long way from that. If anything, she was close to collapsing, and she didn't want that. She was so darn needy. She should have come up with an excuse and stayed home and locked herself inside her room until she had time to pull herself together.

The popular family restaurant was crowded. Even though it was a weeknight, the place was packed. The twins weren't fussy eaters, but their favorite food outside of hamburgers was spaghetti and meatballs with lots of cheese.

Vanessa did her best to hold on to her composure, asking Ralph about his trip. Deep in thought, she picked at the food in front of her. When Ralph asked if something was wrong, she shook her head. Aware of his silent inquiry she reached beneath the table for his hand and slipped hers into one of his, then whispered, they would talk later. He nodded his understanding, giving her hand a reassuring squeeze.

Relieved that the children were busy laughing and teasing each other, Vanessa concentrated on holding on to her smile. It took every bit of her control to succeed. She released a weary sigh when everyone settled on hot-fudge sundaes for dessert.

"What is it?" Ralph whispered into her ear, as they walked hand in hand to the car.

"I'll explain when we're alone." When she attempted to move out of his reach he held on to her.

She looked up at him in surprise when he said, "It's not us, is it?"

She shook her head. She was trembling so hard that she needed his support as he helped her into the car. She blinked back tears of stunned dismay. Suddenly, she realized she didn't have a single doubt that Ralph would be there for her in the coming weeks. All she had to do was ask for his help. The question was, did she have the courage to ask? Or would she let her fear of repeating her mother's mistakes prevent her from reaching out to him? This wasn't Ralph's problem. It was hers. In the end, she had to do what was best for her family. If only she was certain what that was.

After the children thanked Ralph for dinner, she asked wearily, "I've got to go up and get the kids settled. It shouldn't take long. Can you . . ."

"I'm not going anywhere until I find out what has you so upset." Caressing her cheek with a finger, he smiled. "Take your time. I'll be out on the back sunporch."

"Okay." She hurried up the stairs. It took less time than she expected to get the twins ready for bed. After tucking them in, she left Lana soaking in a tubful of bubbles reading a romantic novel.

Vanessa stopped in her room to retrieve the letter she'd casually opened a few hours earlier. Now she felt as if her world were crashing in around her. She hesitated on the threshold, wondering if she was wrong to share this with Ralph. She sighed; if she didn't, she might explode. Ralph was her friend and she badly needed a friend.

Ralph relaxed on one end of the swing, his long legs stretched out in front of him.

He'd switched on the floor lamp in the corner.

"Would you care for a drink?" She braced a hand on the doorjamb. Her stomach was a mass of nerves.

"I'm good." He patted the cushion beside him. "Sit with me . . . please."

Vanessa, who was so close to crumbling and feared she'd end up in a heap of inconsolable sobs, didn't argue. She went over and gave him the letter. "Read this. Then we'll talk."

"This was what stole your smile all evening?"

"Yes. The instant I saw Gregory Cummingham's name, I knew we were in serious trouble."

"Gregory Cummingham?"

"The twins' father. Just read it." When he finished, she whispered, "What am I going to do? I can't believe I am telling you this, but you want to be my friend. So friend, tell me what to do. I can't afford a high-priced attorney."

Vanessa shouldn't have been surprised by how fast he moved; after all, the man had been a professional basketball player. She was in his arms, her cheek against his chest before she could ask for what she needed . . . she craved his strength and support.

"What you're not going to do is hand over custody of the twins," he snarled furiously as he held her tenderly, his hand gently moving over her shoulders and back.

Vanessa did just what she'd tried to avoid, she cried

scalding-hot tears she'd held in all through dinner. Beneath it all was the overwhelming fear that if she wasn't extremely careful, she'd lose the twins.

"Go ahead. Let it out, beautiful," he soothed. "He won't win. I promise."

Vanessa cried harder, then gradually calmed, enough to form a coherent thought. Finally, she said, "How can I stop him? He's not only filthy rich, he's a powerful criminal attorney. And he really is the twins' father." She sniffed.

Ralph's brow creased in concern. "No doubts?" he asked as he passed her a tissue.

"None," Vanessa said, unhappily, as she mopped at the steady stream of tears. "I'm sorry. I didn't mean to break down like that."

"You have nothing to apologize for, beautiful." Reaching for her hand, he led Vanessa back over to the swing. They sat side by side, with Ralph's arm draped around her shoulders. "I'm missing the facts. Tell me about Cummingham. All I know is that he takes on high-profile cases and usually wins. And he recently married a TV journalist."

Vanessa released a tired sigh. "That's right. When my mother met him at her office, she was a legal assistant. He wasn't married then. In fact, he swore he'd never marry." She paused, then explained, "My mother, Leah, had been a housewife until our father died from a sudden heart attack three years earlier. She was forced to go back to the work she'd done before she married.

"While he was busy seducing her, he never bothered to tell her he was a womanizing cheat. He ended up not only breaking her heart, but her spirit as well. She loved him. And how did he repay her devotion? When she told him she was pregnant, he ran out on her and never looked back."

Ralph kissed Vanessa's forehead. "I'm sorry, sweetheart."

"Yeah, me too. My mother was ashamed of being pregnant without a husband. Can you imagine how she felt? Used, degraded, and, most important, the love she so cherished was one-sided." Vanessa bit her lip. "She was devastated. That's when Lana and I lost her." She broke down, sobbing.

"Shush, beautiful. You don't have to explain." Ralph tightened his arms around her, but as quickly as he brushed them away, more tears welled up in her dark eyes.

"I want to tell you. I want you to understand what kind of man Greg Cummingham is. Everyone thinks he's such a wonderful man because he's done so much for the black community. Well, he wasn't wonderful to my mother. He ended up destroying her. She didn't want to live, not for me or Lana, and not for the babies. Yes, there were problems with the pregnancy, but that's not why she died. She gave up, Ralph."

The tears came, and no matter how hard she tried, she couldn't stop them. She had no idea how long the emotional storm lasted, but Ralph held her through it all. Drained, she slumped against him, exhausted.

Unfortunately, Greg Cummingham was still the twins' biological father, and he was seeking full custody. Yet Vanessa felt better, even stronger. And she knew the change in her had everything to do with Ralph's support.

For some reason, Cummingham wanted the twins. She would have to fight to keep them. But she would not be facing him alone.

Sixteen

Ralph didn't say a word. He knew that there was nothing he could say to ease the worry or pain she was facing. She was an incredible woman who didn't deserve this heartache. There were a few choice words that he wanted to say to that lowlife, Greg Cummingham, but nothing that could be said in front of his lady.

"I'm . . ."

He kissed her tenderly. "Stop saying you're sorry. You have good reason to feel the way you do. Tell me, what can I do to help? Would you like me to contact my lawyer to find the top child-custody attorney in the state?"

"I'd love to say yes, but how can I? I can't afford any attorney good or bad." Her velvet brown eyes were swimming in tears. Worrying her bottom lip, she admitted, "I also know I don't have a choice. To beat Cummingham, I need the best. What am I going to do?" she whispered aloud.

"It's going to be all right, sweetheart. I'll contact my lawyer. It shouldn't take long to get things rolling. You have any idea why Cummingham is doing this? What made him change his mind? Until now he was content, pretending he didn't have kids. Right?"

"That's right. When you asked me what was wrong, I'm sure you didn't expect to be caught up in my problems.

Tonight wasn't supposed to end like this. First you had to share me with my family, now you are stuck mopping up my tears." She looked at him with eyes full of disappointment.

"Will you stop apologizing? I enjoyed the time we have together. You and the kids are a complete package. And I've accepted that. What I don't like is knowing you're worrying about money. Let me take care of it for you." Lightly, he pressed his fingertips to her soft full lips before she could get the protest out. "You can't afford it without sacrificing something that I'm sure is for one of the kids. Money is not a problem for me. In fact, I'd love to be able to do this for you. Say yes, beautiful."

Vanessa shook her head. "You know I can't. And you know why."

Frustrated, Ralph snapped, "You gave that a great deal of thought. What did it take? Six, or was than ten, seconds' worth of deliberation?"

Vanessa had the nerve enough to smile at his quip. She ran a hand soothingly over his chest. "Don't be mad."

Ralph rose to his feet and began to move restlessly around the screened porch, which overlooked the Grants' backyard. A warm breeze caused the leaves to dance and flutter in the old oak tree in the yard. Despite the late hour, the scorching heat of the day had not abated.

Ralph cleared his throat before he grumbled, "I've never met a woman less interested in my bank balance. We're not talking about an expensive designer bag or something as frivolous as a week in the islands. Nessa, this is the twins' future we're talking about here."

Stubbornly, lifting her chin, she said, "I appreciate your offer, but I'm really not your responsibility. While I need your support, I don't want your money. I will find a way."

He could tell by the way she worried her bottom lip that her solution involved raiding the piggy bank. Not good.

"How? By going into Lana's college fund? Or the money you set aside for the kids' school clothes? How are you going to get the money?" He was practically shouting. "And don't you dare tell me it's none of my business."

Tears shimmered in her beautiful eyes, but she didn't let a single one fall. Her hands were balled into small fists, as she insisted, "I'm only doing what I have to do. How can I take money from you? It wouldn't be right. There has to be another way."

"Such as?"

"I don't know!"

He quirked a brow. "You are talking about pride, Vanessa Grant. That's the only thing standing in your way. Why are you making it personal? You need what I'm offering, and I'm willing to give it to you. I can give you a blank check tonight. You fill in the amount." He reached into the inside pocket of his sport coat.

She glared at him. "Stop it! You're making light of a very difficult and painful situation. I don't appreciate it!"

Ralph gritted his teeth, knowing she was picking a fight with him. Why, because she could? She was female and knew damn well she wasn't making a bit of sense. He also knew there wasn't a thing he could say because she had stopped listening.

He came toward her with no intention of backing down, while she angled her chin upward and didn't take a single step backward. She was no match for him, and they both knew it. He didn't stop until the tips of their shoes nearly touched. Despite his frustration, he was impressed. There were grown men who would not go toe to toe with him, but, his Nessa did.

"Don't!"

"What?" He grinned at her.

"Don't try to use masculine charm to get your way. Neither fierce determination or smooth-talking trash will get you anywhere with me, Ralph Prescott. Accept it! You're not going to win." Her forehead creased, but her pretty mouth tilted up a bit at the corners.

He couldn't help it, he laughed and leaned down to brush her soft lips against his. "Should I try another tactic? A few hot kisses."

"Nope. My mother made her share of mistakes, but she taught me to respect myself. I can't do that taking your money."

"I could lend you the money, as your friend."

She shook her head. "Why? I can't pay it back."

Staring into her beautiful face, he realized he was hurt. After years of hard work and having a successful career, he was powerless to help the one woman that mattered. He shoved the checkbook back into his pocket, wishing to shove her rejection away. Had he ever felt so helpless? What was a small amount to him was enormous to her. She had him so twisted inside he didn't know what to say to get her to change her mind. But he had to! The consequence of her refusal could be disastrous. Cummingham was a shark. He would win.

He shocked them both when he asked, "Would you take money from your husband?"

She laughed as if he'd told a joke, then said matter-of-factly, "Of course. Everyone knows that married couples share everything."

"Then marry me." His heart pounded in his chest as he waited for her answer.

As if doubting her hearing, she asked, "Did you . . ."

"Yes. I asked you to marry me. If that's what you need to use my money to protect those babies, then let's get on with it. From what you've told me about Cummingham, I agree with you wholeheartedly. He doesn't deserve a place in their lives."

Vanessa wrinkled her pretty little nose when she snapped, "What is your problem, Ralph? People don't marry because one of them is in a jam."

"People marry for all kinds of reasons. You asked for my help. Well, I'm offering in a way that should appease your misplaced pride. Don't be a fool! Take the money."

She crossed her arms, unwittingly drawing his gaze to her lush breasts. His body began to harden with need. For once, sex was not his primary concern. He didn't want to stand back and watch her devastation from losing the twins. Careful not to touch her, he shoved his hands into his jeans pockets.

"You are the one making this a lot bigger than 'misplaced pride.' Why would I want to marry a man I know doesn't want to be saddled with a wife? And certainly not three kids? That's asking for heartache. No thanks!"

"Vanessa, you're forgetting one important consideration. We're friends, as well as lovers. We will both know why we're going into this. Cummingham thinks he's going after a young woman with limited resources. In that case, it's a fight he is assured of winning. Right?"

"Yes! What does that have to do with anything?"

"It's the reason for the suit. He knows he can win. That will change as soon as he learns you are engaged to a man who can more than match his income. He will back off, guaranteed!" Ralph could not believe this crazy discussion. What he hadn't wrapped his mind around was the fact he had actually asked a woman to marry him, and she'd refused.

"You don't know that."

"Sure I do," he said stubbornly, folding his arms over his chest.

Vanessa rolled her eyes. Throwing her hands up in sheer frustration, she hissed, "Are all men so pigheaded, or is it just you? Greg Cummingham is not afraid of you! For all I know he has half the judges in the state in his back pocket. I don't care about what he thinks or feels. All I care about are those two babies asleep upstairs." She paused to catch her breath. "But as much as I love them, I have no intention of ruining your life or mine, in order to play some underhanded trick on Cummingham. Forget it!"

"Cummingham fights to win. He won't back down," Ralph persisted.

"Neither will I. But marriage isn't the answer. I will find a way to fight him, just not tonight. It's late. And I'm tired. Please, do me a favor and go home. I've had enough for one day."

Ralph wasn't ready to leave. If left up to him, he would stay and fight it out. He didn't plan to stop until she quit complaining and took his money. But he could also see by the slump of her shoulders and the quiver of her bottom lip that she had had enough for one night. She was clearly exhausted.

Rather than argue, he dropped his head and kissed the side of her neck, inhaling her sweet feminine scent. "Try not to worry, beautiful. And get some sleep. We'll talk tomorrow. Okay?"

"Yes." She brushed her lips against his jaw. "Good night. And thanks for caring enough to try and help. I really appreciate it."

"'Night." He gave her a gentle squeeze before he walked out the front door. "Lock up. And don't forget the alarm."

"I will, good night." Vanessa closed the door while he waited outside, listening for the sound of the dead bolt, then the beeping of the burglar alarm being activated.

He hurried down the porch stairs, to the sidewalk and to his car. Deep in thought, he started the engine and drove off. But he didn't head home. Instead he drove to Wesley's home. Before he got out of the car, he punched in his attorney,

Russell Morgan's number, on his cell. Russell headed the family-owned Morgan Corporate Law Offices in downtown Detroit. Over the years the two men had become friends. Ralph wasn't concerned by the late hour. Like Ralph, Russell was a bachelor and workaholic. The call didn't take long. Explaining to his oldest cousin what he'd done would take longer.

Despite the fact Wesley was in training, Ralph rang the bell and waited until the porch lights were turned on and front door opened.

"Hey," Ralph said sheepishly. "I know it's late, and you're in training but . . ."

"Come on in." After unlocking and swinging open the decorative wrought-iron screened door, Wesley covered a yawn.

Ralph tried, but couldn't manage a decent excuse for being there, much less his normal easygoing smile. All he could think about was how raw he felt from Vanessa's refusal.

"What's wrong?" Wesley asked as he ran a hand over his unshaven jaw. He wore a pair of worn jeans, his feet were bare, and his close-cut natural needed a brush. None of that mattered. Wes was family. That was all Ralph cared about.

"Everything. I needed to talk." Ralph shoved his hands into his pockets and rocked back and forth from the ball of his feet to his heels.

"Who is it, baby?" Kelli called out from their bedroom, down the hall of the spacious ranch-style home.

"Ralph!"

"Oh. Is something wrong?" Her voice was filled with concern.

Wesley switched on a lamp in the living room. "Make yourself at home. I'll be right back."

"Tell Kelli I'm sorry." Ralph, familiar with the house,

went over to the fireplace and studied the photographs on the mantel. Just then the grandfather clock chimed from the far corner of the room. Midnight.

At the sound of his cousin's footsteps in the hall, Ralph said, "Kaleea is growing so fast. She looks a lot like Kelli in this picture although that chin is all Prescott. She's beautiful, Wes. I hope I didn't wake her."

"Nope, have a seat." He handed Ralph a bottle of beer, then sat in an oversize armchair.

"Thanks." Ralph settled back in the matching chair. "How's that rookie, Bradshaw shaping up?"

Wesley took a swallow of his beer before he answered, "He's coming along. With the new coach, it's looking up. We're going all the way. But that's not why you're here, cuz."

Ralph said what he'd never expected to say, and he was certain Wesley hadn't been prepared to hear. "I proposed to Vanessa tonight." Then quickly clarified, "She turned me down."

Wesley looked stunned for a moment. He asked, "Vanessa Grant? Gavin's secretary?" At his cousin's nod, he asked, "Why?"

"Why did she turn me down?" Ralph quizzed, trying to pretend that just hearing her name wasn't painful.

"No, why did you pop the question?"

"It's complicated." Ralph scowled.

"And," Wesley prompted impatiently, "just because your bed is empty tonight doesn't mean mine is."

Ralph chuckled, stretching his long legs out in front of him. "That's the problem. It's been that way since I got involved with Vanessa. Getting next to her has been as easy as cuddling up with a porcupine."

"Then why bother? I've never known you to let a female complicate your life. The minute things look like they might get complicated, you walk. No, make that run for the closest exit. How come you're not sprinting, little bro?" Wesley quizzed.

"I wish I knew," Ralph mumbled. "Vanessa and I became friends during the planning of Brynne and Devin's wedding. We were thrown together so much that it seemed natural spending so much time together with her. We decided to spend only one night together and became lovers the night Brynne and Devin married. That night changed everything for me. I had no idea I would be her first. To make matters worse, I woke up alone, and she didn't want a thing to do with me. The hell of it was, it wasn't some kind of a game, the lady was dead serious."

"What!" Wesley stared at him in disbelief, as if struggling to take it all in.

"Crazy, isn't it." Ralph could see that his cousin was struggling not to burst out laughing. "Just what I deserve, right?"

"I didn't say that, but I was thinking along those lines." Wesley grinned, then he sobered at the pain in his cousin's eyes. "Rough, huh?"

"Yeah. I've tried damn near everything I could think of to tempt her. Invitations to fly to the Caribbean, or anyplace in the U.S. didn't impress Ms. Grant. I considered sending expensive gifts but knew they'd be returned. Nothing I tried worked. Talk about stubborn! It seems the more she said 'no,' the more I wanted her. She has turned me down so many times." He shook his head in disbelief. Leaning forward, he braced his elbows on his thighs.

"I guess I'm too stupid to give up. Anyway, when she told me she didn't have time to play with me, she has three kids at home waiting to be fed, I realized she was serious. She's a woman with her feet on the ground and her priorities straight. Her family came first with her. Wes, I couldn't help but respect her for it. I admire how hard she works to take care of her brother and sisters. She's not about getting her nails and hair done or pretty clothes. I told her not to worry about food; I'd take care of it. I brought Chinese takeout enough for everyone. That was the first of many dinners I've shared with her and her family."

He laughed, "I know it sounds weird, but getting to know her meant getting to know her family. Now, I'm crazy about those kids, just as I am about her. Everything was going well, until I made the mistake of inviting her and the children to fly down to Orlando with me, in front of the kids. I thought I was helping by offering to pick up the tab."

Wesley laughed. "You really put your foot in it that time."

Ralph didn't waste time defending himself. Wes had gotten it right. He had really messed up. "Nothing like family to tell you the truth," he grumbled.

"If you want someone to lie to you, call one of those silly women you used to date," Wesley quipped.

Ralph ran a hand over his stubbled cheek. "Vanessa is nothing like the women I've dealt with in the past. She won't take a dime from me under any circumstance."

Wesley grinned. "Your problem is you've been around too many females who are after whatever they can get from you. When they look at you, all they see is dollar signs. Vanessa, on the other hand, is her own woman. She's just what you need."

Ralph couldn't help but grin. "Finally, she came to me. We were working things out, until today. She gets a letter from Greg Cummingham's attorney. He's the twins' father and has decided to sue for custody."

Wesley's shot to his feet. "Greg Cummingham, the high-powered attorney, who's defended . . ."

"That's him. Vanessa has been devastated since she got that blasted letter. But she refuses to let me help financially.

She is determined to keep her family together. My lady's a fighter. And if anyone can pull this off, she can."

Ralph began to pace aimlessly around the room. "Wes, it's killing me. When I think of how Cummingham has her hurting, I see red. She's devastated, doesn't know how she is going to pay some high-priced attorney to take her case."

He snapped. "She won't consider even letting me lend her the money. You would think there is something wrong with my money. And it's driving me up a wall. Right now she is probably trying to figure a way to use Lana's college fund and still send Lana to college next year. Man, I've tried everything I could to give her the money, including proposing. It was my last resort. And it didn't work. The only thing she let me do was call Morgan, to get a child-custody lawyer."

"Most women want their man to propose to them out of love," Wesley pointed out.

"Yeah, well some of us don't get that lucky. No, I didn't plan on proposing . . . not ever. But now that it's out there, it makes sense." Ralph glared at his cousin. "You know, desperate situations call for desperate measures. What else could I do? I can't let her lose those kids."

"Tell me something. Are you in love with her?"

Ralph stopped suddenly, one hand braced on a lean hip. "What? This isn't about love."

"Just answer the question."

Thoughtful, Ralph rubbed his jaw, before he shrugged. "I don't know. I'm crazy about her and those kids. Why isn't it enough that I care for her? I care more than I thought I could."

"It's Vanessa's call, not yours. Seems to me that the lady's got her head on straight." Wesley ended with a grin. "She sure has you jumping through hoops."

"Ha-ha-ha," Ralph quipped sarcastically. "Pardon me if I don't laugh." He paused before he said, "What she's doing is driving me up the wall! I don't know what to do to make her see reason. Those twins deserve a lot better than Cummingham."

"All you can do is be there for her. Let her know you care and are in her corner every step of the way. Who knows? She might come around and let you help pay the lawyer's fee. As for marriage, you better make damn sure you are serious. Marriage is not a solution to a problem. And it's not a game. Unless it's about how you feel about each other, it won't work. I'm talking from experience here."

Ralph let out a groan of pure frustration. "You don't understand. I hadn't planned on walking down anybody's aisle. But for the first time, I'm not playing some kind of games with a woman. This isn't about sex, although with Vanessa, it's incredible. I can't get enough of her. It's crazy, I know it. Wes, my only goal is to make sure she has what she needs."

Wes nodded. "Watch your back. Cummingham is not a lightweight. He knows how to fight dirty to get what he wants. Do you know what made him decide he wanted the twins?"

"I have no idea. Rest assured, I won't sit back and let him take the twins and end up breaking Vanessa's heart. No way!"

"And you're willing to risk messing up your own life to protect hers? If that's not love, I don't know what is."

"Who asked you?" Ralph glared at him.

"You did. Now get out." Wes grinned as he stretched his arms over his head and rose to his feet. "I've kept my lady waiting long enough." Then he laughed loudly.

"You are enjoying this entirely too much, big bro." Ralph moved to stand next to Wes, a subtle reminder that while Wes was older, Ralph was three inches taller.

"That's right. Do you recall the night you came to dinner, Dev had stopped in? You told me, Dev, and Kelli how you were never falling in love. Kelli said something about the bigger they are, the harder they fall. And she was talking about you. Wait until I tell her, she was right."

Ralph grumbled, "You're not going to tell her . . ."

"Sure I am. It's the truth." Wesley grinned, folding his arms over his chest.

"It's not true. Do I look stupid?"

"Well, now that you mention it," Wes teased.

Ralph chuckled, shaking his head. "You got it wrong. But I'm not staying to argue." He walked toward the front door. "Thanks for listening." He gripped his cousin's shoulder. "Good night."

As he walked to the car, he couldn't help grinning. If he guessed right, his Aunt Donna and Kelli would be on the phone the next morning, then one of them would call Anna and Brynne, discussing his sorry love life. It was part of being a loving but nosy family. The Prescotts would take some getting used to it, and if he were not careful, Vanessa would be joining their ranks. Talk about being damned if you do and damned if you don't. He was in way over his head, and the only good thing about it was that Ralph was smart enough to know it.

He hadn't planned on marrying at all. But he'd meant what he said. He'd get married in a heartbeat if it was necessary to save the Grant twins from Cummingham.

Seventeen

"Doggone it!" Vanessa glared down at the pattern pieces that she had spread over the dining-room table. "I'm making a mess! I'm not supposed to be making Lana a blouse that has two right sleeves and no left."

It's his fault! It was after midnight, and instead of sleeping, she was sewing.

Although Ralph had called the next morning to give her the name and the number of the child-custody attorney, other than ask about the kids, he hadn't prolonged the conversation. What he'd done was increase her stress level. In addition, he hadn't stopped by for a visit or dinner in four days. Both occurrences were highly unusual.

No matter how many times she went over their last conversation, she didn't recall him being angry or hurt when she turned down his proposal. She tried to push the worry away but failed repeatedly. She couldn't stop wondering if her hasty refusal might have cost her a dear friend.

She'd come to depend on his quiet strength and support, so much so, she'd been unaware of the change. When there was a problem either with her or the children, Ralph was the first person she called. That alone was unsettling. But she also missed him.

Missing Ralph didn't mean she was going to marry him,

so she could spend his money without guilt. Talk about a wild suggestion. It was one she hadn't seen coming. Judging by the way it came up in conversation, it couldn't have been planned. Ralph wasn't a marrying kind of man . . . what he did was love them and leave them. What a mess!

Marriage wasn't the solution. What good could come from marrying for the wrong reasons? Ralph couldn't argue with that. It might explain why he hadn't come around. Was he trying to punish her for saying no? It couldn't be! Could it?

When the telephone rang, Vanessa jumped so she dropped the shears, barely missing her toes. Pressing a hand against her racing heart, she picked up on the second ring.

"Hello?"

"What are you doing?" the deep male voice crooned into her ear.

She couldn't stop the smile or the pleasure he so easily generated. "Nothing important. Why do you ask?"

"Curious. What are you wearing?"

She laughed. "Pajama bottoms and camisole top. Why do you ask?"

He didn't answer, instead he asked, "How do you feel about a late-night guest?"

"It depends on who that guest is," she said in an eager rush. "How soon can you get here?"

His chuckle soothed her earlier worries. "Half a minute. I'm on your front porch."

Vanessa dropped the receiver in her haste to get from the dining room through the living room to the door. Sure enough, his shadow was outlined through the frame of the wrought-iron screen door. She didn't remember flicking on the porch light, disengaging the alarm, and unlocking the doors before yanking them open.

"I didn't expect you," she said as she caught his hand and tried to pull him inside. When he didn't budge, she frowned up at him. "Aren't you coming inside?"

"Can't," he whispered.

"Why?" She sighed, pressing her face to the base of his throat and inhaling his male scent. He smelled of a combination of his favorite aftershave, sweat, and his own special scent, heady.

"I've missed you." He rested his chin against her forehead.

"Why did you stay away? Are you angry with me?" she asked, needing to understand what had gone wrong with them.

"No, if anything, I'm angry with myself for pressuring you when you were already being overwhelmed by Cummingham's demands. You didn't need me adding to it."

"That's why you stayed away?" She pulled back, far enough to see his face.

He nodded. He eased away to reach inside the house to turn off the overhead light. He said, "We don't want your neighbors to see you."

"My neighbors should all be asleep," she insisted, relieved when he wrapped his arms around her again.

"I know it is late, but when I saw the lights on, I couldn't resist. You should be in bed."

"So should you. I don't get it. How could you just be passing by? This is way out of your way."

"Yeah. But since I can't see or talk to you, I had to at least go past the house to make sure you're okay."

Vanessa smiled. "Thank you, but we're fine." Only she missed him terribly.

"You're welcome." He ran a finger down her cheek. "How are you holding up?"

"Fine," she hedged.

"Would you tell me if you weren't fine?"

She smiled. "Probably not."

"Figures. You don't have to be so darn strong, beautiful," he complained, brushing his lips over hers.

"Yes, I do."

"No, you don't. I'm only a phone call away, sweetheart."

"I . . ."

He stopped her before she could say more. "You're not alone tonight." He tightened his arms around her.

She rubbed her cheek against his T-shirt-covered shoulder. "You smell like sweat."

He laughed. "I was playing in a late-night basketball game at the community center."

"Nessa!"

"Excuse me," she turned toward the stairs. "Lana, I'll be up in a minute!" Turning back to him she said, "Ralph, I'm sorry, but . . ."

"I know you've got to go. Call me and let me know when and where."

"Tuesday at three. You'll come with me to see the lawyer?" she asked, trying not to show her eagerness.

"Absolutely." He kissed her tenderly. " 'Night." He began to move toward the door.

" 'Night," she whispered back, wishing he could stay and hold her all night long. But she had more than herself to take into consideration. She had an impressionable teenage sister and little sister and brother to set an example for. They might not even realize it now, but Vanessa knew her actions would impact on the children's lives for years to come.

"Don't forget to set the alarm," he reminded.

"I won't." Vanessa gave him a small wave before she locked up.

"Nessa, where are you?"

"Right here," she said as she mounted the stairs. "Something wrong?" Locking arms with her sister, she walked Lana back into her bedroom. "You should be sleeping."

"I know. I wanted to talk to you about something."

"What's wrong, kiddo?"

"I was talking to Marissa and her cousin Cheryl on the three way. We were talking about colleges. Cheryl goes to Michigan State." They curled up on Lana's bed together. "What do you think about Michigan State?"

"I really don't know that much about it. Why, honey?"

"Marissa wants me to go away to Lansing with her. She's talking about us being roommates. I keep telling her that I'm going to Wayne State, if I get in, but she won't listen." Lana frowned.

Vanessa reached out and squeezed Lana's hand. "Honey, you don't have to stay in Detroit with us. You can go away if you like."

"But it costs so much to live on campus. I keep telling Marissa that, but she doesn't understand. She's got a mother and a father, so she doesn't have to worry about money."

Vanessa hugged her, then said, "If you want to go away to school, we'll find a way. Lana, I don't want you worrying about money or me and the twins."

"I know, but . . ."

"But nothing. We still have plenty of time. We don't have to decide tonight. And you don't have to worry about college right now." Vanessa had decided that for now she wouldn't tell Lana about the letter from the twins' father. She didn't want to upset her.

Vanessa shook Lana playfully. "Stop worrying. I'm going to bed. You can stay up because you don't have school in the morning, but I have to go to work, kiddo. Next time, let's do this in the evening."

Lana laughed. "Okay!"

"Sleep well, baby girl." Vanessa kissed her cheek and gave her a hug.

"'Night, sis. Love you," Lana said as she reached for her bedside lamp.

"I love you, too." Vanessa went in to check on the twins. They were sound asleep in Curtis's room. She covered them both and tiptoed out. She didn't have a problem seeing, since the night-light was on in the upstairs bathroom.

Vanessa went into the dining room to collect her pattern pieces and put everything away. After placing the fruit bowl back in the center of the table, she got ready for bed, doing her best to take her own advice and not worry.

She was still in shock. She had seen Ralph, knew that things were good between them. He wasn't angry over her refusal. He hadn't even brought the subject up. She missed him. She hadn't forgotten that he was a sexy, healthy, good-looking man who was used to an active sex life. And now he was involved with her.

She could count the number of times she'd had sex on one hand. It was a big difference. How long did she have before he became bored with her? She had felt his desire while he'd held her tonight. And he left unsatisfied. There were plenty of women who wouldn't hesitate to invite him to spend the night.

"Enough," she scolded herself aloud. It was late. Pounding her pillow, she closed her eyes, hoping to find solace in sleep.

Although her lids were heavy, her thoughts shifted to the situation with Greg Cummingham. How was she going to pay for this high-priced lawyer? How long could she keep Lana in the dark? And what if things got so desperate that she had to use Lana's college fund to pay for the lawyer? What then?

How could she replace even part of the money intended for Lana's college expenses? Lana wanted to be able to go away to college no matter how much she denied it. Even with the amount of money their father had put aside for her education, it was going to be a tight squeeze getting her through four years of college, especially with today's inflated cost of tuition and fees. There would be dormitory fees, as well as the additional expenses of books, clothes, and food.

A scholarship would help so much. But Vanessa was not going to fool herself. There was a mighty big question mark hanging over their heads. Yes, there was also the possibility that the Mathis college fund might be able to help Vanessa pay for some of Lana's college fees. Unfortunately, there were no guarantees.

No way she could just sit back and let the twins go without a fight. "I have to stop the twins' father," she whispered, wiping impatiently at the tears running down her cheeks. She hated crying, especially when she knew it wouldn't change anything and would, no doubt, give her a headache.

Was Ralph right? Was she letting her pride get in the way, keeping her from doing what was best for her family? Accepting his help certainly didn't feel like the easy way out of a bad situation. But was it right for her? She was running out of time and options.

Naturally, she'd put aside money for all three kids' school clothes. She'd also made some things, but she knew they wanted brand-name clothes. Vanessa compromised, allowing them to pick one special outfit, as long as it wasn't outrageously expensive. Normally, she started saving after Christmas and counted herself blessed that nothing in the house had broken down or needed repair as the year progressed. Nothing could have prepared her for Cummingham's surprise.

The twins would be starting first grade in a few weeks.

They didn't need the added worry that the father they knew nothing about was trying to take them away from her. It was going to be hard enough for them to switch to a new class-room and a new teacher. First grade meant learning to read, write, and do math. Lots of adjustments.

With her lids tightly closed, she remembered the whis-pered promise she'd made to her dying mother. She'd vowed to take care of the babies and Lana. It was a promise she would never break. Greg Cummingham had better get ready because he was going to have a real fight on his hands. She was not backing down.

And she was not going to be alone. She had Ralph on her side. They both accepted that marriage for the wrong reason would ruin their lives. They were lovers but were not in love. Ralph's proposal had been his way of helping. She was not going to let a dream of wearing a beautiful wedding gown cloud her judgment. Not for one minute could she forget that the word "love" hadn't passed his firm, well-shaped lips.

As promised, Ralph was at her side when she walked into Carl Jones's law office. She didn't realized how upset she was until she began to outline what she'd always considered private to a stranger. Mr. Jones's considerate and kind man-ner helped to ease her anxiety and explained why he came so highly recommended. The family-practice attorney spe-cialized in adoption and child-custody cases.

Vanessa didn't realize she was trembling until Ralph took her quivering hand into his own. Her solution to her money problem was simple. The savings that she had been putting aside for emergencies would go first, then her college fund and her 401(k). Lana's college fund would be left untouched until the very end. With any luck, she wouldn't have to ask Lana to make that kind of sacrifice.

She was so relieved when Mr. Jones agreed to take the

case that she could have wept for joy. He was a handsome dignified older man, with a full head of silver hair. He was taking the case as a favor to Ralph. He admired Ralph's skill on the basketball court and his work in the community. He warned them it didn't look good. Cummingham, besides being nationally known for his phenomenal success in the courtroom and being very wealthy, was the twins' biological father.

Cummingham claimed that he'd only recently learned about the twins' existence. That their mother hadn't told him about the pregnancy, and it would come down to Vanessa's word against his. And because he claimed he didn't know about the children, technically he didn't owe back child support.

When Mr. Jones explained his fee, Vanessa nearly fell through the floor. Before she could formulate her apology for wasting his time, Ralph handed him a check. In shock, she simply stared, unable to stop him or push the words out. By the time they left the attorney's office, her head was spinning from details, and her heart was racing with fear.

Once Ralph had helped her into the car and clicked her seat belt, he was smiling when he slid beneath the steering column, and snapped his own seat belt into place. "That wasn't too bad. At least we know that although Cummingham is asking for permanent custody, unsupervised visitation rights, and that his wife was eager to adopt the twins. He's going to have trouble on his hands. Jones has taken the case."

Overwhelmed, Vanessa burst into tears, unable to control the anguish deep inside.

"Beautiful, don't," he whispered as he unsnapped his seat belt and hers so he could pull her close. "It's going to be all right. I promise you. We got the best. Carl Jones knows what he's doing," Ralph soothed, trying to dry her tears.

Vanessa struggled to control the sobs, but nothing seemed to help as all the fears of the last few days bubbled up inside, plus the awareness of what she'd let him do. It was too much, her heart ached.

"I'm so afraid Cummingham is going to win. You heard Mr. Jones. The man clearly has the advantage. He's their biological father. No matter how desperately I wish it were not true. And I still may lose the twins!"

"Shush, sweetheart, we're going to fight him every step of the way. We're not going to just cave in and hand them over because he asked. Hell no," he snarled.

"But there is only so much we can do," she mumbled. "You heard. The only reason he took the case is because he admires you. We're on shaky ground from the start."

"Now you listen to me." He placed a tender kiss against her swollen lids. "Are you listening?"

At this point, all she could do was nod, she was so choked up with emotion. "Cummingham is going to have to prove it to us and the court that he is their father. We're going to delay by demanding a DNA test, not the saliva test but a blood test which will take longer. We can also delay matters by insisting on court-supervised visits. We're going to do everything we can to delay this custody case and make it as difficult for him as possible."

Her tears stopped, and she threw her arms around his neck, pulling his head down to hers. She kissed him saying, "Thank you," over and over.

When he lifted his head, he was scowling. "There is no need for you to thank me. You and the twins are important to me. You're not in this alone. We're a team."

She stared at him through lashes spiked by tears. "I don't want you to think I don't appreciate all you've done for me and my family. I didn't plan on letting you pay Mr. Jones. And when you handed him that check I wanted to stop you, but I couldn't. I finally accepted I had no other options. I will pay you back, every penny."

Judging by his expression, he clearly didn't want her appreciation, which made no sense to her. She was the one left obligated to him. So what if it hurt her pride. The twins were more than worth any personal sacrifice. She kept forgetting this wasn't about her or her relationship with Ralph. Most important, Lana's college fund would remain untouched. Eventually, she'd find a way to pay him back.

"How did you know I don't trust him . . . that I wanted supervised visits?" Vanessa questioned, pushing her financial concerns aside for now.

"After what you told me about the way he disrespected your mother, I don't trust him at all. I don't want the twins left in his care." He surprised her when he said, "I am curious about something. Why didn't you adopt the twins when they were babies? Why the delay? You've taken care of the twins for years without any support from Cummingham."

Vanessa looked away, using a damp tissue to freshen up. "I'm not proud of my reason. I was afraid that if I reminded him of his paternity, he'd change his mind. So I decided to leave it alone. As their legal guardian, I've been able to take care of their needs. That mistake has come back to bite me on the butt."

"There is no point in blaming yourself now. You had no way of knowing he'd change his mind six years later. You okay?"

She smiled. "I am. Thank you, I promise I will pay you back. I'd rather not touch Lana's college fund. But I have some money. I have an emergency fund, my college savings that I've been putting away so I can go back and finish my degree someday. It's not a lot. And then I have my 401(k). And I'm sure if I ask, Gavin might loan me the rest of the money." At his continued silence, she glanced his way. One look told her all she needed to know. He was furious. "What?"

"You'd rather take money from Gavin than me! How do you think that makes me feel?"

"I'm not trying to hurt you. I told you I genuinely appreciate your help. I took the loan from you. I'm just talking it out, trying to figure out how to pay you back as soon as possible."

He stopped her protest with a hard kiss. "It's a loan, beautiful. And it's between the two of us, no one else. I'm not going to ask for it back."

She gasped, shocked, "I can't . . ."

"What I'm saying is the choice is yours. Call it a loan. Or keep it. If you can't handle that, then we will go pick out an engagement ring."

Vanessa closed her mouth so quickly her teeth clicked. "Very funny."

"I'm not joking." After starting the motor and putting the car into gear, he glanced behind him before pulling out into the late-afternoon traffic. He said no more as he headed north on Woodward Avenue.

She had no doubt that he was serious, and it unnerved her. She sat silently, thinking. Why was he making this so complicated? She didn't want to take the money in the first place. Yet she'd done what was best for the entire family. Then she had made the mistake of mentioning Gavin's name.

She didn't want him angry at her. Nor did she plan to follow his lead. She was not keeping his money or getting married. Although she had to admit it was such a relief knowing she didn't have to deal with possible life-altering decisions alone.

Since she'd lost her mother, every decision concerning the children had rested on her shoulders. There were times when she honestly hadn't known the right answer. Often, Vanessa prayed over what to do, then hoped for the best.

Over the years, she'd grown used to making decisions on her own, but she'd never grown to like it.

Many things had changed since Ralph had come into their lives. Clearly, Curtis had bloomed under his guidance. But Curtis wasn't the only family member who had benefited from having a man around. Both Courtney and Lana had gained confidence and enjoyed his attention. The children liked him so much, Vanessa had begun to worry that they were becoming too dependent on him. And now this.

But marriage? There was no point in trying to fool herself. There were a truckload of reasons why her family would benefit if she and Ralph married. And those reasons had nothing to do with his financial success. But the children weren't the only ones who enjoyed spending time with Ralph.

For some time, Vanessa had been reluctant to deal with her growing feelings for him. She not only valued his friendship, she also relished what they'd enjoyed in and out of bed. No matter how hard she tried, she couldn't forget that he was not only gorgeous but an unselfish lover. More important, the two of them enjoyed being together. When she talked, he listened to what she had to say. They also shared the same family values.

She scowled. It was time to get her head out of fantasy land. She needed to concentrate on the facts. Ralph's proposal had nothing to do with love or even the two of them. The goal was to keep her family together. Marriage to him would in Ralph's opinion convince Cummingham that the twins had a powerful backer. Ralph could more than match his income.

Soon she'd have to explain the custody case to the twins. She'd always been as truthful and straightforward with them, without being hurtful. They knew their mother had passed and that their father had never lived with them. They also knew his name and that he was an extremely busy man.

She had no idea why their father had chosen not to be a part of their lives. She simply decided to assure them that they had a family and were wanted and loved. She and Lana were their family, and that had satisfied them.

Vanessa had always believed it was wrong for a couple to marry unless they were deeply in love. Marriage was no picnic under the most favorable circumstances. Cummingham's custody suit and Ralph's proposal hadn't changed her mind.

"Vanessa, which way? How are we going to handle this? Do we need to go now to buy that ring?" he asked, as they approached the expressway. Northwest would take her home, northeast would take them toward an exclusive shopping center.

Without hesitation, she blurted out, "No, please, take me home."

He merely nodded. Vanessa stared at his dark profile. Disturbed by his continued silence, she found herself inquiring, "Are you angry because I think it would be a mistake for us to marry?"

"I'm not angry."

"Then what do you call it? Ralph, you haven't said much of anything to me since we left Mr. Jones's office."

She watched his firm lips tighten. He was angry! He might not be ready to admit it, but it was as clear as the nose on his face. "I don't get it. You aren't making a lot of sense to me, Ralph Prescott. You have been a confirmed bachelor for as long as I've known you. The ladies in your family are on your case about your refusal to settle down. Yet you're spouting out this stuff about marriage like you can't do it fast enough. Why? What happened? Did someone hit you upside your head while your back was turned?"

"Very funny," he sneered.

"I'd like an answer. Something has drastically changed the man we all know and love."

He gave her a sharp glance. "Love?"

"Yeah, I said the L word. I mean it as in the friendship way, not the 'in-love' version. Got it?"

"Got it," he echoed.

"Then please, indulge me and explain."

While not taking his eyes off the road, he let out a frustrated growl. "It's not exactly a secret that you need money to pay the lawyer. Since you've refused my financial help, as a last resort I offered marriage, assuming you have no objections to a husband taking care of his family. Simple."

"There is nothing simple about it when the man in question is you."

"And the woman is you," he finished for her. Then he asked, "Lana should be able to go through her last year in high school without having to worry. She wants to be able to go away to college like her girlfriends."

Vanessa looked shocked. "When did she tell you?"

"A couple of weeks ago. Why?"

"She only told me the other night."

"I'm glad she finally did. It's been worrying her."

Ralph sighed. "Lana's an 'A' student with a bright future. The twins deserve to be happy without fearing they're going to be taken away."

Holding back tears, Vanessa said, "You're right. My family deserved better. Ralph, I can't accept your proposal when I know it is the last thing you want."

"So you're going to insist on paying me back," he said tightly.

"Yes, it's the right thing to do. What I accepted was a loan. And I promise to pay you back, every dime." Vanessa eyed him through the thickness of her lashes.

He didn't speak until he'd parked in front of her house. "Small installment," he clarified.

"Yes, but I don't want you to worry that . . ."

He kissed her. "No more talk of money. I know it's not dark yet, but with the tinted windows, we shouldn't be seen from the street. Let me hold you for a few minutes before we go in. I've missed you."

Vanessa nodded; she was not about to object. She'd missed him, too, missed their intimacy. With her cheek against his chest, she closed her eyes. As she enjoyed his male scent, she was able to admit what she had wisely kept hidden . . . she yearned for his love. Ralph was a special man with a generous heart. He'd not only won her family's respect but hers as well. She hadn't planned to risk her heart. Yet she'd be the happiest woman in the world if she thought his feelings could go deep enough to ensure his fidelity. Unfortunately, with Ralph that was not about to happen.

Eighteen

Laura Murdock's exquisite, high-rise condominium in downtown Detroit overlooked the twinkling lights of the city far below. Everything from the two vibrant green-yellow sofas, facing each other on top of a floral-patterned off-white wool rug. Two Queen Anne armchairs covered in yellow silk damask sat opposite an impressive gold-veined marble fireplace. A large gold-framed mirror above the mantel reflected the pale green washed walls. While the finest cream porcelain lamps with ivory silk lamp shades, trimmed in gold, were placed on elegant glass-topped cream marble end tables. Beauty was everywhere.

Nothing had been overlooked down to the smallest detail in making Laura's home a place of opulence and good taste. No one entering it for the first time would guess that it was the home of someone who had put in years of hard work and determination to transform a poor, orphaned girl into the well-educated, sophisticated woman who hosted the Elegant Five Book Club with exceptional ease and grace. Laura was proud of her accomplishments and made no effort to conceal her humble beginnings.

"More wine, anyone?" She held up the bottle of delicate fruity chardonnay.

The ladies were seated around the pale maple dining

table. The side table was covered with an elaborate array of salads, artichoke-and-chicken salad, berries and walnuts, celery-root-and-shrimp salad, a rice, almond, and bacon salad, orange-and-radish salad, shrimp-and-crabmeat salad. Rounding out the menu was a mixed green salad.

"None for me," Trenna said as she helped herself to more of the mixed green salad before handing the serving dish to Maureen.

"No, thanks," Vanessa said with a smile. "Laura, you go, girl. Everything is delicious, especially the mixed berries salad. Very classy as well as tasty. Love it! Are you sure you didn't sneak Anna in the back door to prepare this elegant spread?"

Laura laughed and playfully snapped her fingers. "Darn! I wish I had thought of it! Well, ladies, if no one wants more, I'll put the coffee on."

"Before you go, I think it's time we faced the painful truth. Our girl, Brynne, has packed up and left. Her home is now in St. Louis. We either need to change our name to the Elegant Four or find a new book club member," Trenna pointed out.

Vanessa frowned. "I hate to admit it, but Trenna is right. We need a new member, but who. Anna and Kelli Prescott might be interested, but both of them are married."

"And I'm not sure if they want to take time away from their two gorgeous husbands for a book club," Maureen surmised. "Besides, we started our group as a single ladies' group. Remember?"

"I don't know about you, ladies, but I don't plan to live my entire life single. The first rich, fine brother who comes along that toots my horn, and I'm running down that aisle," Laura boasted.

"Me too," Trenna put in. "Although he doesn't have to be rich."

"Okay, okay! I propose we stick to one change at a time. I'm sure if we put our heads together, we can come up with a single lady who enjoys reading African-American fiction." Maureen, always the peacemaker, asked, "All in agreement?"

"Yes! I know of someone. She and I are longtime friends. She went to U of D before she moved away to do her graduate work. She's living out of state now, but she plans to move back home to teach at U of D."

"And you're sure she is willing to pick a book of fiction and also read what the others pick?" Vanessa asked.

"Yes, I don't think she will have a problem with that."

"What's her name? And you're sure, she's moving back to Detroit?"

"Jenna Gaines. And she's single. She used to date Scott Hendricks before he went into the NBA," Laura explained.

"Interesting. I'd say let's at least invite her to a meeting after she's moved back," Trenna said.

"I agree," Vanessa chimed in..

"Me too," said Maureen.

Laura said, "Great! It's settled. We'll invite her. Vanessa, help me with dessert, please."

"I'm right behind you." Vanessa began collecting plates. She followed Laura into the pretty green-and-yellow kitchen.

Laura said, "Vanessa, you can put the dishes in the sink. I'll rinse them and put them in the dishwasher later." Laura, having switched on the coffeemaker, lifted the glass dome cover over a three-layer white coconut cake.

"Mm, that looks good," Vanessa said with a smile.

"Thanks. It has lemon-curd filling between the layers. But that's not why I dragged you in here." She turned, one hand on her hip, "What's going on with Ralph? And don't tell me nothing. I saw the expression on your face when Maureen mentioned his speech at some charity dinner."

"Was I that obvious?" Vanessa asked, cupping her warm cheeks.

"Only to me. What's up, girl? Is he still coming around with dinner for the entire Grant family?"

Vanessa laughed. "Oh Laura, he has been my rock. I told you about that horrible mess with Greg Cummingham. Ralph has not only found an excellent child-custody lawyer, but he came to the first meeting with me. He's a wonderful friend."

"Friend? Will you open your pretty brown eyes? The man is more than a friend."

"I know that, but I'd rather not get into that, if you don't mind . . . less complicated."

Laura lifted a brow. "It's fine with me, just as long as you are not trying to fool your own self."

"I'm not! Believe me, I know my back is against the wall." Vanessa sighed. "Just because Ralph asked me to marry me and . . ."

"Marry?" Laura nearly screamed.

"Will you shut up!" Vanessa hissed.

Laura covered her mouth, but her eyes were wide with disbelief. "Now back up! And you better not leave anything out! Go!"

"Did I hear what I thought I heard?" Trenna came into the kitchen with Maureen right behind her. "Did Ralph ask you to marry him?"

"I told you that man was serious months ago," Maureen insisted.

Vanessa put a balled fist on her hip in mock indignation. "Is there anyone in Detroit who does not know my business?"

Laura rolled her eyes. "We're friends. We don't have secrets. So Vanessa, was he serious? Or was he just playing around?"

"No man in his right mind asks that kind of question as a joke," Trenna pointed out.

"Believe me, he was serious. He was so annoyed by my refusal to take his money to pay a lawyer that he insisted if he were my husband I couldn't refuse. So you see, he was only being kind."

"That rich brother can be kind to me any day of the week," Laura teased. "But I would say yes."

"You are so silly." Vanessa laughed, then in somber tones, said, "Seriously, you wouldn't want a pity proposal. No woman would."

"Well, well. It seems our Vanessa wanted a proposal of the serious kind." Trenna gasped, covering her mouth. "You're in love with that man."

Vanessa rushed to defend herself. "Am not! I care about him."

"So you told him no?" Maureen asked.

"Of course I told him no. I had no other choice," Vanessa said quietly.

Laura put a comforting arm around Vanessa's waist. "You wanted to say yes. Didn't you, girl?"

Maureen came up on the other side and put her arm around Vanessa. "It's going to be all right."

Vanessa surprised them all when she revealed, "I would have said yes if I thought he asked because he loved me."

Trenna pushed in until they shared a group hug. "We love you, Nessa. We'll give you the money. Don't worry, we'll do whatever you need doing to keep those babies with you."

Vanessa smiled through her tears. "Thank you. I love you all, too. But, it's settled. I took Ralph's money as a loan. I plan to pay him back as soon as I can."

"I don't know. The brother may be serious." Laura playfully pinched Vanessa's cheek.

"Ouch! Enough about me. We are only halfway through

the book. At the rate we're going, we'll be here until midnight."

"Oh, no, I'm putting you ladies out at ten. I need my beauty sleep," Laura teased, "Maureen, will you bring the coffee. Trenna, if you grab the cups, please. I'll take out the dessert plates and start slicing the cake."

"What do you want me to do?" Vanessa asked.

"Go get Brynne on the telephone. By the time you catch her up on your news, we'll be ready. We'll put her on the speakerphone. And I know she's read the book. Come on, ladies, let's get rolling. We're still the Elegant Five, although I think we should forget the number and call ourselves, the Elegant Ladies Book Club. And if Anna and Kelli want to join, I say, why not. The more the merrier."

"You have too much to say, if you ask me," Trenna put in.

Everyone began to laugh and talk at once.

A few days later, while Vanessa was going through the mail, she paused, to glare at the return address—Greg Cummingham's lawyer. She went into her room and closed her door, then slit the envelope. She was shocked to realize he had managed to stay a step ahead of her. As she studied the hefty check for delinquent child support payments, her heart dropped.

The twins' father was making sure she wouldn't be able to claim that he had neglected the children or that he had ignored them in any way. Cummingham had thought of everything to level the playing field and put his case in the best possible light.

Later that night, as she walked with Ralph down the drive, she pulled the envelope from her skirt pocket and gave it to him.

"What's this?"

"A surprise from Greg Cummingham. It came in today's mail."

"Can't be good," he answered.

"Read it." She waited restlessly as he read the cover letter and studied the check. Before he could comment, she said, "I'm furious. A move designed to make him look good. I would not be surprised if he's got the judge in his pocket."

Ralph shook his head. "Try to sound a bit more positive, honey. This isn't the end of the world. He did what he should have done a long time ago. The twins are his, therefore his responsibility."

"I don't like it, just like I don't like Cummingham." When he put the contents back in the envelope and held it out to her, she held her hands palms up. "I endorsed the back of the check. Keep it."

"Hardly." His scowl was fierce when he snapped, "I know you don't mean what I think you mean."

She nodded. "That's right. I don't want you to be out of so much money. I don't know the final court costs and attorney fees, but it is a hefty start."

He just looked down at her before he said in a cold tone, "Vanessa, that money is for the twins, and that's exactly what it's going to be used for." He curled it into a roll, then put it back into her pocket.

"No, Ralph. This can go toward . . ."

"Don't say it again. Once was more than enough. You and I have an agreement. You will pay me back in small monthly installments. As far as I'm concerned, that hasn't changed." He continued walking toward his car in loose, long strides.

"Wait," she called, hurrying to catch up. "I said wait!" she snapped, catching his arm. She held on. "Why are you acting as if you're angry with me?"

"Damn straight, I'm furious. You think I don't know what

you're doing? You're using Cummingham's money to try to pay me off. And I won't let you get away with it."

Shocked that he swore at her, she missed the underlying hurt beneath the words.

"Of course I'm using Cummingham's money. That's what it's for."

He glared at her. "No! Cummingham is a selfish bastard. And I'm not going to let you use his money to push me out of your life."

"I'm not doing that!"

"That's exactly what you're doing. That money came along right when you needed it the most. You did something you had not planned to do. Taking money from me was the last thing you wanted to do. And don't you dare deny it!"

"I'm not! There is nothing wrong with a strong woman trying to take care of her family."

"There's plenty wrong when you use that money as an excuse to keep me at a distance," he hissed, close to her ear, "The only time I feel close to you, lady, is when I'm inside of you, and you make sure that happens as seldom as possible!"

Confused, Vanessa shook her head in an attempt to sort it all out. Finally, she came back with, "This is about sex? You're not getting enough, Ralph?"

She watched as his hands balled into hard fists, but she felt not even a tiny bit of fear or apprehension. She knew beyond all doubt that Ralph was an honorable man, he would never do anything to hurt her. Didn't he realize the fact that they hardly ever made love was just as painful to her? She didn't need the reminder that she always had kids to consider while the other women in his life were free to welcome him into their beds at any time.

Ralph snapped bitterly, "If that's what you want to think, go right ahead. I can see I'm getting nowhere with this conversation and this relationship. Why are you holding back?

Come on out and admit it? We both know you want out. You can stop searching, beautiful. You want out, you've got it. I won't bother you again. I'm done."

Ralph's long legs moved so swiftly that he was in his car and driving away before she could yell that was not what she wanted.

As hot tears flowed unchecked down her cheeks, Vanessa wasn't aware of the way she crushed the envelope and shoved it back inside her pocket.

The weekend had come and gone as well as part of the next week without a word from Ralph. Vanessa was relieved that at work she didn't have to listen to children complain that Ralph hadn't dropped by. Even her rather awkward explanation to her siblings that he was upset with her, not them, hadn't helped. They took their annoyance out on her.

Vanessa had nearly choked to death while sipping coffee on Friday morning when her baby sister asked what they had done to make him divorce them. While coughing to clear her windpipe, Vanessa had tried to clarify divorce. Then Curtis had cut in to say they didn't want a divorce. They wanted Ralph, and she had to do something to fix it. Still coughing, she looked to Lana for help, but instead of backing Vanessa, Lana had stuck her nose in the air, signaling that she agreed with the twins. They missed Ralph, so she'd needed to apologize.

After a morning of trying to bury herself in enough work to keep her mind off him, Vanessa had nearly decided the kids were right when the telephone rang.

"Mathis Enterprises. May I help you?"

"Nessa, Courtney and Curtis called Ralph on his cell phone. They asked if they could come over to his place to use his pool. He said yes, but only if you said it was okay," Lana told her.

"What!"

"I said the twins . . ."

Vanessa interrupted, "I heard what you said. How did they get his number? And why did you let them call him?"

"Don't be mad at me. I didn't let them do anything. They called while I was fixing lunch."

"I'm sorry, Lana. I'm not angry with you. How did they get his cell?"

"He gave all of us his card in case we needed to reach him, when he first started coming over. I thought you knew," Lana explained.

"I don't remember." Although she grumbled, Vanessa was relieved that the children felt there was someone besides her they could depend on. "So the twins want to use Ralph's pool."

"We all want to go. We haven't seen him in over a week. And since you wouldn't apologize, we had no other choice."

"Whose side are you on?" Vanessa demanded, then thought better of it. It was wrong to put the kids in the middle or expect them to take sides. "Sorry, I shouldn't have said that. Ralph is a friend to the entire family."

Lana whispered, "I'm sorry. Ralph is your boyfriend, and what's going on between you is no one else's business. What should I tell him? Can we go? Oh, I forget he said if its okay with you, he'd pick us up, and then bring us home after dinner. Well?"

Exasperated, Vanessa bit her lip to keep from yelling.

Evidently tired of waiting, Lana urged, "Nessa, can . . ."

"Yes you can go. Be sure and pack an extra set of underthings for the twins and yourself. And take a clean plastic bag to put the wet things in, a comb, brush, hair dryer, and lotion. No running or clowning around the pool area. And make sure you keep an eye on the twins. They get excited around the slide and don't always listen. I'm counting on you, Lana, to be on your best behavior. And remember, Ralph has some very expensive paintings and artifacts in his house. We can't afford to replace so much as a drinking glass. Got it?" Vanessa said, running out of precautions.

"Okay. Ralph said I could invite a girlfriend to come, too. Can I call Marissa?"

"Yes, but make sure her parents understand you will be at Ralph's house. And tell them they can drop her at our place, to save him a trip. I don't want you four wearing out your welcome." Vanessa hoped she had remembered everything. "Oh, Lana, I'll call Ralph to let him know you have my permission. And I will be there as soon as I get off work."

"Nessa, you don't have to come."

"Yes, I do. I can't expect him to take care of four kids on his own. And tell Marissa's mom that I will bring her home after dinner."

"Wait a second, the twins want to talk to you," Lana said, then handed over the telephone.

"Thank you, Nessa," they yelled into the phone.

Vanessa laughed, then said in a firm voice, "You are welcome. And I expect you two to behave yourselves. If I get a bad report from either Lana or Ralph, you're in trouble with me. Got it?"

"We'll be good," Curtis yelled.

"Promise!" Courtney echoed even louder than her brother just in case Vanessa hadn't heard.

"Okay, I'll see you later. Love you."

"Love you, too," all three Grant children chorused.

Vanessa took a few slow steady breaths before she picked up the receiver again. She told herself that there was no cause to be nervous. She already knew he was angry with her. Her call was purely for the children's sake. It had nothing to do with how upset she had been when he'd left in a rage. The famous Prescott charm had been replaced by injured male pride.

It couldn't be anything more. After all, Ralph had grown used to female adoration, used to their giving in to his every wish in the hopes of hanging on to him. Vanessa had her own ideas. If he thought she was going to go along with whatever he decided was best for her and her family, he'd quickly learned she wasn't about to sit back and let him.

The problem was she hadn't expected his reaction. It had been swift and volatile. He'd been so angry, he'd ended it.

Why couldn't he see her decision really didn't have much to do with him? She'd been raised to be independent, to take care of herself. She didn't expect others to solve her problems for her. She borrowed the money against her better judgment. And now that she had the means of taking care of that debt, it seemed like the right thing to do. Unfortunately, their so-called relationship had meant more to her than she realized at the time. But that didn't mean she was prepared to back down.

"Just do it," she muttered, and punched in the numbers from memory.

The telephone rang twice before she heard, "Prescott."

"Hi, Ralph. It's Vanessa." When he remained silent, she rushed ahead, saying "Lana told me that the twins called and invited themselves over. I'm sorry they imposed . . ."

He interrupted, "Vanessa, you don't understand. It's not a problem. I enjoy spending time with Lana and the twins. That hasn't changed. The waterslide is just sitting there. The kids might as well enjoy it. I also invited Kyle and Wayne over. I thought Lana would enjoy having a girlfriend along."

"She told me." With her eyes closed, Vanessa concentrated on the deep timbre of his voice. She missed it. She missed him. Why did he have to be so darn sexy?

"The question is if you trust me to care for them?"

Vanessa gasped, "Of course I trust you to take care of the children. Just as Anna and Gavin and your aunt and uncle trust you to take care of the boys."

"Thank you. I'm picking them up at two and dropping them off around seven, if that's all right with you."

"Two is fine," she said, then rushed on to add, "but it isn't necessary for you to bring them home. I will stop by your place on my way home from work. Four hours of the twins and two giggling teen girls is enough for anyone."

"I don't mind."

"Well, I do. I will be there around five. Bye." Vanessa hung up.

He didn't have to say it. It was clear from his tone that he would rather not see her at all. Even for the short time it would take for her to collect her family.

Nineteen

Ralph tried to kick back, relax, and enjoy the movie playing on the oversize screen in the theater room. Despite the fact he'd just fed them, the kids were happily munching on bags of popcorn. His gaze went to the illuminated wall clock time and time again.

Where was she? Had she changed her mind? Decided he was trustworthy enough to drive the kids home? He swore beneath his breath. He was being unfair but didn't really care. Why was she even bothering to come when she knew he didn't want her here. Well, that wasn't exactly true. He wanted her, and that was the problem. The wanting hadn't eased; in fact, if anything, it had gone from bad to worse.

Maybe Wes was right? Had he fallen in love with her while his back was turned?

If this was love, Devin, Wes, and Uncle Lester were welcome to it. He couldn't remember being more miserable. Naw, this couldn't be what everyone was finding so irresistible. He'd been steamed since he'd left her place. Time and distance hadn't done a thing for him. At the rate he was going, it didn't look as if he would cool down anytime soon.

He'd been surprised when he received the twins' call but glad to hear from them. He was glad to know that they were doing well, and he'd missed them and Lana. He loved all three of them and thought of them as family. Just the thought of anyone breaking up their family unit for any reason made him furious. And he had no doubts that Greg Cummingham's motives were indeed self-centered. Everything connected to that lowlife, as far as he could see, was selfish. Ralph wasn't the kind of man to sit back and let anyone destroy the family Vanessa had worked so hard to keep together.

Even though she was no longer his, and he was furious with her, that didn't mean he had stopped caring about her. Life wasn't that simple. He spent what felt like every minute of every day thinking about her. Talk about a waste of time. Even though he was expecting her to call about the kids, his heart rate had picked up the instant he'd heard her voice, and his body had hardened.

The kids were so engrossed in the movie that they didn't budge when the doorbell rang. Sighing, Ralph headed for the door.

"Hi." He stepped back quickly, making sure her body didn't brush his as she entered. He barely glanced at her, yet he knew she looked beautiful in a short denim skirt that bared a good deal of her incredibly gorgeous long legs and a yellow top that hugged her luscious breasts and warmed her creamy, dark skin. Her thick hair was left to curl past her shoulders.

"The kids are all in the theater room watching the latest *Star Wars* release." He turned, heading back to the theater, expecting her to follow.

"Wait . . ."

He looked back at her from over the width of a shoulder, a frown marring his good looks.

" . . . I mean, since the kids are busy, can we please sit down for a few minutes and talk? How long before it's over?"

He didn't bother to look at his watch. "An hour. But there

is nothing left to talk about. I've said all I intended to say the other night."

"Please, then will you just listen?"

Ralph didn't want her here. He knew his weakness when it came down to this woman, his control was limited. But she deserved his respect and consideration. All he had to do was keep his hands off her.

"This way." He continued down the main hallway, then turned left down a short hall. He opened the door at the end of the hall. The large room had been converted into a home office. Sunlight streamed in from the floor-to-ceiling windows that overlooked the spacious side lawn. Three of the four walls were lined with floor-to-ceiling bookshelves and filled with a variety of books, from fiction to volumes on aviation. The shelves on the short wall displayed basketball trophies, plaques, and a bronzed basketball, as well as his framed team photos, and the team jersey he'd worn when the Lakers had won the NBA championship.

He motioned to the caramel leather chairs in front of his desk and made himself comfortable in the large leather chair behind the oversize mahogany desk.

"Nice." Instead of sitting, she went over to take a closer look at his memorabilia. "Very nice." She studied photos of him with celebrities and politicians. "You have reason to be proud of yourself."

He grunted, wanting nothing more than to get this "talk" over with. Despite the fact she had hurt him as no other woman could, he didn't trust himself to keep his hands off her. He swore beneath his breath, desperate for her just to go, so his need could go back to merely smoldering rather than a raging inferno. Had he ever hurt so damn bad?

"I can't believe it. Why do you hide all these in this room? No one can see . . ."

Frustrated, he prompted, "You didn't come here to talk

basketball." He motioned to the visitor's chair. "Sit. Then say what you need to say." He didn't add, then go, but it was apparent he couldn't wait for her to leave.

As he watched, she took the chair in front of him. He swallowed a groan as she crossed smooth, bare, and perfectly shaped legs. They were so incredibly beautiful, just like she was all over. He shifted, his sex throbbed with need. He was ready for the impossible.

"Well?"

Busy studying her French manicure nails, she was evidently in no hurry to began this oh-so-important discussion, while he could use an ice-cold shower.

"I'm sorry. I really was not trying to get into an argument with you, Ralph. When the check came, I thought of it as a perfect way to start paying the debt I owed you. That was it! I didn't intend to make you angry or to hurt your feelings . . . none of that." She looked at him through the thickness of her lashes, moistening her full rose-tinted bottom lip. "Please, try to understand. Ralph, don't be like this. I hate it when you're angry with me," she ended in a throaty, feminine whisper that left him longing to take away the frown and replace it with a smile.

What was he thinking? She wasn't going to get away with dragging him to his knees, especially when she was in the wrong! No, No, No! Ralph had heard every word while he struggled to hang on to his anger. It was not easy, especially when all he could think about was being inside her. Ralph, lost in thought, was surprised when Vanessa sat down in his lap. He hadn't even seen her move, yet his arm automatically went around her waist.

"What the—" He stopped, then said, "What are you doing?"

"Showing you how much I've missed you. I hate when we fight. No more . . . please." She slid her hands up his chest, to encircle his neck. When she leaned in, pressing her breasts into his hard-muscled chest, and licked his bottom lip, then took it inside her incredibly hot mouth to suckle, he shivered. Releasing a fierce growl of pure need, he tightened his arms around her. Hungry for her, he covered her mouth with his. Suckling her lips, he sponged them again and again.

He barely managed to say, "You are so wrong." Desperate for more, he thrust his tongue inside the sweet cavity to stroke her tongue with his, repeatedly. Her soft moans sent him over the edge. He deepened the kiss even more, suckling her tongue while cupping and squeezing her soft buttocks. The need to breathe forced him to free her mouth.

Amazed by what had just happened, he stared into her sultry dark eyes as he rubbed his thumb over her kiss-swollen lips. He husked, "You would be furious if the situation were reversed."

Vanessa blushed, pressing her face into his neck. She placed soft kisses along the side of his neck and down to the scented hollow at the base of his throat. "So . . ." she crooned, her voice soft and sexy. "But I couldn't help myself." She licked his neck, causing desire to speed along his nerve endings. His shaft was rock hard and throbbing in time to his heart rate. "Are you still angry with me?"

"Yes, but that doesn't stop me from wanting you. This has nothing to do with you being wrong."

She asked sweetly, her beautiful eyes sparkling, "Ralph, have you always been this mule-headed?"

Ralph nearly laughed out loud, then sobered as he recognized that normally he was easygoing. He rarely, if ever, cared enough to become angry with a woman. He didn't believe in giving money to his lady friends. He offered expensive trips and gifts as part of their unspoken agreement. In return, they were happy to please him in bed.

But Vanessa was different. While she had not expected

anything from him, he'd been thrilled to provide whatever she needed. This lending situation had come as a way to ease her worries. And he'd been pleased to do it. The trouble came when she tried to pay him back. He hadn't enjoyed feeling as if he were a bill collector, someone to get rid of as soon as possible. To say he hadn't taken it well was an understatement. He had been hurt, feeling rejected.

"Are you saying I overreacted?" He smiled somewhat sheepishly, placing tender kisses against her soft lips.

Vanessa teased, "Yeah."

Chuckling, he deepened the kiss, then thought better of it. He pulled back. "We better stop. The movie will be over soon." He decided not to push matters and bring up his marriage proposal.

"Okay," she said, sliding off his lap. She asked softly, "Will you get mad if I hand you a check, a small one starting this month?"

He smiled as he rose to his considerable height. He brushed his lips against hers. "If you insist."

"I do." She hugged him tight, wrapping her arms around his lean, taut waist for a few moments, then she took the check out of her skirt, put it into his back jeans pocket, and patted his firm butt.

Grinning, he asked, "How have you been? Have your heard any more from Cummingham?" He didn't bother hiding his concern. He'd been worried, wondering how she'd been handling this all alone, angry with himself for leaving her high and dry yet knowing he had no other choice.

"A phone call suggesting there is more money if I agree to his terms," she said quietly.

"What! He can't be serious."

"Yes. Naturally, I turned it down."

He gave her a tender kiss. "Honey, I'm sorry you have to go through this. It's not fair."

"I know."

"What you doing Sunday?" he asked, folding his arms rather than taking her into them, knowing if he did, he wouldn't let go. He wanted her that badly. A few kisses were not nearly enough.

She shrugged. "The usual. Sunday school with the kids, followed by service, then dinner at home. Why?"

"How about adding dinner with the Prescotts to the day?"

Vanessa looked up into his eyes while smoothing her hand up and down his arm. "Are you sure?"

He blinked in surprise, before he said, "Absolutely."

"Kids, too?"

"Of course. You know how my folks are. The more kids, the better."

"Yes, I'd like to come."

"Good. I'll pick you up at two."

"Vanessa, you didn't have to do all this. German chocolate cake and homemade yeast rolls. From the looks of it, you made both from scratch," Donna exclaimed as she eyed the delicious bounty, before she reached up and hugged the much taller woman. She sent her nephew a sharp look. "Did you tell Vanessa that she had to do all this? Watch yourself." She pointed a finger at him. "We all know that German chocolate is your favorite."

Ralph laughed, his hand resting on Vanessa's shoulder. "Do I look stupid? Of course not, but it didn't do any good. Vanessa has a mind of her own."

Kelli and Anna laughed, exchanged a knowing smile.

Blushing, Vanessa quickly explained, "My mother didn't believe in going empty-handed when invited to someone's house for a meal," while wondering if she was trying too hard to impress Donna.

"She taught you well, dear heart. We're glad to have you. And those twins are so sweet and well behaved. I can't believe how much they've grown." Donna smiled at Lana. "And Ralph tells me that you're starting your senior year in a few weeks. Excited?"

Lana beamed. "I'm excited. And I'm a little nervous."

Donna laughed. "You'll do well. From what I hear, you're an excellent student. Have you decided about college? Where you want to go?"

Vanessa smiled as Ralph reassuringly squeezed her hand. Vanessa relaxed as she listened to them chat. Donna casually displayed warmth and interest that soon had the teen at ease.

She'd always liked the Prescotts because they were genuine and unpretentious, despite their success and wealth. She'd been invited here before, only this time was different. It was different because she was Ralph's date. She found herself wanting them to like her, especially his aunt. It was a little unnerving, but she couldn't help it. She told herself things would be fine as long as she focused on relaxing and being herself.

Soon Curtis, Ralph, Wesley, and Wayne were playing volleyball against Kyle, Gavin, Lana, and Courtney, while Uncle Lester acted as a referee. Anna, Donna, Kelli—with baby Kaleea—and Vanessa were in the kitchen laughing and talking while preparing dinner. The well-organized Donna easily pulled everything together.

Anna prepared sweet potatoes with a brown-sugar-and-walnut topping. Kelli stirred a pot of green beans and diced white potatoes bubbling with a smoked ham bone. Vanessa roasted what seemed like a mountain of diced turnips, carrots, bell peppers, and pearl onions in garlic and olive oil, while Donnie warmed creamed sweet corn on the stove top and marinated racks of prime rib roasted in the oven while

Kaleea napped in the playpen, her thumb in her mouth.

Relieved that there were no pointed questions regarding her relationship with Ralph, Vanessa couldn't say she was surprised that while Anna and Kelli were in the dining room setting the table, Donna said, "Don't worry, dear, I am not going to ask any questions about you and Ralph. But I will say that I like you and think you're good for our Ralph."

Vanessa wasn't sure what to say, so she settled on being honest. "Thank you, Donna. Ralph has been a wonderful friend to me and my family. But I don't want you to think . . ." She stopped because she didn't honestly know how to describe their relationship. Most days they were more friends than lovers. And yes, it was true he had asked her to marry him. But his reason for making that incredibly kind offer wasn't about love.

Donna stopped her by saying, "No, Vanessa. I'm not trying to pry, but I do want you to know I'm pulling for you and Ralph. My nephew is known for his charm. Yet despite the number of women he has dated, he has always been careful not to let any of them get too close. He guards his heart."

She paused, then said, "With you, he's different. If you were my daughter, and we were talking about a known womanizer, I'd tell you to run the other way. But because Ralph's a Prescott, and when the Prescott men fall, they fall hard, I'd say take your time, dear heart, and just be your own sweet self!" Donna squeezed her hand.

Vanessa nodded, then whispered, "Thank you."

Dinner was a lively, noisy affair with lots of teasing all around. There were no awkward moments. Enjoying herself, Vanessa was glad to see that Lana and the twins were laughing at the good-natured teasing.

They were getting ready to leave when Ralph's Uncle gave Vanessa a hug, inviting her to come back anytime. She and the kids were always welcome.

It wasn't until Vanessa and Ralph were alone later that night that she finally asked, "What exactly did you tell your folks about us?"

Instead of answering, he said, "I've been waiting weeks for you to tell me why you chose me to be your lover?"

As they stared into each other's eyes, neither seemed in any hurry to explain. Apparently, they both had secrets and were not ready to share.

"Ralph!"

"Vanessa," he echoed. He surprised her when he leaned down to place a warm, lengthy kiss on her lips.

Instead of pressing for a response, she snuggled close, enjoying his hard strength. Reaching out a hand, she caressed his jawline. "I really enjoyed being with your family. We all had a great time!" After giving him a soft, tender kiss, she whispered, "Thank you for including us."

"You heard my uncle. You're welcome to come back anytime. I assure you, he wasn't being kind. He meant it. And don't think you have to be with me. Uncle Lester and Aunt Donna genuinely care about you and your family."

Vanessa was overwhelmed. The Prescotts had a way of making her feel not only welcomed, but also cared about. Their sincerity and warmth was amazing.

"You have been truly blessed to be part of such a wonderful family."

Ralph nodded. "I feel that way now. It was not always that way. I think I told you some of this before. After my folks died, it took me a long time to accept Donna and Lester's love. I was determined to stay on the outside. I stubbornly held on to the past, telling myself they already had three kids and two of them were boys. There really was no place for me.

"Nothing Lester or Donna said could convince me I belonged." He grinned. ". . . back then I refused to call them aunt and uncle. No matter how much of a pain I was, they never gave up on me. They showed me kindness and love."

"You're too hard on yourself. You were clearly grieving," she reminded softly.

"You know all about that, don't you, beautiful." He kissed her cheek. "Yeah, I was. I was a smart-mouthed kid, who got in trouble mouthing off to a gang member during class. After school instead of waiting for Devin and Wes, I went home alone that day. I was getting my butt kicked when Devin jumped into the fight. We both were pretty bloody, fighting back to back, by the time Wes jumped in.

"We came home pretty beat-up that day, but I learned my lesson. We were family. The Prescotts stick together. Aunt Donna fussed over me just like she did Devin and Wes. When Uncle Lester got home, he got on my case for going off alone. He also got on Devin's case for not sticking with me.

"Wesley was also in trouble for hanging around some girl instead of getting there on time for us to walk together. I think Anna was the only one who got any dessert that night. We were mad because Aunt Donna made peach cobbler."

Vanessa joined in his laughter. Later, as they kissed good night, she couldn't help wondering how long it would be before he was fed up with mere kisses.

He didn't have to say it. He had shown her when they'd last made love that he had a strong sex drive. She'd be a fool if she thought she could keep him without sex. As she closed the door and locked it, she faced the truth. Vanessa really didn't want to lose him.

Twenty

Vanessa knew she was being selfish by putting off telling the twins about the upcoming visits with their father but couldn't seem to help it. At this point, she was grateful for the small victories they'd been granted, the court-supervised visits and the blood test to establish paternity. Nonetheless, she had put off telling the children about any of it until the last possible minute.

Courtney evidently suspected something was wrong because she clung to Vanessa, resting her head against her big sister's arm. Lana looked on from the armchair, worrying her bottom lip. Curtis sat on Vanessa's other side, oblivious to the tension in the air, playing with his collection of small toy cars.

Vanessa was glad that she had tried to answer the twins' questions about their father over the years as honestly as she could without imposing her biased opinions on them.

"What's going on, sis?" Lana asked.

Vanessa forced a smile.

"We need to talk. Courtney and Curtis, do you remember when we talked about your daddy?"

"Greg Cummingham!" Curtis volunteered, excitedly, as if he'd passed a test.

"He lives in a big house in Detroit," Courtney added matter-of-factly.

"He's very busy and can't come to visit," Curtis supplied. Evidently bored, he asked, "Can I go outside and play on the swings?"

"I want to go, too!" Courtney put in.

"Not until we have finished talking. You two are going to the doctor, tomorrow."

"For shots? So we can go back to school, right?" Courtney quizzed.

"Nessa?" Curtis prompted.

"That's right, Curtis. School is going to start in a few weeks. And that's one of the things we have to do to get ready. Everything has to be up-to-date. You're also going to have a blood test, so everyone will know that Greg Cummingham is your dad."

"I don't want to go to the doctor, Nessa. Those shots hurt," Curtis said with a frown.

"I know, but you want to go to school. Everyone has to go to the doctor at some time. Even Lana and I have to go to the doctor sometimes. You know that."

"I bet Ralph don't have to go to no doctor," Curtis insisted.

Vanessa smiled. "Yes, he also has to go."

Courtney nodded. "And then we get to go get ice cream sundaes!"

"That's right," Vanessa agreed, recalling the treat her mother had also used to get her and Lana to cooperate back in the old days. "Only this time, it's going to be different. As soon as the judge says it's okay, you and Curtis will have a chance to go see your dad."

"Judge?" Lana repeated, suddenly sitting up straight, her eyes wide with alarm.

Vanessa nodded, shaking her head in an effort to caution her not to get upset in front of the twins.

"What's a judge?" Curtis and Courtney both asked.

"A very important person who helps us decide on things," Vanessa enthused. "Did you hear? You two are going to go visit your dad." She forced a smile. "In fact, you two are going to see his house. And one day soon, you two can have a sleepover at his house. Won't that be nice?"

Curtis and Courtney looked at her for a long moment, as if they didn't understand what she meant.

Finally, Courtney asked, "Can I take my Raggedy Ann doll?"

"I don't see why not."

"You and Lana gonna sleep over, too?" Curtis wanted to know.

"No, but you're going to have a good time."

"I don't wanna!" Courtney frowned. "Why can't he sleep at our house?"

Vanessa decided that she had put enough on them. Besides that, she didn't know how much more she could say without falling apart. She couldn't let the children see her fears and doubts. It would only make things worse and really scare them.

She smiled. "Well, we don't have to decide now. Why don't you two go out and play on the swings?"

Curtis and Courtney cheered, then jumped up, kissed Vanessa's cheeks. They squealed as they raced each other to the stairs and down to the door and out to the backyard.

Lana waited until she heard the screen door slam. With big angry tears filling her eyes and trembling lips, she snapped, "Nessa! I want to know what's going on! I'm not a baby, so stop treating me like one! And don't tell me some mess about going to visit Greg Cummingham! I know better!"

"I'm sorry, Lana. I put off telling you as long as I could because I didn't want to worry or upset you."

Vanessa opened her arms, and Lana didn't hesitate; she came to her sister and rested her head on her shoulder. Seeking both comfort and assurance as she had when they lost their mother, Lana whispered, "He's trying to take the twins away from us, isn't he?"

Vanessa admitted sadly. "Yes. He's married now. Unfortunately for us, he and his wife have decided they want the twins."

"Well, he can't have them!" she wailed, brokenhearted. "It's been six years!" Fresh tears fell down her pretty brown cheeks. "What can we do to stop them?"

"Fight! We have a good lawyer. Ralph helped me find him. Mr. Jones, our lawyer, is taking this case as a favor to Ralph." Vanessa wiped away her sister's tears and kissed her cheek. "We're not going to sit back and let Cummingham win."

"I'm glad you told Ralph. I knew he would help. Does Mr. Jones think we have a good case?"

Although she was tempted to lie, she couldn't. Vanessa shook her head no. "He warned me that there is no getting around the fact that Greg is the twins' father. The blood test will prove it. That doesn't mean we are going to hand them over because he decided he wants to play daddy," she snapped.

"What are we using for money? We can't afford a lawyer." Before Vanessa could answer, Lana offered, "We can use my college fund. I can always work my way through college. Lots of kids do."

"I appreciate your offer. It's so sweet of you." Vanessa gave her a tight hug and kissed her cheek. "For a while, I thought I might have to do it, once my savings were gone. But I didn't want to do it unless there was no other option.

Ralph offered to loan the money. I didn't want to accept it from him, especially when I found what it would cost. But I did because I had no other choice. Then we got a hefty check of back child support payment from Cummingham."

"It will cover it?"

Vanessa smiled. "Cummingham, in a sense, is paying for both lawyers. I'd much rather put it away for the twins' education." Vanessa smoothed Lana's bangs. "Try not to worry."

Lana shrugged, wiping away a tear. "Can't help it."

"That's where our faith comes in. We have to think positive. No negative thoughts allowed. Remember, we have to be strong for the babies. They're going to need us like never before. Soon the court-ordered visits are going to start. First, it will be with a social worker present, but after that, the twins will be going alone and will stay the entire weekend with the Cumminghams."

"What does that mean? Why can't we go with them? We don't know those people," Lana insisted.

"I know. And we are going to fight them for as long as we can. But, for the twins' sake, we're going to act as if nothing is wrong. It's going to be difficult, especially when we also have to make sure they don't believe that we are abandoning them to strangers. It's going to seem like balancing on a high wire."

Lana whispered, "I hate this!" as a fresh bout of tears filled her eyes.

"Come on, honey. You've got to stop! We don't want the twins to come back and see us crying. If you keep this up, I will be crying, too. And it will only make it harder for them. We don't want to scare them."

Lana sniffed. "I'm sorry, but I can't help it."

Just then, they heard the door slam and stamping feet.

Then Courtney, yelling "I'm going to tell!"

Lana took off, running up to her room.

"Nessa, Curtis Grant is mean!" Courtney posed with hands on her nonexistent hips. Then she jumped in her sister's lap. "Why couldn't he be a girl? Boys are so stupid!" She wrapped her arms around her sister's waist and put her head on her shoulder.

Vanessa kissed her forehead, saying, "Really, I like having a brother. He's so good at finding spiders and taking them outside."

Courtney sighed heavily as she gave it some thought. "I suppose, but he won't take turns pushing. I pushed him three times." She held up three fingers for emphasis.

Vanessa could not help smiling. "I thought that's what big sisters are for."

Courtney studied her eyes as Vanessa said, "Big sisters, like me, love to push. Would you like a giant push?"

"Only me?" Courtney asked hopefully.

"Four huge pushes," Vanessa volunteered.

"Okay!" Courtney jumped up all smiles. Grabbing Vanessa's hand, she urged, "Hurry!"

Vanessa smiled, following her sister outside. If only all her problems were that easy to resolve. She tried to concentrate on enjoying the twins and the lovely summer evening. She was relieved when Lana came out and joined in a game of hide-and-seek. When the mosquitoes came out, the twins curled up on the porch swing with their sisters and listened while Vanessa and Lana took turns reading the last Harry Potter book. It wasn't until the house was quiet, the children asleep, that Vanessa was able to let go and allow her own tears to dampen her pillow.

Even though she'd thought she was prepared for Lana's heartache and tears, she was not. It had been worse than she had anticipated. Her little sister had been crushed, and knowing there was nothing she could say or do to help made it devastating. And this in a sense was only the beginning. They had weeks of uncertainty ahead, with no assurance they would win. Talk about pain. She hated it. Hated what it was doing to their family.

It was close to midnight when the bedside telephone rang. She didn't have to check caller ID to know who was on the other end of the line. She sniffed, nose running, before she picked up the telephone. "Hi, can you hold a second?"

"For you, anything." He spoke in that deep, seductive tone she found impossible to resist.

Hurrying into the bathroom, she blew her nose and bathed her swollen lids with a cool, damp cloth. She raced back to the telephone, somewhat breathless, and said, "How was your meeting?"

"It went well. It's not me I'm concerned about. Tell me what's got you so upset, beautiful."

She smiled, realizing he knew her a little too well if he could gauge her mood from the tone of her voice. "Am I that obvious?"

"To me, absolutely. Start talking, or would you rather I came over there?"

The concern in his voice made her heart pulse from the pleasure. "I wish," she let slip. Then hastily, she said, "I wouldn't ask that of you. You've had a long, busy day. Two meetings downtown. Then you worked on campus the rest of the day. Then you went and volunteered at the community center. That doesn't count the work waiting on your desk at home. You have to be beat. You don't need me crying on your shoulder."

"I'm on my way!"

"No! Honey, please don't. I'm fine really!"

"You didn't sound fine when you picked up the phone. Tell me."

She released an embarrassed sigh. "I was feeling sorry for myself and got a little weepy. That's all."

He sounded doubtful when he asked, "Are you sure you don't need me?"

She released a little laugh. She'd like nothing more than to have his arms around her about now, but she wouldn't ask him to drive across town just to hold her. She wasn't that weak. Nor was she that selfish.

"I am fine . . . truly. As you know, I've been putting off telling the kids what's going on. Well, I told them. Naturally, I gave the twins the limited version of what was going on. Of course, Lana read between the lines, and, like me, she was very upset and took it hard." She ended on a sad little sigh.

"That is understandable. She recognized the threat to your family."

"Then we couldn't really talk it all out with the twins running around. It wasn't until they were asleep that I could spend time with her and hopefully relieve some of the worry. I hate this. And I will be so glad when it's over," she confessed.

"I know. You don't want Lana hurting, but there isn't much you can say or do to make it better. I feel that way about you."

She smiled. "You are awfully good at this, Ralph Prescott. No wonder women find you so charming."

He made an impatient sound. "Very funny, Nessa."

"I wasn't joking. I'm serious. Women do find you irresistible." She frowned, wishing she hadn't voiced the thought.

"Don't start trying to find reasons to push me away. We were talking about you and Lana." His voice oozed exasperation. "So how is she now?"

"She cried herself to sleep. I'm hoping it helped."

"That I don't understand. How can crying make you feel better?"

Vanessa laughed. "You mean, there is something you haven't figured out about the female of the species?"

"That's what I said," he said impatiently. "Why are you trying to pick a fight?"

"I'm not!" Then she frowned, wondering if he might be right. He had his pick of the most beautiful ladies in the city. Sometimes her doubts about herself caused her to wonder why he'd picked her. She was no great beauty. She couldn't afford expensive clothes or to have her hair and nails done professionally. How long before he became bored with her?

"You'd rather fight than tell me what you were crying about when I called." He sighed. "The kids depend on you. They know they can count on you to be there for them. I want to be that person for you . . . the one you, beautiful lady, can count on."

"You don't ask for much, do you?" she said as she released a weary sound. "Ralph, give me some slack. It's after midnight, and I'm exhausted. "

He growled something that she didn't catch. "What did you say?"

"Nothing important," he grumbled.

"So repeat what you said."

"I will, right after you respond to the 'count on me' comment."

"Ralph, I do count on you." Maybe too much, she didn't add. After all, she was afraid of repeating her mother's mistakes . . . growing to depend on a man and caring too much. Did she dare trust him with her heart?

"Okay, beautiful. I know you think I'm pushing, but I'm not. Well, I don't mean to pressure you. I know you have a lot going on right now, but . . ."

She waited a few moments for him to finish. When he didn't, she prompted, " . . . but?"

"I can't help how I feel about you. I'm falling in love with you, Vanessa Grant."

Vanessa covered her mouth to hold in a scream and nearly strangled herself by the sharp intake of air that turned into a coughing fit. When she could finally speak, she blurted out, "Ralph, you can't mean that!"

He snarled, "So now you are going to tell me how I feel? Give me some credit. It isn't something I planned. It just happened."

With her hands curled into fists from fear and doubts, Vanessa bit her tongue to keep from yelling. She couldn't handle his kind of love. How long would it last? A month . . . two, until the next beauty caught his eye? She couldn't believe, not without leaving herself wide open to hurt and pain. No, she couldn't risk it. Maybe if she had only herself to think of. But she had kids depending on her to make the right decisions. No, she had to be careful.

"I really thought we had gotten past the lines, Ralph. Now you tell me this! Why?"

"What did you say?"

"Oh, you heard me. Loud and clear." She glared at the telephone.

Evidently he heard the frustration in her voice. "This is no line, Vanessa. And it's clear your defenses are firmly in place tonight. You're doing your level best to push me away. It's not working."

"It was worth the effort. We both know I couldn't push you if I tried. You're too big!" She forced out a laugh, struggling to make light of it. What a mess.

"Believe it! I am too stubborn to give up and run the other way, gorgeous."

She didn't add he wasn't that stubborn. And she was not blind. She was the flavor of the moment. The minute he had enough he would be gone . . . ready to move on to the next gorgeous challenge. For a while she'd had her head in fantasy land. No more. It was time to deal with the unvarnished truth. Yes, she cared about him, but she was not about to let him know just how deep her feelings went.

"I know it's an effort to keep all the names straight, but mine is Vanessa, not gorgeous. I have my feet planted on God's green earth. No games."

"Thanks for clearing that up for me. Are you done?"

"Yeah," she said tiredly, all the fight having gone out of her. "I need my friend back, badly." She couldn't handle the demanding lover. "Please, don't be angry."

"I'm not." He sighed. "Dinner tomorrow? Do you want to eat in or out?" he said matter-of-factly.

"Out. Can we come by your place? Please."

"The kids need a distraction?" he said quietly.

"Something like that. You don't mind?" She pushed her hair out of her face, too tired to even put it in a braid.

"Nope. I'm looking forward to it."

"Thanks, Ralph. I'll bring the food."

"Not necessary. I'll take a slab of Corky's Ribs out of the freezer."

"What can I bring?"

"You and that new red swimsuit," he teased.

She giggled. "You, Ralph Prescott, are so wrong."

Chuckling, he said, "Glad you noticed. See you around six."

"Okay. And thanks again," she murmured sleepily. "Good night." As long as they both knew where they stood in this so-called relationship, no one would end up hurt when it was over.

Ralph was swearing as he hung up the phone. He told himself he had every right to be ticked, every reason to walk and never look back. Vanessa had managed to hurt him as no other woman had ever come close to doing. And he'd lay odds that she'd done it without realizing what she was doing.

In her attempt to remain up front and honest, his lovely lady had not intended to hurt him, that wasn't her way. Nonetheless, he was left reeling as if he had received a sucker punch to the gut.

He released a litany of swearwords that unfortunately for him didn't do a thing toward easing his heartache. Why wasn't there a law against falling in love?

"As bad as it hurts, it should be illegal," he grumbled aloud. Now she had him talking to himself!

Yet despite his increasing frustration, he couldn't remain angry with her.

What would be the point? She was not trying to hurt him. She was merely stating what she believed to be fact. And she was right, there were plenty of disgruntled females willing to swear on a stack of Bibles that he had taken advantage of them. Even though he knew he'd only taken what had been freely given. Women had the most annoying habit of sticking together.

When had telling your woman how you feel about her become a line? And why didn't she believe him? Throwing his past in his face didn't change how he felt about her. Maybe he was better off this way? Seeing her wearing his ring would be the same as having one through the nose. He didn't need the hassle of her doubting his every word.

It hadn't hurt when he'd been playing around. He had never lied to any of the women. He hadn't cared enough. There was no doubt that this love thing was kicking his behind.

With Vanessa, it was different because he was different. There had been no room for pretence. She was real. And she faced real challenges each and every day, just to survive and do her best for her family. She took her role as single parent and caregiver seriously. From day one, he had respected this very special lady . . . his lady.

"I wish," Ralph grumbled out loud.

He couldn't even blame her for doubting him. He hadn't planned to tell her at all. Tonight, the words had slipped out. And there was nothing to be done about it now but deal with it.

Well, he had to hand it to her. She'd done an exceptional job of protecting herself. It was a pity he hadn't used a little common sense and done the same. Instead he was running around, like the walking wounded. Why didn't he just go and stamp "fool" on his forehead and be done with it. He could almost hear Devin laughing his head off, and Gavin would be right beside him. By now Wes had also figured it out! And Kelli had warned him to watch his step. A fat lot of good it had done. Oh no, he'd gone and done exactly what she had predicted . . . fallen like a ton of bricks.

Ralph went to his den to the liquor cabinet, where he kept the hard stuff. He poured, then downed a squat glass of Jack Daniel's. Even as he felt the burn all the way down, he knew it wouldn't be enough to forget. He could kill the whole bottle and nothing would change. He was falling in love with Vanessa Grant. Even though it scared the hell out of him, he could not walk away. He was in for the duration.

Twenty-one

After yet another restless night, Vanessa knew she did not look her best when they arrived at Ralph's. The kids were glad to see him and didn't bother to hide the fact. Although she'd tried, she hadn't been able to dismiss his vow of love. What if she was wrong? But what if love meant a lifetime for him the way it did for her? No, she just couldn't risk it. And what made matters worse, Ralph had no idea that she secretly longed for the real thing. How had he managed to hit on her weakness?

It made her realize that in this sense, she was no different from the others he'd dated in the past. She cared for him, and because of that discovery, she was vulnerable to him in ways she was only just beginning to comprehend.

Even though she was thoroughly confused by his revelation, when Ralph gave her a hug instead of quickly moving away, she indulged herself. For a long moment, she clung to him with eyes closed, inhaling his clean, male scent, then she pulled back much sooner than she would have liked. Spotting the question in his dark eyes, she gave him a quick, reassuring smile.

She was emotional and knew if he offered even a hint of sympathy, she would break down, and it wouldn't be pretty. Hooking her arm through his and much to the twins' delight, she challenged him to a race across the pool. It wasn't until they were preparing to leave, while the kids had gone off to collect their things, that Vanessa had a moment to speak to him privately. She reached up and brushed her lips over his. "I can't thank you enough for . . ." she stopped abruptly, then asked, "Ralph, why are you scowling?"

He gave her a hard, kiss, then complained, "I hate that you feel you have to always thank me for every little thing. Enough already! So, tell me, how are you really doing?"

She sighed, unconsciously stroking his chest. "I'm holding it together, but only by a thread. I've been a mess since I told the kids about Cummingham. Somehow the telling only seemed to make it more of a threat. I know it sounds weird. But, it's how I feel. I can't bear the thought of losing them. Ralph, they are only babies. They aren't going to understand, no matter how hard I try to explain it to them." Eyes filled with tears, she said, "If we lose this case, what am I going to say to them? They are going to feel as if I let them down!"

He ran a soothing hand over her shoulders. "I know you're scared, beautiful. I've been wracking my brain trying to find a solution. Cummingham may be their natural father, but he hasn't been the one loving and taking care of them for the past six years. It's not fair!"

She blinked to keep the tears from falling while relishing the comfort of his strong arms. "I can't even tell you how badly I'm dreading tomorrow. No matter what I do or say, it won't change the truth. Curtis and Courtney are going to meet their father. Good or bad, Cummingham is going to be a part of their lives. And I have no choice but to accept it?"

He kissed her tenderly. "Is there anything you need me to do to help you through this?"

Tired, she shook her head, running a caressing hand over his hair-roughened jaw. "If only you could make it all go away. I know, I'm being ridiculous. We can't run from our problems. Maybe it would help if I could understand what changed his mind?"

She heard her family coming and took a quick step back, so glad she hadn't given in to the urge to let it all out. The last thing the kids needed to see was her weeping all over Ralph.

He gave her a tender kiss. "Try to get some sleep tonight. You're exhausted."

Vanessa whispered, "I'll try."

"Good. I don't want you up all night worrying. If you need to talk, call me. It doesn't matter how late it is. Promise?"

"Promise."

The twins were up early on Saturday morning. For once they were not arguing over the cartoons they wanted to see. Vanessa was also up. After breakfast, she and Lana helped the twins get ready for their first visit with their father.

While Vanessa was combing Courtney's hair, she realized she hadn't done as well as she thought when preparing the twins. Courtney, dressed in a pretty yellow-and-white sundress, asked why she and Lana weren't also getting ready.

Vanessa explained, "Honey, only you and Curtis are going to visit. Lana and I will be at home, waiting for you and your brother to come back."

Curtis, who until then had patiently waited for Lana to finish brushing his hair, shook his head. "But we want you and Lana to come, too." He was dressed in dark blue pants and a pale yellow shirt.

"I know, but you and Courtney are going to have so much fun that you won't even miss us!" Vanessa encouraged as she finished tying yellow ribbons on Courtney's ponytails.

Her baby sister pouted, saying, "You have to come, Nessa. What if I can't find the bathroom? Or Curtis gets in trouble for not listening?"

"You have nothing to worry about. A nice lady will be going with you. You can tell her or your dad what you need." Vanessa kissed her cheek, trying to ease her fears. "Besides, Curtis isn't going to get in trouble, are you, sweetie?"

"I'm going to be a big boy!" he huffed indignantly. Then he asked, "Is it going to be like school? Lots of kids?"

"No, not like school. You're going to visit your dad and see where he lives," Vanessa said as she smoothed her baby sister's dress that was edged with a white, eyelet ruffle. "You look so pretty, baby girl. And Curtis, you are so handsome." She didn't dare kiss him, making an effort to honor his desire not to be treated like a baby.

Courtney's bottom lip quivered as she asked, her large velvet brown eyes filled with tears, "What if we don't like our dad? Do we have to stay? I don't want to sleep at his house?"

Curtis frowned, tears also in his dark eyes. "I don't want to sleep at his house, either!"

"Now, hush, both of you." Vanessa held one on either side of her. "There is nothing to worry about. You're both going to sleep in your own beds and your own rooms. Just like always. You're only going for a visit. Right, Lana?"

"Right," Lana echoed, struggling not to give in to her tears.

"Promise, Nessa?" both twins asked, looking at her hopefully.

"Promise. Lana and I will be here waiting for you to get back. Later, we can pop popcorn and read your favorite storybook. Okay?"

Curtis and Courtney nodded. Vanessa's heart was aching because she knew that in the not-so-distant future, the twins would indeed be spending entire weekends with the Cumminghams.

"Everything is going to be fine," she soothed softly.

"Courtney, do you have your bag ready? Curtis, do you?" Vanessa had had both of them pack a few toys in a small tote bag.

"Yeah. I have my coloring book, crayons, and four of my favorite cars," Curtis volunteered.

Courtney smiled. "I have my bear puzzle, my Cabbage Patch doll, her outfit and little brush, and my coloring book."

"Sounds like you're ready," Lana offered with forced cheer. "When you get back, you can tell us about your visit."

"Maybe he has a swing set?" Curtis said, hopefully.

"Or a pool, like Ralph?" Courtney offered.

"I heard something." Curtis ran to the front door to peer out. "It's Ralph!"

"No running," Vanessa called, as the twins raced out. She turned to her sister and gave her a quick hug. "I'm proud of you."

"I didn't realize it would be this hard. I keep telling myself it's only for a few hours, but it's not helping much," Lana said softly, clinging to Vanessa's hand.

"I know what you mean." Just then Ralph came in, carrying a giggling twin under each arm.

"Look what I found on the front porch. Should I put them back or keep them?" he teased, playfully jostling each of them.

"Keep us!" the twins called out between giggles.

Vanessa and Lana joined in the laughter, something they all needed, badly. "Let Ralph catch his breath," Vanessa said.

"Want to see what's in my bag?" Curtis didn't wait for a response but took off to get his bag.

"No, he wants to see mine!" Courtney was right behind him, running up the stairs.

Ralph put a reassuring arm around the two sisters. "How are you two holding up?"

"I was just telling Nessa, it's a lot harder than I expected. Do we have to do this?"

"I'm afraid so." He kissed Lana's forehead and gently squeezed Vanessa's hand, and whispered, "Here they come. Smile."

The twins took turns showing Ralph what was in their tote bags. Just then, they heard a car stop in front of the house. They all went out to wait on the porch as a young woman made her way up the walk to the porch.

"Hello. Ms. Vanessa Grant?" At Vanessa's nod, the woman offered her hand.

"Jacqueline Henry, social worker. I'm here to accompany Courtney and Curtis to their visit with the Cumminghams." She handed Vanessa a letter from the court, then she smiled at Ralph. "Hello, Ralph. How have you been?"

"Hi, Jackee. Haven't seen you in quite some time."

Although annoyed by the exchange, Vanessa forced herself to focus on the legal documents. The social worker went on to say, "And this must be the twins."

Vanessa passed the documents to Ralph, then introduced her family. When Ralph looked up from the documents, he said, close to Vanessa's ear, so he wouldn't be overheard, "It looks as if everything is in order."

Just then a limousine pulled into the driveway and a uniformed chauffeur got out and made his way to where they where standing.

"Mr. Cummingham sent his car." The pretty social worker seemed to be having a difficult time taking her eyes off Ralph.

Vanessa told herself it was none of her business. Besides, the twins were leaving, accompanied by strangers. Somehow the sisters managed to hold it together, smiling as they waved good-bye and watched the sleek car disappear into traffic.

Ralph did his best to cheer them up. He talked them into going to lunch and a movie at the mall, all the while reassuring them that the Cumminghams were taking good care of the twins. And they had not won the war.

Although Vanessa had plenty of questions about him and the attractive social worker, she didn't voice any of them. She had enough to deal with by merely remaining calm for Lana's sake. And not falling apart, the way she longed to do.

It wasn't until the twins were back at home that the three were able to relax. Apparently, Curtis and Courtney were more impressed with the mountain of toys waiting for them than with their new daddy and stepmother.

Vanessa was proud that she managed not to vent her feelings until the twins were tucked in for the night and Lana was in her room, chatting on the telephone. She embarrassed herself when she joined Ralph on the screened-in porch; tears of frustration and anger she'd held in all day filled her eyes and spilled down her cheeks.

"I can't believe that man! He's not fooling anyone. He's trying to buy the twins' love. What's he going to do next? Take them to Disneyland?"

Before he could respond, she rushed ahead with, "He's just plain wrong! That hateful man has never even wanted to see those babies . . . now suddenly he's suing for custody. And all I can do is delay the inevitable for as long as possible. It stinks!"

Ralph tenderly encircled her waist, pulling her down to sit with him. "Calm down, beautiful. It's not over. He hasn't won, yet."

"Maybe." She impatiently wiped at her tears. "All I know is it's only a matter of time before he hires a nanny to take care of them until they are old enough for him to send off to boarding school." She was practically screaming, and as she paused to catch her breath, her hands balled into fists.

Moving a stroking hand up and down her bare arm, he soothed, "Hush, love. If you don't calm down, you're going to make yourself sick."

Vanessa nodded, accepting a fresh tissue, "I . . . you're . . . right . . . but I'm so mad . . ."

She let out a gush of hot air. "It's just so hard to keep it all together, hiding my feelings from the kids." Leaning against him, she concentrated on simply taking slow, deep breaths. "I'm a mess. I'm sorry. I can't believe I keep coming apart in front of you."

He kissed her forehead, holding on to her. "Stop apologizing. You have good reason to be upset. Unfortunately, today is just the beginning of these visits." He swore his own frustration, then apologized. "I hate this. You can't help but feel so helpless. You have to keep reminding yourself that you have a good lawyer. Jones knows what he's doing." Ralph paused, his heart picking up speed as he wondered what her reaction would be to his announcement. Finally, he revealed, "Like you, I've been feeling helpless to protect you and the twins. So, I decided to do what I hope will prove to be helpful."

"What exactly did you do?" She tilted her head back so she could study his features.

"I hired a private investigator. Mack Webber is a retired cop. He's a good man, more important, he is thorough. If there is something to find, Webber will find it."

He caressed her cheek. "I've shocked you. Nothing to say? That I don't believe."

Vanessa smiled. "I don't know. But if you think it will help, it's worth a try. Can I afford it?" He cocked his brow, and she let out a giggle. "I know, at this point it doesn't matter."

"That's right." He leaned down until he could brush his mouth over hers. "It's getting late. I should go, but before I do, tell me why you haven't asked a single question about Jackee."

"The pretty social worker, petite and tiny. Just like you like them." Vanessa would have moved away, but Ralph held her in place. She demanded. "Let go."

"In a minute. Jackee is a friend. We dated a few times, nothing came of it. I hadn't seen her in a couple of years. Any other questions?" Ralph held his breath.

"No," Vanessa merely looked at him, no smile, nothing to show if she was secretly relieved. It wasn't as if she didn't know about his past. Did she hate being reminded of how long his list was? Or maybe she didn't care, period? That thought left him ice-cold with a combination of dread and fear.

"What do you mean, no?" he demanded to know.

"Just what I said. Ralph, I trust you." Her eyes locked with his.

"Since when?" he whispered, as longing entered the mix.

He wanted her so bad he hurt from it, but it wasn't just desire. If this was what Wesley and Devin experienced, then he finally got it. He understood why they could not walk away. The need to be with and protect her was stronger than anything else in his life. The need was that powerful. And it was not going away. If anything, it grew stronger with each passing day. All he could do was hang on.

Vanessa did laugh then. "I don't know. You're different with me. You've been my rock. But if you're sneaking around, you're hiding it well." She stroked his cheek, teasing. "Why are you frowning, boo?"

A crease drew his black brows together, "Was that supposed to be a compliment?" He firmly set her away from him and rose to his feet, highly insulted. Did she have any idea what she was doing to him? How she was turning him inside out? His instincts told him to fight this madness in any way he possibly could. His wayward heart was not cooperating. And that back-handed compliment felt like a slap on the face.

"Sorta. What did you expect?"

"If you don't know, I'm not going to waste time telling you, Ms. Grant."

Vanessa raced to the front door and barely managed to get there ahead of him. When he encircled her waist, preparing to lift her out of his way, she threw her arms around his neck and pressed her breasts against his chest and her lips against the base of his throat.

"Don't be angry. I didn't mean to hurt your feelings. Why are you so sensitive all of a sudden?"

"Sensitive? You better believe I'm angry! Doubting my honesty is an insult! How would you like it if I accused you of cheating with another man?"

"I wouldn't like it. But, sweet man, I never said you cheated," she insisted, moving her hands soothingly over his back.

"What do you think not believing I love you meant, Vanessa Grant?" he snapped, struggling to hold on to his anger and not let her softness seduce him.

"It means you're a well-known womanizer, and I would be not only blind, but stupid and dumb if I ever forgot it. But that doesn't mean I don't care about you. Nor does it mean I think you are 'playing' around with women behind my back. For one thing, I can't see how you would have the time, considering your work schedule, family, and volunteer work. But most important," she said as she moved the hot, soft velvet of her tongue over his throat. "Our lovemaking has been limited because of me, not you. You are a highly sexual, intense lover, Ralph Prescott. I've given you a lot less loving than you no doubt are used to or need. And I hate it.

I hate that my problems with my family keep getting in the way. It's not fair to you, sweet man." She kissed him, taking his bottom lip into her mouth to suck, causing hot prickles of desire to speed through his nervous system.

He closed his eyes as her soft fingers stroked the back of his neck. She released his lips, but before he could collect himself, so he could stop feeling and start thinking, she began to tongue the highly sensitive place behind his ear that caused him to groan deep in his throat.

"Sweet man, it has been too long for you." As she slowly rubbed her incredibly full breasts against his chest, he wondered why he was fighting with her. She was where he needed her to be, and that was all that mattered. He wrapped his arms around her.

Kissing her soft mouth, he asked, "Is there a point to this?"

Nodding, she said, "I trust you, but I know that at this moment I can't give you what you need. There is no mistaking that you're hard and ready, that you want me." She bit his bottom lip, then soothed the tiny sting with her tongue. " . . . or that I want you. But considering what the children have been through today, I have no choice but to stay and put their needs ahead of my own. All I can tell you is how very sorry I am, but it doesn't fix the problem."

Ralph groaned again, tightening his arms around her until nothing separated them but layers of fabric. "Don't apologize. I'm not pressuring you, beautiful."

"I know , but I'm not that naive. How long until you are thoroughly sick and tired of waiting? Phone calls and hungry kisses don't get it. We both know that."

His stomach tightened, his heart ached as he watched her lovely eyes fill with tears. "Then marry me, my beautiful lady. If nothing else, you don't have to worry, and I won't have to miss out on your loving."

"Ralph!" She hit him on his forearm. "Will you be serious? You wanted to know why I know you have reason to sneak around, and I'm trying to explain. Why do you make things so complicated?"

"And why do you assume I'm not perfectly serious," he demanded, outraged. "Yes, I'm tired of sleeping alone. Why do you keep turning me down? What? You think I'm running up and down Woodward Avenue proposing?"

"I know you want me. Perhaps more than you want anyone else. Marriage under these circumstances can't work." Vanessa sighed tiredly, leaning her forehead against his chin. "Do we have to get into this tonight? It has been such an exhausting day. Please, babe, can't . . ."

Ralph sighed heavily. He wanted it settled, and he wanted it tonight. But he could also see she was both physically and emotionally drained. The need to protect took over.

"Okay, beautiful. We'll let it go. No pressure." He dropped his head and brushed his lips against hers. "Try to get some sleep. Just give us some thought. 'Night."

"Good night." Vanessa quickly covered a yawn. "I'm sorry," she said as she slipped her arm through his and walked with him outside. After giving him a soft kiss, she stepped back inside.

Ralph stood on the porch, listening until the lock clicked into place. After making his way to his car and absently starting the engine, he wondered how the situation had gone from bad to worse. He felt as if she had ripped his heart out of his chest and was not even aware of it.

As he drove away, he vowed never again. No more proposals. He wasn't giving her a chance to hurt him like this again. He planned to be there for her, do everything he could to help her through this Cummingham mess. If she wanted his love, then she would have to do the asking. He was done.

Twenty-two

Ralph was amazed that his outlook on life had changed so much in the weeks he'd been involved with Vanessa. Despite his frustration, her happiness was more important than his own. This love thing was more profound than he'd ever thought possible. His keen disappointment and bitterness eased a bit each and every time he saw her. The sparkle and joy that was so much a part of who she was seemed to be missing from her eyes. It was clear she wasn't sleeping well. Aware that she had enough to deal with, he'd kept his promise not to pressure her for a response to his proposal.

With the first day of school only two weeks away, Vanessa had been busy getting them ready. Shopping for school supplies and new clothes had been only part of what she'd done. There had been doctor visits and long talks about what to expect and what was expected of them. Ralph was amazed by all the things he hadn't even thought of, let alone considered necessary.

Ralph knew the approach of the upcoming school year signaled the end of long summer evenings spent laughing and talking to Vanessa on the sunporch. He had gained pleasure from the simple hum of the ceiling fan, the gentle sway of the swing, and the flicker of the pillar candles, highlighting the beauty of her dark brown skin.

Was it wishful thinking on his part? Or was she starting to care about him more each day? He tried to listen and give whatever she needed. He had no idea if he'd bolstered what he considered her tremendous courage. All he knew was that, if he was fortunate enough to someday have a child of his own, he wanted Vanessa to be the mother.

It was devastating to watch Vanessa's hope of keeping the twins dim as time passed. He'd never felt more helpless. This custody lawsuit was slowly breaking her heart. The court-supervised visits had ended. Starting this coming Friday, the children would spend Friday and Saturday nights with the Cumminghams.

When the investigator's report came in, he cheered. Finally, there was something he could do. Determined, Ralph went to see Cummingham with a copy of the report in his briefcase. And he had the foresight to make an appointment.

The instant Greg Cummingham realized Ralph's business with him concerned the custody hearing, the man's cordial façade vanished. Leaning back in his costly leather armchair, surrounded by opulence, Cummingham asked, "So, why are you here, Prescott? To show me that Ms. Grant has a wealthy, powerful supporter on her side? It has been duly noted. What does this have to do with you? Are you and Ms. Grant lovers?"

It took all of Ralph's resolve to stay in his seat and not knock the pompous, patronizing smirk off the brother's face. Although his hands balled into fists, home-training was all that kept him from throwing a punch. Instead he tossed the report on the desk. The top page was a detailed list of names.

"It's over, Cummingham. You will find that my private investigator's report is thorough. Names, address, and phone numbers of the three women you've not only had affairs with, but also impregnated and paid off. Who knows, there may be more? The judge will no doubt find it interesting reading, don't you agree?"

Cummingham scowled as he quickly scanned the names and background details. When he finished, he shrugged narrow shoulders camouflaged with padding by an expert tailor. "So what? Last time I looked, sex between two consenting adults is still legal in all fifty states," he sneered.

"Drop the case, Cummingham. If your wife was to receive a copy of this report, what do you think she will do? How sure are you she won't walk? Would you care to risk it? That's fine by me. The choice is yours, and the risk is yours."

"You don't know a damn thing about my wife! Her first loyalty is to me. She won't be swayed by some bogus report!"

"Prove it."

"I don't have to prove anything to you. The law is on my side," Cummingham huffed.

"Really? According to what this report says, Mrs. Cummingham has been trying to conceive for some time. Wonder how she will feel when she learns just how many little Cumminghams are running around? I'm betting she won't be thrilled by the discovery. Wonder if she still wants to adopt the twins? She wanted a baby. It says here that Ms. Burton has two-year-old twin boys. Of course, there is distance, since Ms. Burton now lives in LA. Twins evidently run in your family. It says here that your dad was a twin."

Greg Cummingham jumped to his feet. "Are you trying to threaten me, Prescott? I'm warning you, I will destroy you, if my wife ever receives a copy of this trash. Then I will go after Ms. Grant. She'll never see those cute little twins again."

Ralph would have laughed in the other man's face if he

thought it would make the coward throw the first punch. It was no secret that Cummingham was used to fighting dirty, only his arena was in the criminal courtroom.

Ralph said, as if the other man hadn't even spoken, "Willing to take the risk, Cummingham? It will be interesting to see who comes out of this smelling like a rose." But Ralph knew the decision was not his to make. "If it were up to me, this report would be in the *Detroit News* tonight, but it's not my decision. Ms. Grant isn't interested in your marriage or your career. All she wants is to raise her little brother and sister without interference from you, Cummingham. Call off the custody suit, and your secrets are safe."

Ralph watched him pace restlessly behind his desk, in front of the floor-to-ceiling windows that overlooked downtown Detroit. The street far below was already crowded with rush-hour traffic. Deep in thought, Cummingham suddenly stopped, having lost some of that arrogance. "It's too late. My wife has her heart set on the twins." Sounding like a man between a rock and a hard place, he insisted, "My hands are tied! Perhaps if I met with Ms. Grant, she would be willing to accept a very generous visitation schedule? She can see them anytime she likes, but they would have to live with us."

Ralph stiffened, imagining Vanessa's volatile reaction to that offer. "I'll discuss it with her and get back with you. But I seriously doubt she will agree. Those kids belong with her. She's taken care of them since the day they came home from the hospital."

"Prescott, remind her that she doesn't have a prayer of winning this case. The most she can do is prolong the agony. I'm their biological father!"

"Tell me, something, Cummingham. Why are you so damn sure that none of these ladies are going to tell your wife the truth?"

He sank into his chair, a cocky grin on his face. Lifting his arms and anchoring his hands behind his head, he laughed. "They know better than to cross me. One word to anyone, and the money stops."

Ralph shook his head, amazed by the sheer size of the man's ego. How could one man be so blind to the risk he was senselessly taking, not only with his own health, but with that of his wife, whom he supposedly adored.

Ralph fired back with, "How accepting will your wife be when she learns just how many children you've fathered over the years? Or do you think that just because you weren't married at the time, that makes up for it? And how comfortable will she be when she realizes you may have exposed her to HIV?"

"Now hold on, Prescott!" Infuriated, Greg Cummingham jumped to his feet. He was tall, evidently used to being head and shoulders above most men.

Ralph casually rose to his full height, easily towering over the other man. "We will get back to you after I've spoken to Ms. Grant." He'd had enough of this arrogant jerk. So what if he was wealthy. Did he think because of his money he was a match for Ralph's considerable income? If so, he was sadly mistaken. He'd made his money by using his body and brawn. He multiplied that many times over by using his brain to make wise investments. The airline was making money faster than they could count it.

But that hadn't happened by chance. His uncle had made sure they not only knew how to make money but how to keep it. Up against all of the Prescotts' combined incomes, Cummingham didn't stand a snowball's chance in hell of beating them.

As he walked out, Ralph couldn't believe how stupid one very intelligent man could be. Pushing the elevator button marked down, he scowled. He wasn't looking forward to advising Vanessa to have the twins tested for HIV.

Vanessa could tell that something was going on with Ralph. He called her at work, highly unusual, then asked if she could meet him at his place. They needed to talk. She could tell by his tone that it was serious, and he wouldn't tell her more. He reminded her to drive safely before he hung up.

She was curious rather than alarmed when she left work early. The front door was answered by a beautiful young woman who introduced herself as Madelyn Holmes, Mr. Prescott's secretary. She was everything Vanessa was not, slim, lovely, and unencumbered by children. Vanessa caught herself. She was losing it, jealous of one of his employees. He didn't need her help finding females. He was so attractive, they were naturally drawn to him.

"Ms. Grant?"

"Yes." Vanessa managed to cover her surprise with a smile. She offered her hand and introduced herself, then followed her past the foyer and into her office. The small room was comfortable, decorated in blues and cream, very different than the deep bronze tones in Ralph's office. "Have a seat, Ms. Grant. Mr. Prescott is on the telephone." She motioned to one of the floral chairs in front of a maple desk. The matching sofa with a coffee table were placed against the wall, providing additional seating.

"Thank you. Please call me Vanessa," she said as she made herself comfortable.

"And I'm Madelyn. May I get you something to drink? Coffee, ice tea?"

"No, but thanks." Vanessa crossed her legs, wishing she'd gone home and changed into something pretty rather than the plain, long, denim skirt and white blouse she'd worn to work. She only took time to brush on blush and applied a fresh coat of lipstick. Pitiful! She imagined Laura and Brynne scolding her.

Smiling, the other woman took her place behind the cluttered desk. "I understand you work for Gavin. Do you like working out of a home office as much as I do? I don't miss the big office routine one bit."

Vanessa laughed. "I do enjoy it. It's a huge difference having flexible hours and comfortable surroundings. Gavin trusts me to do my work without him leaning over my shoulders all day. I generally find that I work more hours because I don't want to take advantage of his trust."

"That's how I feel." Madeline laughed. "Most days, Ralph is out of the office, and I'm here on my own. I don't mind. He's a great boss."

Vanessa laughed. "It beats being chased around the desk. How long have you worked for Ralph?"

"Two years. How about . . ."

"Hi, sweetheart. I'm sorry to keep you waiting." Smiling, Ralph seemed unconcerned by the endearment he let slip. Taking her hand, he pulled her out into the hall, pausing long enough to tell his secretary, "Madelyn, we're done for the day. See you in the morning." He ushered her down the central hallway.

"What's going on?" Vanessa asked, but he didn't stop until they reached the den.

Ralph gave her hand a reassuring squeeze, urging her inside. "Anything wrong with wanting to keep you to myself for a few hours?"

"Not a thing." Vanessa smiled as she sat down on the deep-cushioned sectional sofa, crossing long, shapely legs.

He ran a finger along her soft cheek. "Give me a second to get us something to drink. What would you like? Mrs.

Green left a pitcher of ice tea and one of cranberry punch. And there are always soft drinks and juice. What would you like?"

"Cranberry punch sounds good." She smiled, curious if it was only her imagination or if he seemed uneasy.

"Be right back."

Vanessa went to gaze out the French doors. She could see the paved basketball and tennis courts from that angle. Ralph had created a wonderful oasis for himself. There were putting greens and a bathhouse beside the outdoor pool. The soft hum of the ceiling fans throughout kept the large house pleasantly cool.

"Here we go," he said, carrying in a tray. Besides the tall, frosted glasses of punch, he included a platter of corn chips covered with melted cheese, chives, peppers, and tomatoes. "Thought you might need something to hold you until dinner. You're staying for dinner, aren't you. "

Vanessa laughed. "Maybe." She walked over to him, wrapping her arms around his waist. Leaning against him, she released a soft sigh. "I had no idea what you had in mind when you called. It really doesn't matter. I'm just glad that we've found some time to be together." Her plan was quite simple, to enjoy what time she had with him and not let anything intrude. With a smile, she decided he looked especially good in a crisp white shirt, teamed with a pair of well-worn jeans.

"Me too." He rested his cheek against hers. "Mmm, you smell good."

"Thank you." She tilted her head back so she could study his dark features. "So tell me, Mr. Prescott. Exactly what do you have in mind? And don't leave out any details."

"Not even one," he teased.

Delighted, she laughed softly, then placed a series of

kisses at the base of his throat and collarbone. Opening the top three buttons lining his white shirtfront, her lips moved over the dark skin.

When she raised her head, he dropped his in order to cover her mouth with his own. Ralph took hot, lingering kisses . . . one after the other. Releasing a husky moan, he sighed, the sound deep and needy.

"Oh, yes," she said in a small, breathless whisper. Just as she pressed the aching tips of her breasts into his chest, he groaned as he took a step back. Lifting heavy lids, she protested, "Honey . . ." She stopped suddenly. Forgetting her thoughts. Forgetting everything but the way he made her feel and the unmistakable proof of his desire for her.

Resting his forehead against hers, he said hoarsely, "I'm sorry, I lost it for a moment there. We have to talk."

Vanessa didn't want to talk; she wanted him to make love to her. She shook her head, but he held her away.

"I want . . ."

"I need to tell you what happened when I went to Greg Cummingham's office today."

Hearing the man's name was like a face full of ice water. Startled, she quizzed, "What? What about Cummingham?"

"I received the private investigator's report. I was determined to confront him and took the report to his office."

"That's why you asked me to come here?" Even as she asked the question, she knew she had no business feeling so disappointed. It wasn't the end of the world. Yet she couldn't help being upset. She thought he was as fed up as she was with the way things were going. They were both guilty of letting their busy schedules and lack of privacy keep them apart. She'd been thrilled that he'd wanted to spend the afternoon together, hopefully in his king-size bed.

It hurt knowing just how very wrong she'd been. He didn't want to be alone with her, didn't want to make love.

What he wanted was to talk about her custody case.

With her spine stiff, she went over to the sofa, sat down, and crossed her legs and arms. Intent on hiding her hurt feelings, she asked calmly, "What did he say?"

Although she was aware of Ralph's going over to the desk near the windows and opening the top drawer, Vanessa concentrated on maintaining her composure. Bursting into tears of frustration, while it might make her feel better for a few moments, was definitely not an option. She did have some pride.

She murmured thank you as he handed her a thick envelope. Ignoring the way her hands shook as she pulled out the report, she quickly read the document. Her heart rate picked up as she lifted hopeful eyes to meet his brooding gaze. She wasn't conscious of dropping the pages onto the patterned carpet when she asked, "Is he going to drop the custody suit? Surely he doesn't want this made public."

Ralph said with a frown, "He's not giving up. He's more concerned with his wife's reaction than this report being made public."

Exasperated, she practically shouted, "Ralph! It's all in here . . . sex, unwanted children all over the place. I can't believe it. Besides his marriage, his reputation is on the line. Nobody is going to hire a lowlife dog to defend them, even if he's the best. How has he managed to keep these women quiet?"

"Simple. He paid them off. If they want the money to keep coming, they have to maintain their silence."

Vanessa stared at him in stunned dismay. Her heart sank as she realized she wouldn't find help from any of the women, not with Cummingham paying them off. "How can he get away with this? He really is hateful, isn't he?" she ended in an exasperated hiss.

"Without doubt." He squatted until his eyes were level

with hers. "He did waver a bit. He said he can't drop the lawsuit without raising his wife's suspicions, but he did offer to let you see the twins as often as you like."

Vanessa was so angry, she let go with, "That's supposed to make up for what? I'm not the one who did anything wrong. I don't have kids all over the country because I can't keep my pants zipped. What's up with that? Hasn't that jerk ever heard of HIV? Why didn't he use a condom?"

"Makes no sense to me," Ralph echoed. "He may be brilliant in the courtroom, but he does not have a bit of common sense. He has needlessly exposed not only his backward behind but his wife to all kinds of diseases." Then he looked pointedly at her. "Speaking of HIV, have you considered . . ."

"Yes. The twins were tested before they left the hospital. My mother insisted on it. Thanks for asking."

"I should have known you were on it." Taking her hands in his, he said, "I wanted to bring you good news. I'm sorry it didn't work out that way."

"I still don't get it. Why my twins and why now? It took six years for him to decide to play Daddy."

"It's in the last page of the report." Ralph picked up the pages, then shuffled through them until he found what he wanted. As he sat down next to her, he said, "His wife has been unable to conceive, but she wants a baby. "

"So he's willing to take the twins away from Lana and me to make her happy? Why can't they see, the twins are happy where they are, as a part of our family. We've loved and cared for them since the day they were born."

"Good question. I honestly don't believe Cummingham cares about any of his children. Apparently, he has been so caught up in getting his own pleasure, he refused to use protection." Ralph paused, then said, "I don't know for sure, but my guess is he went after Courtney and Curtis because they're right here in Detroit."

"Lucky for us," she huffed, folding her arms beneath her breasts.

"You're angry." He stated it as a matter of fact. "Because of the twins' father? Or is there something else?"

Vanessa didn't realize she was pouting until Ralph ran a caressing thumb over her bottom lip. She sucked it in, holding it with her small white teeth.

"Come on, beautiful. Tell me."

"I'm not angry, just a little upset, about all this. That's all. Look, I should be going. I'm in a lousy mood, and the kids will be expecting me," she said, needing to put some distance between them . . . needing to sort out her feelings, to find out why she felt so vulnerable one minute, so hungry for him the next.

"Why? It's barely four. I thought you were staying."

She quirked a brow. "You don't want me to stay, not in this crazy mood. You're right! I am mad, at everyone and everything."

"Oh, I want you all right," he growled impatiently. "Stay. Let me hold you."

She let out a surprised little squeal when he scooped her up into his lap as if she weighed next to nothing. "What are you doing?"

"Making you comfortable. We're in this together, no matter what. I've missed you . . . missed this." Ralph didn't wait for an answer. He kissed his way up the side of her throat, pausing to suckle her earlobe.

Vanessa, while trying to ignore the heated shivers, managed to say, "That's not why I'm here." Yet she couldn't control the desire that traveled along her nerve endings and settled in her feminine center.

"I'm not in a playful mood, love. I hurt with need for you. It has been too long since we last made love. If your answer is no, then come out with it, before this goes any further."

She bit her lip, wanting to feel him deep within but too proud to admit how much she needed him. Her body and mind were at war. Staring into his eyes only seemed to increase the yearning.

Evidently tired of waiting, he said through tightly clenched white teeth, "Say something."

"It was yes, until you told me your 'only' reason for inviting me here was to talk about the case."

Nestling her neck, he inhaled her scent. "Only? Come on, beautiful." He caressed her hips. "Not wanting you is definitely not our problem. It has been so long since we've been together."

"I've missed you, too." Before she could say more, he rose to his feet, taking her with him.

"What? You think I'm going to let you fall?" He put her on her feet, then used both hands to circle her waist.

"I don't . . ." was all she got out. The next thing she knew he'd tossed her over his shoulder. She landed with her stomach against his shoulder. He'd hooked a supporting arm over the back of her legs. Vanessa let out a squeal, grabbing the back of his shirt to steady herself. "Ralph! Stop! This is not funny!"

He snapped, "Believe me, I am not laughing." Using long, quick strides, he walked into the hall, heading toward the carpeted staircase.

"Put me down! Ralph!"

"Did you say something?" He kept going as if he hadn't heard what she'd said.

"You heard what I said! Put me down right this minute!" Vanessa let out a frustrated screech when he increased his pace, jogging up the stairs with her bouncing against him. "Ouch! You're hurting my stomach." She wiggled, trying to get away.

"Be still before you make me drop you."

She would have punched him if she had not been afraid to let go of his shirt. She settled on mumbling beneath her breath, but she kept her eyes closed and held on as best she could. Her eyes flew open when he tossed her and she landed on her back in the center of his oversize bed.

After she caught her breath, she stared up at him. She looked into dark eyes, smoldering with desire. She could tell by the slight curve of his wide mouth that he thought he'd won that round. He was mistaken.

"No!" Satisfied that she'd finally gotten his undivided attention, she scooted to the edge of the bed.

He finished unbuttoning his shirt and tossed it in the general direction of the long, padded bench at the foot of the bed. Certain he'd heard her, she watched as he unsnapped faded jeans, then slowly eased the zipper down past the considerable bulge. Her breath caught in her throat, her heart rate increased. Annoyed by what she considered being taken for granted, she hissed, "I said, no."

"I heard you."

He rested his hand on a hip, his legs braced. His eyes were on her parted lips as she struggled to calm her breathing. She didn't dare lift her eyes to that broad, beautifully sculpted chest. She had to curl her hands not to reach out and stroke his dark skin. She had no idea why she was clinging to this senseless need to win the game of words they were playing. If she didn't get him, she didn't win.

Stubbornly, she persisted, "Good. I thought I might have to call the paramedics to check your doggone ears."

"You want to fight first? Then make love, beautiful?"

His dark eyes moved from the thick cloud of her dark curls surrounding her shoulders, down to her throat, over-ripe breasts and small waist, to her womanly hips and shapely legs. When he looked at her with such sizzling heat, she could read the need and knew he meant every word.

It still surprised her when he called her beautiful. She knew that was how he meant it, and that was how he genuinely saw her. She wanted him . . . needed him, now. She didn't even know why they were fighting. It made no sense. Why was she wasting what they never seemed to have enough of . . . time alone?

Suddenly, all the fear, confusion, and fight drained out of her. She dropped her lids, whispering, "I want you to make love to me . . . but sometimes you, Ralph Prescott, are the most exasperating man."

Vanessa got up and went to him. She smoothed her hand over the broad planes of his heavily muscled chest, wrapping an arm around his neck and lifting her face to lick his neck before she bit the taut skin.

"You weren't in danger. I had you, baby. I won't ever let you fall." He released a deep groan.

Raining kisses over his dark skin, she confessed, "I was afraid you'd hurt yourself."

"Carrying you? Never. You were made for me. Have you forgotten how perfectly we fit together?"

Twenty-three

Vanessa kissed his chest, lingering on a flat male nipple. He released a husky groan the instant she licked his tight peak. Pleased by his response, she repeatedly tongued the nipple, wanting to give him the utmost pleasure. With his eyes closed and nostrils flared, he kept his hands at his sides. As if unable to bear more of this exquisite torment, Ralph caught her shoulders, holding her away from him.

He shook his head. "You don't need to arouse me." He moved her hand over his rock-hard erection. "I don't think I can get harder."

She shivered, pleased to feel the strength of his need. It matched her own. She whispered, "Please . . . hurry."

His kiss was urgent, demanding, nothing else mattered but the two of them. Ralph unbuttoned, unzipped, and unsnapped. Finally, Vanessa was bare to his hungry, hot eyes.

"Oh, baby. You're so beautiful . . . so perfect for me," Ralph whispered in her ear. After stripping back the velvet quilt and silk sheets, he picked her up and placed her in the center of the bed.

His voice was gruff with desire when he said, "Tell me, Vanessa. Tell me you want me as much as I want you."

"Yes . . . oh yes," she could barely get the words out. Engrossed in watching him, she couldn't look away as he shoved both jeans and briefs down. But he wasn't moving fast enough for her, so she held her arms out, insisting, "Hurry . . . sweet man."

He reached for her, pulling her against him. He suckled her bottom lip until she opened enough to receive the bold thrust of his tongue against hers. Eager for more, she locked her arms around his neck. Their kisses were hot and needy, neither holding anything back.

Rubbing her aching breasts against his chest, she moaned her pleasure. He moved down to lick a hard nipple before taking it to suck. He took his time before he moved to the other dark nipple and repeated the titillation.

When he lifted his head, he kissed her, then said, "Please touch me."

Responding to the husky need in his voice, Vanessa ran soft, silky hands over his broad shoulders to his taut midsection. She smoothed down his concave stomach, then encircled his hard shaft. He groaned her name as she caressed his pulsating length from the thick base to its ultrasensitive tip. She smoothed over the moist peak.

He released a heavy groan, catching her hand in his, holding it still. "No more."

"But . . ."

Ralph cupped her nape, holding her still for his urgent kisses. His hand caressed over her petal-soft skin. He squeezed her breasts before sliding a hand though the thick curls at the apex of her thighs, moving lower into her soft moist folds. Ralph's fingers were soon slippery with her feminine heat.

"Now . . . Ralph," she begged.

"Soon," he said through gritted teeth. He reached into the nightstand for a condom. "Open for me," he said urgently.

Vanessa parted her legs even more, eager for his steely-hard length. Ralph settled between her soft thighs, running his caressing hands up and down her satin-smooth brown skin. She cried out his name as he used the broad tip of his sex to part her feminine folds. He moved against her damp opening until she cried out, as he boldly thrust forward, carefully, eliminating the emptiness, filling her sheath to the point of bursting.

She moaned, welcoming him and lifting her legs to encircle his waist. Responding to his hard, insistent thrust, she sighed with pleasure as her enjoyment continued to build, higher and faster, a sizzling flame. Sparks flared as they moved against each other. His control crumbled as she tightened her inner muscles around his throbbing shaft. All too soon they reached a white-hot peak, beyond anything either of them had ever experienced. Numb from sheer pleasure, he climaxed a heartbeat before she reached her own completion. They drifted down from the stars together. Both equally dazed and spent.

Ralph's cell phone rang while he was out of the room, and Vanessa couldn't stop herself from picking it up from the nightstand. Caller ID told her more than she wanted to know. It was the third call from one woman.

Her hands were shaking when she put it back down. She couldn't say she was surprised. She had hoped she was wrong. That he was seeing only her, that he was really falling in love with her. She didn't dare look in the closet, afraid of what she might find. She blinked back tears. No point in crying. They still had their friendship. It had to be enough.

Vanessa was down on all fours when Ralph walked out of the bathroom.

"Nice view. Can I help?"

She didn't bother to glance over her shoulder; she heard the humor in his voice. He was struggling not to laugh. Hoping to preserve some dignity, she sank back on her heels and held up one sandal.

"I can only find one!"

With dark eyes flashing sparks of satisfaction, he dropped down beside her. Instead of crawling around the perimeter of the bed, he encircled her waist, pulling her close in order to place slow, drugging kisses on lips already swollen from his earlier kisses.

"What was that for?" She studied eyes so dark brown that it was nearly impossible to make out his ebony pupils. Her heart accelerated as she recalled what they'd shared. She'd spent most of the afternoon lost in his magnetic gaze.

He let out a deep, throaty chuckle. "I don't need an excuse, not when I thoroughly enjoy making love to you." He cupped her elbows and lifted her to her feet.

"Hey, I thought you were going to help find the other shoe?" Thrown off-balance, she quickly wrapped her arms around his waist, using his sturdy frame to steady herself.

"No need. You lost it on the landing, at the top of the stairs." He chuckled.

"Evidently you were too busy demanding I put you down to notice."

Vanessa blushed, pressing a hot cheek against his broad shoulder. "Embarrass me, why don't you!"

"Did you enjoy our time together as much as I did?" he quizzed softly as he kissed her on the forehead.

"I did. Our time alone always seems to speed by." It was true. She was so weak for him. Lifting troubled eyes, she asked, even though she felt she shouldn't, "Would I be monopolizing your time by inviting you to dinner with us?" Where was her pride? Why wasn't she kicking him out of her life?

"Perhaps, but you will hear no objections from me. What if I picked up takeout from the seafood restaurant the kids like? Two orders of fish sticks and french fries, fried shrimp for Lana. And, lobster tails and baked potatoes for us."

She nodded. "Don't forget the coleslaw and garlic bread,

enough for everyone." She smiled, glad that he remembered. "Sounds wonderful." She stood on tiptoes in order to brush her lips against his. "Shall I bring the kids here? Or are you coming our way?"

"I'll come to you." Grinning, he said, "Since I don't like you driving at night, it means I will end up following you home anyway. I might as well save myself some time."

She didn't argue. Why bother? She didn't particularly like driving at night. Besides, she was secretly pleased that he didn't bother with concealing his thoughts. He was open about most things. Of the two, she was the one who tended to hold back.

As she recalled a certain look in his eyes while they were making love, she blushed. He'd been deep inside of her, urging her toward completion when suddenly, he whispered he loved her. He had the same look in his eyes the first time he'd said those magical words.

Suddenly, her eyes went wide as she realized Ralph hadn't been teasing or playful or even charming when he said those three incredible words. He truly meant them. He was in love with her. She covered her mouth, shocked by the realization.

"What?" he said, brushing his lips over hers, then tucking thick curls behind each ear.

Holding back tears, Vanessa concealed her eyes behind lowered lids. Her heart pounded as she slowly accepted the depth of his feelings for her. What was she going to do?

As she struggled to find a plausible response, she couldn't help weighing the painful truth that hung in the balance. Until now, she hadn't believed he was capable of the emotion. But what did love really mean to him? There were many definitions for that remarkable word. To Vanessa, being in love meant commitment, fidelity, and forever, all three interwoven in an incredibly beautiful way.

Vanessa's heart sank as she recognized and accepted that it simply was not his way. Judging by his caller ID, Vanessa accepted that love meant something entirely different to him. And she believed that to him it represented incredible sex and lots of it, including exquisite pleasure, pure joy, and sheer excitement. She also believed that when love became difficult, problematic, it would no longer be worth it, and he would turn his back and walk away. He already had someone waiting for his next move.

Had he ever been in this situation? Was this a new experience? She would be extremely naive to think she was the first, considering his history with woman. A much better question would be was how many women had he told he loved and meant it? Good question . . . no answer. Nonetheless, she had a feeling there weren't many, only a precious few. Then again, she could be deluding herself.

This was Ralph, after all. No, she was not going to put on rose-colored glasses. With Ralph, love might never be enough. And she needed more, so much more. She had to be able to trust him. It seemed that love wasn't the sweet joy that she'd read about in romance novels. Vanessa blinked as she suddenly realized she'd yearned for his love because she was in love with him. And because she loved him, she had no choice but to accept that his kind of love was sharp and cutting.

"You're looking in my eyes, beautiful, but you're saying absolutely nothing. What's going on in that pretty head of yours?"

"Would you believe chicken or fish?" she teased. He laughed just as she'd hoped. "I wasn't going to tell you, but I looked at your caller ID when your cell rang. Who is Sue Smith?"

If he was surprised, he didn't show it. "A woman I used to date. Nothing more."

"Not even a friend?"

"Nope. You're my friend and my lover. I don't want Sue."

"Okay," she said, walking out of his room.

"That's it?" he asked.

Deciding to keep her fears inside, Vanessa nodded, taking his proffered hand.

They walked down the stairs and collected her shoe, before hand in hand, they went out to her car parked in the drive. When he reached for the door handle, she stopped him with a hand on his arm. He arched a brow but didn't voice his question.

She forced herself to ask, "Do you think it's wrong for me to go on fighting the twins' father for custody? Maybe I'm letting my own selfish needs overshadow what is best for them."

"What?"

Vanessa slipped her hand into his, needing his strength. "Crazy, huh?"

"No, not crazy. How long have you had these doubts?"

She shrugged her shoulders. "No doubts. It's just that he's their father. If he had stepped in when they were babies, I would not have been able to take them home."

"That was his call. Are you having regrets?"

"Not even one. In everything I've done for them, I've always tried to make sure that I was doing what was best for them. I want them to grow up surrounded by love. I don't want them to grow up not knowing their father. It would be wrong of me to prevent them from seeing him. And that certainly wouldn't be what my mother wanted for them." She sighed tiredly, before she said, "This may sound like a contradiction, but I don't want them to grow up resenting me because I stopped them from being with Greg Cummingham. I couldn't bear that!"

Ralph wrapped his arms around her and held her. She held on to him, needing not only his physical support, but to know he was on her side. She wanted to do the right thing. And she knew he would tell her the truth, not just what she wanted to hear.

"I know I'm a bit jealous that the twins like his wife. She's good to them. And jealous of the very expensive toys they bring home. Things I can't afford. They are spoiling them."

"Money comes easy for Cummingham. Just look at how he has tried to buy you off."

Eventually, she asked, "Do you think I was wrong to seek custody?"

Cupping her shoulders, he insisted, "You didn't start this battle. That was Cummingham's call. Can you honestly tell me of a time when you stopped the twins from talking to him on the telephone or seeing him?"

Vanessa attempted to speak through a throat clogged with tears and failed. She just shook her head.

"Have you?" Ralph demanded.

"No," she finally managed to get out.

"If he had come to you and asked to see the twins, what would you have said?"

"Yes," she said without hesitation.

"So why are you accepting the blame for this custody mess? This is all about Cummingham. He's always known how to get in touch with you. You live in the same house that your mother lived in when he was seeing her. Probably have the same telephone number, don't you?"

Vanessa nodded, looking into his dark eyes. "I hadn't thought about that. Thank you." She brushed her mouth against his in a brief kiss.

"Why are you thanking me?"

"For being you."

Ralph grinned. "You are more than welcome. You haven't forgotten Sunday dinner with my folks?"

Smiling, she said, "I'm looking forward to it. Although I may not be at my best because the twins are spending the weekend with the Cumminghams. I can't stop worrying."

"They are going to be fine. And so are you. Cummingham hasn't won yet. Ready to go?"

Vanessa hugged him for a long moment, not wanting to ever let go. Good or bad, wrong or right, Ralph understood how she felt. He had been both friend and lover. She had come to depend on him without even realizing it. No, she wanted to hang on for dear life, but common sense prevailed. Easing away, she smiled, reminding herself that he wasn't really hers for the keeping. Not for even a second would she let herself forget that Ralph wasn't a one-woman kind of guy. His caller ID proved it. When it came to women, he had an extremely short attention span.

For now, he was devoting himself to helping her and the children. For that, she was grateful no matter how long it lasted. She'd made a promise to herself. She wouldn't make the mistake of trying to hold on when he was ready to move on. In the end, she would watch him walk away with a smile on her face. She was determined that he'd never suspect her heart was broken. She had the rest of her life to mourn his loss.

"Beautiful?"

Brushing her lips against his, she said. "Yes, I'm ready."

Sheila was bubbling with delight, as she leaned back against the plush leather of the limousine her husband insisted she needed. He spoiled her rotten, and she secretly loved every minute. How had she gotten so lucky and found such a wonderful man. Greg Cummingham was also filthy rich, handsome, and smart. Most important, besides being a partner in a prestigious and lucrative law firm, he adored her as much as she adored him. They nearly had it all . . . careers they loved, beautifully furnished homes in Detroit, Paris, and St. Thomas.

Very soon their wonderful life would be perfect . . . they would have a family of their own. Curtis and Courtney were so sweet. So well behaved. Sheila already loved them because they were a part of Greg. His very own flesh and blood. And soon she would be their mother.

Gleefully, she hugged herself, barely able to contain her joy. It was a dream come true, without the hardship and discomfort of losing her figure and labor pains. Finally, she'd have everything she'd ever wanted . . . every one of the fairy-tale dreams she'd longed for as a girl. A rich, loving husband, a beautiful home, children, and a successful career.

Friday evening would be a new beginning. The twins would spend the entire weekend with them! She was so excited, she could hardly stand it. Soon, they would be together always. Wouldn't it be wonderful if they could somehow preserve this magical beginning? A new life for all of them.

Suddenly, Sheila's dark eyes went wide. Why hadn't she thought of it before? Friday just had to be recorded! That way, whenever they wanted, they could look back on their first night as a real family. She imagined that many adopting families wished they had recorded those first, precious moments of connection as a family.

Her television viewers would be thrilled to share her and Greg's happiness. And there were bound to be adopting families interested in seeing it, as well as infertile couples struggling to decide what was best for them . . . to keep trying or consider adoption. Heavens, so many children, especially African-Americans in the foster-care system, longing for a family of their own. It was so sad. Just one airing of her and Greg's story might help. They just had to do it!

Clapping her hands, Sheila laughed out loud. For someone like her, it was a simple matter to get a film crew together. She was surprised her cohost Thomas Redman, hadn't suggested it. But then again, she should be recalling how difficult it had been to talk Greg into allowing their wedding photographs to be in *Jet* and *Ebony* magazines.

While he never hesitated to give interviews about his work, she had no doubts Greg would strongly object to this interview. He'd insisted on keeping their private life . . . private. He could be stubborn. But it really would be such a wonderful, heartwarming story of a man's fondest wish to become a father finally come true! He might not admit it, but she knew he loved the twins and wanted nothing more than to be a great dad. And she loved that about him. When he had learned he was a father, he stepped up and did right by them.

Greg wasn't like the deadbeat man who fathered her. Her mother had to work two jobs the entire time Sheila was growing up. She missed Sheila's school programs, plays, and concerts because of work. By the time Sheila finished high school, her mother's health was deteriorating. When Sheila was close to finishing her last year of college, the hope of finally being able to make things easy for her mother was destroyed. She died of heart failure, at the age of forty-two.

The heartbroken Sheila put the blame squarely on her father's shoulders. He reentered her life only when she became well-known as a television journalist at CNN, which was about the time she met Greg.

The day they brought the twins home to live with them for good was fast approaching. This weekend's sleepover was the first major step toward that goal. No way was she going to let it go down without a film crew standing by, even if she had to hide them in the bushes. Sheila giggled, deciding she would deal with Greg later in the bedroom.

But for now, she had a lot of work to do in a very short period of time. Sheila asked her chauffeur to turn the car around. She had a huge job ahead of her, the first part being to convince her boss that this story was a priority. Once Sheila had Darlene Brownski on her side, what seemed impossible would be done. Darlene was a first-rate newswoman. Even Jeffery Howard, the station owner, would listen. After all, Darlene had a display case full of awards to her credit.

Sheila had a huge grin on her face as she began jotting down notes. If they filmed on Friday night, she'd have the rest of the weekend to convince Greg to let the piece air the following week. Even though he was a criminal attorney, Greg was being courted by the party to run in the upcoming governor's race. Sheila, for one, wouldn't be surprised if Greg made it all the way to the top. He had the credentials and powerful friends. And she planned to be at his side at the podium when he made his acceptance speech. Life was sweet.

On Sunday, during the evening meal, Anna surprised everyone when she said, "Vanessa, is everything all right? You haven't touched the stew."

From one end of the long, round dining table, Donna scolded, "Let her be, Anna. She has enough on her mind."

Vanessa, had been staring at her food on her plate, looked up when Anna said her name. The food wasn't the problem. She'd been self-absorbed since they had waved good-bye to the kids on Friday. It had been even harder than she'd anticipated. It had been so painful just to stand there and do nothing to stop them from leaving. She wanted to run after the big, sleek car as it pulled away. She was grateful for the comforting squeeze Ralph had given her hand from beneath the table.

Vanessa quickly said, "I'm sorry. I didn't mean to upset anyone. Maybe I should go?"

"Absolutely not," Ralph said as he looked at Lana, who was as upset as her big sister. "Lana and Vanessa are really missing Curtis and Courtney. It's the first time the twins have spent an entire weekend with the Cumminghams."

Lester said, "Donna and I both think you've done a fine job of taking care of those twins and sweet Lana on your own. If you need us to testify to that in court, we will be happy to do so."

The tears Vanessa had been fighting all weekend filled her eyes. "Thank you." Brushing them away, she smiled. "You have no idea how much that means to me." She glanced at her sister. "Lana and I have had a rough weekend, but we've managed to get through it. Ralph has been doing his best to keep us from moping around."

Although she appreciated the Prescotts' concern, she was nonetheless relieved when the telephone rang. It was Brynne and Shanna calling to say hello. Vanessa was basically shy and wasn't used to being the center of attention.

Like Kelli's and Anna's, Brynne's man was on the road since the football season was in full swing. After dinner, Wayne and Kyle challenged Lana to play a video game while Ralph and Lester helped with the cleanup. Vanessa joined the ladies in the living room.

The Grant sisters left early. Both were eager to get home before the twins returned. Vanessa didn't protest when Ralph volunteered to wait with them. Even though she tried not to, Vanessa couldn't help worrying that she was becoming too dependent on Ralph. She wasn't willing to examine their situation at the moment. For now, she shoved that thought aside. All that mattered to her was that he was there for her.

Both sisters were restless until the Cumminghams' limousine pulled into their driveway. They didn't wait for the uniformed chauffeur to escort the children to the front door but hurried out to the sidewalk, greeting the twins with hugs and kisses. Courtney and Curtis were happy to see them and were lugging home more toys and luggage than they had left with two days earlier. Vanessa was too happy to see them to worry over the way the Cumminghams were spoiling them with material things.

Later, when they were finally alone, Ralph gave Vanessa a long kiss. He whispered in her ear, "Beautiful, it's really good to finally see a smile on those pretty, red lips."

She laughed softly. "Was I that bad? I didn't realize I was so pitiful." She lifted her arms up to his neck, urging his head down for another kiss.

"Mmm," he murmured. "Now, that's more like it."

She couldn't stop smiling. "I apologize for monopolizing your weekend. You've been so patient with us. And your family was wonderful. I know I've said it before, but I want you to know that I genuinely appreciate all the things you've done to help. I don't know how I would have gotten through the past few weeks without you. Starting with—" She stopped abruptly. "Why are you scowling?"

"You've already thanked me. Drop it, okay." Ralph reached up to gently free himself.

Shocked by what felt like a rejection, she quizzed, "What's wrong?"

"Nothing. It's late. And we both have work in the morning."

"Wait. I don't want you to leave angry." Vanessa hated the way she hung on his arm but couldn't make herself stop.

"I'm not angry, Vanessa."

His mouth said one thing while his taut features and the stiff way he held his torso said just the opposite. Folding her arms beneath her plump breasts, she said, "You're not happy either. Tell me what's wrong."

He leaned down and quickly crushed her lips beneath his in a possessive kiss. "I know you appreciate that I've been there for you. What I don't want is for you to feel as if you owe me a damn thing, including a thank-you."

"When someone goes out of his or her way to be nice, I was taught to at least say thank you."

"Yeah, I got that. So consider it said." He squeezed her hand. "Talk to you tomorrow. Lock up behind me," he said as he went to the door.

"Good night," Vanessa, called after him, automatically locking up and activating the alarm system. She listened to his footsteps as he swiftly descended the porch stairs.

Hurrying to the window, she watched until he drove away. Ralph wasn't the only one upset. She was angry with him for wanting so much from her. He wouldn't be satisfied until she admitted he owned her heart. It was something she was never going to do. She hated showing her weakness, as if her heart were on display. Thank goodness he hadn't guessed the depth of her feelings. Why did it have to be so complicated?

She didn't want to love him! She couldn't stand how it made her feel . . . so incredibly confused and vulnerable. She was determined not to let him so much as suspect how she truly felt about him. Not ever!

Expressing her appreciation was light-years away from what he really wanted. That was fine with her. She had her eyes wide open. He was not going to trap her into a tearful confession. They both knew love signaled the end. No matter what he said—the instant he heard the word "love," he'd run for the hills. He didn't want love, he wanted the challenge of winning, then he could move on to the next conquest.

Twenty-four

"Vanessa, come here quick!" Anna yelled from the kitchen. "Hurry!"

Thinking something terrible had happened, she didn't bother to save the document she was working on but ran into the kitchen.

Anna stood by the flour-covered counter, kneading bread dough, while Kyle sat at the center island eating lunch. Nothing seemed out of place. They had been watching the flatscreen television mounted on the wall above the desk.

"What's wrong?" Vanessa said, looking around.

They shushed her, then pointed to the television. Vanessa's eyes went wide when she saw her little brother and sister playing on the carpet in the background as the lovely Sheila Cummingham sat on a sofa next to her husband, Greg. Vanessa had no trouble recognizing the handsome, lean man that as the twins' father. The couple were apparently being interviewed by Thomas Redman, Sheila's cohost on their morning talk show, *A.M. Detroit.*

"Turn the sound up, Kyle," Anna urged. Her hands covered with flour, she went back to kneading, but her eyes were on the screen.

Sheila said, "Yes , it was a miracle finding the twins after all this time. We had nearly given up having children when we learned from an old friend that the twins' poor mother had died in childbirth."

Tom said, "You mean you had no idea that you had fathered the twins, Greg?"

"None," he said in his quiet dignified tone, the one he must use in the courtroom to persuade the jury to his point of view.

Sheila put her hand into her husband's, smiling when she added, "It was a shame how they were living. They were being raised in poverty by their older sister. But that's all behind them. Things have worked out well for all concerned. And now we are going to adopt them, and our family will be complete. Too many couples fail to look into adoption. So many African-American children are left in foster care, hoping for a family of their own. It's so sad, especially when it doesn't have to be that way. Please consider . . ."

Furious, Vanessa said to Anna, "I can't believe it! It's bad enough that they were talking about the twins right in front of them. But they did an interview about the twins while in the middle of a custody case!"

"They did more than give an interview. Evidently, they were the topic of Sheila's talk show this morning. This is too much! I'm looking at your sweet babies, and they are talking about them as if they found them in some crack house. And it's all lies.

"How could they do something like this? What were they thinking?" Anna said furiously.

Livid, Vanessa was so upset she was shaking. "I have no idea. The twins didn't say a word about the cameras. It's crazy! I don't appreciate it! Excuse me. I've got to make some calls." She kissed Anna's cheek. "Thanks for letting me know about this."

Hurrying back to her office, Vanessa felt so scattered, she merely sat at her desk for a few moments. After taking several deep breaths, she made a point to save the order forms for sports gear she'd been working on earlier. She reached for the telephone to call Ralph, but before she could lift the receiver, it rang.

She automatically said, "Hello, Mathis Enterprises . . ."

"Hey, beautiful. Did you by any chance see the noon news broadcast?"

"Enough to see the twins while Sheila and Greg were interviewed. Anna and Kyle had it on. I couldn't believe what I was hearing! How could Sheila Cummingham say I did not take excellent care of the twins? She has some nerve.

"She doesn't know anything about me or our family. And she claimed that the twins were a surprise, as if Greg Cummingham hadn't known my mother was pregnant. Ralph, we're going to have to talk to that lawyer. Let him know what's going on."

"I spoke to him before I called you. He knows about the interview that aired on Sheila's show this morning. They're doing a series on adoption. Anyway, Carl has talked to their lawyer, and the interview took place Friday evening. The camera crew was waiting when the twins and Cummingham arrived at the house. Evidently, his wife had planned it as a surprise to preserve for the future."

"Really," Vanessa hissed. "No wonder he looked so . . . I don't know." Struggling to come up with the correct word, she settled on, " . . . he looked very uncomfortable. She did most of the talking. He should have stopped it, especially since the kids were in the room while they were talking about our family. It was so rude."

"I doubt the kids were paying any attention. That interview couldn't be in Cummingham's best interest. At this point we have to wait and see what's going to happen."

Letting out a groan of sheer disgust, she complained, "Well, I still don't appreciate her using the twins to complete

their family. It's not like she really loves them. I'm not trying to be mean. I can only imagine how difficult it has been
for her wanting to have children and not be able to. But that
doesn't mean I plan to sit back and let her destroy my family.
Is anyone going to ask the twins what they want?"

"I don't know, but it sounds like an excellent idea to me.
Maybe we should bring it up at our meeting with Carl."

"Okay!" She hesitated, considering whether or not she
should ask. Because she had to know, she inquired, "Are you
still angry with me?"

She heard his sigh before he insisted, "I was never angry
with you. Just disappointed we don't agree." He paused, then
said, "I'm flying to St. Louis this afternoon for a series of
meetings."

Disappointed, she asked, "How long will you be away?"

"I'm not sure. Hopefully, only a couple of days." His voice
deepened when he said, "I'm going to miss you, beautiful."

"I'm already missing you." Sighing softly, she said, "I
wish you didn't have to go."

"I'll be in touch. Maybe we can drive down to Ohio. Take
the kids to Cedar Point before school starts? Think the kids
will like that?"

She laughed. "I know they will, but I'll wait until you're
back to announce it. I have to live with them."

He chuckled. "I'll talk to you tonight."

"I'm looking forward to it. Take care of yourself."

"You, too. Bye."

All three of the Grant youngsters were looking forward to
returning to school. The twins were just as excited about
starting first grade as Lana was about beginning her senior
year in high school.

For an hour each evening they worked at the kitchen
table. The twins practiced writing their names and the al-

phabet while Lana reviewed her math and science textbooks,
her weakest subjects. Vanessa, when not helping the twins,
read her book club's upcoming selection, Kimberla Lawson
Roby's latest novel.

The family called it "getting and keeping it together."
Doing homework around the kitchen table was something
both Vanessa and Lana had done with their parents. It was a
tradition the sisters had continued with the twins.

"I'm tired," Curtis complained.

"Me too. Can we watch TV?" Courtney begged.

Vanessa didn't bother glancing at the clock. They'd only
been at it for about ten minutes. "When the big hands stops
on the six, then you can stop." Just then the telephone rang.
She hurried into the next room, looking for the cordless. She
didn't have to think about who had used the phone last, not
with a teenager in the house. "Where is the phone, Lana
Marie?"

"Living room," she said sheepishly. "If it's Lisa, tell . . ."

"You have an hour to go, Ms. Lana," Vanessa reminded
her as she searched. She found the receiver between the
cushions on the sofa. "Hello?"

"Hi, beautiful."

"Hey, handsome. Where are you?"

"Still in St. Louis."

"Oh." Clearly disappointed, she tried not to show it.
"Here, I was hoping you'd say you were flying over Ohio."
His deep chuckle made her heart race.

"Missing me?"

"Maybe," she hedged.

"Beautiful, have you seen the national news. Or read the
newspaper?"

"Not yet. Why?"

"Where are the twins?"

"In the kitchen, practicing the alphabet. What's going on?"

"Are you in the living room?"

"This is one crazy conversation, Ralph. Yes, I'm on the sofa." She teased, "Want to know what I'm wearing?"

He said seriously. "Turn on CNN. Hurry. And keep the sound low, so the kids don't overhear."

"What's going on?" she asked in a whisper as she hurried to the set, not taking time to look for the remote. Finally, she had the set on CNN, with sound low. "Oh!" She gasped and quickly covered her mouth as Greg Cummingham's face flashed across the screen. Then she whispered urgently, "Ralph, what's going on? I can't hear with the sound down."

"It's taken a few days, but apparently when one of the ladies on that list, Ronda Waters, saw the piece about the twins, she not only hired a lawyer, but she also found a television reporter willing to stand still and listen. Not all of his ladies were as intimidated as he believed. Since Cummingham got that rock star off on that murder charge, and that singer off for rape a few years back, he's gained celebrity status.

"Anyway, when she heard about your twins, she wanted more money. Cummingham refused to give what she felt she was entitled to. Since that interview, two other ladies have come forward. It's only a matter of time before every secret he has is made public, especially with the reporters digging into his past."

Vanessa gasped, "Oh my."

Ralph said, "That's right, all three of them are ready to sue the brother man for back child-support payments, personal damage, and anything else they can get. They're using the money he has paid out over the years as proof he knew about these children."

"I wonder how many babies he has out there."

"According to the private investigator's report four, not

counting your twins. Who knows? There could be more. And all of it because the brother was too selfish to use a condom."

Vanessa knew she was wrong, but she couldn't help it; she let out a scream that brought all three of the Grant kids running into the room to see what was wrong. Lucky for her, she managed to turn the television set off before they could see the screen.

"What happened?" Lana asked anxiously.

Vanessa was laughing so hard, she couldn't speak. Finally, she was able to say, "Nothing really!" She was still holding on to the entertainment cabinet for balance. She finally said, "Ralph told me a joke! I'm fine." She motioned with her hand, "Go back and finish." She was gasping for breath when the children shook their heads at her and went back into the kitchen.

Vanessa whispered into the phone, "I know it's wrong, but I couldn't stop laughing. And don't you say a word. I heard you cracking up, too. Are we terrible people to laugh at someone else's misery?"

"What we are is human. Excuse my French, but the bastard got what he deserved. He has hurt so many people. He made this mess. Now it's his turn to deal with it!"

"Wonder if his wife is going to stick by him?" Vanessa mused.

"Not likely. If I were her, I would run to the divorce lawyer. Clean him out good fashion."

"Yeah, so would I," she whispered, "but that doesn't mean he is going to drop our case."

"I know it doesn't, but we can always hope," he ended.

"Ain't it the truth." Suddenly, she stopped as she wrestled with the depth of her feelings for him. It was a struggle not to confess how she felt about him. She missed him terribly.

"With a little luck, I will finish up my business tomorrow and be on my way home by tomorrow evening."

"Really?" She tried not to show how needy she was.

"Yes, I miss you. Are you missing me?"

"I am," she admitted softly, hoping she had not revealed how much. She had to be careful, remember who she was dealing with. Ralph could be so sweet, so giving, but he was not a one-woman kind of man. When he got bored he would move on, no matter what an otherwise good guy he was. As long as she kept that in mind, she would be fine.

"Good. Take care and try to keep the twins away from the set."

She laughed. "Yeah, piece of cake. All I have to do is move the moon. What time is the lunar landing?"

Chuckling, he said, "I don't envy your having to explain." Then he said, "This trip couldn't have come at a worse time. I feel as if I should be there helping you deal with all this."

"You're helping, but I think we are going to have to put off Cedar Point."

"You sure?"

"Yes." Unable to withhold her emotions, she quickly said, "I've got to go. Have a safe trip back. Bye."

Vanessa was disturbed by what seemed to be her ever-increasing feelings for Ralph. When he showed up at work on Thursday to take her out to lunch, she couldn't seem to breathe easy until he pulled her into his arms and held her close. She'd missed him terribly. She didn't need to be told she was making a complete fool of herself over the man. She couldn't help how she felt, no amount of wishing made it go away, and that frightened her.

Their lunch consisted of a quick hamburger at a nearby fast-food restaurant while staring hungrily at each other's lips. Finally, when they pulled up in the Mathis drive, Ralph, evidently fed up with waiting, pulled her against his strong frame and ended their misery by leaning down to share a long, hungry kiss.

Once he eased back to rest his forehead against hers, "I'm sorry, beautiful. I started what I can't finish. I've gotta get over to the college . . . a meeting . . ."

She nodded. "I should get inside." Not wanting to let him go, she found herself asking, "Will I see you later?"

The instant the words left her mouth, she wanted to call them back. Although embarrassed by her weakness, she waited for his response. No one had to tell her that like most men, Ralph detested clingy women who refused to let go. It was so pathetic. And she'd promised herself she would walk away before she let it get that bad. How close was she to making that relationship-ending mistake?

He smiled, his lips briefly brushed against hers. "Absolutely."

"Bye." Hurrying inside the house, she was relieved that she didn't run into anyone on the way to her office. Vanessa hadn't expected to react so strongly to him. The instant she laid eyes on him, she wanted to throw herself at him. Why was it so complicated? Didn't she have enough to deal with without adding more to the mix?

Determined not to dwell on it, she got back to work.

When the telephone rang, absently she said, "Mathis Enterprises?"

A frantic Lana said, "Nessa, what should I do?"

That morning Vanessa had enlisted her sister's help in keeping the twins away from the television while she was at work.

"What's wrong, honey?"

"Reporters! They've been calling the house nonstop all morning, asking questions about Greg Cummingham and the twins. I didn't know what I'm supposed to say to them, so I've been hanging up."

Vanessa soothed, "You did right, honey. From now on, don't even answer the telephone."

"What if it's important? How do I know it's not you calling?"

"I will ring twice, then hang up and call right back. Okay?"

"Okay."

"Good girl. I'll see you in a couple of hours. And keep a close eye on the twins, make sure they play only in the backyard. No bikes today. And call me if you need me to come home early."

"Okay, Bye."

When Vanessa reached home, she quickly realized Lana hadn't exaggerated—the telephone rang continuously. Reporters determined to learn whatever they could find on Greg Cummingham. It didn't take long for her to grow tired of saying, "No comment." She gave up and unplugged the telephone.

Before she did, she gave Ralph a quick call, told him about the intrusions, and asked him not to come by later. He sounded as disappointed as she felt when she explained they didn't know who might be watching the house. There was no way of knowing what they might film or put in print. She'd spoken to reporters as far west as Los Angeles and east as New York City. Judging by the questions they'd asked, she suspected they wanted to find out whatever they could about Cummingham's connection to the Grant twins. They'd gone on to ask if Cummingham had known about her mother's pregnancy.

It had taken considerable effort to convince a very concerned Ralph that she didn't want him drawn into this mess. And it would be better for all of them if his name was not linked to hers. She'd laughed when he claimed that it didn't matter to him. Well, it mattered to her, and she didn't want his name spread through the tabloids. After a lengthy discussion, she'd convinced him to leave well enough alone, at least for a few days.

Uncomfortable with leaving the kids alone at home, she decided to work from home. She had also sat the twins down and tried to prepare them for the possibility of a crowd of reporters blocking the entrance to the Cummingham property on Friday evening. But she was the one surprised, when the chauffeur-driven limousine didn't come for the children. Her calls to the Cumminghams' went unanswered, and she had no choice but to tell the children the truth. She didn't know the answer.

She got a call from one of Cummingham's past lovers offering to testify that he had fathered her son. Vanessa immediately called her lawyer and Ralph. She also received a call of support from one of her mother's friends confessing that her mother had told her about Cummingham being the twins' father and about his other lady friend. Doubting her testimony would be considered more than hearsay, nevertheless Vanessa was touched by her mother's friend's willingness to help.

On Saturday, they woke up to reporters ringing the doorbell. After an hour of no response, they gave up but didn't leave. Instead they camped out in their parked cars on both sides of the street. The reporters were careful to stay off her property line, so she couldn't involve the police.

The kids were upset because they couldn't go bike riding in the park. After a few hours of entertaining the twins inside the house on this beautiful summer day, an upset Vanessa called Carl Jones, her lawyer, to bring him up to speed and let him know the twins would be with her if their biological father changed his mind.

A quick call to Ralph, then she packed up her family and backed out of the driveway right past the reporters, who hurried out to their cars. One made the mistake of jumping behind her SUV, the kids screamed at the top of their lungs, but she didn't slow down and at the last second, he reconsidered and dove for the bushes and safety.

Terrified, Vanessa couldn't stop shaking, even after she had parked inside Ralph's garage. Before she could unlock her seat belt, Ralph was welcoming them. He helped the twins out and began collecting their bags. She was so glad he lived in an exclusive area of Southfield. They were safe for now.

He teased Vanessa about bringing enough luggage for a week. She was still too upset to find any humor in the situation. Whenever she thought of how close she'd come to hitting that reporter, she started trembling all over again. She didn't have to explain; the kids gave him a detailed accounting.

When he held his hand out to help her from the car, she shook her head. At his look of surprise, she blinked hard, holding back tears, afraid that if he touched her, she would shatter into a million pieces. Several deep breaths later, she got out of the car. On unsteady legs, she went into the house.

While her family went up to pick out their bedrooms, Ralph opened his arms. In desperate need of his strength, Vanessa let out a weary sigh as she moved forward, not stopping until she pressed her cheek against his chest and wrapped her arms around his lean waist.

She whispered, "Thank you for putting us up for, I hope, only a few days. Oh, Ralph, it was terrible." She shuddered. "For one wild moment I thought I had run him over. The kids were crying and screaming, and I was a total wreck.

I'm not sure how I made it here without crashing into something. I could barely hold on to the steering wheel."

"Shush, now, baby," he crooned, as he stroked her hair. "It's over, you're safe, and the kids are fine. You are welcome to stay here as long as you like. A week, two weeks, a month, doesn't matter . . . there are no limits."

Vanessa held on to him until the shaking stopped. She had just lifted her head to tell him how much she appreciated his generous invitation when she heard the children's feet racing to the stairs. She quickly stepped back and dropped her arms.

Smiling, she asked, "Did everyone pick out a room?"

Excited, they were talking at once, trying to outdo each other. Vanessa glanced over at Ralph. "There is still time to change your mind."

"Not a chance." He grinned.

"Enough!" she said, holding her hands up. When they were silent, she said, "Okay. Everyone grab your bags. And we'll unpack, but before we do, what do you say to Ralph for inviting us for a visit?"

"Thank you," they said at once.

"Let's go," Vanessa urged. When she reached for her bag, Ralph picked it up. She was too drained to protest. She smiled. "Thanks." Then she followed her family upstairs.

Ralph was right behind her. As she assured herself, it was only for a few days, she quietly accepted the truth. She was so far gone, she would be thrilled to move in and become a permanent part of his life. No one had to tell her that there was no such word as "permanent" in Ralph's vocabulary, at least not when it came to women. He was not about to change. Besides, she did not go anywhere alone. There was no way she could actually live with a man unless they were married, not with a teenager and two small kids to consider.

She should be counting her blessings. They were good

friends and lovers . . . nothing more. The only reason they were staying under the same roof was because of the mess with the Cumminghams and it was in no way personal.

All she had to do was remind herself of that fact a hundred times a day, and she would be fine.

Twenty-five

They picked from a choice of five luxurious bedrooms with en suite bathrooms. Ralph's master suite was at the end of the hallway.

After the Grant family unpacked and washed up, they went down to prepare dinner. Ralph, with Curtis's help, grilled hamburgers and steaks outside on the patio, while Courtney and Lana prepared a large chef salad, and Vanessa prepared deep-fried potato wedges as well as a banana pudding for dessert.

Over dinner, outside on the veranda, Vanessa explained the Prescott house rules while an amused Ralph quietly listened. No one was allowed in the pool area, the gym, the garage, or Ralph's office without his permission.

He was careful not to display how deeply relieved he was that they were here and out of harm's way. He was amazed that the huge house that he'd bought as an investment felt like a home. When Vanessa had called, he had been touched by the request. In fact he was genuinely grateful that, for a few days, there would be no need to worry about the Grants' safety. They were out of harm's way.

As his feelings deepened for Vanessa, so had his concern for her and her family. They lived too far away for his peace of mind. Between break-ins, the Cummingham situation, plus whatever his fertile mind would come up with, Ralph knew he would sleep better while they were under his roof. The idea of a herd of reporters outside their door irritated him no end. Vanessa didn't need that kind of stress, and Lana and the twins certainly had never done anything to deserve such treatment. This entire mess was Cummingham's doing.

"Ralph?" Vanessa asked expectantly. At his blank look, she repeated, "Do you have anything to add to the list of rules? What about the game and theater rooms? Are the children allowed in there?"

"Absolutely. I will show you and Lana how to run the machines. There is also an indoor basketball court and bowling alley. Would you like to try your hand at bowling after dinner?"

The kids cheered excitedly. They were ready to go right then.

"You have your own bowling alley?" Vanessa asked in astonishment.

He chuckled. "I do, but only one lane."

"Can we play?" Courtney and Curtis pleaded.

"Vanessa?"

Smiling, she said, "Sounds like fun. "

After cleaning up the kitchen, they all went downstairs to what Ralph called the fun house. He explained to Lana and Vanessa that he liked to host parties for family and friends. After four years apart, Brynne and Devin had been reacquainted at one of his parties.

The bowling alley proved to be highly entertaining. Ralph particularly loved watching Vanessa enjoy herself, her fear of losing the twins temporarily forgotten. Courtney had the highest score and was thrilled to have beaten everyone, especially her twin.

In an effort to spend a few minutes alone with Vanessa,

Ralph didn't shut off the equipment and lights but followed her. Before she could climb the stairs with the others, he caught her hand, holding her back. Her sweet smile had his heart racing with excitement.

"Yes?" She paused, her face turned up toward his.

He knew he had no business even getting close to her, especially when his need was so pronounced, but he couldn't help himself. He had to at least taste her sweetness. Dropping his head until he could inhale her scent, he sampled her full, so-soft lips in a hard, but painfully brief, kiss.

"Ralph, if one of the kids saw you," she scolded softly.

Smiling, he whispered, "I know, but I couldn't help myself. Don't worry. I'm not expecting you to sneak into my room tonight." He squeezed her hand. "Beautiful, I'm sorry. I certainly don't want you to feel as if I expect anything from you. I'm just glad to have you and the kids here . . . glad that you trusted me enough to turn to me when you needed help. It means a lot."

Vanessa smiled, then stood on tiptoe to brush her lips against his. "Sweet man, of course, I turned to you. You have been my rock through all this. As for tonight, I can't promise to come to you. It depends . . ."

He stopped her. "No, don't worry about me. The kids come first. We can wait for a more appropriate time. Go on up before you're missed. I've got some things to take care of down here before I turn in. 'Night."

She whispered, "Not good night . . . later." After playfully placing a kiss on his chin, she hurried up the stairs.

Determined not to get his hopes up and to cool his body down, Ralph went into the pool area. Quickly stripping down, he didn't flip the switch to heat the water but dove into the deep end and began swimming laps. He kept going until his arms felt like wet noodles. When he climbed out of the pool, he took a hot shower and pulled on a pair of sweatpants and a T-shirt from the sports clothes he kept stored in one of the changing rooms. His towels and other things went into the hamper. After turning off the equipment and the lights, he headed up to the main floor. Ralph locked up and set the alarm system, but instead of going to bed, he went into his office.

It was after midnight when he went up to his room. All was quiet as he passed the closed guest rooms the children had selected. He paused outside Vanessa's partially open doorway. He couldn't help himself, he peeked inside.

The beside lamp had been turned off, but a night-light from the bathroom had been left on. Vanessa lay in the middle of the king-size bed; Courtney and Curtis were sleeping on her right side, while Lana slept on her left. Her pretty brown gaze met his, and she mouthed the word "sorry." Holding back the chuckle rising in his throat, he smiled, shrugged his shoulders, and whispered good night before quietly slipping out.

He continued on into his room and closed the door quietly behind him. Absently, he moved around in the spacious room that suddenly felt empty.

He acknowledged the unvarnished truth. He wasn't falling. No, he was completely and irrevocably in love with Vanessa Grant. And he was done with fighting what was in his heart.

Restless, he paced in front of the French doors. It took him long enough to figure it out. Finally, he understood what had been going on with him for weeks. The first time he'd proposed marriage, it hadn't been about helping her out of a difficult spot. The next time he'd asked hadn't been about incredible desire eating away at him. Both times had nothing to do with the excuses he'd been tossing around. He'd come up with a boatload of them, all of them centering on improving hers and the children's lives.

Now he saw that his reasons for proposing had been no different than the other Prescott males. He was in love. More than anything else in the world, he wanted to spend his life making her happy.

He would be lying to himself if he didn't admit her refusal had crushed him to his heart. He'd tried to hide it, and he'd hidden it well. She believed his offers were about her need, not his love. Hell, the last time, she hadn't even bothered to refuse. She acted as if his proposal didn't merit an answer. And how had he responded? Like an angry bull. Yet he kept coming back, again and again, like a love-starved fool.

Simple truth was, he couldn't stay away from her. He'd even gone so far as trying to convince himself that he continued to see her for the sake of the kids. Unfortunately, even he wasn't buying that one. He'd stayed because he couldn't bear being away from her.

What was he supposed to do about this love thing? If asked, he wouldn't recommend it to even his worst enemy. His cousins were all married and very much in love. Just because it had worked out for them didn't mean it would for him. He was beginning to wonder what in the hell was wrong with him? There was no doubt in his mind that he'd picked the right person for him. Vanessa was perfect in every way.

He'd never known a warmer, more genuine, giving, and loving woman. Which didn't change the fact that she was not in love with him. Nor did she trust him.

"So what are you going to do, bud?" he mumbled aloud. Was he going to give up and keep on stepping? Or was he going to keep on fighting for what he longed for more than anything else in the world . . . that special place in her heart? The memory of her responses to his lovemaking was the only thing that kept him going. Unfortunately, it didn't ease the hurt deep inside. He longed for her love.

No matter how badly he wanted their problem resolved, he had no choice but to wait until the mess with Cummingham was cleared up. In the meantime, his plan was a simple one. He was going to enjoy what time they had together.

"Are you absolutely positive you don't need my help?" she asked for the third time, her chin propped on her fist. Relaxed after enjoying the huge breakfast that Ralph insisted on preparing, Vanessa felt like a lazy slug for not helping him load the dishwasher.

"Positive," he said with a grin. Pausing, he added, "It's kinda quiet around here. Where are the kids?"

"In the theater watching the new *Shrek* release."

"Again?"

"Yeah. It's a particular favorite."

"So, we're alone." He wiggled a brow suggestively.

Laughing, she teased, "What do you have in mind?"

"Nessa! Telephone!" Courtney yelled as she skipped into the kitchen. She passed the ringing cellular phone. She quickly added, before Vanessa could scold her, "I didn't go into your purse. You left it on the dresser in your room."

It stopped ringing before Vanessa could press the TALK button. She gave her little sister a hug. "Thank you, sweetie. I thought you were watching the movie?" Vanessa said absently, while trying to remember how to activate the caller ID feature.

Blushing, Courtney glanced at Ralph, then said in a loud whisper, "I had to use the restroom."

Vanessa and Ralph shared an amused smile.

"Ralph, may I please have some fruit punch?" Courtney asked.

He nodded, motioning to the refrigerated drawer built into a cabinet that he kept filled with cans of juice and soft drinks.

Vanessa waited until they were alone before she went over to where he was washing a frying pan at the sink. Her smile was gone, replaced by apprehension. "The call was from my lawyer. What do you think he wants? He's never called on Sunday before."

Drying his soapy hands, he cautioned, "Don't start worrying. He could be calling for something as simple as checking on you and the kids." Kissing her cheek, he said, "Call him."

Vanessa's fingers weren't steady as she punched in the numbers. "Hello, Mr. Jones, this is Vanessa Grant." She wasn't aware of slipping her hand into Ralph's. She listened intently. Then said, "Are you sure? There is no possibility of a mistake? Thank you! Thank you, so very much."

Vanessa didn't remember closing the small phone. All she was aware of was Ralph's strong arms around her waist. She held on to him, needing his support. Her eyes were swimming with tears when she said, "The Cumminghams have dropped their lawsuit! The twins are all mine and Lana's. Oh, Ralph . . . oh Ralph," she cried.

Ralph swept her up in his arms and whirled her around, releasing a heartfelt shout of pure joy. Vanessa held on tight.

"I can't believe it!" She was laughing through her tears.

"Neither can I. Did he say why?"

"He doesn't know. He got a call from their lawyer with the news. It's over, Ralph. It's finally over." She leaned up to kiss him, a warm, lingering kiss. "I'm so happy! It's over!"

Grinning down at her, he gave her a tight squeeze. "Finally! And so quickly! Incredible!"

She clung to him, feeling wonderfully safe and secure. "We did it! We did it!"

"No beautiful . . . not we. You did it. You never gave up, or lost faith." Easing back, until he could gaze into her eyes. "I'm so proud of you."

The sincerity in his eyes gave her an extraordinary sense of well-being. She shook her head firmly. "No, sweet man. I could not have done it without you. You were there every step of the way. Hiring that investigator. Keeping me grounded. When I think of all you've done to support . . ."

She blinked, stopping in midsentence at the tightening of his lips. "What is it? What's wrong?"

"Nothing." He smiled suddenly, then asked, "How are we going to celebrate?"

Relieved to see that smile return, she assured herself that she'd only imagined the flash of anger in his eyes. His relief and genuine pleasure for her was all over his handsome face. He wanted the twins to be with her as much as she wanted it.

"Well?"

She smiled up at him. "How would you like to celebrate? I know I would like some time alone with you."

He joined in her laughter. His dark eyes were smoldering with desire. "I'd like that, too. Maybe we can stop by my folks. Drop the kids off there. I'm sure they wouldn't mind a visit."

Vanessa giggled, shaking her head. "I couldn't ask that of them. Besides, the embarrassment of every one knowing what we're up to. No, it wouldn't be right to try to get rid of the twins even for a few hours. We should spend the day together as a family." She reached up and brushed her lips against his. "Tell me you understand?"

He grinned, somewhat sheepishly. "I understand. And you're right. Today is for family."

"Nessa!" Curtis yelled at the top of his lungs as he raced down the hallway.

"Movie is over!" Courtney was right behind him.

"I told you two to stop running!" Lana yelled, only a few steps behind the others.

Vanessa, hands on hips, said as all three entered the kitchen archway on the run. "Do you have to yell? Ralph and I can hear you."

"Sorry," Courtney and Curtis said at the same time.

"Are we going to eat with the Prescotts today?" Lana asked hopefully. "Wayne promised to let me play his new video game the next time we came over. I beat him and Kyle!" She laughed, clearly pleased by the thought.

Vanessa wanted to grab her sister and shout the exciting news that their family was safe, but knew she had to wait until they were alone. With an arm around both twins, she settled for kissing a cheek rather than covering their faces with kisses.

It was revealing that both of the twins weren't bothered that they hadn't seen their father this weekend. In fact, they hadn't asked about him. Yet when they didn't see Ralph in more than a day, they'd bombard her with questions about him, wanting to know where he was and when he was coming for a visit.

"Well?" Lana prompted.

Vanessa looked at Ralph. "What do you think?"

He nodded! "Let's go."

"I'm ready!" Curtis beamed.

"We're not," Lana called, as she and her sisters headed for the stairs.

Vanessa said, from over her shoulder, "Give us a half hour."

Ralph and Curtis exchanged a surprised look. They were comfortable in jeans and sport shirts.

"Want to read the funnies while we wait?" Ralph suggested.

Curtis giggled. "I can't read!"

"I can." Ralph grinned. "Let's go. "

They amused themselves in the den. With Curtis in his

lap, Ralph read his favorite Sunday funnies. Half an hour turned into an hour before the ladies returned.

"We're ready!" Courtney announced, twirling to show off her dress.

Lana had changed into a pink skirt and blouse trimmed in a white border of embroidered flowers, Courtney was in a pink dress, embroidered in white daisies with a ruffled hem. And Vanessa was also in a pink sundress with a long straight skirt, split on both sides, and around her waist were embroidered white tulips. Vanessa had made all three outfits, and each sister wore white sandals.

Grinning, Ralph said, "Wow! You three look so pretty." He tapped Curtis on the shoulder. "Don't they, Curtis?"

Baffled, the boy had forgotten their man-to-man talk. He looked from Ralph to his sisters, then back at Ralph. When Ralph motioned toward the ladies and mouthed the word "pretty," Curtis nodded eagerly before saying, "Yeah, you all look pretty!" After he received the pleased smiles from his sisters, Curtis puffed out his small chest and grinned up at Ralph, who patted his shoulder.

"We're ready," Vanessa announced, trying not to laugh at how pleased the two males were with themselves.

It was an enjoyable yet relaxing afternoon. The Prescotts were genuinely thrilled by Lana and Vanessa's news. The two families shared a small but endearing celebration. Although the twins had no idea why everyone was so happy, they enjoyed their sisters' warm smiles. After dinner, Lester insisted on opening a bottle of champagne. The youngsters were included; they each received a champagne glass filled with sparkling apple juice.

Vanessa was touched by the Prescotts' good wishes. It was a struggle not to give in to happy tears, and, equally relieved, Lana couldn't stop smiling. The added bonus was that there was no longer a threat to Lana's college fund.

With Ralph at her side, Vanessa decided life was especially good. Despite his denials, he had a great deal to do with their success. And she was determined to find a private moment to show him how much she appreciated his kindness.

On the way back to his home, Vanessa asked him to swing by her house to check things out. Evidently the reporters were not aware that the custody suit had been dropped. She recognized two of the three cars parked near the house. One was bold enough actually to park in her drive.

Although furious, she held back her reaction, not wanting to upset the kids. Ralph patted her hand, encouraging her to give it a few more days. Vanessa nodded her agreement.

Once the children were settled for the night, Vanessa came downstairs looking for Ralph. She found him in his office, working on his laptop.

"Last I heard, it was against the law to work on Sunday," she teased, crossing the plush carpet to sit on the corner of his desk.

Stretching his arms over his head, chuckling, he said, "Oh, really." He leaned back in the chair and took her hands and tugged her gently toward him. His laugh was deep and husky when she landed across his muscled thighs. Nuzzling her soft neck, he kissed her soft dark skin. Whispering against her warm, scented throat, he hummed, "Mmm, this is better for me. How about you, gorgeous."

"Gorgeous? I like it." She gazed dreamily into his velvet-dark eyes.

"I adore you." He kissed her tenderly, then asked, "Are the kids asleep?"

"Yeah." She wrapped her arms around his neck. "I'm sorry, you're stuck with us, for at least another night . . . maybe two?"

"Stuck? That's not how I see it." He dropped his head to brush her raspberry-tinted lips with his.

Vanessa sighed, opening her mouth to the hot caress of his tongue. The kiss was tender, giving, just like the man who held her. He'd been so wonderful, especially patient with her family. Her heart swelled with emotion, overwhelmed by his generosity.

"Oh Ralph." She shivered as his firm, smooth mouth warmed the side of her throat before he laved the base and moved to the valley between her breasts, left bare by her neckline. She rained kisses on his forehead, his straight, bold nose, and cheeks. "How did I get so lucky? To find such a thoughtful, caring man? I know you don't like me to say it, but, honey, I simply have to tell you how much I appreciate you."

Immediately, she felt his body stiffen. "You're right, you don't have to tell me. I did what any man worth the label would do for the woman in his life. No more . . . no less," he ended gruffly.

"Ralph, you have to let me say this. And then I promise to shut up and never, not ever, bring this up again. Fair enough?"

He insisted, "No. It's not necessary. All that needs to be said has been said."

She tried to laugh it off, but when she met his dark gaze, she saw that he was serious. The ready charm and playful sense of humor that was so much a part of his personality was notably absent.

Tenderly, she stroked his cheek. "Please, honey. You have been my angel and deserve the words. But more importantly, I wouldn't feel right keeping this locked inside."

"There's nothing faulty about my memory, Vanessa. You've told on more than one occasion how you feel. Please, let it go." Although his voice was quiet, it was also firm.

Vanessa wasn't having it. She rushed ahead with, "You've done so much for us, from the very beginning."

When he parted his lips to what she assumed to be a protest, she lifted her chin, placing her mouth against his. He released a husky moan when she licked his bottom lip before she took it into her mouth to suck. Measuring his response by his hungry groan, she knew she had captured his complete attention.

She kissed him deeply before she eased back to whisper, "Sweet man, you've been so patient with the twins. You've actually listened to Lana and answered her questions about going away to college and how to handle boys. You were open and honest while still being encouraging. I couldn't have asked for more. And when I got that first letter from Cummingham's lawyer, it sent me in a panic. You, Ralph, calmed me down while assuring me it wasn't the end of the world."

Barely taking time for a much-needed breath, she hurried ahead with, " . . . then you found a lawyer, as well as making the appointment. And you were prepared to pay for it, too. How could anyone ask for more? Goodness, you've done it all, including opening your home to us . . . no questions asked. Ralph, I adore you. You're simply wonderful, and I just have to let you know show how much I genuinely . . ."

"Enough!" he growled, in a hard voice brimming with a combination of what sounded like bitterness and resentment.

Alarm warred with confusion as she threw up her hands in disbelief. "No! You aren't making any sense! I appreciate every single thing you've done this summer for me and my family."

He didn't say a word, but his dark eyes flashed sparks of sheer rage as his large hands clasped her waist and lifted her off his lap and onto her feet. Then he stood and just stared down at her, a hand resting on one hip.

Swearing beneath his breath, he snapped, "Why Vanessa? Why did you do it?" Not giving her time to respond, he went on to hiss between clenched teeth, "What I don't get was, why you just couldn't leave it the hell alone?"

Twenty-six

While Vanessa stared back at him, Ralph struggled for control. A combination of hurt and rage rose like a thick cloud over him. It took all his willpower not to yell at her. She'd gone too far! Despite his warnings, she'd said it anyway.

Overwhelmed by rage, he was afraid of what he might say. Despite his fury, he couldn't forget the three innocent ones upstairs asleep. He'd invited them here. And none of this was their fault. No, this was about the beautiful Vanessa. Or was it? It wasn't as if he hadn't known what was coming next.

He had stayed, and now he had to deal with the consequences, the crushing pain of knowing that the woman he loved beyond all reason didn't even come close to returning his feelings. But what made it truly unbearable was that she had no idea what was wrong.

How could she have been so blind? How could she not know what he desperately wanted from her? He'd done every last thing he could think of, short of begging for her love. Crawling on his knees was the one thing he wasn't prepared to do. It was enough that she'd had him jumping through hoops for weeks now. All he had left was his pride.

"Don't you think you're overreacting . . . just a little? All I said was . . ."

He swore hotly. "I've heard nothing for weeks but how grateful you are for my help. Well, guess what. I don't want your gratitude! Damn it! I never asked for your appreciation."

He balled his hands until his dark knuckles were pale from the pressure. He held his normally full lips taut. "I'm sick to death of hearing those two words coming out of your mouth. It's the last thing I want from you!"

As if mystified, she said, "You're acting as if I cussed you out. I was merely attempting to put into words how much you mean to me and my family. Surely, you know I could not have made it through this nightmare without your support." Her lovely eyes pleaded with him to understand. As if she begged him not to be angry.

An excruciating pain, generated from the wounded place where his heart should have been, gave him the strength to look past her sweetness, her beauty, to hang on to the anger and resentment eating him alive. What was she trying to do? Destroy him? She'd already stamped on his heart, crushing it beneath her high heels.

Enough! He had enough! He knew how little she thought of his tender emotions. She'd thrown his love back in his face enough times. Shaking with anger, he closed his laptop. "I think it best that I sleep somewhere else tonight. Stay as long as you like." Grabbing his briefcase, he shoved the laptop inside, along with several file folders on his desk, and closed the case, all without sparing her a glance.

"Leave?" she repeated. "Where are you going?"

He didn't recall moving past her, yet he was at the door, looking back at her when he asked, "Does it matter?"

"Yes, it matters! Ralph, please, don't do this!" She came over and grabbed his arm. "Please, can't we talk this out?"

"I've already said all I plan to say. Keep your blasted gratitude and appreciation." He spit the words out as if they left a foul taste in his mouth.

"No, this is crazy. If anyone has to go, it should be me. After all, this is your home." Vanessa was wringing her hands. "Look, I'll wake the kids. We'll be gone in less than an hour."

"Hell, no!" Then Ralph stopped, realizing that he'd been swearing, something he'd been raised never to do in the presence of a lady. He was losing it. He took a few calming breaths.

"Ralph, it won't take . . ."

"Look! Have you forgotten the reporters? Let the kids sleep. Why upset them? They don't need to be dragged out of bed and into the middle of our mess."

At her nod of consent, he released a pent-up breath. He carefully put the briefcase down. Leaning a shoulder against the doorframe, he folded his arms over his chest and requested, "Explain one thing for me?"

"Funny. You haven't been interested in listening to anything I said tonight." Her beautiful brown eyes were brimming with anger.

Ralph frowned, realizing that to her, his anger might have seemed sudden. In truth, it had building for weeks. He was tired of waiting, living on hope, wondering when she was going to take it into her head to put him out of his misery and walk.

"I need answers. I need to understand why you picked me. Yes, we were thrown together because of Brynne and Devin's wedding. But that doesn't explain why you asked me to be your lover? Or why you didn't bother to tell me you were a virgin? What? You didn't think I would notice?"

Vanessa stared at him wide-eyed, then she turned away.

She took the visitor's chair in front of the desk. She did everything but answer his question!

The small measure of cool he'd regained vanished in that instant. "It was a mistake from the start. I was insane to have ever touched you. I gave you my love while you gave me friendship. Hell, I asked you to be my wife, not once but twice.

"My guess would be, you don't even remember your response." He didn't wait for an answer, but rushed ahead, saying, "At least, the first time, you were courteous enough to answer . . . thanks but no. Lady, the last time you didn't even bother to give me an answer. And to think, you claim you don't get it. Let me break it down for you. I've had enough. My part in this pathetic guessing game is over."

Pushing away from the doorframe, he picked up his briefcase. "I will be out of town for at least a week. By then, I'm sure the news that Cummingham is dropping the case will be out, and you should be able to go home." He hesitated long enough to jot down a note. "This is the code to the alarm. I'll leave an extra set of keys on the hall table. You can give them to Anna when you're ready to leave."

Vanessa jumped to her feet. "Ralph, please! Don't leave like this. You don't understand! At least stay long enough so that I can explain. I deserve that much."

He gestured impatiently. "Go ahead. This should be good."

"Yes, you told me you loved me. Yes, you asked me to marry you twice. And yes, I did refuse the first time. But, Ralph, you know why. How can you act as if you don't know why? I explained it to you."

He quirked a skeptical brow.

"I told you," she insisted. "You just didn't take it seriously. That's not my fault. What woman wants to marry a man because he pities her? Not me! And don't act as if you don't know what I mean!" She hissed at him. "That proposal didn't have a thing to do with love. It was your way of fixing my problems with Cummingham."

He came back with, "I wouldn't have asked if I didn't mean it."

"Oh, you meant it. You meant to save me from the big bad wolf. In my case, Cummingham was the monster. The second time, I didn't think you took that proposal seriously, so why should I."

He was so angry, he didn't trust himself to speak.

"What? Nothing to say?" she challenged.

"Why bother? You were right. We were a gigantic mistake from day one. We made much better friends than lovers. That should make you happy."

"Will you stop? You act like I wanted us to fail. And that's just not true. You claimed you loved me. But how could I take you seriously? I had no idea your so-called love would last."

"So-called!" he snarled.

"That's what I said! You are not exactly a one-woman kind of man. Like Cummingham, you have your fair share to pick from. You know your history better than I do. Just because you've been involved with me longer than anyone else doesn't mean I can trust you. And I know that because your family told me. According to them, you never bring a woman more than once to Sunday . . . dinner . . . that is . . ."

"My family has nothing to do with this. I keep Cummingham out of this. I asked you, Vanessa Grant, to marry me because I want you." He surprised himself when he admitted, "You're wrong about me. I haven't been near another woman since we slept together last spring. I've given you no reason not to trust me."

But Ralph held back. He couldn't reveal that he hadn't

slept with anyone else since their first dance at Brynne and Devin's engagement party months earlier. That was information he hadn't shared with anyone. It was bad enough that he'd left himself wide open . . . vulnerable to her in a way he'd never even come close to doing with anyone else. But then he wanted her desperately.

"Don't lie to me, Ralph!"

He stared at her. The hurt that she didn't believe him was incredible. He blinked, refusing to let the crushing weight of it show on his face. Well, she'd just proven him right. There was no longer any doubt that she, alone, had the power to bring him to his knees. And he had been the fool who had placed the weapon in her pretty hands.

"Believe what you like. I won't stand here arguing with you."

"Ralph, you're the one who brought that other girl to your family's Fourth of July party! It's not a secret. I'm not accusing you of sneaking around. I don't think you'd sneak for me or anyone else. I don't think you would bother. You don't have that much emotion invested in it."

"I didn't sleep with her. I don't sleep with every woman I take out. And you're right. I've never cared enough to go around trying to hide anything. That's not my way."

"Why did you even bring her? You knew I would be there."

"Vanessa, I didn't know you were coming. Besides, you told me to do whatever I liked. You told me to go out and enjoy myself with whomever. You said you didn't care!"

"I know."

"I hope so. Because I cared enough about you to ask you to be my wife. I won't ask again," he said, unaware his voice was edged with bitterness.

"You don't have to throw it in my face. I get it! You're asking a lot, for a man I can trust about as far as I can throw him! I don't want that kind of marriage. And you're not a forever kind of man."

Ralph dropped his lids, determined to protect himself from further hurt and pain. When his cousins talked about love, no one mentioned this excruciating pain tearing at his heart. He'd done it. He had put himself out there, and he had asked that all-important question. And her answer made it clear that she cared for him, but she was not in love with him.

"Ralph!"

He didn't look at her, he couldn't. He had to concentrate on numbing the pain. "I'm waiting for you to say what you need to say."

"So you can leave?"

"That's right. Are you done?"

"Completely!" She gestured wildly. "Talking to you right now is about as easy as trying to talk to that wall!"

"Then we're done," he said, case in hand. "If you need more than a week, let my housekeeper or secretary know. They know how to reach me. Bye."

Ralph stayed long enough to place a call to his pilot and pack an overnight case. He passed Vanessa's door without slowing down. He'd already said too much. Evidently, the only woman that mattered didn't trust him enough to take the risk. It was a shame he hadn't followed his instincts when she'd asked him to become her lover. He should have said no. That error in judgment had cost him. Whoever said love and friendship don't mix hadn't lied. He'd found out the hard way. He'd lost both, his friend and his love.

Blinded by tears, Vanessa sat at her desk, trying to make out the figures on her computer screen. She repeatedly wiped at the tears blurring her vision. It was Thursday. The reporters were gone. Her family had been home for two days.

The kids had enjoyed themselves so much at Ralph's place, they'd come up with one excuse after another not to leave. As much as they loved the high-tech toys and gadgets Ralph had acquired over the years, it was the man they missed and asked about. They'd grown tired of her answer that he was away working. And they were not pleased when she told them they could not call him, period. It had not been easy to stick to it, but she had not backed down. Her nerves were stretched to the limit, and she was nearing the point where she was ready to go after whoever was unlucky enough to say his name with her grandmother's cast-iron skillet.

Life wasn't fair. She'd spent the entire summer trying to take care of everyone else. Now that the kids were in school, it was her turn to concentrate on herself. Yet all she could think about was that she'd blown it. She had missed her chance at happiness. Ralph not only didn't want her gratitude, he didn't want her.

The press had finally moved on once Sheila Cummingham had made public her intentions of suing her husband for divorce. There was no longer a custody question. Greg Cummingham had bigger concerns from back child-support payments, past lovers' claims of personal damage and upcoming paternity tests, plus there were rumors that Cummingham had gone into the marriage without a prenuptial.

There was no question that the twins were all hers. More important, Vanessa was relieved that Curtis and Courtney were not negatively affected by the experience of getting to know their father. Unfortunately for him, he'd made no lasting impression on the twins.

Vanessa made a point of starting the steps to adopt the twins. She was not going to repeat the mistake of leaving it to chance.

Ralph was the one who'd lingered in their thoughts. And

she had no idea how to fix it. She'd put off telling her family that he was no longer a part of their lives. Instead of celebrating that the stress and worries of the summer were gone, she was walking around pretending she'd not lost her best friend, and her heart wasn't broken. Her fantasy man . . . her dream lover . . . the man she loved was gone. What they shared was over. And there was no hope of him coming back.

It was time for her to pull herself together and get on with her life. After blowing her nose and drying her eyes, she let out an exhausted sigh. She wasn't getting any work done here. She would be better off at home. The house would be quiet. Maybe she could take a nap, get some sleep. She hadn't slept an entire night since the argument with Ralph.

Mind made up, Vanessa turned off the computer, straightened her desk, and grabbed her purse from the bottom drawer. Judging by the wonderful smells coming from the kitchen, Anna was baking.

As she passed through, Vanessa said, "I'm leaving early, Anna. Tell Gavin I will make up the time tomorrow. Bye."

"Not so fast," Anna looked up from the scale she was been using to measure flour. Grabbing a damp dishcloth, she cleaned her hands. "What's wrong?"

Trying not to look as pitiful as she felt, Vanessa forced a smile. "What makes you think something is wrong?"

"That's a joke, right?" Anna teased.

"No!" Vanessa was genuinely offended. "I'm serious."

"Girl, you didn't even put a brush through that hair this morning. You never wear bleach-spotted, faded jeans and a plain white T-shirt to work, It's not your style. You seemed fine at dinner on Sunday, but you've been down in the mouth all week."

"I'm just tired. I haven't been sleeping well," Vanessa admitted reluctantly.

Anna smiled, playfully. "Maybe you're just missing Ralph? He should be home by next Tuesday."

The mention of his name caused her eyes to fill with tears, and a sob of anguish escaped, despite her best efforts to hold it inside.

"What did I say?" Anna asked with concern.

"His name," Vanessa mumbled in misery. Wiping her eyes, she managed to get out, "Look, I'm sorry. I shouldn't have said anything. I'd better be getting home."

"Not so fast. Come on, sit down so we can talk." Anna was not about to accept no. Taking Vanessa's arm, she urged her to the kitchen table. Once they were seated, Anna said, "Okay, what did he do? And don't tell me nothing because I know better. Don't forget I grew up with him. My cousin can be just as stubborn as the other Prescott males."

"We had a fight. There's no point in going into all the gory details. It's over between us. He wanted out. There is nothing left to say!"

"That makes no sense. You two were perfectly happy on Sunday." Anna asked, "What set him off?"

Rattled, Vanessa said, "He asked me not to, but I did it anyway."

"Did what?"

"I thanked him for all that he's done to help hold my family together," she confessed.

Baffled, Anna quizzed, "Are you telling me my cousin was angry enough to end your relationship because you thanked him? Come on, Vanessa, that doesn't make sense."

"Ralph warned me not to do it. He was tired of hearing about how much I appreciate all he's done for me. He has been so sweet to me. You wouldn't believe all the things he's done to make life easier for me and the kids, especially after Cummingham decided to sue for custody. He's been there for me, from finding the best lawyer, willing to pay the legal bills, to taking a genuine interest in my family. If you told me what a nice guy he was before Brynne's engagement to Devin, I wouldn't have believed it. I had all these preconceived ideas about him, and most of them, I learned later, were wrong."

"So you two broke up because you thanked him? There has to be some other reason," Anna persisted.

"That was a big part of it. He deserved my thanks. He deserved a lot more than my thanks," Vanessa confessed. "He asked me to marry him twice. I refused."

Incredulous, Anna repeated, "My cousin asked you to marry him, and you turned him down?"

Vanessa nodded. "He even told me he loved me."

"Ralph?"

"Yes. Shocking, isn't it?"

Anna laughed. "Incredible. So why aren't you designing your wedding dress?"

"We're talking about Ralph. I'd be out of my mind not to have serious doubts about his ability to commit. The first time he asked was because I was in serious trouble. I needed a lawyer and money, and lots of it." Vanessa paused before she explained, "He knew I would never take money from a man. So he proposed, and I refused. It couldn't work under those circumstances. The second time, I didn't even answer the question. I didn't see the point. He was still trying to solve my problems with a marriage proposal."

"Vanessa, you may not believe this, but Ralph wouldn't have asked you if he didn't care about you. He has been happily single for a long time. He wasn't looking to change that. It's you that made the difference for him." Anna went on to say, "No woman has even come close to getting a marriage proposal out of him. Ralph likes the chase. If he asked you to marry him, believe it, he's serious and has deep feelings for you."

Vanessa hesitated for a long moment, before she revealed, "Anna, I know he cares for me. He's told me he's in love with me."

"So what's the problem? Tell me why we're not planning a wedding?"

"Because I don't trust him enough to marry him. You know as well as I do he's a player. How long do you think he can remain faithful? A year? Maybe two, if I'm lucky? Besides, Anna, I have more than myself to consider. I don't want the kids to become more involved with him. Anna, they already adore him. I can't take that risk it might not work. It wouldn't be fair to them or me if he messes up."

Anna took Vanessa's hands and squeezed. "I'm not defending Ralph because he is my family, and I love him. Everything you said is true. I've known him longer and maybe better in some ways. Right?"

Vanessa nodded. "True."

"Then you'll try to listen with an open mind?" Anna waited for her answer.

"I'll try," Vanessa promised.

"Ralph was twelve when he first came to live with us. I was around ten and not thrilled to have yet another big brother. I already had two. Mama was expecting, and I was hoping for a baby sister, but no one bothered to ask me." Anna smiled before she sobered, and said, "Ralph was devastated by the loss of his parents. He was an only child, and, through no fault of his own, he was living in a new house, with a new family. At least he knew us because we spent part of every summer down South, but that wasn't the same. It was hard for him, and my folks did everything they could to let him know he was loved and wanted. Despite the fact my folks treated him as if he were one of their own, Ralph wasn't having it. He kept to himself even though he and Devin were the same age, and the three older boys shared a big room. This was back before Wesley made it into the pros, and we lived in a three-bedroom house.

"Anyway, it took most of that year before that stubborn boy let us into his heart. It took a major fight with kids in a neighborhood gang before Ralph believed we were his family. My parents didn't give up on him, any more than they would give up on any of us," Anna insisted, and added, "Ralph hasn't changed. He is still as mule-headed as he was as a kid. If he decided he wants to marry you and help you raise those kids, then that's what he intends to do if you give him the chance. He doesn't make promises lightly."

Vanessa shook her head. "I know that's what you believe, but Anna, it may only be wishful thinking on your part." She held up her hand, "No, Anna. Let me finish." Vanessa waited until the other woman nodded her agreement. "I, also, know how devastating it is to lose a parent. None of that means Ralph is ready for marriage.

"I've never seen him so angry. Ralph told me that I'm treating him as if he's no different than Greg Cummingham, which is a terrible thing to say, especially considering how I feel about the twins' father." Vanessa said sadly, "At first, I did compare the two men."

"Well, Vanessa, if you truly believe Ralph is no different than Greg Cummingham, then you're correct to protect yourself. You should keep on walking and never look back."

Stunned, Vanessa felt an overwhelming need to defend Ralph. "No, you don't understand! Ralph isn't cruel, and he's not out to hurt anyone. His ladies all know that he's not looking for love. Of course, that doesn't stop the ladies from going after him. What I meant, they are both womanizers, and I can't forget that. Ralph has enjoyed years of going from female to female. And he gets away with it because he's gorgeous and irresistible."

Anna laughed, "If I didn't know better, I'd wonder if you're in love with my cousin."

Vanessa's eyes locked with Anna's. She blinked back tears, as she whispered, "It's true."

"I didn't catch that. What did you say?" Anna prompted.

Vanessa lifted her chin. "You heard me."

"Yeah, I did. You said you're in love with Ralph." Anna went around and hugged her. "I knew it. But it sure took you long enough to admit it."

Vanessa hugged her back. "Stupid, ha?"

"Life is crazy. I also fell in love with and married a womanizer. Gavin was so bad that Ralph, Devin, and Wesley ganged up on him and demanded he leave me alone!" Anna laughed. "It's funny now, but at the time I didn't find it amusing.

"I knew what they said about him was true, but I loved him so much, I had to at least give us a try. If I ended up hurt, that was okay. It was worth the risk. Can you honestly do any less?" Anna quizzed.

Twenty-seven

Vanessa worried her bottom lip. "I don't have your confidence, Anna. I've hurt him. I know I have. And I hate it. He really shocked me when he admitted he hasn't had sex with anyone else since we made love."

Although she looked stunned, Anna asked, "Do you believe him?"

"I don't know. I called him a liar. I kept remembering the woman he brought to the Fourth of July picnic. He insisted he didn't sleep with her."

"I repeat, do you believe him?" Anna reminded her. "He's the same man who put his needs aside to help you. Tell me if I'm wrong, but hasn't he been at your side through the worst of it?" Before Vanessa could respond, Anna said, "He's the man who never turned his back on you. We were raised to be proud of the Prescott name. It's a name we have to live up to. Although all the Prescott men are strong, they also have big hearts and an amazing supply of love and loyalty. Once given, the Prescotts never break their word. If you don't believe me, then all you have to do is call Kelli, Brynne, and my mother. They also not only love Prescott men, but have exchanged vows with them. Also, they had to decide if they loved and believed in each man enough to risk it all. You already know that Ralph loves and believes in you enough to take the big risk."

As Vanessa silently asked herself if she loved and believed in Ralph enough to take the ultimate risk, tears slowly filled her eyes. They slowly ran down her cheeks to drip onto her chin. Using her hands, she tried but failed to wipe them away.

Absently, she thanked Anna for giving her a napkin. Deep in her heart she knew that everything Anne said was true. Ralph had never lied to her. He never really broke a promise. He'd come after her because she hadn't kept her word that first night.

The problem was hers alone.

She was the one with the doubts, not the children or Ralph. Did she have the courage to gamble on love? Did she? Or was she going to run? Was she strong enough to stick and stay to the bitter end? Would she be able to fight for what she wanted? Because that was what it would take to get him to even listen to what she had to say. How badly did she want him? Was love enough?

"What are you going to do?"

"I'm not going to let Ralph Prescott get away without a fight. Can you tell me where he's gone?"

"Ralph's in Dallas." Anna grinned. "Now stop wasting time. Pick up the phone and call him."

Vanessa shook her head. "I can't do this over the telephone. I have to face him when I tell him how I feel." Her heart was galloping like a runaway bronco when she asked, "Do you know where he's staying?"

She couldn't help wondering if she could do this. But what choice did she have? He was both angry and hurt. She'd be lucky if he even let her speak to him.

Smiling, Anna said, "No, but I can find out." She went over to her desk and picked up the telephone.

Vanessa didn't listen to Anna's end of the conversation. She was suffering from a bad case of nerves. She nearly jumped when Anna held out a slip of paper.

At her questioning look, Anna said, "I called my mother. This is his hotel. I also called my brother, Devin. In two hours there will be a plane waiting for you at the airport." Anna beamed in satisfaction. "And don't worry about the kids. I'll be happy to look after them until you get back."

"Are you sure? When I said I wanted to see him, I didn't take time to figure out all the details. I just . . ."

Anna interrupted. "It's no trouble at all. This house is so big, we have plenty of room. And Kyle is here to help entertain Lana and the twins. Besides, it will be good practice for me." Anna's eyes were sparkling with pleasure when she admitted, "Gavin and I are pregnant. I'm only a few months along, but we're excited."

"Oh, Anna! That's wonderful news!" Vanessa hugged her, genuinely happy for her.

Anna gushed. "Thank you. We decided to keep the news to ourselves for a little while. You're the first person I've told. My mother doesn't even know yet."

Vanessa smiled. "I'm honored. I promise not to tell."

Anna laughed. "Don't worry about that. We're going to tell the whole family at dinner this coming Sunday. Maybe you and Ralph will be back by then?"

At the mention of Ralph's name, all of Vanessa's worries returned with a vengeance. She said unhappily, "Anna, I don't know. I could be making a huge mistake. What if Ralph doesn't want to hear anything I have to say? He was so upset when he left. He might not want to talk to me."

"Stop that! You're only scaring yourself. Ralph has had days to think and cool down. Hopefully, he's ready to listen to what you have to say. Besides, you don't have time to worry. You have too much to do. You've got to go home, and

get you and the kids packed, then find something to wear
that's going to make his head spin. Plus, you have to drop the
kids off and drive to the airport. There is no time to waste."

Vanessa kissed Anna's cheek. "Thanks for everything.
I love you. Bye." She waved, then hurried to the side door.
Anna was right. She didn't have a moment to waste.

As Vanessa made herself comfortable in one of the plush
leather armchairs in the main cabin of the private plane, she
felt as if she'd been caught in a whirlwind. The good thing
about getting herself and the kids ready so quickly was that
she hadn't had time to worry or reconsider her decision.

Surprisingly, Lana hadn't asked a single question when
Vanessa told her she was flying to Dallas for a few days. For
a moment, Vanessa had been tempted to lie, to say she would
be visiting a newly discovered relative. Looking back, she
was thankful she had decided against it. Lana was a smart
girl. Besides, Vanessa respected her sister enough to tell her
the truth, that she was going to see Ralph.

Vanessa hadn't known that Lana suspected that something was wrong between her and Ralph. It wasn't until she'd
taken the kids to Anna and Gavin's and Lana had kissed her
good-bye, that Lana made a point of wishing her good luck.
Knowing Vanessa had her sister's support helped.

"Would you care for a magazine, Ms. Grant?" Jan Black-
man, the attractive, smiling flight attendant, had introduced
herself the instant Vanessa stepped on the plane. She held a
selection for Vanessa, the only passenger, to choose from.

"No, thank you, Jan." Vanessa nervously smoothed the
skirt of her red suit. It was Ralph's favorite. She assured herself it didn't matter if she'd worn it the last time he'd taken
her to church.

"May I get you something to eat or drink before we take
off, Ms. Grant?"

Already tense, Vanessa was uncomfortable with the attention, pasted a smile on her face. "No, but thank you."

"If you need anything at all, just let me know."

Just then a bell chimed, and the seat belt sign came on. Vanessa automatically clicked hers in place. The flight attendant smiled before moving to the front of the cabin and taking her own seat.

Vanessa was too self-absorbed to notice the beauty and luxury of her surroundings. As she stared out the window with her hands clasped in her lap, she told herself it was a good thing she'd turned Ralph's proposal down. She'd never become accustomed to the opulent lifestyle he took for granted.

Yet despite his wealth, he was levelheaded and down-to-earth. He was a good person with a quiet strength she couldn't help but admire. For so long, she'd done her best not to fall in love with him. She had no idea how it had happened or when. But there was no doubt in her mind that she loved him with all her heart.

Vanessa smiled as the plane rose into the late-afternoon sky. Ralph had a wonderful family. And she had no trouble understanding why Ralph and his cousins were so successful. They'd patterned themselves after two strong yet loving parents. Lester loved his wife and family. Most important, he was not afraid to show that love.

She had no trouble picturing Ralph someday, surrounded by a large family of his own. And she desperately wanted to be included. How could she have been so incredibly blind? She had stood in his face and practically told him he was no different than Greg Cummingham. Talk about an insult!

Covering her face with her hands, she shook her head in despair. If he never spoke to her again, she wouldn't blame him. It was a credit to the fine man he was that he hadn't thrown her and the kids out of his house and into the street. Instead he had left.

She bit her bottom lip, determined not to cry. Here she sat, like one of his exes, hoping that he would reconsider and take her back.

"Ms. Grant, a telephone call for you."

Vanessa murmured a thank-you, as she put the receiver to her ear. Assuming it was Anna checking on her, she said, "Hello, Anna."

"It's not Anna. Hi, girlfriend."

"Brynne!" She laughed. "It's so good to hear your voice. Anna told you."

"Of course, we're sisters now. I hear you're going to be a Prescott soon," Brynne teased.

Vanessa couldn't find even a tiny bit of humor in this situation. Instead she was struggling not to cry. "Oh, Brynne he has to hate me. I made such a mess of things."

"Vanessa . . . stop! Ralph is crazy about you. Do you know of any other woman he's proposed to?"

Vanessa covered her mouth as if that would muffle the scream rising in her throat. "Was there anything Anna left out of our conversation?"

"I sure hope not. You, Miss should-have-told-me-your-own-self, what's with the secrets? You know I love you and those babies. Devin and I would never have gotten back together without your encouraging me every step of the way.

"Now, I really know you're exaggerating. You were in love with that man before you moved back to Detroit. How's my little Shanna doing?"

"She's fine, getting bigger every day. But this call isn't about me and mine. How are you holding it together?"

"I'm a mess. And I can't stop shaking," she whispered, careful not to be overheard. She went on to tell Brynne about their argument, then ended with, "So you see why there is a good chance he won't open his hotel door."

"He'll let you in. If for no other reason than to let you know how angry he is with you. That's when you use your best weapon."

"I don't have any weapons," Vanessa insisted.

"Sure you do. At times like this, you have to play dirty and walk right into his arms and press up against him."

Vanessa broke into a peal of laughter. "You are so wrong. But I like how you think. If all else fails, go for the sex appeal."

"That's right. You're packing the kind of heat he finds irresistible. That man may be angry, but he still wants you. I saw the way he could not take his eyes off you at the family picnic. He was checking you out, my friend."

Vanessa couldn't help smiling at the bittersweet memory. "It seems so long ago. I never expected to fall in love with him. I fought it as long as I could, but nothing helped. I don't know if I should kiss you or hit you for starting this mess by asking me to be your maid of honor."

"A kiss, of course. Don't forget Devin's part. My honey asked Ralph to be his best man."

"Oh Brynne, what am I going to do if he says no? What if he doesn't give us another chance?" Vanessa sniffed, searching until she found a tissue in her purse.

"He will. But if he's stubborn enough to say no, don't worry. You know where he lives. You even know all of his relatives. And you are too smart to give up. You just keep on talking until you wear him down and get him to listen. Right?"

"Right," Vanessa repeated with less conviction. "Wish me luck."

"You've got it, girlfriend. Call me when you can?"

"I will. Bye, Brynne. I love you."

"I love you, too. Bye."

Vanessa leaned back against the seat, closing her eyes to review the words she planned to say to him. If only she could convince him to listen. She hoped that Devin had not called Ralph to warn him that she was coming.

Ralph had just returned to the hotel after a business dinner when Devin called to tell him that Vanessa was flying in to see him. He swore angrily, but it didn't release the tension inside of him.

What he could not figure out was why she was coming. What did she hope to gain by rehashing their argument? There was not a doubt in his mind that it would be more of the same. He certainly hadn't changed his mind, and he would be willing to bet that the stubborn beauty hadn't changed her mind, either.

So what if she was on her way. That didn't mean he would open the door and let her anywhere near him. Damn her for following him! Why couldn't she leave it alone? She'd hurt him enough to last for a lifetime. What was she trying to do? Grind what little pride he had left to dust? He didn't need to be reminded of what he couldn't have.

First she'd tempted him to take what he could never have. Why? Why had she let him inside her sweet body? She'd given him a slice of heaven only to plunge him in to hell when he discovered she was a virgin. That night of lovemaking had turned into his own personal nightmare. No matter how desperately he wanted her, he'd never have touched her if he had known. When she approached him, she deliberately kept that bit of choice information to herself. And he didn't like it. At least that's what he told himself.

After that first time, he found he could not stay away from her. But she could have easily stopped him with a simple no. Yet she let him wear her down, all the while knowing that he couldn't get enough of her sweetness. Each taste of her left him mad with hunger for even more. For the first time in his life, no other woman would do. There could be no substitution for his Nessa.

Swearing bitterly, he paced the confines of the sitting room of the luxury suite. He sat down at the desk with his laptop but found he couldn't concentrate.

He should have insisted she marry him as soon as he realized that she was an innocent. It would have been the honorable thing to do. He should not have backed down but kept at it. Eventually, he'd have worn her down, and she would have seen it was their only recourse, under the circumstances. She might even be pregnant by now. It certainly would have saved him months of heartache. Her kids needed a man in their lives, a stabilizing influence.

None of that was important now. She had refused his proposals. Whatever might have been was not destined. Once she said whatever she'd come to say, they would be done.

When she was gone, he would face and deal with the heartache alone, then move on. If he never saw her again, it would be too soon. He wanted nothing from her. Not even the time of day. Why couldn't she see that she was wasting both of their time by coming here? Not even for her precious kids would he put himself through this kind of hell ever again. It was over.

He'd heard the best way to get over one woman was a new woman. He planned to get out his Blackberry, call the first cutie willing to go out with him, and hopefully sleep with her. Certain of what he needed to do to get his life back on track, he decided to end the night hitting the hotel's night spots.

"Sounds like a plan," he said aloud.

At the sound of the brass knocker hitting the door, he smoothed his damp palms down his thighs and began moving toward the door. As he reached the doorknob, Ralph straightened his shoulders and took a deep breath.

After swinging one of the double doors open, his large frame blocked the entrance. With powerful arms folded across his chest, he waited. Vanessa stared up at him, not saying a word. Her large beautiful eyes were velvety brown, her full, glossy, red-tinted mouth was lush and looked good enough to taste.

He swore beneath his breath as he slowly checked out how good she looked in that short red skirt suit and the red strappy heels that showed off those incredible, long, shapely, bare brown legs. Talk about unfair, she'd left her thick, hair down to curl, framing her beautiful face. She was made up and clearly loaded for bear. What was she trying to do, bring him to his knees? No way! As he stiffened his spine, another part of his anatomy was hardening.

Despite the fact his shaft pulsated with need, he silently repeated *I am in control* again and again. He intended to make sure it stayed that way. This wasn't about desire. They both knew he wanted her. That wasn't exactly news.

Determined to stand his ground, he said impatiently, "Say what you came to say and leave. I have plans for the evening."

Shaken, Vanessa lifted her chin, determined not to turn and run. "You obviously were expecting me. Someone told you. Who was it? Who told you I was coming?"

"Devin. What did you expect? Devin and I jointly own the jet on which you flew out here. You evidently played on Anna's sympathy. What I don't understand is why you bothered to come."

"May I come in?" she asked politely.

Ralph's frown hadn't eased, but he stepped back and allowed her to enter.

Although she was shaking so badly that she feared her

legs would give out, she made it to the sofa and took a seat. She barely glanced around the expensively furnished room.

He coldly repeated, "Vanessa? As far as I'm concerned, we said it all the other night."

Determined to ignore the way her stomach hurt from nerves, she crossed her legs and held her clasped hands in her lap. Having rehearsed her speech so she wouldn't leave anything out, she said, "I know I should have told you all this on Sunday night, but I couldn't seem to get the words out. In fact, I never told anyone this because I was too embarrassed to admit the truth."

She quickly went on to say, "I've made a point hiding it all this time. I didn't want you to know I've been infatuated with you for years. Your face and strong body have played repeatedly in my dreams. You're my fantasy man. I've imagined you making love to me hundreds of times. Getting to know you before the wedding made it worse."

"What?" Ralph said in disbelief as he sat down on the arm of the love seat across from her.

"You heard me. And it's true. That's why when we were in Atlanta I finally found the courage to tell you I wanted you. Being away also helped. And I decided to take advantage of what felt like a golden opportunity. I found the courage to ask you to be my lover."

Reading the doubt in his eyes, she whispered, "You don't believe me, do you?"

"I don't know what I believe." He shook his head as if to clear it. "You've certainly surprised me. Why are you telling me all this now?"

She released a nervous laugh. "I didn't have much choice. You walked away. It was now or never."

He still looked doubtful, confused. He admitted, "I'm not sure I know what to believe. We spent most of the summer together. Not once have you even hinted you felt this way."

Twenty-eight

"*I know.* And I was wrong. I should have told you on Sunday night. While you were able to tell me how you felt, I held back. Look what happened! Everything went so horribly wrong." She threw her hands up in helplessness. "And it was all my fault that you left angry. Ralph, please. It's time we really talked. I'm so sick of trying to keep it all inside. I can't do it anymore."

He stared at her so long, not saying anything, that she came close to panicking. She rushed ahead with, "I should have told you all this when I first asked you to be my lover. I knew you had a right to know, but I was too embarrassed to tell you. I think . . . no, I know, I was falling in love with you way back when we were planning Brynne and Devin's engagement party."

She could tell she'd shocked him. She smiled for the first time since she arrived. "Should I wait for you to catch up?"

"I'm glad one of us finds this amusing," he growled, clearly frustrated.

"I don't, not really. I'm just trying to lighten the mood." She covered her face with her hands for a moment, then dropped them into her lap. "This is so hard. I don't want you to be angry. I'm really trying to make you understand why I did what I did."

He folded his arms over his chest. His face closed, not allowing her to guess what he might be thinking. "I'm listening."

Nodding, she took a deep breath before revealing, "While we were planning the engagement party, I used to wait to call you until it was late. Sometimes it was something I easily could have told you during the day. I liked to turn off all the lights, after the house was quiet, then climb into bed, close my eyes, and concentrate on listening to the sound of your voice. It didn't matter what we talked about. Ralph, I adored that deep huskiness of your voice. It was as if you were in bed with me. Yours was the last voice I heard. And I'd dream about you . . . sensuous dreams."

Afraid to even look at him, she said in a nervous whisper, "I was falling in love with you. It frightened me, yet I didn't want it to stop. After the engagement party, the calls stopped. And it hurt. I needed to talk to you. I wanted it back. I wanted you back.

"Then we had that surprise trip to Atlanta. And you were there. I had an unexpected opportunity if I had the courage to just ask for what I wanted. Somehow, I did ask." She took a deep breath. "I was so scared the night I asked you to be my lover. I just knew you were going to turn me down. But you didn't. I didn't realize I was in love with you. All I knew was that I wanted to be with you. You . . ."

Before Vanessa finished, he was in front of her. He pulled her against his hard frame. His kisses were deep and hungry. Vanessa melted, locking her arms around his lean waist. Then suddenly, she was pushing against him, shaking her head. She said, "Let me finish. I need to tell you . . . all of it."

He nodded. When he sat back down, he brought her down with him until she sat across his thighs. With his face against her soft throat, he said, "Go ahead. Say it."

"No, let me up. I'm heavy. Besides, I can't think with you so close."

"Don't ever complain about your size. I adore your curves. When I look at you I see nothing except a beautiful woman. I love you, Vanessa Grant. I love everything about you. And I'm not going to ever let you go, again."

Vanessa blushed, unable to control her happy tears.

"Don't cry, sweetheart."

"These are happy tears," she said, kissing him.

"Marry me."

She shook her head no, then instantly felt his entire body stiffen.

"Was that a refusal?" he demanded.

"I love you." She brushed his lips with hers. "I love you so very much. And I want nothing more than to be your wife." She let out a breath when she felt him relax beneath her.

"When?"

She moved a caressing hand over his biceps. "Honey, please. We need to talk. I don't want there to be any more misunderstandings between us. It hurts too much."

When Ralph placed a finger under her chin, she lifted her face until her eyes met his. What she saw made her heart ache at the depth of love and vulnerability he didn't try to conceal. She felt as if she were seeing into his heart.

He'd put himself out there, and she could do no less than be completely open with him. "I've made so many mistakes this summer. I've been so busy taking care of the children and dealing with the twins' father, plus struggling to handle my fears and doubts while fighting my feelings for you. With the twins' situation sorted out and the kids back in school, finally I was able to focus on what was important to me. You, my love . . . only you."

Through a haze of unexpected tears she let him see into her

heart. She wanted Ralph to be her all . . . her partner . . . her heart . . . her mate. If they were going to make it as a couple, there could be no secrets. Vanessa fully accepted what would be their reality. They would do it . . . all of it . . . together.

"Happy tears?" he questioned.

"Absolutely." She smiled back.

They shared a long, gentle kiss.

"I see the love, but I need the words," he said quietly. "For so long it has only been wishful thinking on my part."

"I mean it. I am so in love with you, Ralph Prescott. More than I can possibly say."

He smiled, before whispering, "Good. I'll need you to tell me often. Get used to it because I'll never get tired of hearing those magical words."

"Ralph, I'm sorry I kept you waiting, and it took me so long to tell you how I feel. I let my insecurities that you might not love me enough to commit keep us apart. Never again."

Gathering her close until her breasts pressed against the plane of his chest, he said close to her ear as his warm breath sent shivers along her skin, "You, my love, are worth the wait. Do you have any idea how much you mean to me? I meant every word when I told you that I haven't been near another woman since the night of the wedding. What I didn't tell you is that it was since our first dance at Devin and Brynne's engagement party.

"The instant I held you close that night, my heart started racing. You not only felt right against me, you fit me perfectly. In that moment I knew I wanted you, more than I've ever wanted any woman. I forgot all that stuff I'd been telling myself about you."

She pressed her lips against the side of his neck and felt his shiver. "What kind of stuff were you telling yourself about me? Be careful, I'm listening closely."

Ralph's chuckled throatily. "Oh yeah."

"Yeah. Go on."

"I thought you were too much of a good girl for me to get involved with. You were Gavin's secretary. I knew he and Anna held you in high esteem. And I tried my best to ignore the way your late-night voice on the telephone turned me on," he teased huskily. "Satisfied?"

Vanessa giggled. "No. So tell me. What do you mean, I turned you on?"

Ralph laughed, "You want details?"

"Oh yeah . . . every single one," she teased.

Ralph chuckled, kissing her forehead, tightening his arms around her. "Well, I've always thought you were cute. Loved those curves, sweet girl, but you were off-limits to me. Until then, I liked the wild, willing, out-there types. I was not about to mess with you."

"What? You thought I was a virgin, and you were turned off?"

"I knew you were around Anna's age. So I just assumed you had some experience. You weren't my type. So I intended to keep my distance, despite that sexy voice of yours." He chuckled. "But, man, when I felt those dangerous curves, I was instantly hard and ready. Sweet girl, you know you were wearing that dress that night at the party. I could not take my eyes off you all night. You were so beautiful. Not only did you feel right in my arms, you smelled so good."

"Thank you, sweet man." She couldn't stop the smile that came from the inside out. Caressing his cheek, she said, "And I'm glad you didn't keep your distance."

"I tried, believe me, I tried. But I couldn't stay away from you. I was so jealous of any man who danced with you or looked at you too hard. When I got on that plane to Atlanta, all I could think about was keeping Ron Daniels away from you. He wanted you. I planned to make it my business to make sure you didn't fall for his lame lines and pretty-boy looks. "

"Wow." She stared at him. "I never, ever, thought of Ron that way." Caressing his lips, she said, "You were the one I dreamed about, fantasized about. The one I wanted to be my first lover."

He insisted, "Your only lover!"

Then he rained kisses down her throat. Eyes closed, she began to tremble when he unbuttoned her white silk blouse. He placed kisses down the scented valley between her breasts. Releasing a moan, she looked up into sizzling-hot flames of desire in his dark eyes.

He growled possessively, "Say it, Vanessa."

Reaching up, she cupped his nape. "I don't need to say it. You know I didn't want Ron. He doesn't even compare to you, my big handsome man. You're my heart. You're the only man I want to make love to me . . . only you. I'm all yours. And you're all mine. Remember, Ralph Prescott, I don't believe in sharing."

Vanessa gasped when he kissed her and swept her up into his arms. He carried her into the dark bedroom. Her arms were locked around his neck. "What are you doing?"

He let her legs go and her thighs brushed against his. His arms were around her, holding on tight. His mouth open and hungry over hers. "Oh, my love," he whispered as he savored her lips in kiss after kiss. He said huskily, "I need you, beautiful. I need to be inside you, now."

"Yes–yes, my love, "Vanessa managed to get out.

While he attacked the buttons of her blouse, she did the same with his shirt. When she reached his waist, he pushed the jacket and blouse off her shoulders. Then he started at her waistband and zipper. His hands were unsteady, so what normally only took seconds seemed to take forever. But soon, there was nothing separating them, they stood dark skin to dark skin, trembling with need.

Ralph backed her up to the bed until they came down on it together. His body cushioned her descent. His kisses were hard, insistent. Lost in his sweet magic, Vanessa concentrated on nothing beyond the way he made her feel.

She mumbled a complaint when his mouth left hers, but she was soon moaning in pleasure, as his kisses traveled down the side of her throat to her shoulders until he tenderly squeezed her soft breasts.

Then Ralph kissed and licked his way over the plump globe of each breast. Vanessa whimpered as the pleasure intensified. When he took an aching nipple into his mouth to lick, then suck, it hardened into a taut peak. He didn't stop there. He smoothed his hand down her stomach to trail his fingers through soft curls covering her feminine mound. Cupping her plump folds, he rhythmically squeezed her softness again and again.

Vanessa was beyond all reason. She stroked down his spine down to his firm buttocks, all the while opening herself even more to him. Her breath fast and uneven, it picked up speed even more when he slid a finger deep inside her wet heat.

"No," she protested. "I want you inside of me now. Hurry." When he slid off her, she shook her head vehemently. "Honey, where are you going? You can't stop now," she said in disbelief.

His voice rough with desire. "Just give me a second, sweetheart."

He walked over to his suitcase on the luggage rack. He searched an inside pocket before he returned with a box of condoms.

She watched as he returned to the king-size bed, ripped

open the condom, and quickly covered his shaft. One look into his dark eyes told her all she needed to know. He wanted her as much as she wanted him.

She covered his lips with hers, and they both moaned with desire and incomparable need.

"Touch me, sweetness. I need your hands on me," he whispered.

There was no hesitation on her part. Her only thought was pleasuring him. She eased back until she could stroke his hot, dark skin from the base of his throat, over his chest and nipples. She worried them with her nails until they were pebble hard. He let out a ragged breath as she caressed his ribs and stomach before she stroked the pulsating length of his thick erection. She smiled as he let out a husky groan. She was thrilled by the pleasure and hunger displayed in his eyes. Vanessa's soft hands stroked him again and again until he called out her name.

Kissing her, he said, "No more, beautiful. It feels too good, and I don't want to spoil our enjoyment."

Exchanging hot, tongue-stroking kisses, he kissed his way over her breasts, tonguing each of her aching nipples in turn. Then, kneeling, Ralph teased her moist folds open. He caressed her slowly, repeatedly with the wide crest of his shaft until she was begging him to hurry. Quivering with desire, she tilted her pelvis forward, wanting every hard inch of his shaft. Unable to hold back an instant, he thrust forward. They both groaned from the intense pleasure as he entered her dewy, slick sheath. He groaned her name as he pushed until he completely filled her. Vanessa cried out as she felt his entire length, and instinctively tightened around him.

"Yes, my love . . . oh yes," she whispered as she lifted her legs and wrapped them around his waist. He groaned his pleasure as Vanessa closed her eyes, focusing on their closeness. He gave her a tongue-stroking kiss as her muscles caressed him from deep inside. When Ralph pulled back, Vanessa moaned in protest, then he kissed her again and again. He dropped his head, took her hard nipple into his mouth, and sucked as he plunged back in and out. Shivers of need raced along her nerves, and the pleasure continued to mushroom as he repeatedly stroked her. She was unsure if she could contain the enjoyment. As if he sensed that she was holding back, he slid a hand between their bodies to find her feminine nub, and he worried the ultrasensitive peak, again and again. He teased, causing her to tighten even more. Numb with pleasure, as Vanessa's control crumbled, so did his. He lifted her legs until they rested on his forearms, opening her even more to his persistent strokes.

He called her name, increasing his thrusts, each one harder and deeper than the last. Vanessa screamed his name, losing track of time and place. Her heart pounded wildly in her breasts as she reached an earth-shattering climax. Her strong contraction triggered his own release. Ralph's arms tightened around her, and his body shook and jerked from his convulsion as he experienced an incredible release that seemed to go on and on. They clung to each other, their sweat-dampened bodies touching from chest to hips, legs intertwined. Ralph was the first to recover as he moved to slide off her, but Vanessa protested, tightening her arms around him. He placed a series of tender kisses over her face and throat, lingering on her kiss-swollen lips.

"No," she pouted. "I don't want you to move."

He chuckled, "Believe me, I don't want to move, but I'm too heavy. I'm crushing you, sweetheart."

"Never," she persisted, needing their closeness. She whispered, "You feel so good."

He kissed her gently. "So do you, my beautiful lady." Ralph solved the problem when he rolled onto his back, taking Vanessa with him. Their bodies were still connected.

Vanessa sighed when she found herself cradled on his chest, her face tucked beneath his chin. He moved a caressing hand down her back, settling on her bottom, squeezing her again and again.

"I'm sorry," she whispered.

"Sorry about what?" he quizzed.

When she sniffled, burying her face between his shoulder and neck, he shifted until he could see her eyes. "What is it, beautiful? Are you crying?"

"It's nothing," she mumbled, as her tears dampened his skin.

Ralph stroked her back, soothingly moving from her nape to her hips. "No secrets, remember? Don't tell me those are happy tears. I'm not buying it."

"It's not you. It's me. I was wrong not to believe you when you told me you haven't been with anyone else. I was so afraid of being hurt. So much so that I compared you to Cummingham. It was a terrible thing to do. You're a loyal, giving man of your word. Cummingham is self-centered and weak," she ended in a sob.

Ralph kissed her forehead, wrapping his arms around her as he focused on the beat of their hearts. He used the top sheet to dry her tears. He said close to her ear, "No, my sweetheart. You weren't wrong. You had a good reason for doubting me. Until that night at the engagement party, all I was looking for was to get laid. Nothing else mattered, not the women, not their dreams. You changed all that. You made me see what was missing in my life . . . you. I needed you to love me, to be mine."

He covered her face with gentle kisses. "I'm going to prove it to you that you have nothing to worry about concerning other women. That part of my life is over. I promise you."

"And if that changes?" she asked, yet afraid to believe.

"It won't change, but if I'm that much of an ass, then I

deserve to be kicked to the curb. We're not going to have a prenuptial. If I mess this up, you can have it all."

Vanessa tilted her head back until she could study his eyes. "That's crazy."

"It's how it is going to be. We're going into this on trust."

"You mean that?"

"Absolutely. It's all-or-nothing on my part. You got my heart and soul. There is no turning back for me. All I ask is you to trust me to do right by you and your kids. I love them."

She nodded. "I know."

"You know what? That I love the kids?"

"I know that you love the kids. I know you love me. My answer is, yes, to all of it. Ralph Prescott, will you be my husband, my heart, my man?" Vanessa asked.

He let out a deep, throaty sound that she felt deep in his chest. His arms cradled her. His eyes shimmered with tears. He vowed softly, "Absolutely."

"How soon can you marry me?" she asked.

He grinned. "Soon." His kiss was filled with warmth and love. "You mind if I adopt your kids? I want us to be a family."

Vanessa smiled. "I'd say yes. But it's up to the kids."

"Fair enough. How soon, Vanessa?"

Vanessa couldn't stop the pure joy bubbling up inside of her. Kissing him, she said, "One month."

"Not a minute longer. Promise," he said, kissing her throat.

"Promise." She smiled. "To think, you could have said no when I asked you to be my lover."

He chuckled. "You've got that wrong. I could never have said no."

She laughed. "I'm glad."

Epilogue

Vanessa stepped out of the patio doors off Donna and Lester's crowded family room, onto the snow-cleared veranda. Gazing up into the dark blue sky, with only a deep red cashmere shawl that matched her turtleneck sweater and cream leather slacks, she ignored the cold. She sought a few moments alone to whisper a grateful, heart-filled prayer.

Christmas with the Prescotts was even more wonderful than Vanessa had imagined. She teared up whenever she recalled how, from the very first, everyone in Ralph's family had welcomed and accepted her and the children into their family.

This Christmas had been the best ever, from the moment she'd opened her eyes and found herself wrapped in her husband's arms. The house had been filled with joy, from the children gleefully opening their gifts to sharing a cheery breakfast around the kitchen table.

Vanessa smiled, remembering the few minutes alone with her husband while the children were getting ready for church. Ralph had found her in their family room, checking to make sure they didn't leave a single gaily wrapped gift behind. Laughing softly, she recalled how he'd teased her about her long list, asking if she was the same woman who didn't intend to use any of the money he routinely deposited in her checking account.

But she'd teased him right back that he was spoiling them rotten with the expensive gifts he'd piled under the Christmas tree for all of them, but especially her. She still hadn't gotten over the thrilling surprise he'd given her. A honeymoon cruise on the *Queen Mary 2*, a week starting tomorrow. They would be flying out in the morning to meet the ship in New York for a six-day cruise ending in Southampton, England, with the promise that their family would take the entire cruise next summer.

But what he spoiled them with was love . . . so much love. And the love they shared seemed to keep growing, making her wonder how much joy she could stand. Every morning and night he made a point of thanking her for marrying him and making an honest man out of him. Since their October wedding, not a day had passed that Ralph didn't tell her how much he loved her and vowed to love only her. And he never forgot to remind her how genuinely happy he was that they were a family. She often felt like pinching herself to make sure she was not dreaming. She had done the impossible, she'd found a man who had not hesitated to gain a ready-made family.

All those fears and doubts that had nearly torn them apart during the summer had vanished. She no longer worried about his ability to commit to her or her family. With love came trust.

Their marriage had not been all sunshine and roses. There had been tons of adjustment for all of them from the instant they moved into his huge house in Southfield. The children adored their new rooms, especially Lana. She had a teenage girl's dream with her own telephone, bathroom, and I-pod. All the children liked their new school and teachers, and they were making new friends. And all three of them loved their new brother-in-law.

They also had adjusted surprisingly well to the changes that Prescotts brought into their lives. Ralph's aunt and uncle insisted that Lana and the twins call them Grannie and Grandpa, like their other grandchildren.

Their plan to adopt the children was moving full speed ahead, thanks to Greg Cummingham's cooperation. For now he continued to pay child support, but had bowed out of all parental rights including visitation. Vanessa was grateful that the twins didn't miss what they'd never had . . . their father's love.

With Ralph's support, Vanessa, after giving her notice, was busy designing evening and bridal gowns full-time. In that department, things were going better than she'd dreamed possible. The orders were coming in droves from her sisters-in-law and their society friends. She was getting to the point where she was going to have to decide if she wanted to open her own boutique or go back to college to earn her degree in business. She was leaning toward opening the boutique, especially if she could find a good location close to home. The last few weeks, she enjoyed working in the beautiful home office her husband had set up for her. She especially liked being close to her family.

Had she ever been happier?

"Hey, beautiful. It's cold out here," Ralph said as he stepped outside, closing the door behind him. "Looking for a little peace and quiet?"

"Something like that." She smiled as she felt him drop his sport coat, still warm from his body, over her shoulders before he wrapped his arms around her waist from behind.

Closing her eyes, Vanessa leaned back against him. "Did your aunt send you out here to find me?"

"Nope. I missed you. Do you mind a little company?" he said, close to her ear.

Familiar shivers of desire raced up and down her spine.

"Mind your company? Never. I was wondering when you'd remember me."

"I never forgot you, sweetheart. How could I when you're my heart? Everything all right?"

"Perfect. I just needed a quiet place to say a thankful prayer."

"Mmm, Good Christmas?"

"Wonderful, marvelous, magical Christmas. I'm trying to decide if I've ever been happier."

His voice was rough with emotion, when he asked, "What did you decide?"

"I've never been happier. You do that for me just by being you, sweet man," she whispered, tilting her head back for his kiss. He didn't hesitate. His lips were warm and giving. "How about you? Have you been happier?"

"Never. Not since you and the kids made a family man out of me. Have I told you how much I love you today?"

"Of course. But don't let that stop you," she teased.

He chuckled, before whispering, "I love you, Vanessa Grant Prescott."

"Thank you, because I love you, Mr. Ralph Prescott. Thank you for my fabulous gift."

"You're welcome. Can you be ready to go tomorrow. Or do you want to wait another day to get ready? The kids are packed to stay with my folks."

"No delays. We are leaving in the morning. I can sleep on the ship. How did you manage to keep the twins quiet about this?"

He laughed. "Believe me, it was not easy. I was sure Curtis was going to cave in and tell you. He has been so proud of himself for keeping quiet."

"He had a right to be proud. When did you tell him?"

"Day before yesterday. The girls have known all long. Lana helped Curtis and Courtney get packed, so you don't have to worry that they have everything they need, including clean underwear. Besides, the folks have keys. They can bring them back to the house if they forgot something."

"That is so much trouble for your folks. Are you sure they want to keep all of the grandkids over the holiday?" Vanessa questioned.

"Stop worrying. My folks have had plenty of practice. They are looking forward to it. And you and I can spend as much time as we like in bed." He squeezed her waist.

Vanessa laughed. "Why do I get the impression you are looking forward to it?"

"Because I am. How about you?"

"Without a doubt," she said, rubbing the back of his hand. "Remember, it was your idea to take the kids with us on our honeymoon."

He chuckled, "Universal in Orlando was more a family vacation than a honeymoon. Besides, it was too soon for the kids to be away from you. They had enough adjustments to make."

Vanessa turned, wrapping her arms around his waist. She lifted her face to kiss him. "I can't wait to have you all to myself."

Chuckling, he covered her lips with his.

"Behave," she scolded him tenderly, before asking, "Any regrets?"

He stared into her eyes. "Not even one. I didn't know what happiness was until you became my bride." He felt her shivers. "We'd better go in. I don't want you catching a cold."

Vanessa nodded. He caught her hand and escorted her back into the spacious family room, where everyone was seated.

The tall spruce had been beautifully decorated with ornaments that held sentimental value to the family; most had been made when the boys and Anna were children. A fire blazed in the brick fireplace, and the mantel was crowded with family photographs, as was the top of the old upright piano that had once belonged to Donna's grandmother.

"You're just in time to help us sing," Donna said from where she sat at the piano bench, her husband, Lester, beside her.

The children were all seated around the piano on the beautifully patterned area rug.

"Let's hope your side of the family can sing," Anna teased from her place beside Gavin on the love seat.

Everyone laughed, including Lester. At Vanessa's blank look, Lester explained, "Donna and Anna are the only Prescotts who have any musical talent. Both our ladies play the piano and sing beautifully. Unfortunately, the boys and I can't carry a tune, but that hasn't stopped my beautiful wife from insisting we try."

"We've been lucky," Devin said from where he was seated on a floor pillow with Shanna in his lap and Brynne seated in the armchair beside them.

Wesley interrupted, "That our wives can sing. That way they can drown us out." He was seated at one end of the sectional sofa with his wife, Kelli, beside him. Keleea was in her grandfather's lap, clapping her hands eagerly.

Vanessa laughed. "I'll do my best." She smiled at the twins seated side by side at the piano, eager to join in.

Despite the empty seats on the sofa, Ralph took the armchair and pulled Vanessa down onto his lap. Just then Lana and Kyle and Wayne came in carrying bowls of microwave popcorn. They grabbed pillows and squeezed in on the floor.

"Are we ready," Donna called as she began playing the chorus for "Jingle Bells."

Looking around the room filled with love, Vanessa snuggled against Ralph, truly content with her life.

The Prescott children had gifts waiting for them under the brightly lit tree from their aunts, uncles, and grandparents. The adults had not exchanged gifts, but donated the money they would have spent to a selected homeless shelter. The families would receive Christmas gifts for their children that included toys and warm clothing for all of them, with the added assurance that they would have food and a warm safe place to sleep during the winter months.

As Vanessa joined the Christmas caroling, her gaze rested on Kelli and Wesley. They held hands, both thrilled that they were expecting a second baby in the new year. While Kelli was hoping for a boy, Wes insisted he didn't care as long as both the baby and Kelli were healthy.

Brynne curled with her arms on Devin's shoulders. Her dream of founding a women's crisis center in St. Louis was moving forward. They had not only selected the building, but if all went as planned, they would open their doors by June 1.

Brynne and Devin had never been happier. Shanna was thrilled to have Curtis, Courtney, and Lana as her new cousins.

Everyone was happy for Anna and Gavin as they awaited their first baby, especially Donna. Gavin was thrilled. The couple was also looking forward to their first anniversary in February. Gavin's brother, Kyle, while pleased to be an uncle, was excited that he and his best friend, Wayne, would get their driver's licenses in the new year.

Lester and Donna were clearly still very much in love and proud of all their children. They were delighted to have the children and grandchildren all together to celebrate the holiday.

When Ralph lifted Vanessa's hand and placed a kiss in the center of her palm, Vanessa sighed contentedly. She was looking forward to a future filled with love and joy.

Author's Note

Dear Readers,

I'd like to take this opportunity to sincerely thank you for all the prayers, letters, e-mail, cards of encouragement, and support that you have sent on my behalf. You have no idea how much they mean to me.

Can't Say No is the last book in the three-book Prescott Series. Ralph and Vanessa are an unlikely pair who fall in love around the backdrop of his cousin and her best friend's wedding. I hope you enjoyed it. *Unforgettable* is Anna and Gavin's story and *An Everlasting Love* is Brynne and Devin's story. As always, I'm looking forward to hearing from you. You may write to me in care of Avon Books. Visit my website at www.bette-ford.com. Thanks again.

Best wishes,

Bette Ford

Soulful Love With A New Attitude

Jewel
by Beverly Jenkins
978-0-06-116135-3

Reckless
by Selena Montgomery
978-0-06-137603-0

Always True to You in My Fashion
by Valerie Wilson Wesley
978-0-06-101552-6

Deadly Sexy
by Beverly Jenkins
978-0-06-124639-5

The Sweet Spot
by Kayla Perrin
978-0-06-114392-2

Marrying Up
by Nina Foxx
978-0-06-114391-5

Unfinished Business
by Karyn Langhorne
978-0-06-084789-0

Hitts & Mrs.
by Lori Bryant-Woolridge
978-0-06-114389-2